Louise Millar grew up in Scotland. She began her journalism career as a freelance sub-editor on magazines such as *Smash Hits, Kerrang!*, the *NME* and *Empire*, before moving on to commission and write features for women's magazines and newspapers. She was a senior editor at *Marie Claire* for five years, before leaving to produce 'ordinary' people's private memoirs and write her first novel. Millar lives in London with her husband and two children

THE PLAYDATE

Sound designer Callie Roberts, a single mother, has come to rely on Suzy, her best friend and neighbour. Suzy has been good to Callie and Rae, her daughter; welcoming them into her large, apparently happy family. But Callie knows that Suzy's life is not as perfect as it seems. It's time she pulled away — and she needs to get back to work. So why does she keep putting off telling Suzy? And who will care for Rae? The houses in the anonymous city street hide families, each with their own secrets. Callie's increased sense of alienation leads her to try and befriend a new resident, Debs. But she's odd — you wouldn't trust her with your child — especially if you knew anything about her past . . .

LOUISE MILLAR

THE PLAYDATE

Complete and Unabridged

CHARNWOOD
Leicester

First published in Great Britain in 2012 by
Pan Books
an imprint of
Pan Macmillan
London

First Charnwood Edition
published 2013
by arrangement with
Pan Macmillan
a division of
Macmillan Publishers Limited
London

British Library CIP Data

Millar, Louise.
  The playdate.
  1. Large type books.
  I. Title
  823.9'2–dc23

  ISBN 978–1–4448–1450–7

Published by
F. A. Thorpe (Publishing)
Anstey, Leicestershire

Set by Words & Graphics Ltd.
Anstey, Leicestershire
Printed and bound in Great Britain by
T. J. International Ltd., Padstow, Cornwall

This book is printed on acid-free paper

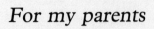
For my parents

FRIDAY

1

Callie

The water is cold. I knew it would be, despite the disco ball of early summer sun that twirls through the willow trees onto the dark green, velvety pond. I pull my foot out quickly and rub its soft, icy edges. A small yellow leaf sticks to my ankle. I'm not sure I am up for this.

'There's something slimy in there,' I say.

Suzy adopts the pout she uses when she's trying to get Henry to eat broccoli. 'Come on — it's yummy.' We both laugh.

She stands up, towering above me at her full five foot ten. With one swift movement, she pulls her grey towelling dress over her head and kicks off her flip-flops. She stands at the water's edge in a black bikini and looks out. An elderly lady glides towards her with smooth, long strokes, a blue rubber hat perched on wire-wool hair. Suzy smiles and waits patiently for her to pass.

I sit back on my elbows. There are about twenty women on the grass, in various small groups or alone. Some are reading, some talking. Two are lying close together, laughing, their legs entwined. I look back at Suzy, who is still waiting for the old lady to move safely out of her path. It takes me a minute to realize I am staring at her body. It's not that I haven't seen it a hundred times before, marching naked round the swimming baths' changing room after the kids, or whipping off her top in her kitchen when she gets gravy on it. No, what is strange is to see her body unfettered by children. In the two and a half years I have known Suzy, there has almost always been a child attached to it: feeding at a breast, astride a hip, wriggling under an arm.

Suddenly I notice how young she is. It's amazing how well her body has recovered from three children. She has a thick waist, and a flat stomach with no hint of the soft pouch of flesh that Rae has left on mine. Her substantial bust sits high, politely accepting the support of the bikini, but not really needing it. Her skin is creamy and smooth, her frame strong and athletic. Taking a deep breath, she lifts her arms with the confidence of a girl who's spent her childhood lake-swimming in the Colorado mountains, and dives into Hampstead Ladies' Pond, ejecting a startled duck.

I lie back and try to concentrate on where we are. A fly buzzes at my nose. There is an air of calm around the pond. A hidden world behind the trees of Hampstead Heath, where women swim and stretch and smile; far from the company of men. Perhaps this is what the inner sanctum of a harem feels like.

Yes, I think. What could be better than this? Sitting in the early summer sun on a Friday afternoon with no kids and no work to worry about.

Yet that is not really how I feel at all.

The hot sun pricks my face a little

4

unpleasantly. I try to focus on the sounds around me to relax. I used to collect interesting sounds, storing mentally the tiniest hum or echo, or whisper of wind that I heard and liked, in case one day I might need them. Today there is birdsong from a warbler, the soft swish of Suzy's strokes, the crack of a squirrel on a twig.

It is no use. However much I stretch my legs out, the tension that makes my buttocks and thighs clench won't release. My mind is racing. I need to tell Suzy. I can't keep this secret from her. There is enough I hide from Suzy already. I sit up again and check where she is. She's travelled to one side of the pond and is working her way back.

Oh, what the hell. I am here now. I stand up and walk over to the ladder, and begin gingerly to climb into the murky water. The noticeboard says there are terrapins and crayfish in here.

'Good girl!' Suzy calls across, clapping to encourage me.

I roll my eyes to show her I am not convinced. The water is cold and earthy as I lower myself into it, shivering. Bit by bit, the icy ring moves up my body until I am almost immersed.

'Just swim,' calls Suzy. Her bright American tone echoes out across the pond and the female lifeguard looks over.

I launch myself off the edge. I am not a good swimmer. Suzy approaches me.

'This is so great,' she says, turning on her back and looking up at the clear sky and treetops. 'Next week, I'm going to book us a day at that spa you told me about in Covent Garden.'

5

My legs dip, and water goes in my mouth. I splutter, kicking hard. I can't touch the bottom.

'Hey, you OK?' she says, holding my arm. 'Let's swim to the middle then turn back.'

I take a breath, clear my nose and follow her.

'Suze,' I say, 'I can't spend money on stuff like that at the moment.'

'Don't be silly, hon, I'll get it,' she replies. I know she means it. Money is never an issue in the Howard house. Jez's business is thriving even in these uncertain times. For Suzy, money does not have the emotion attached to it that it does for me. It doesn't hang around her house like a critical mother, interfering in every decision she makes, squashing dreams, telling her 'maybe next year'.

Satisfied that I am OK, Suzy leaves me to swim alone. I wonder which direction to take across the pond. It is a strange sensation swimming in a natural pool, with no tiled edges to aim for, just gentle slopes of black earth veined with slippery tree roots. There is no rectangular structure to measure my lengths. It is lovely, Suzy is right. It's just that right now my mind aches for corners and edges, for beginnings and ends.

I hear a splash and turn round. The old lady is climbing the steps out of the pond. Stunned, I realize she is about ninety. Tanned, loose flesh hangs like draped curtains from strong old bones. I think of my own grandmother, sitting for twenty years after my granddad died, watching telly and waiting for the end. How does that happen? That one old lady watches telly and another walks to an open-air pond on a summer's day and floats around among water lilies and kingfishers?

The woman's lack of self-consciousness about her body gives her an air of confidence as she walks past two young women gossiping animatedly, eyes hidden behind overlarge designer sunglasses, thin limbs spray-tanned the same dulled bronze. Probably business wives from Hampstead. I decide the woman could be an old suffragette or a famous botanist who spent her younger years travelling round remote South America on a donkey, finding new plants. Whatever, I sense she has no time for young women like them. And me. She's probably earned the right to spend her days doing such wonderful things. She knows someone else is paying for ours.

This is not right. This has to end.

Taking a deep breath through my nose, I swim as fast as I can back to the steps and reach up to the railings with dripping hands. Pulling myself from the water, my body feels oddly heavy. Heavy, I suspect, with the weight of my own guilt.

I have to find the words to tell Suzy. I can't do this any more.

★　★　★

It became apparent at Easter that Suzy had a lot of plans for her and me. She has never had a daylight hour without children, she claims, since she moved to London. Even when Jez is home, he says he can't manage all three of them together, so she always has one, whatever she does.

So since Peter and Otto both started private nursery in May, and Henry and Rae are now reaching the end of their first year at primary school, Suzy finally has the chance to do the things on the list she has been compiling from *Time Out* magazine and her London guidebook. All through June, we have been out most days. She knows I have no money, so we have done free things. We have rollerbladed in Regent's Park, ignoring the sign that says 'No skating'. 'They'll have to catch us first,' said Suzy furiously when she saw it. She has waited too long to take long, gliding strokes through the flat paths of the rose garden unhindered by our children's buggies and scooters. I don't like breaking rules, but I go along with it.

Another day, we ate sandwiches in Trafalgar Square after a visit to the National Gallery to see Botticellis and Rembrandts. We've peered through the railings at No. 10 Downing Street and seen Big Ben up close. Suzy even made me come with her to the Tower of London, insisting on paying the entrance fee. As I stood waiting among German tourists to see the Crown Jewels, I had to smile to myself. These are not the things I did with friends in London before I had Rae, but I remind myself that Suzy is from America and not Lincolnshire, like me, and that she wants to do the touristy stuff in the way that I wanted to climb the Empire State Building when Tom and I spent that one precious weekend in New York.

And today it has been Hampstead Ladies' Pond. 'We should come here every day,' Suzy says, as we get ourselves dressed. 'People do.'

Sometimes when she says these things I feel like I did in the pond today. I flail around, trying to find something solid and familiar to hold on to, but there is nothing.

★   ★   ★

It is 3.25 p.m. It has taken Suzy sixteen minutes to race from Hampstead Heath across North London in her yellow convertible to Alexandra Park. She skids to a stop outside the kids' school, completely ignoring the 'No drop off' sign.

'Go get 'em, pardner,' she shouts to me over the horrible American soft-rock music she likes to play loud in the car, oblivious to the looks we get from mothers walking through the school gate.

I laugh despite my embarrassment, and jump out. We both know the routine. I pick up Rae and Henry, she fetches Peter and Otto from nursery. We do it without speaking now, guiding each other through our shared daily routine like dressage horses, with a gentle nod or a kick towards school or soft play or swimming.

'I'm going to take them to the park,' I say, shutting the door.

'Coolio, baby,' shouts Suzy cheerfully, and drives off, waving a hand above her head.

I turn and look at the arched entrance with its

9

century-old brick 'Girls' sign. Instantly, my shoulders hunch up. The massive wall of Alexandra Palace rises dramatically behind the school, like a tidal wave about to engulf the little Victorian building. I run through the gate, turn right into the infants' department and smile my closed-mouth smile at the other mums. Everyone told me that having kids is when you really get to know your neighbours in London. They must have neighbours different from mine. A few mums nod back, then continue arranging playdates with each other in the diaries they carry around. I've tried so many times to figure out what I've done wrong. My best guess is that it's because in Rae's slot on the class parent contact list 'Callie' and 'Tom' sit separately at two different London addresses; unlike 'Felicity and Jonathan' and 'Parminder and David' and 'Suzy and Jez'. Suzy says if the mothers are not going to be friendly to me because I'm a divorced, unemployed, single mother who lives in a rented flat, she and Jez won't accept their invites to stupid drinks parties in their double-fronted Edwardian houses in The Driveway, the only road apart from ours with a guaranteed catchment into this tiny, one-form-entry infant school. She says this is the price we pay for 'getting our kids into a posh, oversubscribed primary school' and that 'they're a bunch of stuck-up, middle-class cows for ignoring me', and that I am much better than they are.

I try to believe her, but sometimes it's difficult. Sometimes I think it would be nice to belong.

Sometimes I think that if one of these mothers invited Rae to her house for a playdate, I would fall on the floor and kiss her feet.

The classroom door opens and Henry and Rae burst out looking grubby and stressed. 'What have you got to eat?' Rae murmurs. I give them the rice cakes I always carry around in my bag. She has red paint in her mousey hair and her hands are greasy as if she hasn't washed them all day. As usual I search her eyes for signs. Is she overtired? Too pale? I scoop her up and hold her too tight, kissing the side of her face till she squirms and laughs.

'Are you all right, Henry?' I say. He looks dazed and wired, checking behind me to see if Suzy is there. If she were, he would be whining by now, making his disapproval of her abandonment apparent. I put Rae down and hug him to show that I understand. He leans into me a little, and sighs. Then the pair of them head out of the outer door, gnawing their food like puppies.

At the school gate, Henry starts to run. He does it every day, yet I am so busy trying to shove their scribbled drawings into my bag that it still catches me unawares. 'Henry!' I shout. I chase him along the pavement, grabbing Rae who is following him blindly, dodging round a man, a woman and two girls. The man turns. It is Matt, a divorced dad from another class. Or The Hot Dude That Callie Must Get It On With, as Suzy calls him. And I have just shouted in his ear.

'Sorry,' I say, lifting a hand to emphasize it. He

smiles coolly, rubbing his hand over a new crew cut. Embarrassingly, I blush. 'Stupid, stupid, stupid,' I mutter. As if.

I catch up with Henry at the play park behind the school. 'Henry,' I say, 'you mustn't run like that. Remember, Rae follows you and it's dangerous for her in case she falls.'

He shrugs a 'sorry', jumps on a swing standing up and throws himself in the air with violent jerks, as if trying to shake out his excess energy like ketchup from a bottle. Rae sits on the next swing, playing with the tiny doll that she manages to keep hidden about her person however much I search for it before we leave for school. I am going to look up her sleeve on Monday. They don't talk much, Henry and Rae. But, as their teacher says, they seem joined together by an invisible wire. Wherever one is, the other is never far away — just like me and Suzy.

I wonder what Rae feels about that sometimes. I wonder if she feels like me.

I watch Rae, and I think about Suzy, and I can't even bring myself to imagine what it will be like for them both when I'm not here.

2

Suzy

So — he was back.

As soon as Suzy opened the door of her house at No. 13 Churchill Road at 3.55 p.m., she could see from the discarded shoes in the middle of the hall that Jez's meeting in town with Don Berry had finished early.

'OK, little boo-boos,' she said to Peter and Otto, releasing them from the carry she had given them from the car. Without breaking the broad smile she used like a tractor beam to keep them from teetering over the edge into hysteria after nursery, she kicked her husband's loafers into the shoe rack with its sweetie-shop rows of bright sandals. 'Who wants a drink?' she called, moving Jez's jacket from the banister onto a peg. The boys nodded, dazed. 'And who wants a cookie Mommy made?' she growled in a goofy voice. The boys nodded more enthusiastically. 'Coolio!' she shouted, tickling them as they wandered into the kitchen.

Peter laughed.

Otto cried and hit her hand away, his brown eyes flashing a warning.

This little baby would need more help today, she could see.

'Hey, buddy?' she said, picking him up again.

13

He resisted, squealing angrily and grabbing her hair.

'No,' she murmured in his ear, holding him tightly. His little body, heavy with toddler chunkiness, began to relax. His fingers let go. She kissed them gently, smelling exhausted salty sweat and baked beans. 'My very beautiful boy,' she said. Just holding him made her body ache for more. And a girl this time. A girl called Nora, with Suzy's own childhood freckles and strawberry-blonde hair, not the rich darkness of Jez's domineering, upper-class English genes.

Otto brushed his nose across the front of Suzy's dress, marking her territorially with snot, and sighed.

'It's OK, hon,' she whispered, pressing her cheek against the wet thickness of his. 'You're tired.'

'Hmm.' He nodded. She put him down, sighing with the satisfaction of getting it right, and watched him toddle into the kitchen behind Peter, his raven curls bouncing.

The mid-afternoon sun beamed in through the glass wall that ran across the back of the house, making her Italian kitchen gleam. The boys climbed on the giant sofa. She loved this space. It was impossible now to remember what it looked like as a collection of cramped Victorian rooms. She thought Jez was joking when he told her the price of the house. You could buy a small ranch for that in Colorado. Then he explained how the vendor had just received planning permission to knock the rooms together and extend at the back — just as he and

14

his girlfriend decided to split up. Suddenly Suzy had seen how it could work. A huge family room filled with toys and the new friends they'd make in London, and her serving everyone great steaming bowls of pasta; children running around, playing; she and Jez opening wine together. Jez was right. The room had worked out well.

He just hadn't been in it much lately.

Suzy took paper and felt-tip pens out of the drawer of the kitchen table, and placed them with a cookie and a drink each on top, kissing each boy as she helped him up. She turned on the oven, pulled a tray of meatballs that she'd made earlier from the fridge and turned to wash her hands.

It was then that she saw it.

He had done it again.

A newspaper was spread out on the quartz worktop beside a white mug whose sparkling interior was violated by a muddy tide line of coffee. Crumbs lay beside it. The remnants of a sandwich eaten without a plate or thought for who would clean it up.

Discarded shoes, jackets, cups and crumbs. Shaving foam left out. Undrained baths. Uncapped olive oil. A house full of Jez's semaphores for things he wouldn't say.

Clamping her jaw, Suzy folded the newspaper and put it in the recycling box. She and the boys looked up as heavy footsteps came down the stairs and towards the kitchen. Jez filled the doorway like a dark cloud about to rain.

'Hi . . . good day, boys?' he muttered gruffly.

15

Peter smiled shyly, Otto began to grizzle again. Jez glanced at his wife briefly, then looked around the kitchen.

'Can't find the phone charger.'

'I put it back on your desk,' she said flatly, picking up Otto for another hug. 'I needed to use the kettle.'

He raised his eyebrows and began to walk back out of the room. She couldn't help herself.

'Would you like me to put this away, too?' she said, nodding at his dirty mug.

He paused, then shrugged. 'Or leave it there.'

She held Otto closer, like a shield.

'All right, little man?' Jez said, ruffling his hair as he walked back out the door.

She put Otto down again and began to cut up an organic cucumber, focusing on its uneven ridged bumps to distract herself from the urge to follow Jez. With a start, she realized Peter was watching her silently, his gentle face fixed in a frown. Of the three, Peter was her sensitive one. The one who stood back and let Otto and Henry grab their favourite toys first, gently stroking Suzy's arm when his brothers bit and kicked each other. She blew him a kiss to show him everything was all right, and began laying the table with plates, trying to concentrate on the polka-dot blue plastic.

Three plates for her three boys, then one for Rae just in case. Now, did Rae like meatballs? Yes, she did, it was sausages she'd gone off . . .

How could Jez say that?

Putting down the jug, she pointed the remote control at the widescreen TV on the wall.

16

Cursing under her breath that she was breaking her own rules of no kids' telly during the week, she flicked through till she found *Postman Pat*. The boys' faces turned to the wall, amazed.

'Mommy go pee-pee,' she said, beaming. 'Back in a minute.'

Checking that they weren't following behind her, she tiptoed up the stairs past the first floor to the office Jez had converted out of the loft. The door was firmly shut.

She nudged it.

It swung open to reveal Jez at the computer, in front of a wall covered with charts and projections that had no meaning for her apart from when money appeared in her bank account. She had given up trying to make him explain what he was working on. 'I just want to understand, hon, so I can be there for you if you need support.' But he had said there was no point. He'd let her know if there were any problems.

Jez was still wearing his grey Paul Smith suit trousers with a charcoal shirt from his earlier meeting in town. Even on days when he didn't have a client to meet, he dressed impeccably. He turned to look at her, his six-foot-three, fifteen-stone frame forcing a squeak out of the leather swivel chair. Jez looked big in any setting you put him in. Even among the Midwestern men of her home town with their cowboy-sized hands, who spent their weeks in office suits downtown and weekends hunting in the mountains, Jez had held his own, standing shoulder to shoulder with them in the local bar, meeting well-meant jibes about his English accent with a dry humour that quickly earned him a slap on the shoulder and a shot of bourbon.

At the time, his strength had made her feel safe. She hadn't imagined what it might be like to be on the wrong side of it.

'What?' he said, turning to meet her with eyes that said nothing.

What? What do you think? she wanted to say. But right now they were past words.

So on an impulse she did something else.

She reached behind her back and undid her bikini top through her dress.

Jez watched. It took him a second to realize.

'Oh . . . no,' he said firmly, shaking his head and turning back to the screen with a half-smile to show how ridiculous he found the idea.

The rejection stung. But it was too late. She walked over and put her hand on his shoulder, pulling him round with the momentum of the swivel chair.

'No. Really — get off,' he said, the humour disappearing rapidly from his tone, the hard muscles in his shoulder twisting easily away from her fingers.

But she was only five inches shorter, and before Jez could stop her, she had straddled him with one long leg and pushed her chest towards his face to stop him propelling her away.

'Suzy!' he growled. 'I said STOP. I don't want to. Leave it.'

How could she stop? Fighting back the humiliation, she pulled his hand and tried to put

18

it inside the top of her dress, needing some kind of connection with her husband, even for him just to laugh at her desperation. Then she could join in and they would hug and joke about her wanting more babies. Anything that broke the silence.

'Oh, will you fucking stop it!' he shouted suddenly, grabbing that wrist and the other one, and holding them high beside her shoulders. 'You are not listening. I don't want to.' Their eyes met inches apart. She could see the blackness in his now.

Looking down at her bare legs that smelt faintly of pond water, and the bulk of loosened straps underneath her dress, she felt shame. Blood ran into her cheeks.

'OK, then. Let me go,' she whispered.

The doorbell rang downstairs. Callie with the kids.

Jez held her wrists for a second more. Then she felt his grip loosen.

'OK, then,' he said, lowering his voice. His expression softened for a moment.

God, she saw it now. He felt sorry for her.

There was a knocking downstairs.

She dropped her gaze.

'I am your wife,' she whispered, so quietly she was not sure he even heard. And with that she walked out of the room.

3

Callie

By the time we have wandered through the park back to Churchill Road, Rae and Henry are holding hands. We walk along our quiet street of Victorian terraces, looking at neighbours' window boxes. I say 'neighbours', but the truth is, apart from Suzy, the people on Churchill Road are just people with whom I happen to share a postcode. There was a nice woman my age at No. 25 when I first arrived. I asked her once where she got her wrought-iron window boxes. She was friendly, and I thought I'd ask her in for a cup of tea soon. Then two days later I saw a removal van outside her house and she was gone. I didn't even catch her name.

We turn into Suzy's gate at No. 13. Empty boxes sit outside No. 15, next door. A little surge of hope rises in me. Perhaps the new people will be nice.

I ring Suzy's doorbell, and wait. No answer.

I knock.

Nothing.

That's weird. I open the letterbox and hear the murmur of telly. They must be in the garden. I search my bag and find the spare set of keys Suzy and I swapped long ago, and put them in the lock, praying we don't walk in on Jez

20

wandering around jet-lagged and naked like that first time, after which I couldn't look him in the eye for a month.

There is a pounding of feet down the stairs as I start to open the door.

'Sorry — in the loo. Hi, sweetie!' Suzy squeals at Henry, sweeping him up high into a hug and covering his face with kisses. 'How was your day? I missed you.' Henry struggles, trying to contain his grin.

'Stay for tea?' she says. 'We're having meatballs!'

'Sure?' I say.

'Absolutely.'

I can never resist going into Suzy's when I am asked. I should try sometimes, but I don't. It is the choice between her house, or going home and hearing that jailer's click of our flat door that says I am not going to see another adult till tomorrow.

Suzy lifts Rae up and kisses her, too. 'You look so pretty today, sweetie.'

'Thank you, Aunty Suzy.'

'Good girl,' says Suzy, and kisses her again before putting her down. Rae always looks so safe in Suzy's arms, and I am always grateful when Rae looks safe.

In the kitchen, I put the pens and paper back in the drawer, and help Suzy prepare tea for the kids.

'Jez here?' I say, slicing a pepper.

'Uh-huh,' she says, motioning upstairs. 'He's got the pitch for that big Canadian contract coming up next month. After that, though, he's talking about taking us to some hotel in Devon where they have kids' clubs and nannies so he and I can have some mommy-daddy time. You know it?'

'Er . . . no,' I sigh.

She sees my face.

'Oh, hon — sorry.'

'No, it's OK. Tom'll be back soon. Then I'll get a break.'

She makes a face. 'A break?' she says sarcastically.

I shrug.

'Cal, this thing about him ringing you every ten minutes has got to stop,' Suzy says, lowering her voice, as Rae looks over.

'I know,' I sigh. 'It's because he doesn't see her regularly — he thinks every little cold means something. He's worse than me . . . '

Suzy puts an arm around my shoulder. 'Well, he needs to learn to deal with it — you are burning out. Anyway, you know, you can always leave her here if you want to get away.'

Get away? I almost snort. Get away where? And paid for by what? But I don't, because I know she means well. So I smile. 'You have enough on your plate, but thanks for offering.'

Suzy kisses me on the cheek and starts to clear the kids' plates.

'Anyway, guess who I spoke to today?' I say, grinning as she spins round.

'No? You bugger!'

Suzy makes me laugh when she uses English swear words. They lose their power and become funny, like the Queen calling someone a motherfucker.

'I bumped into him when he was talking to Maddy in our class's room.'

'Nooooo!' Suzy protests again, with huge comedy eyes. 'Right, that's it. Rae and Henry have to invite his kid, what's-her-name, round for tea.'

'They don't even know her!'

There is a creak of stairs. We stop talking instantly. Jez wanders into the kitchen.

'Hi, how are you?' he says, leaning down to give me a token kiss on the cheek.

'Good, thanks,' I say. 'How was Vancouver?'

'Cold,' he replies. He takes a beer out of the fridge, picks up some cheese from the pile Suzy has grated and chucks it into his mouth. She smiles up at him and strokes his back lightly.

'You want to eat, hon?' Suzy asks as he opens the beer.

'No. Remember, I'm out tonight. Don's over from the States.'

'Oh — yeah.'

'So. I'm going for a shower. How was the pool?' he asks me.

'Good, thanks,' I say. 'Cold.'

He half-smiles, then heads back out the door, his duty done. The boundaries are very clear. I am Suzy's friend.

Suzy never complains, and is always telling me about all the sweet things Jez does for her, but it's amazing how often I see him need to make an important phone call just as she's about to bathe the boys or a nappy needs changing. So today, after the kids have eaten and she pours us both a glass of wine, it's me who changes Otto, with Rae pulling funny faces at him behind my shoulder to make him laugh, while Suzy encourages a reluctant Peter to use the potty. While she runs the bath for the boys, I put the dishes in the dishwasher and turn it on.

'Right, we're off,' I say, gathering up Rae and her stuff, and heading out the front door. 'Thanks for tea.'

'You're welcome — and come over this weekend. We haven't got anything planned.'

Outside, the empty boxes on the pavement remind me. I nod my head next door at No. 15 and mouth, 'Have you met them yet?'

'Seem OK.' Suzy shrugs. 'Oh, hon, let me get us that spa day next week,' she calls, lifting up the twins. 'Call it an early birthday present.'

My birthday is not for three months. I look back at her, a boy under each arm. Her dress is stained with tomato sauce. Suzy. Always doing so much for her kids. And Rae. And me.

For so little in return.

This is wrong, I think. This has to stop.

'I'll call you in the morning,' I wave. Saturday evening, I promise myself. When the kids are asleep. I'll tell her tomorrow night.

4

Debs

Debs sized up the women through the gap in the voile curtains that the previous owners had left for them till they put their own blinds up. The women were younger than her, early thirties perhaps, and had that confidence a lot of women seemed to have round here. She could see it in the languid, sure way they carried their bodies. The loud voices that called their children's bold, individual names across roads and from one end of shops to the other without self-consciousness. What did these women, or their husbands, do to afford property so young and in this part of north London? Here Debs was, nearly forty-eight, buying her very first house.

She had seen the American woman before. She had been entering No. 13 next door when they arrived with the removal van yesterday. Debs had been so exhausted, she hadn't listened properly when the woman said her name. Sue? Susan?

Debs pushed her eye closer into the curtain to see what was happening, inadvertently making a voile tent with her nose. The American woman was standing by the gate, waving to the other woman, who crossed the road with a child and went into No. 14. Debs counted the children left

playing in the front garden. One . . . two
. . . three . . . three boys? Three? Oh Lord. She'd
already heard one having a tantrum in the
garden yesterday evening, screeching repetitively
like a high-pitched parrot till she thought she
would get a migraine.

'Debs, don't start,' sighed a voice behind her.

She turned to see Allen, holding a screwdriver.

'I wasn't . . . ' she exclaimed, jumping back,
but he turned and walked out before she could
finish.

How annoying. Now he'd be watching her
again.

That was no good.

Lifting her head, she looked at herself in a
mirror above the marble fireplace, and smiled
hard till her eyes joined in behind her glasses.
Then she walked out of the sitting room into
their new Victorian hall. The hall was still making
her uneasy. Compared with the tiny box rooms
of her purpose-built flat in Hackney, which an
architect had seemingly designed by stretching
out a human then drawing a line for walls by
their head and feet, this hall felt like a cavern. A
cavern she was lost in. It stretched up to the
crumbling ceiling cornice, where spiders hung
watching, then soared up the stairwell to the
darkened first floor far above. No. She didn't like
it. But she wasn't going to tell Allen that.
Quickly, she walked along the corridor to the
dining room at the back of the house.

'We have our own stairs!' she called, trying to
make her voice light. Allen smiled a tight smile,
and continued erecting a shelf unit, pushing his

glasses up his nose where they'd slipped.

What was she saying? What did he care? God knows he'd trudged up and down enough stairs in his mother's gloomy little King's Cross mews, taking her cups of tea.

'Can you hold this upright a sec, love?' Allen said.

'Course, love,' she replied, holding a piece of MDF shelving as he pushed against it with a screwdriver.

No, she mused, looking down at Allen's squat, freckled hands twirling the screwdriver, his eyes screwed up in concentration, perhaps she'd been too quick to assume the value of having her own stairs in this new house.

But what could she do? It wasn't her fault. It was all those months. All those months of the woman upstairs coming in at 12.30 a.m. Clicking her court shoes on the vinyl floor of the communal hall. Always eight steps. Then fifteen thuds up the stairs, eight more clicks past Debs's door, then fifteen more thuds up to her front door.

'Come on,' Debs would say, lying in bed, her ears stuffed with earplugs, a pillow held round her ears. Surely tonight the woman would get the right key? But no. Mostly she tried two, delaying the inevitable banging shut of her front door, and then the padding across the floor above Debs, before the telly started up, invading Debs's blackened bedroom with its muffled rumbling for the next two hours as she lay supine, her jaw aching with the grinding, her eye sockets heavy and bruised from hours of staring angrily at the ceiling in the dark.

Allen took the MDF off Debs, making her start.

'Right. I've got it. You don't want to make us a cup of tea, do you, love?'

'Good idea,' she said cheerfully.

Debs wandered into the kitchen, where a box of her own familiar mugs sat next to a box of china teacups from Allen's mother's house.

Yes, stairs, she thought, putting teabags in Allen's mother's teapot. She'd spent so much time focusing on finally having her own stairs, she'd forgotten something very important.

Sides.

Terraced houses have sides, too.

And now Allen was finally occupied with a task, that was something she was going to explore.

'Thanks, love,' he said as she set a cup of tea beside him with a custard cream.

'Right, I might do another box,' she said, trying to sound casual. 'If you're all right here?'

She held her breath. Allen nodded as he drank his tea, his eyes already fixed back on the instructions for the unit.

Trying not to run, Debs returned to the hall and grabbed one of the boxes Allen had so carefully colour-coded. Orange for kitchen, red for books, orange and red for cookery books. Grabbing a yellow box — clothes — she headed up the stairs and into the large bedroom at the front of the house that straddled the hall and sitting room below. She shut the door quietly, crossed to the windows and closed the curtains, sinking the room into a velvety pink glow.

Debs returned to the door, and put the box of clothes gently down on the floor. Then, kneeling beside it, she pushed her ear firmly into the wall that she shared with the American woman. The patterned floral wallpaper smelt of dust. She smoothed her face along it until the raised stalk of a wisteria rested against her cheekbone.

'Aaahh,' she wanted to say; 'Aaahh,' with the relief of it.

There was nothing at first. A tiny rustling.

Dust mites, she told herself, pushing her ear harder against the paper. Or ants.

Another moment passed. What was that now? If she held her breath and stayed still she could just pick up a faint tick-tick-ticking. Water pipes, perhaps? Now, that would be OK. She probably wouldn't even hear that from a few inches away, and certainly not from the bed.

So far so good. She moved herself closer and waited. A minute passed, then another.

Then another. There was no more sound.

She pulled her head away from the wall a little and, as she waited, began to sort through the box, putting Allen's ties in one pile, and his brown and grey socks in separate ones.

Could she be this lucky? That there would be no . . .

'CAN YOU JUST WAIT TILL I'VE FIN-ISHED, JEZ?'

The muffled shout was such a shock, Debs jerked her head away from the wall, feeling a ping in her neck.

What? Where on earth had that come from?

29

She stayed crouched on the floor, looking around nervously as if the owner of the voice was in the room.

Debs waited a second, then carefully placed her ear back at the wall. There was a new noise now. Like a tap dripping. No. Lighter, like a . . .

It couldn't be.

The flush of the toilet right beside her head almost threw her back on her knees. A great gurgling and groaning of pipes followed.

A toilet. There must be an en-suite bathroom in the bedroom next door. With a great big noisy toilet that she would hear throughout the night?

Palpitations hammered in Debs's chest like a brass knocker. A pressurized sensation started in her head, as if someone had put a hand on her scalp and was pushing down.

All of a sudden, the bedroom door nudged her leg.

Allen.

With a start, Debs jerked upright, plunged her hands back into the box of clothes she'd brought up and pulled them out, sending one of Allen's cricket ties flying right across the room.

'Everything all right, love?' Allen asked, putting his head round the door and looking at the tie now dangling off the dressing table, then at the closed curtains. He walked over and opened them.

She smiled hard, rubbing her neck. 'Just unpacking.'

He wrinkled his nose. 'Probably best to wait till we've cleared the hall,' he said.

'Hmm, maybe you're right,' she replied, standing up.

Allen put out his hand to help her. Then he looked around at the large bedroom. The sunlight burst through the windows and spread a great buttery beam across the walls. The bed was freshly made with a cream eiderdown they'd bought, with matching wooden lamps on either side.

'Yes . . . We're going to be happy here,' Allen said, nodding his head.

It sounded like an order, she thought. And after the last six months, she couldn't blame him.

Debs heard the front door slam next door and someone leave through the gate. Were they going to make that noise every time they left the house?

'Oh yes, love,' she said, turning back and smiling at Allen. 'Yes.'

5

Callie

It takes me a while to realize it's a phone I can hear ringing.

The thing is, sometimes I dream in sounds. I know most people dream only in pictures, but not me, not since I was a child. Typically, the scenario is that I am sitting somewhere empty like Dad's potato field in winter under that flat, mouse-grey Lincolnshire sky, hearing nothing but silence. Then the sounds start to build up around me, each tone perfect and unadulterated in my ear. Maybe it begins with the wind breathing past me, rustling branches of a tree. Music starts, like gusts of air blowing through empty irrigation pipes in discordant notes. Then a heartbeat joins in. A heavy, booming heartbeat. That's usually when I wake up and find myself sweating, my own heart thumping with panic. I jump up, run into Rae's room and check she is still breathing.

But it isn't my heart beating, or a dream, or even Rae whimpering in her sleep that wakes me up tonight. In fact, it is Tom.

'Hi,' he shouts down the phone. 'I got your message. What is it?'

'Hang on,' I say, scrabbling to get the phone

32

by my ear. There is a faint echo from his end. Satellite phone.

'What's up?' he says, sounding concerned.

'Oh. No. Rae's fine,' I say, trying to sit up.

'Well, what?' he snaps.

'Tom?' I reply, opening my eyes and blinking. 'You know it's two in the morning?'

There is a silence as he works out that in Sri Lanka he is five hours ahead, and not behind, UK time.

'Shit. Have I done it again?'

Tom is a skilled wildlife cameraman who could tell you everything you'd like to know about the breeding habits of a golden jackal or fennec fox, but when it comes to numbers, he is bordering on the equivalent of dyslexic. In the old days, I found it sweet and funny when he woke me at 2 a.m. from Uganda or Papua New Guinea, hearing his apologetic disbelief that he had cocked up again. 'Go on then, tell me what you've been doing,' I'd say, burying into blackness under the duvet so I could pretend he was lying beside me, hearing about his day spent searching a cave for a rare wolf spider or getting stuck up a tree with a camera while his guides chased away the mountain lion underneath.

But Tom and I don't joke any more. Ever.

We just get to the point.

'I rang because I've got some news,' I say.

'What?'

'Um . . . well, I'm going back to work.'

There is a pause. A great big pause that stretches from London across the starry night of the Arabian Sea to Sri Lanka.

Maybe I'll be lucky, I think. After all, I was lucky with Rae when I told her earlier this evening. She was so excited she spat out the popcorn we were having for our weekly Friday-night 'midnight feast'.

'You're going to work?' she had shrieked. 'What, like Hannah's mum? A farmer?'

'A pharmacist,' I laughed, picturing Caroline tossing hay in her Karen Millen suit and highlighted bob. Rae has already told me that Hannah is her big hope for a best friend.

'No, I've got a different job. But you know what that means? It means that I won't be here to pick you up after school.'

'Yippee!' Rae shouted. 'So I can go to after-school club with Hannah?'

'Uh, yes,' I replied, confused. Grateful. Already missing her.

So that was Rae. But Tom is Tom.

'What — is that a joke?' he growls on the phone.

'No.'

I sigh.

'Tom, listen. I can't stay at home forever. It was only meant to be six months, then it was a year. Now it's five. I have to go back to work some time.'

He says nothing, so I tiptoe on.

'I actually just rang Guy at Rocket on the off-chance he had a few days' freelance work, and then he just asked me out of the blue to do the sound for Loll Parker's first short film — the Swedish artist, who did the thing at the Tate?'

I pause, fighting the small involuntary smile

34

that keeps pulling at the corners of my mouth since I spoke to Guy on Tuesday.

'Bloody hell, Cal!' I want Tom to say. 'Well done! Well done for being so good at your bloody job that your old boss has snapped your arm off the minute you ring after five years!'

'Sorry, Cal. Am I missing something?' he actually says. 'So, who's going to look after Rae?'

It still feels like the universe has shifted off its axis when that coldness emerges from Tom's lips. My Tom always spoke as if there was a joke coming at the end of his sentence. My Tom never spoke like this. Not once in four years. I try to remind myself he's just worried about Rae.

'Well, she'll go to after-school club for a few weeks,' I say, trying to remind myself he'll need time to get used to the idea, just like I have. 'Which she's really excited about, by the way. And the staff are trained in first aid, like teachers. But if the Loll Parker job goes OK and I like it, and Guy offers me more work, then I don't know . . . I'll probably find a childminder who can fit round my hours.'

There is another, even longer pause.

'Tom?' I say.

'What?' he replies curtly.

I take a chance. 'Look — I know this is a lot to ask, but could you talk it through with me? Guy said that a lot of the tech's moved on. I said I'm sure I'll be fine, but actually, I'm completely petrified . . . '

There is another silence.

'Actually, Cal, I couldn't give a shit. I can't believe you're dumping Rae with strangers. After everything we've been through with her. And I'm five thousand fucking miles away. What am I supposed to do?'

Tonight Rae and I celebrated my new job. We made 'cocktails' of lemonade, apple juice and pink food-colouring, and danced to Girls Aloud.

I take a long breath. Stay calm, I think.

'Tom. I don't know — maybe . . . You have been away a lot this year, and . . . '

'Yeah, well, that's what happens when you have two lots of rent to pay, Cal.'

I exhale.

'OK, but the thing is, I don't think you realize how good she is. She wants to do stuff on her own. I found out from her teacher last week that she took herself off to join the lunchtime choir all by herself, and now she's excited because they're doing an end of term concert. And you should have seen her today, trying to run to the park with her friend. She's just desperate to get away from me. She just wants to be normal. I mean, Tom, really, she is normal.'

And then I throw my last attempt into the ring.

'And, you know, it means I'll be earning my own money again and not asking you all the time. So maybe you won't have to work away so much . . . '

He actually snorts now.

'You know what, Cal? That's the thing. It's always about you.'

What? I feel Mum's temper rising in me. I gulp.

Count to ten.

'I actually don't think for a second this has anything to do with what is good for Rae, Cal, I think it's about what is good for you . . .'

'Tom — that's not fair!' I hear myself exclaim down the phone.

Please, I think. Don't do it, Callie. Don't let him do this.

'Yeah?' he says. 'You reckon? That's exactly what it's about, it's . . .'

It's no good. When Mum's temper comes, it comes out of some place deep down inside me. I wish, not for the first time, that she'd been around long enough to teach me how to control it.

'Tom?' I say. 'Why don't you just . . . oh, just . . . oh, FUCK OFF!'

And it's all too late. Slamming the phone down, I turn over in my bed and scream into my pillow.

Idiot!

Stupid, stupid, stupid.

I've done it again. Every time.

I lie there, keeping my face buried in the soft cotton, annoyed with myself. It dampens quickly with my breath. Somehow the warmth is comforting.

Oh God. I bet Kate, his camera assistant, was there, listening to all of it. I bet she was lying with her head on Tom's shoulder, with that amazing hair, the colour of blackberries, tumbling all over him.

Why do I let him get to me?

Groaning, I roll out of bed and walk through to the sitting room, shaking my head. I will not cry. I will not cry. I will not let Tom rip away the tiny bit of forgotten self-esteem that Guy gave me back this week.

Aimlessly I pick up my address book, desperate to talk to someone, already knowing there is no point. The grubby pages are tattered, full of crossed-out contacts and out-of-date entries. I keep meaning to replace this book but secretly I know that if I removed all the school friends I left behind in Lincolnshire, and the college and work friends who eventually gave up calling when I gave birth to a child with a heart condition at twenty-seven and was too tired to meet them for a drink or even answer the phone for three years, there would be hardly anyone left.

I look at the few contacts who have hung on determinedly. They are fading away of their own accord, the ink blurring with age. I consider them for a second. Fi's dad died three months ago in hospital in Lincoln and I haven't been in touch since she first rang from home to tell me, because, to be honest, she mentioned that her friends were 'helping her through' and I realized, with a pinch of pain, that she didn't include me in that category any more. I can hardly ring in the middle of the night and ask her to listen as I pour all this out. And then there is Sophie. I count the months she's been in Zurich on secondment. Four already, and I still haven't got round to writing in the Swiss phone number she sent me on an ironic postcard of a mountain milkmaid — an almost-forgotten reference to the night she cried with laugher while I drunkenly tried to show her how to milk a cow on our bemused old cat — and have now probably lost it altogether. I suspect she sent it as a formality anyway, out of loyalty to a friendship that has gently dissipated into air.

I put the book down.

When did I lose the ability to keep and make friends? When did it become just Suzy?

Even though it's only June, the air is balmy and thick. I undo the latch on the old wooden sash window. It lifts with a heavy creak. The tiny crack in the corner pane is spreading, I notice. I keep meaning to tell the landlord. One day I will open the window and it will just fall out.

A light catches my eye. The new woman at No. 15 is up, too. She is standing up, putting books on the shelf in her sitting room. There are hundreds of them. Just like Mum used to have. The shelves are nearly full, packed around the fireplace.

A book, I think, watching the woman. When was the last time I read a book? Mum and I used to devour them, passing them between us, waiting to see what the other one thought. Now I am just too tired even to open one. Tired with what, I sometimes think? Shopping and cooking. Washing and drying. Taking lots of things to lots of places: Rae to school, the bins to the gate, our ancient car for its MOT. My mind has become like a car engine with a faulty clutch. It revs too fast, without actually going anywhere.

The woman's presence is oddly comforting. She looks quite old, with a thick, greying bob and black-rimmed glasses. I saw her husband coming back from the shop earlier. He is shorter than her, with longish sandy hair, sideburns, thick glasses and a nose that looks too big for his face.

The woman turns round. That's funny. She is wearing one of those soft velour dressing gowns that Mum used to wear, too. I touch the cracked windowpane and test it gently with my finger.

Up and down Churchill Road, darkened windows stare back.

Oh God. I can't live like this any more.

Rae's illness has sucked us dry. I am a husk. An empty shell. No wonder other women avoid me. They sense that I will suck them dry, too. Maybe Tom is right. Maybe it is all about me. Me and my endless problems. Women sense I need everything and have nothing to give back in friendship. All of them, that is, apart from Suzy.

I watch the woman a little longer, staring at a cover. Will I ever meet her, I wonder? Or will we pass wordlessly in the street like I do with everyone else around here?

A memory drifts back to me. A warm evening the colour of buttercups. I am eight, and walking shyly towards our farm cottage, entrusted with a tray of lasagne to take to our new farm assistant and his wife. It is almost too hot, the tea towel placed carefully on my outspread hands no longer absorbing the burning heat. I walk among the dried-mud tractor ruts of the farm track to a patch of nettles on the corner, where our cat, Tuppence, lies grooming herself beside a pile of rusty old fence posts. The couple are lifting a sofa in through the cottage gate. The woman,

40

who is wearing a spotty headscarf, turns and looks at me, and I see her eyes drop to my tray. My stomach lurches with doubt. What if they don't want the lasagne? How does Mum know they will want it? Panic overcomes me. I stop and turn. Mum is watching me from the farmhouse window, willing me on with a fluttering hand, and I just know then, in my eight-year-old way, that sometimes you have to make an effort with people. You have to be brave; put yourself out there to get to know them.

And I did that for a while. I did it fine when I grew up. Then I forgot how to do it, and Mum wasn't there to wave me on with her fluttering hand and reward me with a kiss when I returned.

I watch the woman across the road. She shuts her book and turns off the light. Maybe it's because her dressing gown reminds me of Mum, but right at that minute I decide that it's time to change things. She just looks nice.

6

Suzy

Suzy woke up with a start.

Something was wrong.

'Mummy . . . ' Henry murmured.

She rolled over, and pulled Henry's body close to her.

'It's OK, hon,' she said, not sure if it really was.

She lifted her head off his little wooden bed, where she'd been lying with her long legs tucked up, and looked at his bunny rabbit clock, its ears timed not to pop up till 7 a.m. The face said 2.40 a.m.

She turned round and sat up. 'Jez?' she called into the darkness of the house.

Nothing.

Slowly, she pulled away from Henry limb by limb, till she could manoeuvre her body out of his warm little bed. Pulling her cardigan around her pyjamas, she padded silently down the stairs to the hallway, where a single lamp continued to perform its duty of waiting for Jez to come home. Nothing. His shoes and coat were not there. Still on his Friday night out with Don Berry. His third night out in town since he'd got back from Vancouver on Monday.

She padded upstairs again and sat in the

hallway. If she looked up to the second-floor ceiling above, then down to the hallway below, this is where she had the most space. God, how she craved space.

She shut her eyes and summoned a picture of home: hiking out onto the mesa, through silver birch and juniper bushes dotted like bristle across a plain, above which pristine clouds scudded at breakneck speed against a deep blue sky; finding a place to camp against a rock, where she could sit and watch the deer trail past, the crunch of their feet on ice the only sound out there apart from the occasional plane landing in Denver, twenty miles away. If she tried hard now, she could even conjure up in her mind the soft dusk there, and the way the light bathed her skin in gold dust before twisting into great swirls of violet and crimson across the atmosphere. And oh, the stars. Millions of them — not the occasional dim glow you saw in the mean piece of murky sky that topped London like a badly fitting lid.

Homesickness knotted in her stomach. Surely he couldn't have just forgotten Colorado. Who she was?

A new memory floated into her mind. Of Jez appearing at work one Friday and motioning her over with a smile. In his hand, he dangled a key.

'Bob's lent me his cabin for the weekend,' he'd said in that deep English voice that sent teasing reverberations through her body. He raised his eyebrows and dropped his arm behind her back.

'Cool,' she said, smiling, feeling his fingers stroke her gently, desperate already for more.

She had taken him for his first wilderness hike
that weekend. They'd climbed down into a
ravine hewn by water from towering rock over
millions of years, and walked along the sunlit
river for hours till they reached one of her
favourite lakes. Nobody else had been there so
they'd laid out a blanket on the bank and swum
naked out to the centre of the lake, her arms
round his neck, feeling him close. There was
something about the fact that she knew he
couldn't get home without her that had thrilled
her that day. Jez was all hers.

'You like it?' she'd asked.

'Yes,' he'd smiled, rubbing one hand down
over her buttocks and thighs, her skin taut in the
chilled water.

'There are lots of places like this. Where
nobody goes. I can show you.'

'Don't you get scared?' he asked her. 'Out here
on your own?'

'Of what?'

'I don't know,' he said. 'Bears?'

'Bears are OK,' she replied. 'You just throw a
stone — shout. Wave your arms.'

She remembered how he laughed. 'You're an
interesting girl,' he said, pulling her further into
him.

Back at the cabin in the late afternoon they'd
found a hot tub out back.

'You know, I think this may be the best day of
my life,' she'd murmured drunkenly in his ear, as
they'd sat naked, their legs entwined, drinking
beer, steam floating around them.

'Hmm,' he'd said, nuzzling further down into

44

her neck. She'd waited for him to agree.

But he never did. And she was going to have to face up to it — he never was going to.

Her husband had been an enigma then, and he was an enigma now.

Suzy yawned and headed past Henry's room to her own bedroom, and climbed into the middle of her empty, king-size bed.

The sheets were cold. She hugged herself close for warmth.

Tomorrow. Tomorrow she'd make the phone call. What choice did she have?

SATURDAY

7

Debs

It was eleven o'clock in the morning when the doorbell rang. Debs lifted her head in the bedroom upstairs, surprised. Who was that? Who would be calling on a Saturday morning? Had Allen's cricket match been called off?

The sun was back in the bedroom today, projecting laser displays of dust beams. She had held out her hand to touch one earlier, watching particles of human skin, loam and hair left by the people who had slept here for a hundred years dance round her fingers.

She hadn't slept too badly in the end, dropping off about 3 a.m. Thoughts of the Poplar girl hadn't kept her awake, for once. Allen had spent the night, in his green paisley pyjamas, firmly on the other side of the bed. She had wondered if that would change when they moved to the new house, but so far there was no sign of it.

She'd heard the toilet next door flush once and not again. That would be bearable, she supposed. She'd have to wait and see. She hadn't noticed her neighbour upstairs in Hackney for three years. And then one night she heard the door opening, her heels clacking on the stairs. Then it never stopped.

49

Rubbing her stiff neck, Debs pulled herself up and headed out the bedroom door, picking up the last empty yellow box labelled 'Allen' on the way. Allen's sock drawer was now full of brown and grey pairs that still whiffed slightly of shoes, even though she'd washed them. This was one of the strangest things about living with a man for the first time. The foreign odours.

With the empty box held in front of her, her vision of the upper landing was blocked. 'Aargh!' she shrieked as she felt the hard edge of something catch her knee, sending her toppling sideways into the wall with only time to put out her left hand. A vicious stabbing pain travelled up her arm, through her shoulder and into her sore neck. 'Oh,' she moaned. Too late, she remembered Allen's final words before he left for his cricket club in Barnet this morning: 'I've popped another box outside the bedroom for you, love.'

Limping down the stairs, she rubbed her sore knee with one hand and held her neck with the other. Her neck had been painful all night. That's all she needed, a sore knee, too.

The doorbell rang again. Oh, for goodness' sake!

'Coming,' Debs called, reaching the hall. The morning sun was bursting through the stained-glass roses in the front door, creating a prism of reds and pinks on the mirror of the old-fashioned hallstand Allen's mother had left him. It was carved fussily with twirls and pleats, and offered racks for tall umbrellas and hooks for hats and shelves for God only knew what. Allen's mother had left him lots of things that made Debs uncomfortable, including an ugly mini-grandfather clock that now hung opposite the hallstand, and the china cabinet in the sitting room, which overwhelmed the room with its brooding, mahogany doors and teetering stacks of 1930s lime Burleigh wedding service, much of which was veined with brown cracks. It was as if the presence of his mother was still with them, reproaching him from every corner.

She took a deep breath.

'Hello?' she said through the glass.

'Uh — hello?' said a voice on the other side. It was a young woman. She sounded nervous.

'Can I help you?' Debs called again.

'Um . . . I'm just . . . it's just . . . um . . . '

Debs looked through the spy hole. A woman with long, soft corkscrews of dark blonde hair stood on the doorstep with a little girl who looked just like her, but with slightly blonder hair and darker eyes. She was holding a dish covered in tinfoil and a bottle.

Oh no.

Feeling sick, Debs opened the door.

'Yes?' she said faintly, poking her head round.

'Hi,' the woman said. She seemed unsure of herself. 'I'm Callie, from across the road?'

'Oh. Yes?' said Debs.

'Sorry — are you OK?' the woman asked, looking at the way Debs was rubbing her knee.

'Oh, yes. I just had a little fall,' said Debs.

'I've probably come at a bad time?' said the woman.

Yes, thought Debs. You have.

51

'I just wanted to drop in this lasagne and some wine to say welcome to the street. I live across the road with Rae.'

Debs looked at them both, up and down. Could she just take the food and shut the door?

What would Allen expect her to do? She made herself think hard.

'Oh, how kind of you,' she forced herself to say. 'Would you like to come in?'

The young woman's face lit up. 'Thanks, that would be lovely. We'll just stay a minute.'

Debs motioned them in, smiling at the little girl. The woman, Callie, was very slim, she noticed, wearing jeans and an embroidered tunic and sandals. She looked like one of those effortlessly small-boned, thin girls Debs used to envy at school. Self-consciously, she pulled her long navy jumper over her generous hips. The little girl wore a summer dress on a tiny frame that revealed skin the colour of bread dough.

'I'm Debs, by the way. Now,' said Debs, trying to stop her fingers from shaking as she took the gifts from Callie, 'can I get you a cup of tea?'

'Well . . . thanks, if you're sure?' said Callie, looking round at the piles of boxes.

'Absolutely,' Debs said, walking ahead of them. 'Just give me a second to find everything. We're still in a muddle. So have you been in the street long, Callie?' she asked, putting on the kettle and taking the teapot down from a shelf.

That usually worked. If she asked people questions, they usually talked about themselves and left her alone.

'About two and a half years,' said Callie, smiling.

'And are you from round here?'

Callie shook her head. 'Not really. Not at all, actually. We were in Tufnell Park before. But we, er . . . ' She glanced at Rae, then shrugged. 'Well, there's lots of lovely park space here. And what about you? Where have you come from?'

'Hackney, dear,' said Debs, putting teabags in the pot. 'Allen and I just got married, actually . . . ' She looked at Rae and winked, seeing the little girl's ears prick up. Debs could see her summing up this old lady and wondering what she'd look like in a white wedding dress. Her face looked revolted.

'Oh, congratulations!' Callie said. 'That's wonderful.'

'Thank you,' Debs said, taking the teapot over to the kettle. Oh no. Now the woman might ask about the wedding and that was something Debs wasn't discussing with anyone.

'So, what about you, dear?' she said. 'What do you do?'

Callie looked at her in surprise, and suddenly laughed out loud.

'Actually, it's funny to be asked that. Years ago I was a sound designer — you know, doing the sound effects for TV adverts and films? And I'm actually going back on Monday for the first time in ages and . . . '

It was no good. Debs could feel the shaking in her fingers getting worse. Too late, she tried to place the teapot on the worktop, before feeling it slip between her fingers.

It hit the floor with a loud crack and splintered in ten different directions.

There was a stunned silence.

'I'm so sorry,' Debs said, looking at Rae's shocked face. 'Deary me, what a silly. What will Allen say? That was his mummy's teapot.' She smiled, steadying herself on the table.

Callie looked mortified. 'Sorry, it's my fault for distracting you. Let me help you with that.'

'No!' Debs said, louder than she meant to. It was all she could do not to let the word come out as a shriek. 'Please. Leave it. I do apologize, I'm just very tired from the move.'

'Oh, this is a bad time, I'm sorry. We're just barging in on you,' the young woman said, her face flushing. 'Why don't we do this another time, when you're more settled?'

'Of course,' said Debs. 'Give me a couple of days, and when everything's unpacked, come over and have a proper cup of tea.'

Except from now on she'd be on alert. She wouldn't answer the door.

'Actually,' the young woman said, her voice with a slight quiver in it. 'This might be a bit presumptuous, but I noticed all your books . . . '

'Oh, yes,' Debs replied warily. 'I have far too many. Allen keeps asking me to clear some out — but I do like my books.'

'It's just that it's ages since I read a book. I need to get myself going again. I was wondering — ' the young woman grimaced nervously — 'if maybe I could have a look at them some time?'

Oh Lord. What was Debs getting herself into here?

'Mum . . . ' A whine came from the hall. They both looked to see the little girl standing at the front door. 'I want to go home.'

'Sorry,' said Callie. 'We better go. Rae's a little tired today.'

'Well, it was kind of you to bring the lasagne,' Debs said, relieved, following her through the hall. 'Allen will enjoy that when he gets back from the cricket.'

At the front door, Debs stopped, and looked down at a box marked green for 'loft'. She had a thought.

'Rae, is it? Do you like little puppets, dear?' she asked.

The little girl nodded.

'Would you like this?' Debs pulled out a revolting Christmas reindeer puppet with felt antlers and a scarlet pom-pom nose from a box. 'This was Allen's mummy's. She made it.'

Rae took the puppet wordlessly from Debs. She fixed the puppet over her fingers with a smile, then looked up at Debs. Without any warning, she ran the puppet up Debs's arm, and banged it hard on her nose.

'Rae!' Callie shouted.

Debs took a deep breath. 'Oh, goodness!' she said.

'I am SO sorry,' Callie said. 'Rae — that's not like you! She's usually very well behaved. Rae, say sorry.'

'No,' said Rae, looking at Debs sullenly.

'I don't know what to say,' Callie said. 'I'm so embarrassed.'

'Oh, not at all, dear,' Debs said. 'I'm sure she didn't mean it.'

'Well, I'm sorry,' said Callie, grabbing the puppet from Rae and putting it back in the box. 'I will have a word with her when we get home. And thanks again.'

Debs waved goodbye, and shut the door behind them.

'Oh,' she groaned, falling against the wall. Her thighs felt as if they had heavy weights strapped on them. She rubbed her sore knee and her sore neck, then her sore nose. The ugly puppet sat back in the box, its blue button eyes laughing at her.

Not to worry, though. She'd met little girls like that before and she knew how to deal with them.

★   ★   ★

By the time Allen arrived home from the cricket at 3 p.m., she had recovered herself. Most of the green boxes were on the upper landing for him to put up in the loft, and she was sorting through more books.

'Love, have you got a minute,' he called from the front garden.

What now? she thought.

She came out and found him standing with the American woman from next door and a man with dark, wavy hair pushed back from his face. He was towering over Allen, with a jowly face and hooded, tired eyes. Her palms went clammy.

'Love, this is Suzy and Jez from next door,' said Allen. 'They were just telling me that Thursday is pick-up day for the rubbish and recycling.'

'We've met!' Suzy said, waving at Debs. 'Hey, how's it going?'

'Fine, thank you,' Debs stuttered.

'Debs, this is Jez.' Suzy pointed at her husband. He was so handsome Debs could hardly look at him. She had never looked men like him in the eye, in case for even one terrible second they thought she was flirting with them. The thought of their contempt was much more difficult to handle than their complete blindness to the fact that she was there.

'Hello,' he said. He was English, with a deep, clipped voice. He gave her a polite smile, hardly registering her at all.

'Listen, you must come round for a cup of tea,' said Suzy. 'I'll invite Callie, she lives across the road.'

'Oh yes,' said Debs. 'The lady who does the sound effects?'

'Sound effects?' said Suzy. 'Uh, no. I mean, she used to . . . '

'Oh — ah, I think she said she was going back to work next week?' said Debs. Why couldn't all these people just leave her alone? Was she getting confused again?

The woman's face changed a little. 'I don't think so.'

Debs stared.

'Come on, love — it was nice to meet you,' said Allen, beaming at Suzy.

The couple turned into their own gate, the man nodding politely.

'OK, love?' said Allen.

Debs gave him a peck on the cheek. 'Not bad. Had a little fall and hurt my knee, but it's feeling better now.'

'Oh dear.' Allen patted her arm.

As he bent over to put his cricket bag down, she spotted a small piece of the Burleigh teapot lying on the floor outside the cellar door. Oh Lord. It must have fallen through a hole in the plastic bag that she had taken down to the cellar earlier to hide under the floorboards. She marched ahead quickly, before he stood up, and picked the china shard up, pocketing it in her trousers.

8

Suzy

'Hmm, well, at least they don't look like they'll be having loud parties . . . ' Suzy said as they shut the door to their house.

'Who — the trolls?' Jez muttered.

'Jez!' she giggled, hitting his arm. 'Don't. The boys will hear you and repeat it.' Jez winked at Henry, who sniggered, delighted to be involved in the joke.

'She does seem a little spaced out, though. She thinks Callie works.'

'That was the best restaurant ever,' Henry shouted, running upstairs to play in his bedroom, holding a balloon the waitress had given him.

Suzy smiled. 'Yeah, that was nice, thanks.'

'Good,' Jez said.

They caught each other's eye for a moment and . . .

Jez's phone shrieked.

'Hang on . . . ' he said, answering it. He disappeared into the front sitting-room, shutting the door.

God, she could throw that phone out the window. It burst into their lives every hour, every day, bringing news or messages that took him away from her. Who on earth was ringing him on a Saturday?

Suzy followed Peter and Otto into the kitchen, trying to ignore it, and put out their train set for them. Things had been brighter this morning and she didn't want it spoilt. OK, so Jez hadn't got back in from his night out with Don Berry till 4 a.m. this morning, and OK, he'd woken Otto up by slamming the door drunkenly and then left her to deal with the two-year-old's cries. But ever since he'd got up this morning he had been in a great mood. He'd even put his hand round her waist as they'd been talking to the couple next door in a way that strangely reminded her of that day at the lake in Colorado. The smell of him so close had put all her senses on alert. The warm scent of wine and garlic on his breath. The proprietary weight of his hand on her back.

No, it was exciting, if she thought about it. Something had changed since yesterday.

Maybe this had all been in her mind. Maybe there was nothing to worry about after all, she thought, replacing the sofa throw that Jez had used as a blanket during the night then dumped on the floor. Maybe he'd just been stressed after all these months of trying to land the Canadian contract and talking it through with Don Berry last night had allowed him to blow off the pressure of it all?

Suzy walked over to the kitchen area and put on some fresh coffee to sober them both up after the bottle of wine they'd had at lunch. The calendar caught her eye. She counted the days since the beginning of June. Ten, eleven . . . She

60

was probably starting to ovulate right now.

She opened the fridge, suddenly excited about planning the evening. Asparagus fought for space with strawberries at the top of the fridge. There were a couple of steaks on the middle shelf and two bottles of white wine. Good.

All she had to do was get the kids to bed early, have a bath . . .

Jez wandered into the kitchen, his head turned backwards to listen to something Henry was shouting from upstairs. Suzy glanced at his face as she went to fill the coffee pot.

Wait a second. What was that?

She looked back.

Jez's head was fixed at an upward angle as he answered Henry's question about something to do with planets. There. There it was. Where the dip of his cheek normally was, a new layer of flesh subtly flattened out the contour.

Was he becoming heavier around the face? When did that happen?

Her eyes scanned his body quickly for more evidence, and settled on his stomach. He had always been big, but there, too, there was a change. His shirt pushed a little ahead of his jacket.

Suzy watched, amazed. How had she not noticed before? It wasn't that surprising, perhaps. She couldn't remember the last time she had seen her husband naked.

As he turned and walked towards her she saw it more clearly. There. Under his chin. A slight curve. It made him look older; gave him a vulnerable look.

The idea of an old Jez was comforting. He would need her then.

'Hey, hon,' she said in her gentlest voice. 'Come here — please.'

Jez put down his phone and walked over to her, glancing at the boys.

'What?' he murmured.

She reached up and put her arms around his neck, pulling him lightly towards her, feeling no tension this time. Just the velvet heat of his neck connecting with hers. At the touch of his skin, a tremor ran through her at what might happen later. It made her involuntarily flex her body towards him.

'What do you want to do tonight?' she whispered.

'That was Don,' Jez murmured back in her ear. 'His boss at the bank is throwing a party tonight out in Hertfordshire. He reckons I could make a few contacts. The guy's invited us to stay over and play golf tomorrow.'

She held him close, finally allowing herself to recognize the familiar hard tension in the muscles beneath his skin. It had never gone away; the wine had just softened his resolve to push her away again. Instead, he was standing patiently in her arms, waiting for her to let go. So he could leave again.

Lunch hadn't been for her. It had been for the boys.

'OK, hon,' she said, lowering her eyes. 'If you think that's a good idea. Can you pour the coffee? I'm going to use the bathroom.'

Her cheeks burning, she fought her way

blindly up the stairs and into her room, shutting the door behind her.

She sat down on the bed — the bed that she had slept in alone last night while Jez lay drunkenly on the sofa downstairs. No foetal position for her husband. She'd found him this morning on his back, snoring, his arms splayed out, like the king.

Be strong, she told herself. Be strong. Do not give him an easy excuse to leave.

Time was running out. First she had to make Nora happen. Nora would make everything all right. A daughter would soften him. A cute little girl would crack through that armour.

And, in the meantime, she would just have to do everything she could to prepare for the worst. Jez's father already looked at her like she was a bad smell. Just think what he could ask his old boys' club friends to do to her in the divorce courts.

No — she needed evidence, just in case Jez did leave, so she could protect her babies.

Suzy took out her own mobile and finally did what she had been putting off doing all day. She dialled a number.

9

Callie

'If I do this, it feels like I'm in an aeroplane.'

Rae stands on a bollard in the ice-rink car park, her arms spread wide, pushing her face into the wind.

From this angle, we could be standing on a cliff edge. Below us lies London, six miles away, the London Eye and Gherkin tiny miniatures from this distance.

It was Rae's idea to come up to Ally Pally this evening. It's her favourite place. She almost squeals with delight as she does her carefully paced half-run that I have taught her, along the stone terrace in front of the palace. I worry that it's a little late to be up here. Saturday night is when families visiting the ice rink and duck pond go home and groups of kids take their place in the empty car park, leaning with their dogs against the gerbil-cage runs of fire escapes that cover the side of the palace, eyeing up anyone who walks past, with loud music bursting from battered cars. But it is still light enough to feel safe. A pretty silver sky hovers above.

I walk behind Rae, watching her, as always. She dashes in and out of the Victorian lamp posts and walkways that run along the front of the palace's honeyed-brick façade, counting the lion gargoyles on its walls. At a pair of blue doors, tall enough for a giant, she begs me to lift her up to look through the portal windows at the Great Hall that lies empty behind. In some places there is nothing behind. The great arched windows stand alone, like a film set, birds fluttering through them, the palace's innards long ago ravaged by fire. All front, with nothing behind. Everything behind destroyed by one catastrophic event.

'Can I look through that, Mum?' she shouts, pointing at a telescope.

Normally, she knows we can't afford to waste 50p on such trivia, but today is special. I sit on the wall beside her and look around.

Children go skidding by on scooters, screaming, followed by their parents. A black crow flies off the steps and soars over the parkland below.

My wall. Our wall that we have sat on a hundred times.

As Rae turns the telescope one way, then the other, that month when we moved here from Tufnell Park comes back to me.

It's funny. I didn't even know the palace existed then. I stumbled upon it by accident at first, of course, not realizing it was actually a building, not just a park. After an afternoon of following steep pavements uphill with Rae's buggy, trying to walk off the pain of splitting with Tom, I gasped my way up to the top — and there it was. This beautiful old shell of a palace, overlooking the city below. From then on, each day I'd wait as long as I could before the walls of my flat closed in on me and then I'd burst out of the door like a free-diver coming up for air. I'd push the buggy up here and sit for an hour, Rae wrapped up warmly. Not that it took away the loneliness. Even when training athletes sprinted up the near-vertical hills towards me, blowing hard through shiny cheeks, and large groups in turbans and veils strolled past me showing their visiting families this view of the city, I felt more by myself than I ever had in my life, up here. I'd look out at the famous landmark buildings, so far in the distance I might as well be back on the farm in Lincolnshire dreaming about them.

'Mum?'

I look up to see Rae struggling with the weight of the telescope, blinking hard to focus.

'Here,' I say, standing up to help.

'You see that building that looks like a big rod,' I say, moving the telescope towards the west and holding it for her. 'That's the Post Office Tower.'

'Mmm . . . '

'That's near where I'll be on Monday, so not far away.'

I say it to reassure her, but the truth is, I can't quite believe it myself: that on Monday, I will be back in the city.

Rae shrugs. She jumps down and we sit back on the wall.

'Hannah and me played sunbathing at school. We lied on the ground and pretended to put our sunglasses on.'

'Did you?' I smile. 'What, yesterday, when it was sunny?'

'No, the day after yesterday,' she says.

I laugh out loud. She sounds like Tom with his back-to-front timelines. Rae looks up at me, confused. She joins in anyway, pleased she has made a joke. I watch her. It's a shame not many people see Rae laugh. She has a dirty laugh, like Muttley the dog, pushing the air through her teeth with a 'shee shee shee' noise. I put my arm round her and pull her close.

'And where was Henry?'

'He was in Mr McGregor's office because he hit Luke,' she says.

'Really?' I say. I am so glad Rae is starting to make other friends. Now, she and I are both trying. It's funny that Suzy didn't tell me about Henry, though.

'Does he hit you?' I ask.

'No,' she says. 'Henry says he is going to marry me.'

★ ★ ★

We pick up our Saturday-night chips on the way home and walk along the peaceful avenues, sharing them. It becomes so quiet around here in the evenings. Curtains shut. Children stop crying. Dogs stop barking. The dusky summer evening is lit by a trail of little outdoor lamps that people have beside their front doors to help them see their keys and welcome visitors.

When we reach our flat, there is no welcoming light. Our landlord did not instal one and I have no power to do so myself. Not that we have many visitors to welcome, anyway.

67

I hurry Rae through the door, trying not to think about it.

Rae runs to her bedroom without being asked. Every week, it seems, she becomes capable of doing something new and more difficult; things that Tom and I thought she might never do. She puts on her own seat belt in the car now. This morning she took food from the shelves in the supermarket and put it in the trolley. Tonight, she wants to do her favourite new job of getting herself ready for bed, while I pour myself a glass of wine from the second of the two nice bottles I managed to buy on offer earlier, one for the woman across the road, and one for Suzy coming over later.

'Mum, I'm ready!' Rae shouts from her bedroom. I walk in to find her sitting up in bed, her fairy lights already switched on, her favourite Dr Seuss book ready to read on the duvet cover Suzy bought her for Christmas that is covered in embroidered princesses. Rae looks at me defiantly. She is wearing one of Tom's T-shirts again, her curls tumbling down across it. She has a drawer full of pyjamas and nighties but insists on rifling through his shelves every time she stays at his flat in Tufnell Park. Tonight she sports an old red Clash T-shirt that droops off her shoulders. I flinch momentarily at the sight of Paul Simonon smashing a bass on her tiny body. A memory of Tom wearing it at a gig in Camden comes back to me. Of his body inside it, hot and damp from dancing in the packed venue. Of him looking at me with those sleepy, relaxed eyes, then pulling me into his arms, where I rested my lips on the sun-bleached down of his skin, safe from the squash of the crowd.

I've been trying to persuade Rae to wear something warm at night but can see from her face that she is determined. So I can't help it. I lean forward and bury my face in the T-shirt, just for a second, just to remember. Rae kisses my head, and holds on to it for a second.

'Love you,' I say, kissing her back, and turn off her main light.

She turns over and is asleep before I leave the room.

$$\star \quad \star \quad \star$$

Saturday nights are the worst.

Once, before Rae, they were the nights to look forward to, after a day of sleeping off our long working week. Like vampires, Tom and I would emerge at dusk from a mess of warm sheets and newspapers and legs, to head out to Islington or Soho or Camden, depending on whose friends were going where. A few hours was all Tom needed. Then the energy levels that sustained him through the most tortuous of week-long shoots would soar sky-high again. He'd herd me and everyone else into the long hours of a night that could just as easily end up in a club in Camberwell as on the beach in Brighton. You never knew with Tom. All you knew was that the week was finished, if he had his way. Finished, celebrated, drunk over, joked about, yelled at, laughed at, then discarded; ready for a new dawn on Monday.

Now I dread Saturday nights. I dread them.

I look out of my window. There is nothing about Churchill Road tonight that says it is any different from Friday night or, say, Monday night. I just know it's different. I know that behind those curtains, couples are sitting on the sofa, shoulders and legs touching, sipping wine, watching a DVD box set; other people have already headed out for a night with friends in a city that I have always loved but no longer know.

In desperation once, when Tom had Rae one weekend, I even suggested to Suzy that we go into Soho on the Saturday for a drink. But she said she couldn't leave Jez on his own with the kids and that she wouldn't trust a stranger to babysit them, either. So it never happened.

I walk around my flat impatiently.

Where on earth is Suzy? She was due at 9 p.m., and now it is 9.40.

I am on my second glass of wine. I sip it again, too fast.

It is Suzy's reaction to my news that I have worried about the most this week. Because we both know that I will be leaving her alone. I never asked her to ignore the school parents who have so pointedly turned their backs on me. Yet she did it anyway. So now, because of me, there will be no one for her to roller-skate with or swim with or talk to over coffee in this lonely corner of the city during those weekdays that stretch into infinity.

The thing is, I remember how it feels.

Suzy once told me, shortly after they moved

70

in, that Jez thought he might have made a mistake basing his communications consultancy back in London. At the time, Rae and I were at Northmore every few weeks for check-ups after her second op, the big one, before she started school. The thought of knowing I might have to return from the brittle stink of hospital without Suzy's new but already welcoming arms across the road, sent me into a night of anxiety dreams that my desperately welcome new friend had already left, her house replaced by a fish-and-chip shop.

I check the clock again: 9.41 p.m. Where is she? Putting down my wine, I walk into my bedroom to look through my wardrobe in the vain hope I'll find something to wear to work on Monday. Ruefully, I recall hacking through it one afternoon years ago, after the news came that Guy could no longer extend my endless maternity leave. Sartorial self-harm, if you like. By the time I had tearfully bundled my carefully chosen work clothes onto the bed for eBay there were just folded piles left: T-shirts, jeans, jumpers and a padded coat. Not much good in a Soho design studio where image is everything. Great for the play park.

Mentally, I calculate how much Dad sent me for Rae's swimming lessons. I could spend that tomorrow at Brent Cross shopping centre on something to wear, then pay it back out of my first pay cheque. Is that a bad thing to do?

The thought of going back to Guy's studio on Monday sends my stomach into a roller-coaster plunge.

The intercom buzzes. Suzy. Thank goodness. I push the thought from my mind and open the door.

'Hey, hon. I can't stay long,' she says, breezing in. 'Jez just put Peter to bed without his eczema cream.'

'Oh no — call the police,' I say, following her back into the kitchen.

She pretend-punches my arm. 'Shut up.'

'Glass of wine?' I say.

She nods, motioning a half-glass. Moving around the kitchen, my body is tense and upright in anticipation of its difficult duty.

'So . . . ' she says, checking her mobile distractedly. 'What's up?'

'Suze,' I say, handing the glass to her. 'I'm really sorry — there's something I've been meaning to tell you for days . . . '

She looks alarmed.

I take a breath. 'I'm going back to work — on Monday. At my old studio.'

She shrugs slightly, and puts her hand over her mouth. It slides further up over her eyes.

'Sorry . . . ' I say, wrinkling up my face. 'I just have to.'

Suddenly I hear her sniff.

What is she doing?

She sniffs again.

'Suze!' I exclaim. 'It's just a three-week project to start with to see if I can still do it, and I'll be round at the weekend and . . . '

She lifts her face. It takes me a horrible second to realize she is smiling.

'I know — you bitch,' she says, pretending to

72

hit me on the arm again. 'The woman next door told me.'

She rolls her eyes with comedy effect to emphasize how bad this is.

I already know.

'Oh God, I'm so sorry. I don't know why I told her.'

'Hey,' she says, 'don't worry about it. I think it's great.'

'Really?'

'Absolutely. I thought you seemed a little down. But what about Rae?'

'She's going to after-school club.'

'Really? What does Tom say about that?'

I grimace. 'What do you think?'

'You want me to keep an eye on her?' she says.

She, more than anyone, knows how hard it is for me to leave Rae.

'Thanks,' I say, putting down my wine glass and hugging her. 'I don't know what I'd do without you.' I try to ignore the hypocrisy of my own words.

'Oh, you're welcome,' she says. Even though she's been here for more than two years, Suzy has never stopped replying like an American to each and every 'thank you' she receives, and sometimes I want to tell her to stop, but I don't. 'I know you'd do it for me.'

For some reason, I can't leave it there. I feel I owe Suzy something back. I have to meddle.

'Do you ever think about doing something else now the kids are at nursery — working, or studying or something?'

I realize I can't remember what Suzy did

before kids. I think she met Jez when she was temping in an office that he was contracting for in Denver.

Her expression shifts.

'No,' she says. 'Oh my God, no. Really. I just want to be there for my kids, Cal. It's important to me.'

A picture of Rae pops into my head: she is coming out of class on Monday, not into my arms, but to the back of the queue of exhausted kids led off by the after-school club teacher to yet another stuffy room full of more chaotic noise and childhood germs, where they will wait till tight-jawed parents dash from the Tube to grab them at 6 p.m.

'Listen, don't worry about me — here's to you,' Suzy says, lifting her glass. 'Good luck, you know I'll miss you.'

All of a sudden, I don't want my wine. She looks at me quizzically.

'What's up? Are you nervous about going back?'

'Incredibly,' I say. I am actually feeling hurt but I'm not sure why.

She looks at her phone screen.

'Oh, hell,' she says.

Jez probably can't find the nappies. Four minutes, I calculate. That must be a record. The bottle of wine sits on the worktop, not even half-drunk.

'Got to go,' she says. 'Listen, just ring me if you're worried. And, hey, don't be nervous, I know you'll be brilliant.'

No, you don't, I think. You have no idea

74

whether I'll be brilliant or not because we've never really spoken about my job. I am not sure that you even know what a sound designer does and you certainly don't know what it took me to become one. Because you've never asked.

But I hug her anyway, knowing I should be grateful that she cares enough to say it.

As she leaves she turns.

'What was she like?'

'Who?'

'The woman next door.'

'Really nice, actually. She gave Rae a little toy when we went round, which I'll tell you about another time. And I'm going to borrow a book from her, she has hundreds,' I say.

'Maybe I should invite her in for coffee,' Suzy murmurs.

'I see — gone five minutes and you're already replacing me,' I say, trying to sound cheerful.

'You think she likes spas?' she says, doing a giant, comedy wink. If I did that I'd look stupid. When Suzy does it she looks like a model in a Vogue spread, all elfin blonde bob, long pale lashes and sexy full lips.

I stay on the doorstep watching her.

A strange sensation comes over me. I feel the way people describe feeling when they sense their loved one's plane is going to crash. As Suzy lifts her foot off the road and onto her side of the pavement I have an urge to shout at her that I won't go to work. That we'll go to The Sanctuary next week after all, and lie on our fronts having sandalwood and lotus oil rubbed into our skin.

But I don't.

Because I have to let her go, just a little. It is time.

So I stay fixed to the spot as she enters her gate. The front door opens and she is gone.

I look up. The silver sky has oxidized into black. A breeze makes me shiver. The weather forecast said rain was coming.

10

Suzy

Suzy opened the door of her house and walked in. As soon as she shut it behind her, her shoulders slumped and she pulled her cardigan round herself.

So it wasn't a mistake. A ball of pressure shot up inside her chest like a high-speed elevator. She held her breath for a second, trying to contain it. There was no noise.

Tiptoeing upstairs so as not to wake the children, she passed the blown-up studio photo of her three boys hanging on the wall. Ruefully, she turned away. Just the other day her new cleaner, Clara, had mentioned how nice the photo was. Suzy had nodded, keeping the truth firmly to herself: that Henry's grinning face had been Photoshopped onto his body from the last of fifty shots after he'd screamed in all the others because Jez hadn't turned up at the studio. Traffic, Jez claimed. She hadn't been so sure. She knew he'd hated the idea anyway. 'Bit tacky, isn't it?' he'd grumbled when she told him she'd booked the session. So instead of the five of them, there were just three. Of course, she could have been in the photo, too, but the image of a single mother with three boys was tempting fate too much. If you looked closely you could see

77

the swollen redness of Henry's cheeks above a smile paid for with a bar of chocolate the photographer had brought out of a drawer without asking her, clearly having reached the limit of his patience.

Suzy reached the top of the stairs, picked up the cordless phone she had left by the open doors of the boys' bedrooms and pressed the 'end call' button, immediately terminating the call to her mobile. She turned that off, too, and quickly checked the sleeping bodies. The faint cry she had heard on her mobile at Callie's must have been one of them calling out in their sleep. She sat down, wrapping her arms round her waist and rocking forwards and backwards. Callie. Oh no. Callie.

The thought of empty days as well as empty evenings ahead was more than she could take right now. To her shame, she'd kept Henry up till 9 p.m. tonight just to avoid being alone for another evening, risking the inevitable tantrum when he became overtired.

How long had Callie been planning this? She mulled over the last few months in her head. Of course, she'd noticed Callie becoming restless, even before Rae started school last September. That's why she'd planned so many things for them to do together. And when Callie looked worried or miserable, she had done everything she could to be a good friend — listening, hugging, making her laugh. Once, just once, when Sasha had rung and left a flirtatious message on Jez's business phone when Suzy was looking for a pen on his desk, she'd nearly

78

confessed to Callie about her marriage troubles, but she could see from Callie's eyes there was only so much more stress her friend could take. Instinctively, she knew Callie needed her to be strong. So what had gone wrong?

She groaned quietly. Now this — on top of what was happening with Jez?

Her husband, the enigma. Out again for the fourth night.

Her phone beeped. She took it out. It was a text from Vondra, saying she had received Suzy's phone message and would ring back at 10 p.m.

She sighed. So, it was time.

Vondra had been asking her a lot of questions recently about her relationship with Jez. It had stirred it all up in her head.

'Was he like this when you married him?' she had probed gently, looking at Suzy over a cup of tea in a workers' cafe in King's Cross, her soft eyes full of sympathy.

'Yes,' Suzy had been forced to admit. All the clues had been there, so obvious, she couldn't deny it even to herself now. The British diplomat parents who'd moved every few years from Syria to Malawi to Taiwan, leaving Jez in a boarding school from the age of seven. The violent, primal adventures that took place in that school, recounted to her as she lay wrapped in his arms those first months in Colorado. The fires in the school woods in the middle of the night; being hung by his legs, and hanging others, out of dormitory windows. Stuffing people in boxes and lifting them onto shelves for being 'a bloody girl'. The ritual of chanting songs before strange team sports she'd never even heard of. It all seemed so eccentrically, exotically English.

It was when they finally got to England, she'd revealed to Vondra, that she'd realized her mistake. It was the way Jez spoke so politely and guardedly to his parents, who met the attempts at warmth from his new American wife with barely concealed distaste suggesting that she had stolen their son from some Home Counties girl called Arabella or Belinda. And the friends from school and university who communicated with Jez in a muttered, posh, secret code laden with cruel in-jokes. Jez, she suddenly saw, was intimate with nobody. How else could he live and contract in Hong Kong for three months, then Denver, then Melbourne? No. There was no excuse. It had all been there on show from the start. She just hadn't wanted to see it.

The pressure ball was now expanding so quickly inside her chest that she had to stand up to breathe. Before she could stop herself, she found herself walking straight into the bathroom and opening the cabinet door. The pack of razors that Jez kept high on a shelf, out of Henry's way, sat innocently in their cardboard packet. If she closed her eyes, she could imagine the sharp cut already on the skin of her inner thigh, and felt the relief of the pressure ball escaping out of the slit.

'Damn it,' she said.

A loud bleep burst into the silence of the bathroom. Suzy felt her phone vibrate inside her jeans pocket and pulled it out. The screen read 'private'.

'Hello?' she said quietly.

'Hi, Suzy? It's Vondra,' said a cheerful-sounding woman with a soft Jamaican accent.

'Hey, hon,' Suzy said. She sat down on the toilet. Well, she'd asked for it and now she was going to get it.

'You ready, my love?' Vondra asked.

'Mmm,' Suzy replied, placing her other arm between her legs and leaning forwards.

'OK, I'm afraid it's not looking so good. I waited outside Churchill Road. I was expecting him to turn right towards the A10 to Hertfordshire. He actually turned left into town . . . '

Suzy sighed quietly.

'You OK, my love? Now listen, I followed him in. He went all the way into Soho. He parked in the NCP car-park on Wardour Street and walked to Ellroy's. Do you know it?'

'No,' said Suzy faintly.

'It's a private members' club on Frith Street. He went there about an hour ago and he hasn't come out. Now what else do you feel you'd like to ask me?'

Suzy gathered her courage. 'You know what I need to hear, Vondra.'

'Sasha? You have to remember I only have the photo from your husband's company website. But as far as I could see — and I've been outside for an hour now — she definitely hasn't gone in. What I can't swear to you is that she wasn't in there before I arrived.'

Suzy took it in. She'd only met Sasha once, at a party for Jez's clients that she had forced him to let her attend, but the young woman's face was fixed in her memory: long-lashed doe eyes that searched Jez too longingly as he spoke, without bothering to turn to Suzy; the glossy, loose ponytail that she teased slowly around a tanned shoulder as he spoke: a mouth that rolled softly into a pout as she sipped wine.

Suzy had seen it all before, in Denver. The kind of women who liked Jez — and there were a lot of them — usually didn't bother to hide it.

Her thigh throbbed for her attention. No, she thought. Not since the night she found out she was pregnant with Henry, and never again. Jez would not drive her to that.

'Now, my darling, I can stay here as long as you like. What do you want me to do?'

Suzy thought. 'Does the club have bedrooms? Could they stay there all night?'

'I think it does, my darling,' Vondra said. The kindness in her voice always made Suzy want to cry. She knew what Vondra had been through with her own errant husband, and how running this business was more than just a money-making exercise. The first time Suzy had rung her, nervous and guarded, Vondra had listened to her for half an hour. At their meeting in the cafe Suzy had talked for two hours, warming to the woman's kind voice and concerned expression.

'Suzy. You know I'm here for you. And I'll stay here till we find out what you need to know.'

She thought for a second.

'OK, can you just give him another hour. See if she turns up?'

'I will. And Suzy, one more thing. I've been checking on those bank accounts as you asked . . . Do you know of a Flock Ventures?'

'Uh . . . ' said Suzy, searching her mind. 'There's something familiar about it, but . . . no, I don't know. He doesn't let me near the business. Why, is it important?'

'Maybe. Maybe not,' Vondra said. 'Nothing to worry about now, anyway. Now listen, my love. Go and have yourself a nice hot bath and relax. We'll get to the bottom of this, and everything will be fine. Remember what I told you. Whatever happens, you're back in control.' She lifted her voice to a singsong, chanting tone, like a preacher at church. 'And THAT, my darling, is where we ladies HAVE TO BE!'

★   ★   ★

Ten minutes later, Suzy went to brush her teeth, Vondra's words still repeating in her head. She looked up at the razors, then spat a mouthful of toothpaste into the sink, closed the cabinet door and climbed into bed.

She pulled her knees close to her, and tried to close her eyes. But the image of where Jez was right now — what he was doing — made them spring open again, and an involuntary groan come from her lips.

Sitting up, she stepped back out of bed, and

looked out of the bedroom window. Callie's light shone softly in her sitting room.

Jez was leaving her, and Callie was going back to work.

She padded down the hall and climbed quietly into Henry's bed, pulling his sleepy little body close for warmth.

SUNDAY

11

Callie

I'd forgotten how much fun shopping could be.

Rae and I arrive home on Sunday afternoon from Brent Cross, our crisp new shopping bags filling up the communal hall as I pick out the silver key to our flat from the ring.

Just as I put it in the door and turn it to the left, I sense someone behind me. I turn to see the Somali woman from the rented flat upstairs coming in the front door behind us, holding a plastic bag filled with what looks like meat wrapped in anonymous white paper and a cluster of tall, knobbly cream vegetables I don't recognize.

'Oh, hello. How are you?' I ask, waving a hand, already knowing there's no point asking.

She waves back, and touches Rae's cheek, looking at her with gentle brown eyes.

'Ah,' she says, smiling.

Rae stares at the woman's pregnant stomach, and then at me, shifting her eyes sideways for me to have a look. The woman laughs, and holds up four fingers. I think this means she has four months to go. But it could mean she is four months pregnant. I nod and smile, and hold up a thumb to say 'good luck'.

I tried to exchange names when we first met,

87

but she shouted back Arabic words at me in this pretty, sing-song voice and I couldn't work out which of the words were her name. I checked her post once, and worked out it is probably Nadifa, but, as that isn't one of the words she shouted at me, I'm too scared to use it in case it's her surname. And now it feels too late, too rude, to ask again.

So, I think to myself, with a nagging sense of failure, our lives will probably pass by one another's, with no connection between us other than a street name, like the woman with the wrought-iron window boxes.

The woman waves and heads up the stairs, her long dress swishing around her feet, to her shy husband who also smiles but never looks me in the eye, and a world that I know nothing about, apart from the soft footsteps above my head, and occasional interesting cooking smells that drift down into my flat and make me nostalgic for something I don't even understand.

'Can you try on your dresses now, Mummy?' Rae shouts, rushing ahead into the flat. She loved Brent Cross, grabbing a hundred different items in ten different shops and shouting, 'What about this, Mum?' till I had to tell her to stop because the shop assistants were starting to look cross. She also persuaded me to have my make-up done in John Lewis and now it sits oddly on my face in thick powdery layers. It is so long since I've worn make-up, I feel like I've been coloured in with crayons.

'OK, come on then,' I smile. I need a cup of tea but, to be honest, it's better to keep going.

Every time I stop and allow myself to imagine walking into Guy's studio in Soho tomorrow, an electric shock of nerves bolts through my stomach.

We go straight into my bedroom and lay out the new things on my bed. There are two dresses, a pair of dark, well-cut jeans, three tops, a pair of sandals and some make-up. My purchases have the effect of cut flowers, filling the room with a new, fresh smell and bright, unadulterated colours.

'The shiny one first,' Rae says, clapping her hands gleefully. She is wearing the pink sunglasses I bought her, with a lollipop for 'being good' sticking out of her mouth.

I pull off my T-shirt and pick up a silver shift dress. It took me three visits to the shop before I felt brave enough to buy it. It is made of silver sequins, which gives it the effect of being beaded with a thousand tiny light bulbs. I pull it on carefully over my made-up face, enjoying the factory-fresh chemical odour of new clothes, and the sensation of how it clings to me, crisp and unsagging, unlike my old T-shirts.

Rae stands back and stares at me.

'What?' I say.

'Don't know,' she replies, looking shy.

'What?' I repeat more forcefully.

She shrugs, and comes over and falls into me, pulling my arm around her.

I bend down to look in the dressing-table mirror and see why she has gone quiet. I look completely different.

With a shock I recognize this woman. I am

89

looking at myself before Rae. I blink heavily, focusing through the thick mascara.

'You are all lighted up,' Rae finally blurts out.

'Hmm,' I say. I'm not sure I like her seeing me like this. I realize what she's thinking. That the woman in the mirror is taking me away from her.

'It's going to be fine, you know,' I say as she wraps herself silently around my neck. 'Listen, Hannah will be at after-school club and that will be fun, and I'll be at work, so we can have more money to do nice things by ourselves, like go on holiday, maybe.'

'Can I have a party if we have money,' she murmurs in my ear, 'a big one for all my class?'

'Well . . . ' I pause. She's only been invited to two class parties this year, both of them thrown open to all thirty children by parents rich enough to do it, or too uncomfortable to leave anyone out. The thought that Rae might invite the whole class to her party and find no one wants to come apart from Henry, and maybe Hannah, is too painful to contemplate. 'Let's see how we get on, but it's nice of you to think about doing that. I hope your friends realize how lucky they are to have such a kind girl in their class.'

I take her into the kitchen to get a drink, then put her in front of a DVD. Back in my bedroom I look at myself again in the mirror.

I can't stop staring. If I subtract the wan, tired woman in the dark clothes from this shining, made-up woman I am now in the mirror, I am left with five years of loss. That's what the difference is. Five years of lost everything.

I hear the Somali woman padding about above my head.

Idly, I pick up my address book and flick through it again, trying to remember. Wasn't friendship easy before Rae, evolving gently and meaningfully out of one moment of laughter at school, a long talk in the pub after college, or a shared moment of late-night drama at work?

Now, it simply doesn't exist. On any level. Apart from with Suzy.

I've been thinking a lot about Suzy this past week.

Sometimes, in the dead of night, I feel bad. One of the reasons I feel bad is that I have always known something about Suzy that I have told no one. It became clear to me after those first few flurried, intense weeks when we met that, apart from babies and children, we had nothing else in common. A cursory glance at each other's CDs, and music was never discussed. There are no books to share. Suzy owns none, apart from London guides and baby books. Even the wide-open spaces that we both experienced growing up as children — the ones she still craves are the very ones that I ran away from when I came to London. So we talk about me and my problems. And we talk about her latest purchase from Heal's or her new car. And we talk about school corridors and park swings, fish fingers and period pains, and make jokes about a relationship that is never going to happen with Matt, The Hot Dude That Callie Must Get It On With, because it would take Matt precisely one evening of chat to realize that I am an empty husk inside with nothing to offer. Eaten up by myself. Incapable of a normal relationship even with my so-called best friend.

I have been pretending for a long time that it is OK for me to depend on Suzy, to allow her to believe we are so close. But in the black of the night, I know it is not right. Our friendship is not a friendship of choice, but one of need. An American stranger in London and a lonely single mum stuck together. It's wrong to rely on her so heavily when I am not honest with her about who I really am; to allow the truth to stay hidden in a dark corner, like a ghoul, waiting. But I carry on because I need Suzy. I can't survive without her. Not yet.

And what makes it worse is that she appears to have no idea. Crucial elements are missing from our friendship, but she doesn't even seem to notice. She seems happy just the way we are.

Yes. Some nights, I feel very guilty indeed about Suzy.

I look in the mirror some more.

Rae is right. There is something about this dress. The iridescent sheen seems to be lighting me up. Charging me up. Giving me power to return, finally, after five years, to the world outside.

I need this. I need to get back to Rocket. I need this to make things right.

Nerves shoot through my stomach with such intensity, I get up and go to find some food.

12

Debs

The children had been screaming for an hour now.

Debs checked the old clock in the hallway. Nearly seven o'clock. What time did those boys go to bed on a Sunday night? Didn't they have school tomorrow?

'Don't want my hair washed!' she heard the older one scream, followed by a long, agonized cry like he was being tortured.

'Hold still, hon!' she heard the American woman shout. 'Nearly done.'

They were all having their hair washed by the sounds of it. If one wasn't screaming, the other was.

She had walked all round the house trying to escape it. Allen didn't seem to notice, sitting in the front room doing his crossword.

'Gosh, those little boys don't like having their hair washed, do they?' she exclaimed cheerfully, checking him with sharp eyes.

'Hmm,' he said. 'Sorry?'

'The little boys next door. Screaming about having their hair washed?'

'Really?' he said, turning back to his newspaper. 'You know me, love, I'm a bit deaf.'

She turned away, frustrated. How could he not

93

hear it? The anguished howls were bursting through their hall wall, upstairs and down, as if one child was upstairs and another one or two downstairs. She walked up the stairs trying to escape it, trying her bedroom at the front first. That was just as bad. A child seemed to be in the bedroom next door and there was a roar of a hairdryer.

The spare room. That might be the best idea. It shared no walls with the American woman's house and was as far away from their bathroom as it could be.

She hadn't been in this room much. It was long and narrow with a sash window that overlooked their garden, with its little lawn and shed. A bare light bulb hung above. The room felt as if it hadn't been used much. The Hendersons' children had left long ago to get married, they had told her, so it had probably been the couple's spare room, too.

She sat on the old oak bed she and Allen had brought from his mother's house, opposite its matching oak wardrobe. The new plastic-covered mattress squeaked beneath her weight. That was one item of his mother's she had refused to hold on to — the mattress where the woman had lain for twenty years, shouting for her uncomplaining son to fetch and carry for her. Allen hadn't argued with Debs's plans for the old mattress at all. He'd taken it to the dump in her car, both of them averting their eyes from the sallow stains that seeped among the faded stripes.

Debs swung her legs, kicking the sides of a purple — 'miscellaneous' — box. She could hardly hear the screams from the children next door at all in here. That was fine. She'd just stay here till they stopped. Turning her head, she looked around at the green striped wallpaper. Maybe they would be able to decorate it in time for Alison staying at Christmas. If her sister would actually accept their invitation.

Or maybe Allen would eventually move into this bedroom permanently. Debs looked around it. The pretence of him coming to bed each night as if they behaved like a normal married couple would eventually wear out. One night, she knew, he would walk through the bedroom door in his pyjamas as usual, and say, 'Goodnight, love,' but instead of climbing into bed and gently turning his back on her, he would politely walk back out and disappear into this room.

As she thought about it, the familiar flash of memory burst into her mind.

'Oh no,' she groaned, shaking her head to brush it away.

But it was no good. There it was. She and Allen walking up the stairs of their hotel, her a little tipsy from the wine, Allen nervous and upright, and then . . .

A sudden loud noise made Debs jerk her head round.

She stood up and looked round the little bedroom. It was a distant scraping whine that was getting louder by the second, like a skateboard down a rough tarmac road.

The whining rapidly increased in volume, breaking into a loud rumbling over her head.

'What on earth?' she muttered, going to the window. It sounded like a plane, wheezing and roaring right above her. It was as if it had appeared out of nowhere and almost landed on her roof.

Looking straight out of the back window, across the roofs of the terraced houses behind and towards the tall transmitter mast on the top of Alexandra Palace, she couldn't believe what she saw. A second plane was advancing towards their house, from a mile or so away.

As she watched, the noise started again. A long whine that became louder and louder as the plane descended towards her house. With a crack like thunder, it came over Churchill Road and rumbled heavily above her head.

'Allen!' she shouted, running downstairs and into the sitting room. 'There are planes flying right over the house — did you hear that?'

He looked up over his glasses and frowned.

'Um, I'm not sure, love. There are planes everywhere in London.'

'I know that, love, but these two were . . . ' As she said it the whining started again, as a third plane began to approach. 'There!' she exclaimed, excited. He couldn't have been deaf enough to have missed that, could he?

But Allen just shrugged. 'No worse than King's Cross. Really, Debs. You're a right live wire tonight.'

Oh, this was ridiculous.

She walked back out of the sitting room and went to open the front door, remembering at the last minute to take the squashed cardboard boxes they had left in the hall and stuff them in the recycling box. Replacing the black lid firmly, she stood up and raised her head. A jumbo jet glided above her, sounding as if its pilot was revving its engines just for her.

Where had they come from? She hadn't heard a single plane since they'd moved in on Thursday.

Shutting the front door, she walked briskly into the kitchen and hunted through the pine dresser left by the Hendersons until she found the phone book. She marched back to the hall and picked up the phone.

'This isn't right, Allen. Really. Something has changed,' she called into the open door of the sitting room.

It took her a minute to find the number, and she then waited another five till someone answered her call at the end of a very long list of automated services about flight arrivals and parking. Her own query seemed to have no category of its own so she pressed and pressed each option for 'another query', until a man eventually picked up her call.

'Heathrow. Can I help you?' a voice said.

'Hello. I'm sorry. I'm ringing about your planes,' Debs gabbled into the phone. 'I have just moved into Alexandra Park in north London and suddenly they've started coming over my house and making a ridiculous noise.'

There was a pause at the other end of the line.

'Madam, north London is on the landing path to Heathrow. Depending on the prevailing wind, planes will sometimes fly over Alexandra Palace.'

'What? But we came here lots of times before we moved in and never heard a plane once. Now, it's so noisy. It's as if there's a motorway above my head.'

'Well, very occasionally, it might be over your house.'

As he spoke, another plane roared overhead.

'Can you hear that?' she shouted. 'Can you?'

'Can I hear what?' the man said.

'That plane!' she shouted.

'Madam, I work at Heathrow.'

'Well, OK, but I want to make a complaint.'

There was silence.

'About what?'

'About the planes coming over my house.'

'Uh . . . '

* * *

In the end, he gave Debs an address to write to and she put the scribbled note on the fridge under a magnet. She'd do that first thing tomorrow.

At least it had taken her mind off the children next door, she thought. They were quieter now, just one of them apparently still awake, his tantrum diminished into a distant whimper. She walked back to the spare room and sat, bracing herself for the next plane.

Allen popped his head around the door five minutes later to see her with a pillow wrapped around her head.

'Do you want a cup of tea?'

She looked at him and put the pillow down.

'Allen, I'm worried we've made a terrible mistake. Can you not hear these planes? They have been non-stop for half an hour. Endless. Flying over our heads every minute. And that's not all. The children next door screamed for over an hour. And the woman on the other side of us isn't even there at the moment. What happens when she gets back and starts thumping around in her house, flushing toilets and . . . '

He came into the room and sat beside her on the bed. He said nothing for a moment, and in that silence she heard her own words echoing back at her, and wished she could keep her mouth shut; wished she could take it all back.

Finally, Allen lifted his hand and patted her leg. 'Come on, love, you're just very tired from the move. Come downstairs and have a cup of tea. I think you should try to get an early night tonight.'

Easy for him to say, with his deaf ears. How on earth was she going to sleep with that toilet flushing through the wall? And the planes now, too. Don't tell me it's not real, she wanted to scream. I can hear it!

'OK, love, good idea,' she said, getting up and following him out of the door.

As she went down the stairs she stopped for a second. There was complete silence now from next door. Beautiful, still silence. The children must all finally be in bed.

It wasn't the children, really, she reasoned as she followed Allen down the stairs. She didn't mind the noise of children very much at all. What she hated was when children shouted and their mothers did nothing to stop them. It wasn't that difficult, after all.

MONDAY

13

Callie

I am running. I am running so hard I can't breathe.

I haven't run this fast for years. My new sandals are clicking on the pavement on Oxford Street, and I am darting between a man holding a board on a stick that says 'Trainers sale this way' and an actor I recognize from an American TV series, a baseball hat pulled firmly down on his head.

It is 5.20 on Monday afternoon. I have just finished my first day at work. I have forty minutes to arrive back at Alexandra Park and pick Rae up from after-school club, which, I was informed by Ms Buck, closes promptly at 6 p.m. The train journey takes thirty minutes alone. How could I have been this stupid? To forget that any trip around London needs a safety margin of at least fifteen minutes for unexpected signal failures and gridlocked traffic. Especially, I now realize far too late, when a child is involved.

I keep running, my head spinning with what has just happened at work.

★   ★   ★

In the end my nerves about returning to Rocket were justified. The moment I walked into the

103

newly refurbished studio this morning and saw the white marble floor, reception desk carved out of an interior designer's idea of lunar rock, and soundproofed sound rooms each with a new £50,000 sound desk, reality hit.

This was not a game. It could not be a whim.

I am back in the real world, where you are paid for doing a job, and sacked for not doing it properly.

'Callie,' Guy shouts with a smile, coming towards me with a welcome hug. Since I last saw him, his tight black curls have relaxed and turned grey, causing his deep-set brown eyes to emerge. In a black skinny knit and jeans he looks like a rakish, older, Calvin Klein model. 'Great to see you, mate. How does it feel to be back?'

Absolutely bloody terrifying.

'Brilliant!' I smile, nodding at the new receptionist, Megan, who could be Alice in Wonderland's older, sensual, sister complete with pretty white chiffon dress, long tanned legs and a blue ribbon in her hair. Self-consciously, I pull down the short sleeve of my silver dress, which now makes me feel as if I am trying too hard.

'I'll show you round the new features on the software, then I've got a promo for you to try out on,' Guy says, straight to business. 'Megan will show you where the new kitchen is.'

'Oh,' I say, picking up my bag and following him. 'OK. Sure.'

What was I expecting? A long chat over coffee where I could apologize for being a tearful wreck the last time I saw him, and thank him for helping me out? Where I could ask him how it's going with Ankya, the leggy Polish fashion photographer? No. I am on the clock again, I realize, slightly bewildered. Every minute I stand here, I am earning money. In the time it has taken me to say hello to Guy, follow him to the sound room where I will be working and sit down on a client seat shaped like a satellite, I have probably earned enough to pay for a sandwich at lunchtime.

Responsibility weighs heavily on my sequinned shoulders.

* * *

It is 5.25 p.m. I have nearly reached Oxford Circus Tube, and am forcing my protesting legs to take me the last few yards when my phone rings.

'Yes?' I say, gasping. This is ridiculous. I need to start doing some exercise.

'Cal?'

Suzy's voice is so out of place in this crazy, frenetic street it takes me a second to recognize it.

'Oh, hi. Hi,' I reply, holding one finger in my ear to hear. 'Is everything OK?'

'Um . . . ' she hesitates.

My face goes cold.

'What?'

'Hon, don't worry. She's fine — well, I mean, she's not ill. But I just thought I better tell you that when I picked Henry up at three-thirty she was kind of upset about going to after-school club.'

'Really? What do you mean, upset?'

Taxis flash by in rows of black and yellow neon. Two teenagers carrying Topshop bags push past me, banging my leg, shrieking with laughter. I am finding it difficult to hear.

'Well, she was crying. She said she wanted to come home with me and Henry. So I gave her a hug and told her Mommy wanted her to go to after-school club, and that you'd pick her up as soon as you could. I'm sure she was fine when she got there, but I thought I'd better warn you, anyway.'

'OK, thanks. Listen, I'm running so late,' I shout. 'I've got to get on the train, but I'll pop in later.'

I run down the stairs into the Tube. That hadn't even occurred to me. Rae seemed so happy to go to after-school club. What if she doesn't want to go back? After the day I have had, I cannot allow myself to contemplate that right now.

★   ★   ★

Once Guy finally left me this morning, it all went wrong immediately. I pressed three buttons and lost half an hour's work.

'Sorry, it just disappeared,' I say, pointing at the blank computer screen as he walks back into the room.

'Didn't you switch on autosave?' he murmurs.

I groan inwardly. Novice mistake. I bet he's wondering what he's done asking me back. Should I offer to pay him back for the lost half-hour?

By lunchtime, however, some of the old confidence is returning to my fingers. My job is to add sound to a TV ad for a new digital cooking programme that promises to teach budding cooks skills such as filleting, chopping and skinning. The visual, which I play on a plasma screen above my sound desk, shows a chef expertly juggling ten different sharp knives, each one landing in a different food ingredient around his kitchen, till he is left with one.

Biting my lip in concentration, I access the massive digital library of sound effects on the updated software, and pick five or six for each ingredient, then meld them together into one noise for a tomato being split with a mild squelch by a filleting knife or the dull thump of a bread knife in cheese.

To my surprise, it isn't too difficult. I don't know why, but my ears just know instinctively which sounds to mix together, in the way that some people just know which herbs and spices work and never need recipe books.

'You're either born with sensitive ears, or you're not,' Guy told me when I first came to Rocket, aged twenty-three, to work as a studio assistant. 'I bet you loved music when you were a baby.' The comment left me open-mouthed. Just that weekend, on a visit back to see Dad, I had found a photo of me in old-fashioned earphones as a toddler, smiling, with one of Mum's captions underneath. 'Callie can't stop dancing!!'

I keep meaning to go for lunch, but before I know it, the clock says 4 p.m. There is a basket of muffins for clients in reception, I remember. I pop out and Megan looks up.

'Can I take a couple of these?' I say, not sure.

'Course!' she laughs.

So I take one to eat, and put the other in my bag for Rae. I look back at the screen and plunge back into my work. The strange thing is, I am not really hungry.

* * *

It is 5.31 p.m. Aha! I am lucky tonight. There is no signal failure on the Victoria Line after all. I run down the crowded escalator at Oxford Circus, wind my way through the slow-moving passengers onto the packed northbound platform and manage to squeeze onto a train that's just about to shut its doors. Even as I jump on, I know there isn't enough room, and can only blame myself when I have to travel three stops with my head bent into the curved side, worrying about Rae. It doesn't help that the group of French students around me are all talking at each other at the same time. To my newly re-sensitized ears, it sounds like three TV channels on in the same room.

At King's Cross, the carriage finally half-clears and I grab a grubby tartan seat. My face looks flushed in the reflection of the window in the dark tunnel. I rub it. My skin feels raw as if it's been slightly burned by all the artificial wall lights and computer rays emanating from around the studio. It's as though the dead cells have been zapped away and the blood has pumped near to the surface of my cheeks.

As the train roars off through each station, I realize I am perching on the edge of the seat, not sitting back. Energy has made me rigid, given my stance purpose. I have finished one job today, and now I have another ahead of me. To pick up Rae.

Two purposes, I think. Mother and sound designer. Each clearly defined. Corners and edges.

And then exhaustion hits. As the train rumbles on through dark tunnels, the adrenalin that has powered me all day unexpectedly drains away. I look round. Women like me are dotted up and down the carriage, some perched on the edge of their own seats, some slumped. Some have mascara smudged under their eyes, others creased skirts and suits.

I am joining a tribe, I think. Women who work all day in London then go home to look after a child. Women who choose to do that in a big city, despite the fact that they probably live far from their extended families in places like Lincoln-shire, and in London streets — if they are anything like mine — where they don't know their neighbours.

They make it work. So this could work. With some adjustment, maybe, I can really make this work.

Then I remember Suzy's call. What if Rae refuses to go back to after-school club? Who could I ask to look after her?

As I jump out at Highbury & Islington and race across the platform to the overland train to Alexandra Park, a memory comes back to me of the day I heard a bang at my door and I opened it to find a panting woman, sweat pouring down her face. She was dressed in a huge black dress, with a child asleep in a buggy wearing just a nappy.

'I'm sorry,' she said. 'Can you help? I think I'm going into labour early. I saw the child seat in your car outside.'

Wet slick down her legs told me she was right. Her waters had broken.

'Oh my God, of course,' I said, ushering her in. 'How far on are you?'

'Thirty-three weeks,' she gasped.

'Don't worry,' I said, running for the phone. 'I'll get an ambulance.'

The next minute was a flurry of dialling 999 and grabbing a chair from the sitting room.

The woman nodded thanks and kneeled down, carefully putting her head and hands on the chair before moaning with another contraction.

'Oh hell, I think they're coming.'

They?

'Twins.'

Jesus. 'Can you hurry up?' I shout down the phone. 'It's twins.'

I run into the kitchen, grab a wet cloth and run over and wipe the woman's forehead. She smells a little greasy and sicky. I rub her back, too, remembering how much it helped when Tom did it to me.

'Thanks,' she says, gulping for air. 'I'm sorry — my husband's away and we've just moved in.'

'Don't worry,' I say for the second time, struggling to find more words to comfort her. 'I've helped my dad deliver lots of sheep.'

My words hang in the air for a second, as we both realize she is on all fours with her bum pointing towards me. We both burst out laughing.

'Suzy,' she says, before taking a sharp gasp of air.

'Callie,' I say.

* * *

I check my watch for the hundredth time: 5.47 p.m. A worry starts to gnaw at me. What if being a working mother in the city makes me even more dependent on her, rather than less?

The problem is, after my day at Rocket studio, I don't think I can give up work ever again.

* * *

At just after 5 p.m., Guy came to see my finished soundtrack for the promo. If I wasn't tense enough already, he then called in Megan and three male sound designers, including an edgy-looking twenty-five-year-old called Jerome, in retro black-rimmed glasses and Nudie jeans, whom Guy had described to me earlier as an exciting find — 'The new you,' he said, without irony.

'OK, go for it,' Guy says, looking up at the plasma screen.

Nerves flutter in my stomach. I press 'play'

and sit upright, gauging Guy's reaction out of the corner of my eye. The knives slice through the air with a sharp, metallic whizzing noise and land in each piece of food with a subtly different effect. Only designers know how much work goes into making each sound so imperceptible that it doesn't intrude on the message of the advert.

There is a silence.

Then he claps.

'Great work, Cal,' he laughs, turning round. 'What did I tell you? That's how to do it, guys!'

My mouth bursts open into an unexpected, happy smile whose muscles I can't control.

'Thanks. Look, Guy, but is it all right if I slip off? I have to get Rae?'

'Course,' Guy smiles, resting his hand on my shoulder for a second, and gets up to leave. 'Good work, Cal. Remember, Loll Parker's in at ten tomorrow. He's looking forward to meeting you.'

★　★　★

It is 5.54 p.m. One stop from Alexandra Park. So much for escaping signal failures tonight. I have been blindsided by the good old passenger alarm.

Our train driver informs us cheerfully that one has been activated in the train in front of us and we will be held here while an elderly lady who feels unwell is helped off the train. Eleven minutes to reach Rae. I am so far forward on my seat now, I am in danger of falling off altogether if the train takes a particularly fast bend. A woman in the opposite seat catches my eye and makes a face. Surprised, I nod back.

My phone shows no signal. What will they do if I am not there at six?

Luckily, the elderly lady is taken off quickly, and I stand up and hold on to a pole for the rest of the journey, bursting through the opening doors as soon as there is a gap, and ascending the steep stairs to the pavement in great, unladylike gallops.

I check my watch again: 5.59 p.m. I am not going to make it. It is starting to rain, too. I set off running along the steep main road up to the school, trying not to slip in my sandals. A woman in heels and a tight suit jogs ahead of me, looking equally harried. She is shouting into a mobile at her ear: 'It's on my desk, Ian, just look!'

It is 6.04 p.m. I can hardly breathe. My lungs ache. I turn left up the last hill and there is the school in front of me. I race past it and through the iron gates of the red-brick Victorian building next door, which was once a swimming pool. The woman in front of me, who clearly exercises more than I do, has already arrived and buzzed the intercom of the big wooden door, so I manage to squeeze through just before it swings shut.

A warm, yeasty smell greets me. The grand former hall might be empty now, but the frenetic disturbance of twenty-eight recently departed children is still evident in the air. The mother in front of me has already grabbed a grumpy-looking child and is on her way out, still shouting into her mobile: 'Well, try the printer, Ian, maybe I left it there.' I rush up to the after-school leader, Ms Buck, who is clearing tables, and try to look as apologetic as possible.

'I'm so sorry . . . first day . . . passenger alarm on the train . . . won't happen again,' I splutter.

'Don't worry,' she says, looking a little like it does matter. 'Rae's over there with Mrs Ribwell in the painting area.'

Through a brick arch, I see Rae in an area decorated with children's drawings. A teacher is kneeling down in front of her, talking to her intently.

'Hi, sweetheart,' I call.

Rae looks at me without smiling. In fact, she looks cross. My heart sinks.

Mrs Ribwell turns round. I am so concerned about the look on Rae's face it takes me a second to realize that I recognize her.

'Oh, hi. What are you doing here?'

'Oh — I work here,' she smiles.

'Do you? How funny,' I say. 'Oh. Well, that's great. Rae will be pleased. I hope she's behaved herself?'

'Oh, yes. We've had a nice afternoon, haven't we, Rae?'

Rae looks at the ground.

'Want to go,' she whines, and begins to walk away from me, towards the door.

'Sorry,' I say.

'Bye,' the woman calls. But Rae has already

114

slipped out of the wooden door, so I wave in her place.

'So, how was it?' I say when I find her outside and we head out through the iron gates and along the side of Alexandra Palace.

'Hannah left early,' she says quietly. 'She had a playdate at Grace's house.'

My heart drops.

'Well, that will happen sometimes,' I say, trying to keep the sadness I feel for Rae out of my voice. 'You'll just have to play with someone else. That's the fun bit of after-school club, you'll meet lots of other children not in your class.'

I wouldn't have been convinced when I was five years old, but it is the best I can do.

'When can I go to someone's house?' she says quietly.

'Soon, darling, it'll happen soon,' I say, putting an arm round her, hating the sound of my own lie. 'Listen, what's that lady's name, you were talking to — it went right out of my head, I was so surprised to see her.'

'Mrs Ribwell,' Rae says. 'But she says when no one else is there I can call her Debs.'

★ ★ ★

I take her hand, and we make our way down the hill on the main road that leads to Churchill Road.

Cars flash by us. The traffic is heavy, I think. Of course, six o'clock is the busiest time on this road. Sometimes, when Rae and I have tried to cross the road from the park, we have had to wait

115

here for three or four minutes.

Rain starts to fall heavily now, turning the road wet and slick. Traffic crashes by my ear, spitting and screeching.

And then, with no warning, Rae lets go of my hand.

'What are you doing?'

She starts to run. An image of the racehorses a family used to keep in one of Dad's fields comes to mind. At the end of the day, I would watch them from my bedroom window as they were released from their bridles and let loose, jumping and kicking their heels high, daring anyone to try to catch them again till tomorrow.

'Rae?' I call. 'What are you doing?'

She is not just doing her careful half-trot. She is actually trying to run, her little sandals flying up in the air.

'Rae!' I raise my voice, speed up and grab the back of her coat. 'I mean it.'

Cars skid past, ignoring the 30mph sign, people as desperate as me to get home.

She staggers a little as she turns.

'That's so naughty,' I say. 'So dangerous. You know you could fall. And then what would happen?'

'It's not fair!' she shouts, pulling her shoulder away from me. 'I can't NEVER do anything.'

Her face is angry and confused, her big eyes flashing. I put my hand on her shoulder and kneel in front of her.

'You're right, darling, it's not fair. But I don't want you back in hospital, and I don't think you want that either, do you? So you always, always

116

hold my hand on the road, right?'

She shrugs. I open my bag and pull out the muffin I took from Rocket.

'I brought this for you from work.'

Rae's eyes open wide and she grabs it, taking a bite.

'Sorry, Mummy,' she says, taking my hand again.

'I'm sorry, too, for being late,' I say. And we wait at the side of the road for the traffic to break.

* * *

At Suzy's house, we stop. I can hear a child shouting behind the front door.

'Oh, it's you,' she says when she opens the door. She gives us both hugs and ushers us into the hall. Rae runs off to find the boys in the kitchen.

'How is she?' she whispers.

'Bit tired. It'll take her a few days to get used to it. Oh. By the way, can you believe it? That woman next door, Debs, works there.'

Suzy spins round, surprised. 'Really? I didn't know she was a teacher.'

'I know. It's great, isn't it? It means Rae will have someone she knows from home at after-school club. And I'm hoping Debs might keep an eye on her because she knows her.'

Suzy looks thoughtful and nods. 'Well, she doesn't KNOW her.'

'No — but you know what I mean. She's a neighbour.'

Suzy seems distracted, checking her watch.

'So, how was your day?' I ask. 'OK?'

'Yeah,' she says absentmindedly. 'I kept the twins off nursery. We baked brownies.'

'Are you OK?' I ask. She seems quieter than normal. A little deflated.

'Oh, yeah — no. I thought Jez would be back by now. He took Henry swimming.'

I stare. 'He did?'

'Yeah, he says Henry should have learnt by now.'

Maybe if Jez ever bothered to take him, he might have done, I think.

'So — did you decide whether you're going to the spa this week?' I ask carefully, trying to judge her mood.

'Oh, I'm not sure. Jez is around this week — maybe I'll go for lunch on Hampstead Heath with him instead, or something.'

I nod and wait.

And wait.

She doesn't ask me.

'So . . . ' I whisper. 'Suze . . . '

'What?' she says.

'Work. It was SO amazing.'

'Oh — yeah?' She turns her head round to check the twins in the kitchen.

'The studio was incredible. You should see it. It's all been done up like a spaceship, and there are these toilets where it took me five minutes to find the soap because it was hidden under this stainless steel bar . . . ' I laugh, but I am not sure she's listening. 'And I was so nervous. But Guy liked my work. And being back in Soho. And hey, who's that American actor that . . . '

She leans forward and touches my shoulder. 'That's great, hon. I told you you'd be brilliant. Listen, I have to get the boys ready for bed. Do you want to stay and have some tea? I've got some chicken left in the oven?'

As she says it, I realize I've been smelling something. That's what it is. But behind the cooking smell, there is another odour.

I inhale silently.

Urine.

The familiar tang of wet nappy is hanging in the hallway, in air that is stale with the breath and body odour of people who have been trapped inside all day. Suzy's T-shirt is stained again with sauce. Her cheeks are pink and sweaty from cooking, and there is a slight sheen of perspiration around her hair-line, turning her blonde hair darker at the roots. Behind her, through the hallway, I can see a trail of toys littered about the kitchen. Crayons and pens without lids are scattered on the white porcelain tiles. And the kitchen. The kitchen that yesterday looked like it came straight out of an interiors magazine now looks a little homely after the top-end industrial aesthetic of Guy's studio.

Perspectives shift like a kaleidoscope in front of my eyes.

Peter toddles to the door of the kitchen, and I wave to him. A thick stream of snot runs down his nose and he wipes it away with a pen-stained hand.

No.

No. I don't want to stay for tea.

'Suze, it's really kind of you, but I think Rae needs some quiet time,' I say.

And that is true. But what is also true is that I don't want to be here tonight. I was here last night, and the day before, and the day before that. I want to go home. I want to pour a bubble bath for me and Rae to share, and have a chat to reassure her about after-school club. Then I want to work out some notes for my meeting with Loll Parker tomorrow, and maybe have a glass of wine and pluck my eyebrows.

The thought of eyebrows makes my mouth twitch.

* * *

It was just before home time when I pushed open the heavy metal door of the toilet at Rocket, with its black granite 'V' for Venus ('M' for Mars on the men's), to find Megan standing looking in the mirror.

'Great promo,' she says. 'Guy's so chuffed to have you back. We've all heard about you, you know.'

'Really?' I frown, not knowing how to reply. Instead I watch her applying red lipstick, presumably on her way out for a night in Soho.

'Your eyebrows are amazing,' I blurt out, pointing at the arched, penned creations above her huge blue eyes.

'Thanks,' she says cheerfully. 'This woman at my dry cleaner's threads them for me. She says the arch shapes your eye better.'

'Oh really?' I mutter ruefully, poking at the

little advancing army of mousey hairs that I notice have crept below my own eyebrows. 'Yeah, well, mine don't so much frame my eyes as keep them warm.'

And this is the bit that is making me smile in Suzy's hall.

Megan laughed.

Not the neat little laugh that Suzy emits when I attempt humour, followed by the comment: 'That's a good one,' as if she understands I'm making a joke but not why it's funny. This was a proper laugh. First Megan snorted through her nose. Then she threw her head back and let out this warm, joyous, throaty chortle, and touched my arm warmly.

'It's going to be so great having another girl here,' she exclaimed happily, heading out the door. 'See you tomorrow, Callie.'

★ ★ ★

'What?' Suzy says. 'Why are you smiling?'

'Oh,' I say. 'Nothing — just something at work. Anyway, listen, I meant to say. Rae tried to run down the pavement tonight — if you are with her, can you make sure you hold her hand? She nearly fell.'

'I always do, hon.'

'I know. Thanks.' I touch her arm. 'And, thanks for being here when I'm at work. Next time she stays at Tom's, I'll baby-sit to say thanks.'

'Cool,' she says, still looking distracted.

What happened to 'coolio', her favourite

stupid word? I watch her. What is up with her? She's not sulking about the spa, is she? Suzy and I have never had a cross word in two years. Not for us the carefree, drunken arguments Sophie and I used to have about who locked who out of the flat last night by accident, made up croakily over cereal bowls in the morning and hugs in pyjamas and last night's mascara. I can't risk that with Suzy. Who knows what might be said?

'So . . . ' I say, carefully, forcing myself to remember that I only want to pull away a little from Suzy right now. Not lose her completely.

'So,' she replies. 'See you tomorrow.' She hugs me and Rae again, and we walk across the road to our front door. I pull out the key, already dreading the mess of discarded pyjamas and breakfast bowls waiting behind it.

Tiredness washes over me. Rae sighs, too, leaning into my side. At least her cheeks are bright. They have definitely taken on a new, rosy hue. I put my arm round her shoulder and guide her inside the house. As I pull the door behind us, I look up and see Suzy standing at her gate, peering anxiously up towards the main road.

No. That has nothing to do with me, I reassure myself. Not this time. And shut the door.

14

Suzy

Suzy turned back from the gate, shut the front door, and returned to the kitchen, biting her lip. Wordlessly, she removed the plates, cups and cutlery she had laid out for Callie and Rae on the kitchen table and put them back in a cupboard.

She looked at the oven clock. Where on earth was Jez?

She ran upstairs to turn on the taps for the twins' bath, poured in some baby oil and threw in a few plastic trucks and ducks, then came back down to the hall and picked up the phone for the fourth time since five o'clock.

'Jez,' she said into the receiver. 'Hon, where are you? I thought you'd be back by now and I'm getting worried. Henry needs to eat his tea. It's six-thirty. Ring me.'

Just as she replaced the receiver, the phone rang.

'Hey!' she said. 'Where are you guys?'

There was a pause.

'James here,' said an impossibly genteel voice.

'Oh. Hi, James,' she replied, her voice automatically taking on a more refined tone. She hated the way he did that to her.

'Is Jeremy there?'

For such a well-bred man, he was severely lacking in manners, Suzy thought, not for the first time.

'No, no he's not, James. He's taken Henry swimming. I was actually expecting them back by now . . . '

Her father-in-law made the strange snorting noise it had taken her a while to get used to. A mix of a horse's whinny and a grunt.

'Give Jeremy a message, will you? I've booked lunch at the club on the twenty-ninth, one o'clock, for our meeting.'

What meeting? Why didn't he just say 'lunch'? Suzy tried to think quickly. How much could she ask her father-in-law without appearing too suspicious?

'Will it just be the two of you?' she said, trying to make her voice sound casual.

He repeated the odd noise again, a kind of 'harrumph'. James Howard was not used to being questioned by anyone, and certainly not a young American woman, daughter-in-law or not.

'Jeremy knows about it,' he replied. 'Tell him Michael Roachley has confirmed. Please pass on the message. Goodbye,' he said without warning. And with that, he replaced the receiver and was gone.

'Yes, James, the twins would love to say hello to Grandpa — let me fetch them,' Suzy trilled sarcastically into the empty handset. 'And how is Diana? Are you looking forward to your break in South Africa?' She put the phone down and sat on the stairs, biting her thumbnail. Who was

Michael Roachley? A divorce lawyer friend of James's?

'Come on, boys,' she said, marching into the kitchen. 'Bath time.'

She picked up their chubby little bodies, one under each arm, and swiftly moved up the stairs. Removing their clothes gently and popping them in the bath together, she left them giggling as they put bubbles on each other's heads. Leaving the door open, she ran up to Jez's office and sat down at his computer. He had left it tidy as usual, the small bold capital letters written on yellow sticky notes on his keyboard presumably there to remind him to do certain tasks when he came home. None of them, she noted, mentioned Sasha or her initials, 'SW'.

She moved his mouse and a blue screen appeared. Nervously, knowing that he hated her to be on his computer, she called up a search engine and typed in 'Michael Roachley', before jumping off the chair to the open door to check she could still hear the twins shrieking and splashing downstairs.

The first search offered little of any interest, just a few genealogy sites mentioning Sir Michael Roachleys from the nineteenth century.

Frowning, Suzy tried again, inserting 'lawyer' after the name, to no avail. Once more she tried, this time adding James' name alongside Michael Roachley in the search box.

Maybe she was spelling it wrongly. She checked the twins quickly, then tried again: Rochley. Rokesley. Roshley. Roachleigh. Still nothing came up that looked significant.

Too late, she heard the heavy tread on the stairs. She swung round, one hand desperately trying to grab the mouse, to see Jez at the study door. His eyes sprang to the search engine page, which she just managed to delete before he could see it.

'Er,' Jez said. 'Why are the twins alone in the bath?'

'They're not alone in the bath, I'm checking them every few seconds,' she retorted, her cheeks flushing at being caught out. 'Peter has a rash and I was just checking the symptoms on the Internet. Where on earth have you been? I was getting worried.'

'What do you mean, where were we? I told you. I took Henry swimming then we went for something to eat,' Jez said, looking again over her shoulder at the computer.

Downstairs, there was a shriek as Henry entered the bathroom.

'Henry!' Suzy shouted, running past Jez, glad to have a reason to escape. She could hear the hyperactive excitement in Henry's voice from here as he teased his brothers. She couldn't blame him. An outing on his own with Jez by himself was so rare he must have been hyperventilating. It would take her hours to get him to sleep tonight.

She walked in to find Henry shooting water at Otto out of a toy water pistol, his dark eyes flashing with fun. 'Henry!' she shouted, grabbing it from him as Otto finally found enough breath to let a long, piercing wail out of his shocked mouth. She tested the water before she put the gun on the side. It was freezing. Henry must have filled it from the cold tap.

'How could you do that to Otto?' she admonished Henry.

To her horror, Henry ran past her, picked up the gun and squirted Peter, then ran out of the room laughing.

Jez caught him at the door, and swung him high up in the air before landing him firmly back on the bathroom floor.

'What the hell are you doing?' he demanded. Henry's laugh slid downwards on his face and turned into a howl.

'Mommy,' he whined, holding his hands out to Suzy. Automatically, she lifted her arms.

'Come here, boo-boo.'

'No,' Jez barked, frowning at Suzy. 'Look at me, Henry. You'll listen to me. Now, say sorry, then go to your room.'

'Mommy,' Henry started to scream, trying to wriggle free.

'I said, NO!' Jez shouted, giving Henry a firm shake.

'Jez, give him to me,' Suzy cried, seeing that Henry was going to reach the point of no return soon.

'He'll do what he's told, Suze. Don't undermine me. It's this type of behaviour that's turning him into a bloody mummy's boy. Now go to your ROOM and stay there.'

She gritted her teeth as Jez took a screaming Henry to his bedroom. Putting her head in her hands to block out the noise, she knelt down beside the twins in the bath. Henry's tantrum continued, in long agonized bursts, as Jez repeatedly stopped him from running back out of the room, and placed him back in his bedroom.

'Stop it, stop it,' she whispered again and again. She felt Peter's little wet hand emerge from the bath and rest on her arm, and grabbed it tight in hers.

This was unbearable. Hearing her baby so upset. Desperately, she fought the urge to run into the hall and take Henry from Jez and give him the big cuddle she knew he would need. Each time Jez shouted, 'No! Back in your room!' at Henry it felt like he was punching her in the stomach. 'Leave my baby alone!' she wanted to shout.

She knew better, though.

When it was finally over, and Henry's wails had diminished into long, self-pitying sobs, and he accepted the 'time out' in his room, Jez returned to the bathroom and stood in the doorway with the repentant little boy.

'Now, say sorry to your brothers,' Jez said.

'Sorry,' Henry sobbed.

'Good boy, now go and tidy your room till the bath is free.'

Suzy refused to look at Jez, instead sitting up to wash the twins and take them out of the bath. She would hug Henry later in his bedroom when Jez had disappeared back upstairs to his study or gone out. She would sneak him up a cookie. Whisper to him how much she loved him and that she was sorry Daddy had shouted.

'How's the rash?' Jez said after a minute, as

she was wrapping Peter in a towel.

'What?'

'Peter's rash. How is it?'

She pulled the towel tight, gulping. 'Probably just eczema.'

★   ★   ★

She and Jez finally sat down to dinner on their own at 8.30 p.m. in a tense silence.

'How did Henry get on at the pool?' asked Suzy, going to unscrew the top off a new bottle of red only to find Jez had already opened it.

'Useless,' Jez murmured, offering his glass for a top-up. 'He should be swimming by now. Couldn't even get him to put his head under the water.'

'Well, it's kind of tricky, hon, taking three of them on my own.'

'Well, get him lessons then. I was swimming lengths by his age — on the school team at eight.'

God, he sounded like his father sometimes. She half-expected him to start harrumphing.

'I don't think they have a swimming team at Palace Gates Infants School,' she teased, watching him lift his glass to his mouth. How many had he had? Three was usually when his jaw began to soften. There was no point giving up yet. Not while there was still a possibility of conceiving. The top button of his shirt was undone, and her body ached to kiss the triangle of warm skin that it revealed, to feel his weight on her again.

'Well, he's not likely to be there when he's eight, anyway,' Jez said sarcastically, standing up and going to fetch the salt.

'No. He'll have moved up to the junior school,' she said warily.

He shook his head. Even from behind, she could tell the expression on his face was one of irritation. 'That's not what I meant.'

'Then what do you mean?' she whispered.

'I mean, he's not going to be staying at that school. At all.'

'What are you talking about? Are we going back to the States?'

'No.'

'Then what do you mean?'

Jez rolled his eyes. 'Nothing. It doesn't matter. Don't worry about it.' He walked towards the door. 'Right, I've got work to do.'

'Jez!' she said. 'What are you talking about?'

He shrugged as he walked out of the kitchen door with his plate and glass, and headed for the stairs. 'I'm not getting into it right now. I said, don't worry about it.'

She pushed her plate away, frightened.

TUESDAY

15
Debs

The phone rang on Tuesday morning, injecting a panicked squeal into the bedroom. Debs woke feeling she was inside a cloud. She shook her head from side to side, moaning with the effort of coming to, then forced her arm to reach over, pick up her glasses from the bedside table and put them on. A little dizzy, she tried to focus. The clock said 9.05 a.m. She'd slept in. 'Have another couple of hours, love,' she remembered Allen saying. He knew she'd had a bad night. At 11 p.m., the spectre of Daisy Poplar had finally returned to visit her just as she was about to fall asleep. At 1 a.m., she'd given in and taken a pill to get rid of the girl.

She blinked her eyes and looked round the room. Who was that ringing? With a second surge of effort, she mobilized her sleep-heavy limbs and sat up, pulling round her shoulders the dressing gown that Allen had presented her with for Christmas. He said she couldn't wear her old sage robe any more.

The phone stopped. Never mind. If it was important they would ring back.

Time to get up. She forced her legs out of bed, and leant over to lift the curtain to see what the weather was like. It had changed overnight. The sky looked like a wet grey blanket. She heard a bang. Callie came rushing out of the gate opposite, in a smart dress. Debs frowned. She'd hardly recognized the young woman when she'd come into after-school club yesterday. When she had turned up with that rather odd lasagne, she'd appeared so nervous. Now she looked like all the other stylish, professional women Debs walked past with her head bowed on her rare visits into central London.

Hang on, she thought, it was after nine. They must be late for school. Callie was calling from the pavement to Rae, who was dawdling inside the gate. From up high, Debs saw Rae bend down behind the wall and, with a rapid hand, take something out of a plant pot by the gate. There was a flash of yellow as she put it in her pocket and ran to her mother.

Debs watched. Later. At after-school club. She'd find out. When the little girl was on her own.

★ ★ ★

She had just stepped onto the stairs when the phone rang again. Debs limped down the steps, trying to protect her knee.

Just as she got off the bottom step, the phone stopped.

How annoying.

She picked it up and dialled 1471. Number withheld. Probably someone selling something.

Now that she was downstairs she made a cup of tea. She'd made all the tea since Saturday and

134

Allen still hadn't noticed the pot was missing. As the kettle boiled she looked round the kitchen for a mug. Where were they all?

The dishwasher the Hendersons had left stared back at her.

She opened it up and found all six of them in there, washed from last night. How strange. For so many years it had just been her plate, her cup and her cutlery arranged neatly on the drying rack. She had no idea when to start stacking her and Allen's things into this cavernous machine — wouldn't they run out of dishes before it was full?

She took her tea back upstairs to the large front bedroom, and started again on her own clothes boxes. Just as she was hanging up a navy-blue work skirt, the phone rang again. Honestly. She stood up, straightening out her sore knee, and padded back down the stairs. Suddenly, she had a horrible thought. What if the people who'd bought her flat had tracked down her number and were ringing to complain about their first night under the woman upstairs, and her noisy footsteps on the stairs?

As she got to the phone, she decided to pick it up anyway. It might be Allen.

Just as she put her hand out, it stopped again.

She shook her head. Very strange. Checking the connection at the back to make sure she wasn't stepping on something, she frowned. Everything looked fine. For a minute she waited to see if the caller would ring back. When they didn't, she turned back upstairs, remembering at the last moment to take another box from the hall with her. She was halfway up when the phone rang again.

The muscles across her chest pulled tight. What on earth?

She put down the box and ran down the stairs, this time flying off the last step to grab the receiver.

It stopped.

Debs's face went cold.

The phone rang again.

She grabbed the receiver.

'Hello!' she shouted, her voice rising into a shriek.

Dead. The phone was dead.

'Oh no,' she murmured. 'Oh no.' Grasping the phone with shaky fingers, she quickly dialled a number.

'Allen!' she said in a panicked tone. 'The phone's been ringing and cutting off. I think it's them. The Poplars.'

There was a long silence. 'I'm in a meeting,' he said neutrally. 'Can we speak about it at lunchtime?'

'Yes, love, sorry,' she said

'Why don't I pop home for lunch?' Allen said. Yes. Yes.

* * *

She didn't hear him come in through the front door. The sky had finally cleared to reveal blue patches, so she was weeding a flowerbed of pink peonies and blue irises that the Hendersons had left, to keep her mind occupied.

'Hello,' Allen called, walking into the kitchen and putting down his briefcase. He was wearing one of the two grey suits she'd helped him buy at M&S. She'd tried to persuade him to buy one version with a stripe but he had wanted them plain. 'Don't want to be a show-off,' he had said.

'Hello,' she called, trying to keep her voice from wavering. 'Soup's just on.'

'OK, love,' he replied.

The word 'love' made her shoulders instantly drop down. Perhaps it wouldn't be too bad.

'Good morning at work?' she said lightly, coming in to wash her hands and kissing his cheek.

'Yes, I think it was,' he said, wandering past her and out into the garden, looking pleased with himself. 'I put forward my idea for the bus stop by the library and I think the planning officer liked it.'

'Mmm,' she said, not really listening, pouring out the chicken broth she had made earlier and bringing it outside on a tray with a spoon, buttered bread, a napkin and a glass of water. 'Uh-huh.'

'Of course, Ali said he'd already mentioned it last year and they'd said no, so . . . ' he started, sitting down on a garden chair and taking the tray from her. 'But I thought . . . '

'I am so very worried about these phone calls,' she blurted out.

'Hmm,' he said, looking down at the ground.

'Well, Allen, I'm sorry — it's strange, isn't it? I mean, why would the phone keep ringing like that . . . '

Allen lifted up a spoonful of soup and put it in his mouth. She waited for him to say something and when he didn't she continued, desperate for something. She knew what he was thinking. She just needed some reassurance. Acknowledgement. Anything.

'Because I just think, how have they found my new number? And does that mean they know where I live, too?'

Allen screwed up his mouth and blinked hard.

'Debs, love.' This time the word 'love' had a different tone.

He took another breath.

'I don't know. You have no reason to think they'd call. The matter is finished with. It's probably just one of those computerized phone companies that ring you automatically to enter you in a lottery or something.'

She looked at him.

'Do you think? Really? Do you think that's possible?'

'I think it is,' he said, nodding. 'Really, love, you've got to stop yourself getting worked up like this. This business with the planes, for instance . . . '

Planes. She looked up and checked the sky before she could help herself. Why did he have to say that? She hadn't noticed them since last night. Now she would start hearing them again.

'You know, love,' he continued. 'Maybe you should do something to occupy yourself during the day. Some volunteering, perhaps, just to get you out of the house.'

'That might be a good idea,' she nodded,

trying to show how much she appreciated his efforts to calm her down.

'Maybe a few hours in a charity shop?' he said.

'Hmm,' she said, trying to look more interested than she was. The thought of speaking to strange adults she didn't know all day was more than her nerves could manage right now.

'That's what Mum did,' he said, popping a piece of bread in his mouth. 'Got her out of the house Tuesdays and Thursdays.'

She looked at him, horrified.

His mother?

Is that what she had become to him? One burdensome woman exchanged for another?

'Hmm, good idea, love,' she stuttered. 'But the after-school club does take it out of me, you know. I know it's only two and a half hours, but the children are very tired after school and it's quite demanding. I want to keep myself fresh for that.'

He looked at her. He looked like he had something to say that was difficult to get out. 'The thing is, love . . . The way you've BEEN recently . . . ' He said the word 'been' as if it had a hundred meanings. 'After what happened, I'm not sure it's really a good idea for you to be working with children again at all . . . '

Behind them there was a rustle. Suddenly, a creature leaped over the fence, streaked across the garden in a blur, scrabbled up the other side with a loud bang and was gone.

'Aargh!' shrieked Debs. 'What was that? Allen, what was it?'

'Goodness. How strange,' said Allen. 'Must have been a fox.'

'No,' Debs protested, with haunted eyes. 'Allen, that was not a fox. It couldn't have been. It was huge.'

She looked around her, shaken, as if it were about to jump back over the fence and attack her. Allen cleared his throat. She turned and saw him rubbing his brow, his eyes fixed firmly away from her as if he were seeking an escape route.

Oh no. Quickly, she reached out a hand and touched his sleeve, pausing a second as her fingers absorbed the forgotten fleshy softness of his arm under the cotton.

'No. No. You're probably right, love,' she nodded, dropping her fingers so that she wouldn't have to suffer the pain of him pulling away politely. 'I'm seeing things. It must have been a fox.'

That was no fox, though, she thought, forcing herself to smile. The creature had been evil-looking. Strange. Like a devil's hound.

16

Callie

Bloody Tube.

I'm late. On my second day at work.

Now it really is a signal failure, this time at King's Cross. I jump off the fast Victoria Line train and run to the Piccadilly Line. I glance at my watch. This is a disaster. I'll have five stops on the Piccadilly line, not three, and will have to get off at Piccadilly Circus, which is five minutes' walk further from the studio in Soho. To make it worse, everyone else at King's Cross has the same idea and I have to push onto a crowded train, where the only space is beside the open window of the door that connects two carriages. As soon as the train sets off, a blast of wind blows through, pushing all my hair forwards, so that I look like an Afghan hound, much to the amusement of two boys standing opposite me.

I shut my eyes to stop hair going in them and think about Rae.

She is the reason I am late.

'I'm not going to after-school club,' she said, sticking her chin out defiantly, the minute I woke her up at 7.30 a.m.

I stared at her. Where's this come from?

'Well,' I stuttered. 'Rae, you have to. I'm at work today.'

'It's not fair,' she cried suddenly. 'I hate you. And I am not getting out of bed.'

I was so shocked I had to go to the kitchen and made sandwiches for work. When I finally tempted her out of bed with the offer of pancakes, she announced that the school shirt I've just bought her was suddenly 'too tight'. Then she refused to eat the pancakes, deciding she wanted porridge instead. Her pièce de résistance, however, was kept for last. When I finally persuaded her into the bathroom to do her teeth, she 'accidentally' dropped her soft doll with the plastic head and arms down the toilet and flushed it before I could stop her.

'What are you doing, Rae?' I shouted as the water in the toilet bowl rose up and refused to drain away. The doll had disappeared apart from one pink finger sticking out, fittingly, out of my reach.

She just shrugged. I was so confused, I marched her to school without talking, and handed her to her teacher, Ms Aldon, trying not to feel upset when Rae refused to kiss me goodbye.

So now I am late for work, worried about Rae. I forgot to talk to Ms Aldon about Rae being upset about after-school club, and I have no idea how I am going to find a plumber to fix our toilet.

I jump off at Piccadilly Circus and cut away from the tourists on Regent Street through the back alleyways of Soho, past the sex shops and market stalls, hoping I can remember the way to Wardour Street.

'Come on, Cal!' Guy shouts at me from his

142

glass-fronted office when I run in the door of Rocket, my hair buffeted from the Tube and now also frizzed in the morning rain. 'He's been here ten minutes.' Guy's warm brown eyes have darkened dangerously. I might have been away from work for five years but I still know the score. In Soho sound design, the client is king. And turning up ten minutes late for a meeting with the king is simply not showing the appropriate amount of respect.

'Sorry, sorry,' I whisper, running into Guy's office, looking for somewhere to put my coat.

'Here,' Megan says, coming in and taking it off me. 'Coffee?'

I nod gratefully.

'Right, let's go,' Guy snaps.

He takes me into the client room, which boasts luxury cinema seats and a giant plasma TV that is currently screening some of the studio's latest prestigious commissions: in this case, a Japanese car advert.

Parker stands up when I come in and, to my relief, offers me a beaming smile. I recognize him from a BBC art programme I watched. He is tall and slim, with coffee-coloured skin, startling deep blue eyes and Afro hair woven in tiny plaits, wearing a stylish pinstripe suit and an open-necked white shirt.

'Nice to meet you, Callie,' he says with a mild Scandinavian accent. 'Heard a lot of good things about you.'

I almost laugh out loud. The idea that Loll Parker has heard of me is funny. He is clearly just being kind.

Guy shoots a look at me. 'Lucky for you he's a nice guy,' it says.

Suitably admonished, I sit down. 'Right,' he says. 'Loll? Will we run through?'

Parker nods and Guy turns down the lights. A film starts to play on the plasma screen, with no sound apart from a rough of the actors' voices.

Parker's ten-minute short film opens on a remote Swedish lake that is surrounded by pine forests. On the empty shore-line sits a lone cabin. The narrative starts. The cabin belongs to an overweight, retired lawyer from Stockholm, who arrives every weekend, makes himself a luxurious breakfast of herrings and cheese, sits on his balcony overlooking the tranquil lake in his straw boater with his newspaper and gives a self-satisfied sigh.

Except this weekend, he wakes to a banging sound. He looks out to see a giant thug of a man laying the foundations for a cabin right in front of his.

'Who are you?' the lawyer booms off his balcony.

'Your little brother,' the thug booms back.

He is in fact the man's long-lost brother who has been in jail abroad for thirty years for murder, and has been left equal rights to the land around the lake. 'Our father favoured you,' the thug shouts at the lawyer. 'It's his fault I turned to drugs and crime.'

'But you're stealing my view,' whimpers the older brother, sensing the menace of his brother.

'I haven't had a view for thirty years. It's my turn now,' the thug growls.

The film follows him as he continues to saw and hammer and build his cabin, stealing his brother's tranquillity hour by hour, till the film ends with the lawyer suddenly finding his bravado again, and fixing a chair to his roof. It finishes with the thug erecting one even higher on his.

Guy and I clap at the end, and Parker beams. 'I'm exploring ideas of global population migration,' he tells us, with his slight Scandinavian lilt. 'You know, two hundred million people right across the world no longer live in their country of origin. At the same time, more of us than ever before are choosing to live in cities, cramming in together, searching for cultural identity and space.'

I watch him, fascinated. Parker can't be any older than me. Yet while I've been sitting at home for five years, he's been doing this. Developing ideas, learning, taking on the world.

The possibilities hit me. The doctors keep telling me that Rae is fine now; that she will live a normal life, bar a few extra risks. If we have really reached that point, we can both start finally to live a little. If I can really allow myself to believe that — well, the things I could achieve . . .

It's an art film, and visually stunning. Parker says he wants two things from the sound. He wants me to capture the stillness of the lake and forest, so that the intrusion of the sounds of the building contrast as violently as they can.

The challenge, I can see, is immense. Frightening. To create the perfect background of 'nothing'. Already my ears are mixing sounds: sparrow wings flapping on the current, breeze through reeds, insects creeping through undergrowth. I'm excited for the first time I can remember in years. But as Parker smiles that big smile at me expectantly, I also feel like a fraud. He expects something from me that I'm not even sure I can do any more.

★   ★   ★

Parker heads off to see his agent and leaves me to it, and I work on a few ideas, forcing myself to concentrate every time my stomach turns with nerves, and I have to fight the urge to bolt out the door and down Wardour Street. It is only when I go to the bathroom that I remember the broken toilet at home, and manage to ring my landlord to get a number for his plumber, and arrange a visit with the plumber's wife for sometime Thursday, all whispered from inside a toilet cubicle. I have the feeling that Guy will not appreciate domestic dramas interfering in our day today. I turn off my mobile as I walk out of the bathroom, in case the plumber himself tries to ring me to confirm the time, and head back to my office.

'Ready for us?' Guy asks, popping his head round the door just before lunchtime.

'Er,' I say, my heart thumping. 'I think so.'

He and Parker walk in and sit on the cinema chairs. I work around them calmly, making sure I don't do anything stupid, running through the sequence in my head. I am just about to press 'play' when Megan comes into the client room holding a handset.

'Callie, there's someone called Suzy on the phone?'

Guy looks at me. 'Need to take that?'

'Um . . . '

What do I do?

'Do you mind? It might be urgent.'

'Go on, then,' he says, his expression giving nothing away.

'Sorry.'

How did Suzy get this number? I'm sure I didn't give it to her for precisely this reason.

'Suze — everything all right?' I say, turning my head away from them as much as possible.

'Hi, hon,' she says. 'Yeah. I was just phoning for a chat. Your mobile is going straight to message.'

A chat? I look up at Guy. He is sharing a joke with Turner Prize nominee Loll Parker, drumming his fingers on the table.

'Um. Suze . . . '

'Sorry I was a little weird last night — I was just worried about Jez and Henry. I wanted to check how Rae was this morning?'

I stare at the carpet. 'That's nice of you, but actually I am in a meeting . . . '

'You can't talk?'

'Quite an important meeting.'

'Oh, OK. I'll leave you to it. Hey, hon? I must tell you before I go. This morning? You know Rae and Henry are doing this history assembly? It was the funniest thing. Henry told me he had to dress as a pheasant.' She laughs.

147

I say nothing, just smile inanely and nod as Guy looks over. What is she doing?

'He meant a peasant!' she says.

'I know,' I say. 'That's a good one. Listen, I really have to go — sorry. I'll call you later — bye.'

'OK, hon, bye . . . ' she trails off as I firmly press the 'off' button.

Avoiding Guy's eye, I go back to starting my rough soundtrack again.

'Everything OK?' Guy asks.

No, it's not.

'Yeah, sorry. Anyway, what I was thinking . . . '

* * *

Loll Parker likes my ideas for the 'stillness'. Guy catches my eye and winks.

'Good. Right — lunch. We better go,' he says, checking the clock on the wall. 'Table's at one-thirty.'

I let out a silent sigh of relief, and busy myself at the desk as they stand up and walk to the door. I could do with half an hour just to sit quietly and recover my nerves.

Guy stops at the door.

'Cal? Ready?' he says, waiting.

Parker holds the door open expectantly.

'For . . . ' I try faintly.

'Lunch?'

'Oh. I'm coming, am I?' I stammer. Guy shoots me a subtle but admonishing look. We're on show — pull yourself together, it says.

'We'll meet you in reception,' Guy barks,

motioning Parker to go ahead of him.

Shit.

I find a lipstick in my bag and quickly apply it in my reflection in the computer screen, rubbing my lips together to squash it into some sort of even tone. Pushing my Afghan-hound hair back, I dash after them into the reception area. Guy is already opening the front door and ushering Parker out into Wardour Street.

'Do you know where we're going?' I whisper to Megan, rummaging desperately to see if I have enough money in my bag for a sandwich.

'That restaurant that chef off the telly has just opened on Wardour Street, I think,' she says, reapplying her own lipstick in a pretty little compact. A compact. Of course, Megan would have a compact.

'Really . . . ?' I turn pale, looking hopelessly at my maxed-out debit card.

'Callie — Guy's paying,' she says. 'It's a client lunch.'

'Is it?' I say more loudly than I mean to. Of course it is.

Megan lets out a giggle like a tinkling bell. 'You do make me laugh,' she says. 'You've got to come out one night.'

'Oh,' I say, taken aback. 'That would be nice.'

'There's a launch party at Universal on Thursday — my flatmate works there. A few of us are going. Come.'

'Really?' My mind spins. What would I do with Rae? I'd have to ask Suzy . . .

'Cal?' Guy barks, his head appearing back in the door.

'Go on — you know what he's like,' Megan teases, as I rush towards the door.

She's right. I do know what Guy's like. I'm remembering fast. Demanding, challenging, forces you to think quick and live on your nerves. Encourages you to do things you didn't think you could do.

Exhilarating.

Guy and Parker are already twenty feet ahead, deep in conversation. I trot behind them on my new sandals. I can hear Guy's voice booming even from this distance, as he moves confidently through the bicycle couriers and pavement tables, past film and music and advertising companies. I watch him. He walks these Soho streets where deals are done like he owns them. Like he belongs.

The restaurant is only two minutes from Rocket. As Guy and Parker stop at the door to wait for me, I notice two women in their sixties pass the cool glass and wood exterior that says 'Asian fusion' and glance up. I can tell from the women's pastel suits, carefully accessorized scarves and coiffed hair that they are on a day trip to London to visit an exhibition, do some shopping and take in a musical, just like Mum and Aunty Jean used to do once a year.

One is whispering loudly to the other as they reach me.

'Who?' the taller one is saying, animatedly.

'That show we saw at the Tate?'

'Ooh!' the taller one replies, glancing back. 'Yes. I think you're right. Parker, or something? Loll Parker, was it?'

I am so taken aback, I accidentally meet their eyes. The women realize they have been caught.

'Loll Parker,' one of them murmurs conspiratorially at me, pointing with hidden pantomime hand gestures and wide eyes back towards the restaurant.

'Ah,' I nod, smiling, walking past them.

'OK, Cal?' Guy calls out loudly as I reach the door.

In the reflection of the window, I see the women's heads turn and watch me. I see Parker place his hand politely on my back, and guide me through the door that Guy is holding open into the restaurant. The women turn away, with wide eyes and embarrassed hands over mouths. If they are anything like Mum and Aunty Jean, I know they'll be in hysterics on the train home, recounting their story in peals of laughter.

An urge overcomes me to shout after the women, 'No, really, honestly, trust me. This situation is as weird for me as it is for you.'

But I realize that they see me, like Guy, as someone who belongs here.

★　★　★

In the end, the lunch lasts a couple of hours, during which Parker tells us about growing up in east Stockholm with his Swedish mother and Nigerian father, and the sense of displacement he felt as they moved to Lagos, then back.

'OK, this might sound a bit mad,' I venture after we finish the second bottle of wine. I feel Guy's eyes boring into me. Be careful, they say.

'But OK, I think what you are after is that idea of the harmony of an environment shifting and changing.'

Parker watches carefully. He's listening, I realize. He's taking me seriously.

'So . . . ' I continue, praying that Guy is with me, 'I know you're thinking of using actual building sounds, but what if we use natural sounds instead? Sounds that we pick out of the 'silence' mix and distort to create a shift in the harmony. So, say, for the sawing, you could have the buzzing of flies amplified until they're overwhelming and unexpected. Or a really high-pitched, screeching bird song for the drill.'

Parker thinks for a minute. 'Interesting,' he says, tapping his fingers on the table and looking at Guy.

Then he nods.

He NODS.

'I like it. Could you do another rough of that, Callie?'

Did he really just say that?

My cheeks burn. 'Of course. I'd love to.'

'Good. Let's do it,' says Guy, raising his eyebrows at me, and waving for the bill.

Maybe it's the alcohol, maybe it's elation. I feel like someone has just plugged me into the wall and switched me on. Inside me, darkened rooms light up.

'Thanks, Cal,' he says. 'Listen, call it a day. We've got a lot done today. You can start tomorrow.'

'Really?'

'On the dot, though, mate. There's a lot to do.'

I walk on air.

My legs feel like they have been extended to twice their length as, an hour later, they effortlessly race up the hill that takes me from Alexandra Park station to Rae's school. The pavement is bathed in cheerful June sunshine. It's difficult not to smile. Parker liked my ideas. He liked them.

And then there is Megan's invitation to go out in Soho on Thursday.

This is working! I can't believe it. It's really working. Already I can feel myself mentally separating from Suzy.

I stride on towards the after-school club, wondering how Rae will be after this morning's grumpiness. Checking my watch, I realize I'll have plenty of time to chat to Ms Buck about how she is settling in.

To my surprise, however, Rae greets me right inside the door with a huge grin on her face.

'Mum!' she yells. 'Can I go to Hannah's house?'

What?

'Can she?' Hannah shrieks, appearing from the cloakroom and grabbing Rae's hand. They jump up and down together, giggling.

'Um, I don't know, Rae, I mean, how's . . . '

Flummoxed, I look up to see Hannah's mum, Caroline, emerging from the cloakroom behind Hannah with her rucksack.

Has Caroline offered Rae a playdate? My heart hammers. Caroline always did seem a little warmer than the other mothers, even asking me if I'd like to come to the parents' school quiz with her and her husband shortly after school started last September. But then Suzy needed me that night when Jez was away and one of the boys was ill. And after that, Caroline and her friends seemed to form a clique and she never spoke to me again.

'Hi, Caroline,' I say. 'Rae was just saying . . . '

There is a small twitch on her face.

Her nose. It wrinkles almost imperceptibly.

Oh God. My breath. It smells of alcohol from the restaurant.

'It's just, Rae was just asking me if . . . um . . . '

'Yes,' Caroline replies. Her tone is not unfriendly. Just neutral. 'That should be fine.'

Fine?

'But not today, I'm afraid. Hannah's got piano.'

'Tomorrow then, Mummy?' Hannah yells.

'Yes, tomorrow?' Rae squeals.

I watch Caroline for her reaction. She smiles a closed-lip smile. What is happening here?

And then I see it. With horror, I realize that Caroline has not asked Rae for a playdate; Rae has become so desperate, she has asked Caroline if she can come to her house. Caroline is being put on the spot. There is no way she can possibly say no.

I freeze.

Caroline nods, and looks at me. 'Yes. Tomorrow should be fine. I'll pick Rae and Hannah up early from after-school club. You can get her about six-thirty?'

Rae's mouth drops open in excitement, and she runs to hug my legs.

I hug her back, but the word 'fine' is still reverberating through my head. Maybe it's my embarrassment, or an early hangover from lunch, but internally I feel myself bristling in defence. 'Fine?' I want to say. 'Excuse me, Caroline, but that is really not good enough. My daughter is not 'fine'. She is beautiful, and sweet and kind. She has an amazing laugh, if you ever gave her the time to hear it. She has survived more than you can imagine, and deserves more than 'fine'.'

Then I catch sight of Rae's face, pink with excitement.

Oh, poor Rae. If only she knew. It is me who is unpopular with the school mothers, for a reason I have given up trying to understand. It is me who has ruined her chance of a playdate. And me smelling of alcohol at 5 p.m. is not going to help.

So I bite my tongue. An unwillingly donated playdate is better for Rae than nothing right now. 'She'd love to come, thanks.'

Caroline opens the door to let Hannah pass through. We follow them out, and through the after-school club gate onto the pavement.

'Our address is on the class list,' she calls back.

'Brilliant,' I nod.

Caroline leads Hannah off down The Driveway, her eyes fixed firmly on her daughter's face in what appears to be an attempt to impart a secret code. Hannah

155

wisely keeps her eyes firmly on the ground.

'I've got a playdate!' Rae squeals, holding my hand tightly and jumping up and down till it hurts.

Today has been the best day both of us have had for a long time. There's no point, I decide, telling Rae off about her behaviour this morning, or about pestering Caroline.

We start to head off towards Churchill Road. Then I think of our empty flat with the broken toilet, and Suzy, waiting across the road, like always.

Not today. No, I can't.

I stop and dig out the coins that I found in the bottom of my bag at lunchtime.

'Rae. Suzy told me there's a new milkshake bar near the roundabout in Muswell Hill,' I say, counting out £6.30. 'Shall we go and try it?'

Rae's hopping about becomes even wilder, with a 'yippee' thrown in. I take her hand, grinning, and head up the hill for the fifteen-minute walk to the Broadway, Rae skipping at my side.

Too late, I remember I forgot to tell Caroline about holding Rae's hand in the street after school tomorrow, and to make sure she has my mobile number in case of medical emergencies.

I turn, but Caroline has disappeared down the hill.

Not to worry, I'll ring her tomorrow from work.

17

Suzy

What on earth was Jez doing?

Suzy moved round her kitchen, shutting cupboard doors and turning on the dishwasher.

This was ridiculous. It was nearly 7.30 p.m. and he still hadn't emerged from his study. He'd been in there since after breakfast, with the door firmly shut. At one point, after she had returned from a four-hour shopping trip to Brent Cross, she had crept up the stairs and tried to listen at the door. But there was no clue. No rumbling of his voice on the phone, or the music he played sometimes in the afternoon, or the tap of his fingers on the keyboard. Just silence.

She picked up a dishcloth and began to wipe the kitchen surfaces she had already cleaned twice today, once after breakfast, and again after lunch. Cereal and milk, followed by drips of vegetable soup and crumbs; now it was cold baked potato and broccoli remnants that she pushed into her palm. At six o'clock, as the children fought and sang and yelled, she'd shouted up to ask when Jez wanted to eat, hoping he might help put them to bed.

'Later,' he'd called down. 'Leave it in the oven.'

That was an hour and a half ago. Something to

do with a presentation he was giving in Birmingham on Thursday, he'd mumbled this morning. She'd dealt with the kids by herself.

The urge to barge in there and ask what he meant about Henry's school was overwhelming. Instinctively, however, she knew it would just make him withdraw even more.

No. She'd have to be patient. Wait till he was out of this mood. When she had rung Vondra this morning, from Brent Cross, she had promised to chase up the Michael Roachley lead as soon as possible. And there were other things Suzy could still try in the meantime.

With a long sigh, she threw the cold potato and broccoli in the bin, washed out the cloth, walked into the front sitting-room, and shut the door.

Checking that she still couldn't hear Jez on the stairs, she walked over to the white sofa. Carefully, she pulled it away from the wall so that it didn't scrape the stripped floorboards. The corner of a dark-green plastic bag became visible. She leant over and pulled at it. It emerged with a satisfying weight.

'OK,' she murmured, sitting down on the sofa and opening it. Checking the door again to be sure, she tipped it out on the floor. Various tubes and tubs of designer make-up tumbled out, much of it with the price sticker still on. A £53 foundation rolled to the side, and she trapped it with her foot, beside a £77 moisturizer.

She picked up the shiny wands and shimmering pots. Taking as many as she could carry, she stood up and went to the mirror above the

158

mantelpiece. Donning a new pink hairband, she pulled back her hair and wiped her skin with a cleansing wipe from a fresh packet. Then she applied the rich, creamy moisturizer with the tips of her freshly manicured hands. Now for her make-up. Oh, she knew how to apply make-up. That, she would never forget. Marianne, a girl at work back in Denver, had shown her how. Then she had met Jez, who had told her she didn't need it. Well, now perhaps she did again.

Carefully, she applied the foundation, smoothing out her pale freckles. A picture of Sasha, with her smoky eyes and pale pout, came into her mind. She took a light-brown eyebrow pencil and stroked it through her pale brows, bringing it down harder towards the end to achieve a more defined shape. Silver and navy shimmering eye make-up followed in deep sweeps. Then she reached back down and took out a little plastic box. Two rows of spidery eyelashes sat waiting. With an expert hand she applied the glue and stuck them onto her upper lids, applied some navy-blue eyeliner with a steady hand, and a couple of coats of mascara, then stood back to see the effect.

Even she was shocked at the transformation. Her turquoise eyes smouldered sexily from behind thick lashes. She dusted rose-coloured blush across her cheeks, and smoothed pale lip gloss on her lips.

Pulling herself up to her full height, she threw back her shoulders, making her neck long, and pouted a little. On impulse she undid a few buttons of her checked shirt and dropped it off her shoulders to hang around her jeans, revealing a rose silk camisole she'd also bought this afternoon and already tried on in the bathroom.

If this is what he wanted, she'd give it to him.

'Suze?'

His shout took her by surprise.

'Damn,' she whispered. In a panic, she tried to sweep some of the make-up off the mantelpiece back into the green bag. It would do her no favours right now if Jez discovered the cost of today's expedition to Brent Cross. She hadn't meant to buy so much. The day had just stretched ahead so emptily without Callie.

As she pushed everything into the bag, the open pot of silver make-up fell onto the white rug, sprinkling it with sparkling dust. She knelt down, scrabbling to pick it up.

'You in here?' he said, suddenly opening the door. She stayed bent down, the green bag clutched into her stomach, her back towards him, her shirt flapping around her sides.

She felt Jez's eyes boring into her, wondering what the hell she was doing.

'Dinner's in the oven, hon,' she said breezily. 'Give me a minute, I've just dropped a needle on the rug.'

'Don't worry, I'll take it up — going to be a late one,' he said quietly, and walked out of the door.

A late one.

She stayed where she was, shaking her head gently. With a sigh, she stood up and walked over to the wall. She placed the green bag behind the sofa again, then sat down on its firm cushions.

Pulling her shirt up and back around her shoulders, she waited for the clank of the oven door and the clatter of the cutlery drawer to turn into heavy footsteps as Jez took his tray back up to the study and shut the door once again.

Doing up her last button, she opened the sitting-room door, and padded gently up the stairs in his wake. At the top, she sat down in her usual place in the space and the silence, and took hold of each end of her false eyelashes.

Rip.

She pulled them so quickly they tore at her eyelids.

Suzy sighed, rubbing the patches of stinging flesh left behind.

It helped, but not enough.

So she pushed one hand up the sleeve of her shirt, where nobody would see it, and dug her newly manicured nails into the flesh of her arm. She kept them there, like a claw.

WEDNESDAY

18

Callie

Rae is so excited about her playdate with Hannah after school, she dresses herself within minutes of jumping out of bed and runs around collecting various bangles and stickers that she wants to take to Hannah's house.

'So you're all right about going to after-school club, then?' I venture, as she scoops up the last spoonful of her porridge and we head into the hall.

She starts to smile, then looks confused. 'Yes. I don't know.' Her face suddenly drops. 'I miss you, though.'

'Well, I miss you, too,' I say, brushing her long curly hair in front of the hall mirror and dividing it into the plaits I know will be pulled out long before home time. 'But soon, we'll have lots of new things to look forward to. If you're really well behaved and do what Hannah's mummy asks you, maybe we can invite Hannah back some time.'

'Yes!' Rae squeals.

'And you know what?' I smile at her in the mirror. 'I might have a new friend, too. A girl at work called Megan.'

Rae stares at me in the mirror. 'What is she like?'

'Nice,' I smile. 'Friendly. You'd like her — she looks like Alice in Wonderland. And she thinks I'm good at making jokes.'

Rae opens her eyes wide, then pulls a comedy cynical expression that I recognize as Tom's.

'Oi — monkey,' I growl, grabbing her sides and squeezing.

★ ★ ★

We head out of the door with plenty of time to spare.

'Hey, hon!'

My eyes drop to the floor at the sound of Suzy's voice. For some reason, it makes me feel panicked and trapped. I force myself to smile, then look over to see Suzy coming out of the gate with Henry.

'We didn't see you yesterday.'

'Sorry,' I say, crossing the street with Rae. 'We got back late but we might come over later and use your toilet if that's OK? Ours is only half-working and the landlord's plumber can't come till tomorrow.'

'Sure. How are you, sweetie?' Suzy says, patting Rae's shoulder as we head down Churchill Road together. 'You tell Mommy about after-school club?'

Rae's face drops.

Suzy makes a questioning gesture at me.

'I'll speak to Ms Aldon this week,' I say. 'Haven't had a chance yet.'

'Well, good luck getting any sense out of her, hon,' she sighs. 'I can't wait till Henry's out of that woman's class — one of the mums was telling me the other day that she . . . ' She lifts up her hand and gestures taking a drink. 'Don't you think she looks hungover sometimes?'

But before I can answer, Rae pipes up.

'Mummy's got a new friend at her work. She looks like Alice in Wonderland. And she thinks Mummy is good at jokes.'

She makes her comedy expression of disbelief again at Henry, and he laughs out loud.

Oh no. Poor Suzy. That will hurt her.

'She's not my friend,' I gabble to Suzy, out of earshot of Rae. 'She just works there.'

But Suzy doesn't seem to have heard any of it. She is concentrating on Henry's backpack, which is hanging open, and trying to do it up as we walk.

I watch her, thinking about Megan.

Should I ask Suzy? Is it hypocritical?

But then if I start to make friends away from Churchill Road, it could do Suzy good in the long run, I reason. She might not realize it yet, but she needs to break free from me, as much as I do from her. In a roundabout way, I'm giving her her own freedom, as well as grasping mine.

'Suze . . . ' I venture when we reach the main road.

'Hmm.'

'Actually, there is a work thing on Thursday night. I'm really sorry to ask, but would you mind babysitting Rae for a couple of hours? It wouldn't be till later, once the boys are in bed.'

'Sure, if Jez is around.'

'Really?'

'Of course.'

'Thanks,' I say, taking her arm. 'When I'm back full-time, I'm going to find a childminder so I won't have to ask you any more.'

She stares at me.

'Callie, really, hon. You don't need to do that. I'm happy to help. You never know who you can trust with your kids, anyway. Talking of which, why don't you head off to the station? I'll take Rae for you.'

'Really?'

'Course. I'll talk to Ms Aldon and find out what's going on with her, if you like. I'll do my best, anyway.'

'OK, thanks,' I murmur appreciatively. I know I should do it myself but Rae seems better today, and if Suzy takes her into school, it would give me a twenty-minute head start on the day with Parker.

I wave as Suzy takes both Rae and Henry's hands firmly in hers, and crosses the main road.

'I'll pick you up at Hannah's,' I mouth at Rae. I would have shouted it, but at the last moment, instinct tells me Rae hasn't mentioned her playdate to Henry yet.

★　★　★

By the time I reach Rocket, my head is buzzing with ideas for Parker's soundtrack.

He drops in for an hour to talk through it, then leaves for the morning. For inspiration, I Google 'Swedish lakes' to find out about the wildlife that lives in and around them, then start

168

to search our massive sound library for a match. I am so lost in thought about the exact noise a freshwater roach makes when it grabs a tiny water snail in its mouth that I don't even notice it's lunchtime, till Megan comes in and offers to fetch me a sandwich.

'So, can you make it tomorrow night?' she asks, wafting delicious perfume past me and wearing a leopard-print top.

'I think I can,' I smile. 'If that's OK?'

'Course it is! It'll be good. OK, so anything with cheese from Pret?'

I hand her the money, embarrassed that she's doing this for me, but also a tiny bit thrilled that I can hand over one of the many menial tasks that have filled my day for so long to someone who is genuinely happy and paid to do it, and carry on with my work.

* * *

I am so engrossed with sourcing sounds for the house-building that I jump when my mobile goes off.

I don't recognize the number. Who is it?

'Callie, it's Caroline, Hannah's mum,' a voice rings in my ear.

It takes me a minute to place it.

'Oh God, Caroline — hi!' I say too loudly, glancing at the clock. How did it get to 3 p.m. so quickly? 'I'm glad you rang. I meant to ring you this afternoon to say that Rae is a bit tricky on the road at the moment. It's a bit complicated, but when she had her big heart operation before school started, there were complica — . . . Well, she lost some oxygen and it's left her with poor coordination. The trouble is that at the moment, she's desperate to run and I'm — '

'Callie, can I just stop you there,' Caroline says.

'Yes. Sorry.' I must sound mad. She'll think I'm drunk again.

'I'm sorry, but I'm ringing to say I'm going to have to cancel Rae's playdate.'

I stop breathing. Oh no. Please no.

She carries on. 'I completely forgot that Hannah had an extra piano lesson at five tonight that's been rescheduled from last week when she was ill.'

She pauses, waiting for me to reply.

How could she? What on earth have I done to this woman?

And then I see it. Caroline never had any intention of having Rae to play. She just said yes last night because she couldn't think of an excuse to get out of it quickly enough.

Disappointment courses through me. How on earth is Rae going to feel?

'Oh, that's a shame. OK, don't worry,' I mumble. 'Caroline, would you tell her at five, when you pick Hannah up from after-school club?'

'Yes, of course. And I am sorry, Callie,' Caroline says. 'Maybe another time.'

'Maybe,' I say, knowing there will not be one.

'Well, bye.'

'Bye.'

There is no time to be upset. My sadness for Rae sits in a lump inside my chest like indigestion. Guy is flying in and out of the studio all afternoon checking on me. He confides that if Parker's short film is well received, he may end up moving on to feature films like Sam Taylor-Wood and other artists. If we impress him now, it could bring in new and bigger sound design contracts in the future.

Parker has to be in New York next Wednesday, so we are tight for time. Parker pops back in to see what I've done at the end of the day. We're playing everything back when I look up at the clock. I freeze. How is this happening? A minute ago it was 4.10 p.m. Now it is 5.20 p.m.

'Guy?' I gasp. 'Is that clock right?'

He checks his watch. 'Yeah — problem?'

'I am sorry, but I'm so late — I have to go.'

He frowns.

'We did say five . . . ' I mouth at him.

'Can you do another ten minutes, Cal?'

The implication is clear. We're under pressure here. He let me off at four yesterday. I owe him.

'OK, but I have to make a call.'

I run to reception and Megan gives me her phone. I bash in a number, hating my own hypocrisy. One minute I am trying to break away from her; the next, I am relying on her like family.

'Suzy,' I whisper. 'Listen, I am SO sorry. I've been held up. I don't think I'm going to make it to after-school by six. Is there any way you could pick up Rae if I ring them to tell them you're coming?'

There is a pause.

'Suze?

'OK, hon, that's fine . . . ' she murmurs.

'What?' I say. 'You sound annoyed.'

'No — not at all. Not with you. It's just that Rae was kind of upset again when I picked Henry up at three-thirty.'

'Really?' I say, bewildered. She wouldn't have known about her cancelled playdate yet at 3.30 p.m. — she should have been excited to go to after-school club with Hannah.

'Yeah, she lay on the floor, and screamed. Ms Aldon had to take her to after-school in the end because she wouldn't go with Ms Buck. And now if you're not picking her up at six either . . . I mean, hon, I am just wondering. Are you sure you're going to manage this?'

Oh God. And now Rae's going to be devastated about her cancelled playdate when Suzy picks her up, so she'll have to deal with that, too. I can't take this right now. Guy emerges from the studio and waves me back in.

My stomach is hurting.

'Suze, I know. But, please, can you just do it this time? I'll call you as soon as I get away and explain everything.'

'OK, hon. Listen, don't worry about it,' she says, and rings off.

I put the phone down and roll my eyes at Megan.

'You'll work it out,' she says. 'It took my sister ages.'

Why couldn't Suzy say that, I think as I walk back into the sound studio? Now I feel so worried I can hardly think straight.

*   *   *

In the end, Guy keeps me for forty — not ten — minutes, by which time I am almost hyperventilating. Eventually Parker picks up his jacket and Guy gives me the nod to go.

'Good start,' he says. 'Let's pick this up tomorrow.'

I burst out of the studio a respectable one minute after Parker, and start teetering along fast on my heels to the Tube, trying to ring Suzy's house on my mobile. No wonder you see so many women running round London wearing suits and trainers.

Suzy's phone rings out six times then goes to answerphone.

Maybe they went to the park. I try her mobile. That goes straight to voicemail, too.

That's odd.

At Oxford Circus station I stop and stand at the entrance, wondering what to do. Once I am on the Tube I won't have a phone signal for half an hour.

Flustered, I ring both her phones again, and leave a horribly apologetic message on both saying that I'll be back around 6.45 p.m.

I am just putting my first foot on the top of the Tube stairs when my phone rings.

'Hi, Suze?' I shout above the roar of traffic and a newspaper seller shouting, *Come and get it!*

173

'Did you get my message?'

There is a sudden scream right beside me. A tall woman in a business suit, with groomed hair and perfect make-up, is marching down Oxford Street towards me with a sharp, military stride, screaming in French into a phone headset. The sight is so bizarre I stop talking for a second to watch. She lifts her long legs up high with each step, verbally tearing a strip off somebody with such ferocity that one mother pulls her children towards her. Must have been dumped by her boyfriend, I think. Blimey. He messed with the wrong woman there.

'Cal?' I hear Suzy say.

'Sorry,' I say. 'There's this really bizarre woman walking around . . . '

'Cal,' she repeats.

'What?' I say.

I hear a noise that I don't understand. A noise down the phone that sounds like a sharp intake of breath. Then silence.

'What?' I say. 'Suze? What? Speak up, I can't hear you.'

The French woman stops in front of me, and carries on screaming. I turn my head away, desperately trying to hear Suzy.

' . . . into the road . . . ' I hear her say.

'What?'

The French woman carries on her tirade.

'Oh will you be QUIET!' I shout, silencing her and making her walk off with a haughty stare.

'You tell her, love!' jeers the newspaper seller beside me.

'Rae . . . fell into the road . . . '

174

'What?'

' . . . hurt her leg . . . she's fine . . . '

'What do you mean, fine?' My voice splutters away as if it has run out of petrol.

' . . . cut her leg a little . . . '

'Her breathing, Suze — how's her breathing?' I shout.

'OK. I think . . . you want me . . . take . . . A&E?'

'Yes. Please,' I shout. 'They need to check her out. Go to Northmore. Tell them to contact cardiology as soon as she gets there . . . '

There is silence at the end of the phone. I stare at it. Suzy's cut off.

Shaken, I turn and knock into the newspaper stand.

'You all right, love?' the newspaper man shouts in a rasping voice.

I shake my head, and turn one way and then the other.

He takes my shoulders, and I can smell stale cigarette smoke.

'I've got to get to Northmore — my daughter's fallen in the road.' I jerk away from him, panicked.

'All right, love. You stay there,' he shouts, and sticks his arm up and whistles. A black cab stops, and he opens the door and pushes me in it.

'Northmore A&E, mate,' he shouts. 'It's her little girl.'

And the cab pulls away before I can thank him.

19

Debs

She had an hour to change out of her work clothes and get the evening meal ready for Allen. She walked around the kitchen, concentrating hard, to keep the bad thought from her mind. Shut them in a box, her therapist had told her. Put each bad thought in a box, then imagine closing the lid and locking it. Fill your mind with other new, harmless ones.

For instance, this new oven. This new oven seemed very hot for only 180°C. The lamb casserole smelt dry and smoky. She prodded the potatoes with a fork. Undercooked. She took milk out of the fridge, poured it in the pan and put it back over the gas ring. Mash it, she thought. Allen hated lumps. Mash it. Again and again. There should be no lumps.

By the time she heard the sharp click of a key in the door ten minutes later, the potato had been beaten into a watery purée.

Allen walked in with his briefcase and put it down.

'Hello,' she called, trying to keep her voice relaxed. 'Dinner's nearly ready.'

'OK, love,' he replied.

Putting cutlery on the table, she walked into the hall.

'Here, let me help you,' she said, taking his overcoat off his shoulders.

'Thanks,' he said, leaning in for her to kiss his cheek. She wanted to lift up her hand and touch his cheek, but these moments of intimacy were so difficult now that she was frightened of how he might react. At the last moment she lost her nerve, and used her hand instead to brush away something invisible from his lapel. He stroked her arm lightly as thanks.

'What's for tea?'

'Stew.'

'Lovely.'

He went upstairs to change into the cords and jumper she'd left out on the bed, giving her a chance to get the dinner on the table. Concentrate, she thought, piling on the stew. Don't let your mind slip. Put the bad thing in a box.

Trouble was, the lid of one particular box was desperately trying to get off.

Mash, mash, mash. Squash, squash, squash, she thought. Squash the lid down.

Allen walked back into the room and placed his newspaper on the side for later.

'Good day?' she said, dishing out stew, carrots and potatoes. The potato ran towards the gravy and disappeared into brown mush.

'Yes, I think it was,' he said, looking pleased with himself. 'It looks like the bus stop idea will go to planning.'

'Oh, well done, love,' she said.

Allen smiled and sat down to his dinner with a contented sigh. 'Mmm, lovely.'

177

She sat down and watched him pick up his cutlery, leaving her own where it was on the table. She would watch him for a moment enjoying the food she had cooked for him. For a second she let herself pretend that it was last night again. That they were nearly finished their tea, and she was looking forward to the night they'd spend together on the sofa watching *Coronation Street* then the ten o'clock news, Allen doing his *Guardian* crossword, her helping him with the ones at the end he couldn't get.

Because tonight that wasn't going to happen.

'So, how was your day?' he said finally.

She looked down at the table.

'Not very good at all, I'm afraid, love. Something very bad has happened.'

Allen watched her, his eyes concerned, chewing the same piece of meat over and over.

20

Callie

'She's over there.'

I am already walking swiftly through the security door, past Suzy, to get to Rae, who is sitting in the paediatric section of Northmore A&E watching a telly on the wall. We've been here so many times, I already know what to expect. Stale air. Strip lighting so bright it scratches your eyes. Grubby toys scattered on the floor that smells of bleach. A cleaner wiping up yellow bile.

'Mummy,' she murmurs, pointing at the telly. 'Henry's got this film.'

'Hi, sweetheart,' I say, taking her face firmly between my hands and scanning it, inch by inch, starting my mental checklist. Lips — pink, if a little pale. Skin pale, too, but not out of the ordinary. Eyes . . . OK. Strangely bright, actually. Breathing normal.

'Has she been seen?' I call to Suzy, ignoring the curious stares of other waiting parents.

'Yes, hon, they've checked her leg and her blood pressure and pulse. The cardiology guy's going to get here when he can.'

'Show me your leg, Rae,' I demand, whipping off the blanket. Suzy has already stuck a large Winnie the Pooh plaster on it. Rae lifts her hands to show me skin engraved with bloody scratches.

The innocence of the baby plaster infuriates me. There is no such thing as a little cut when it comes to Rae, as far as I am concerned.

'How do you feel?' I bark.

Hold her hand tightly, I had said to Suzy, twenty-four hours ago. Hold her hand tight on the road.

Rae recoils a little at the unfamiliar tone of my voice. She looks up at Suzy then back at me.

'OK?' Rae tries.

'Not breathing funny? No pains?'

'No!' she says, frustration entering her voice. 'The lady just asked me all that.'

I look up at Suzy. She makes a sympathetic face.

'You want me to get the nurse?'

I turn away from her. She waits a second.

'Hon? I said, you want me to get the nurse?'

'No.'

She hesitates, then tries again.

'Sure?'

'I'll speak to her when I'm ready.'

There is a heavy silence for a second. Rae looks at me, and then at Suzy. She starts to smile, then bites it away nervously.

'Well, you know best.' Suzy moves away towards the door. 'You know what, I'm going to give you girls a couple of minutes to yourselves.'

I nod numbly, and go to put my arm round Rae. But before I can, she stands up and limps over to sit beside a child with a patch on his eye, and looks back up towards the TV. A toddler runs past bashing a tambourine. Each shrill bash crashes through my temples. 'Rae?' I call, softly.

She keeps her eyes on the screen.

★ ★ ★

How many times have I told Suzy about Rae's poor coordination?

I bite my thumbnail. She was supposed to hold her hand.

Out of the corner of my eye, I can see the security door opening again, and the shape of a tall person carrying two cups of coffee.

Suzy stands for a second. She puts one foot experimentally in front of the plastic chair beside me as if to test the water. Then another. She slowly sits down and hands me a coffee. The hot acrid smell turns my stomach. She puts hers on the floor with her right hand, then gently touches my little finger, which is resting on my knee. She leaves it there, and looks at me.

'Suze,' I whisper, pulling it away before I can help myself. 'I'm sorry. But what happened?'

She takes my hand again and leans gently into me.

'Hon?' Her voice is hurt. 'You OK?'

'It's just — I thought you understood about Rae falling over. I feel like I've said it a hundred times. Sorry, I know you were helping me out, and I wasn't there, but . . . '

'I do know that.'

'So, what happened?'

'OK, well, you know you rang me from work to pick her up? So I had to leave the house about ten-to-six to get her from after-school club? Well,

181

I'd just put the twins in the buggy and was going out the door, and Peter started to throw up. I didn't tell you on the phone but he's got a temperature, and just before he was sick I noticed this rash on his arm. Anyway, he just kind of projectile vomited everywhere. All over Otto, some over me. To be honest, I was concerned he might be real sick, you know, maybe — ' she checks my face before she says the word — 'meningitis . . . '

My anger deflates a little. 'Why didn't you say when I rang?'

She lets out a deep sigh. 'Hon, you sounded so stressed when I rang yesterday, I was scared to ring again in case I was interrupting something and I got you in trouble. I didn't know what to do. The twins were covered in vomit. I couldn't leave the house, so I took them back inside and rang the after-school club. I spoke to the leader — Ms Buck? — and told her that I was going to be twenty minutes late, at least, to pick up Rae. She sounded kind of pissed. And then I remembered you said the woman next door worked there, so we agreed that she would bring Rae back with her to Churchill Road when the club closed, and leave her with me till you got here.'

It takes me a second to realize what she is saying.

'So it wasn't you that was with her when it happened?'

This wasn't Suzy's fault.

Suzy shakes her head and pulls me towards her. A stupid, embarrassed smile breaks out on my face. 'No — oh, you silly person. Is that what you thought? Oh God, hon. You know how careful I am with her. No wonder you were angry. No — she was with that woman. And now I feel so bad that I asked her to bring Rae home. I didn't even question it — she's her teacher, for Christ's sake. I was worried about Peter, and you sounded so cross on the phone, I just had to make a decision.'

'So how did it happen?'

'Well, I don't know. I was changing Peter and I heard this shouting at the end of the road. I didn't think much about it, then I remembered Rae was coming back. So I ran out to the gate and I saw this pile of people in the road. I ran over and I realized Rae was lying on the road, with a teenager beside her with his bike.'

'A bike?'

'Yeah. He was trying to get up — he was shouting something at Debs, then he got up and rode off.'

She pauses and looks at me.

'Suze. Are you telling me Rae was hit by a bike?' I stammer.

'Yeah, no — I don't know, Cal — you're going to have to ask the police.'

'The police?' Other parents look up as my voice blurts out sharply.

'Hon, please try to stay calm. Yeah — someone called them, I think a woman on our road who thought Rae had been knocked over. Look, I really don't know what happened, but I think Rae tripped over on the pavement, and started to fall into the road just as this boy was turning the corner. I don't think he hit her. I think he probably just lost his balance trying to avoid her. Now, whether she cut her leg on the bike, or the road, I don't know. She didn't know.'

Each detail flashes at me like a strobe light, as I try to take it in.

'The bike cut her leg?'

'Yeah, maybe, but, hon — listen, they've checked her over. They don't seem worried.'

'And he rode off?'

'I think so.'

I look at Rae. She was hit by a bike. And this is my fault. Suzy was too scared to ring me because I was being such a selfish bitch on the phone, asking her to pick my kid up when her kid was sick, while at the very same time planning a way to cool down our friendship. It serves me right.

Suddenly, a thought occurs to me. I turn to Suzy.

'So where is she?'

'Who?'

'Debs.'

'I don't know.' Suzy looks down.

'What do you mean?'

'I don't know, Cal. It was kind of weird, actually. She was just staring at Rae, like she was frozen or something. I don't even know if she followed us up the road. I was too worried about Rae.'

'But, Suze, you did tell her that Rae had to be held tightly on the road?'

'Of course I told her. I specifically told her on the phone when we arranged it. I just . . . I just feel so bad. Like this is my fault. I don't know what to do. I was worried about Peter throwing up . . .'

'No. It's not your fault. It's my fault for being late and putting you in this position.'

Suzy looks at me and bites her lip.

'What?'

'OK, well, I'm glad. But there is something that you are going to be mad at me about.'

'What?'

'Um. Tom.'

'What do you mean, Tom?'

'I rang him.'

'Oh, Suze — why?'

'I know. I'm sorry. There was just this moment when I couldn't get through to your phone and I kind of panicked. I know how worried you two get.'

'So he knows what happened?'

She nods, her mouth screwed up apologetically.

With a loud bang, the A&E door flies open and the frame of a large man fills the doorway. For a second, I think it's Tom, but there's no way he could get here this quickly from Sri Lanka. I refocus. It's Jez.

An awkwardness quickly descends. Jez stands there with the twins asleep in the buggy and a tired-looking Henry holding on to it. He is wearing a beautifully cut suit and looks completely out of place among the screaming toddlers and exhausted parents wearing anything they could throw on in five seconds for the run to the hospital.

'Hey, baby,' Suzy says. 'Hey, hon.'

'I need a pee-pee,' Henry whines, coming over and pulling her arm.

'Come on then, little boo-boo,' Suzy says, standing up and leading Henry towards a toilet door at the end of the waiting room.

Jez parks the buggy and approaches me awkwardly, his eyebrows lowered, his mouth upturned, as if attempting to show empathy.

I find myself curious. I've wondered in the past how Jez would react if a woman had a crisis in front of him. Whether that rigid exterior would soften and he would put an arm round her, or not?

I sit up straight and try a smile.

What am I doing?

It's amazing. He's done it already. I am acting the way Jez wants me to. Polite, emotion hidden away.

'How is she?' he says, looking at Rae. I wonder what he's thinking.

'They think she's OK — we're waiting for a consultant.'

I pause. What will he come out with next?

Jez clears his throat.

'My father knows the hospital director here. I'll get him to have a word.'

'Thanks,' I say, looking up as Suzy emerges from the toilet with Henry.

Jez follows my eyes. This is ridiculous. I want to laugh. Instead of offering me a hug and to do something practical, he is offering me one of his networking contacts.

'Sorry you've had to come out so late with the kids,' I say. Again, I bite my tongue. Why did I

186

say that? Why am I apologizing?

'Cal, do you want me to stay?' Suzy says, walking back in, carrying a half-asleep Henry. We both know it's for show. Jez would probably spontaneously combust if he had to put three kids to bed by himself.

'No, go. Really. We could be here for hours.'

'OK, well, I'll ring you later.'

She hugs me and Jez half-smiles, and they're gone through a large white door. Free from this place.

* * *

I hate this hospital. All hospitals. I hate the stupid plastic chairs that press meanly into your back. The smells. The sense of doom. The coffee that tastes like chlorine.

Gloomily, I look around the A&E, wondering how many times Tom and I have dashed here with Rae at all hours of the day and night, worried that every little sniffle and cough meant something. This was just supposed to be the place Rae was born. Where we'd stay for a day or two before returning to Tufnell Park and getting on with the challenge of being accidental parents.

In fact, she was so normal, our only concern was to learn how to do the simplest of tasks for her. To learn how to wash between the tiny creases of her knees, and wipe her tiny mouth with cotton buds.

How long was it — two weeks later? — when we gently carried her round to the local cafe,

187

desperate to get out of Tom's flat in Tufnell Park, and in the bright light of the day we suddenly noticed how pale and limp she was becoming, and realized she hadn't fed for hours. A woman in the cafe with three kids told us to go straight to A&E.

'It's her heart,' the doctor said, with no time to sugar-coat it. 'She has a coarctation of the aorta — a narrowing of the artery.'

It all happened so fast that now I realize I don't know when I fell in love with Rae. All I felt was an overwhelming, primal need to keep her alive, broken up with moments of terrible regret at what might never happen. That I'd never get to see if she'd escape my maddening curls. That she'd never get to sit with me, as I did with Mum, in her bedroom when she was a teenager, having long chats about boys as I folded the washing. For some reason, I got particularly upset that she'd never get to have sex.

'The medication isn't opening up her artery, so we need to operate,' the doctor said. 'We'll insert a tube through her groin into the femoral artery with a balloon on it, then inflate it.'

'OK,' we both said numbly. Neither of us had even taken out a mortgage or made a will. Now we were telling a heart surgeon what to do.

'Even after this, it's not going to be easy,' he said bluntly. 'She'll need regular check-ups and an operation before she starts school to repair the artery.'

'Any good news?' Tom said, a catch in his voice.

I recall closing my eyes and wishing for a

second that none of this had ever happened. That I was sitting watching telly in my old flat in Islington, deciding whether to make it out to the pub with Sophie. That I'd never met Tom.

Then I opened my eyes and saw the way he was looking at Rae in the incubator, a tube inserted in her nose. The miracle child that he thought he'd never be able to conceive. Her heartbeat rang out in the hospital room, not in the deep thump of my dreams but a tinny, fragile beep. I went over and held Tom tight.

* * *

It is two hours before Dr Khatam eventually appears and starts to look Rae over. I have learned to read Dr Khatam's face over the years. There is the way the cheek area below his eyes tightens when there is bad news to come, like the first time we met him. Then there is the swish of his white coat — if it flies as he walks towards us, I know he is pressed and only has time to impart crucial information, not reassure anxiety. Today, however, it hangs gently around his knees. He stands back from Rae and gives me a rare smile, showing short boyish teeth under a thick moustache. The sight is so unexpected, I have to stop myself looking at them.

'She seems fine,' he says. 'We'll send her for an MRI and an ECG to be sure, then she can go home.'

I stare at him. I see his face twitch. Dr Khatam and I have been here a few times. He knows what's coming.

189

'Hmm,' I say. 'I just worry that . . . '

He screws up his mouth. 'Here we go,' it says. Dr Khatam spends a lot of his time reassuring parents whose child has had an aortic coarctation that, in most cases, the child will be fine for the rest of his or her life.

He nods. 'Look. Why don't we wait for the results of the scans?'

'But . . . ' I start. I hate this. When my anxiety goes into over-drive. When I can't control it. 'I'm sorry. Could she just stay in? Till tomorrow, in case? I'm just so scared of . . . '

He pauses for a second, then pats my shoulder. 'Let's find her a bed.'

I nod shamefully, avoiding the impulse to hug him.

★ ★ ★

Rae is so sleepy after her scans, she quickly falls asleep in a room the nurses have found for her in the paediatric ward, snuggling into her pillow greedily while I lie beside her on the pull-out parent's bed, stroking her cheek with my finger. The radiator pumps heat into the room despite the warm evening outside. If you squeeze your eyes up this could be a hotel room. A cosy little hotel room. Except for the tubes and masks fixed to the wall, ready for the next emergency; the furious screaming of two babies from down the corridor; a television blaring from the room across the hall, where I saw a tearful mum sitting earlier, looking like she needed help.

A nurse walks in with a blanket.

'Hi there!' she whispers with a cheery wave. 'How's she doing? Do you remember me — Kaye?'

I nod and smile, and try to look pleased to see a friendly face. It's not that I don't appreciate all the effort the nurses made during Rae's big operation to lighten the mood for Rae, me and Tom, but I don't want to know her face and her name any more. We live in the outside world now.

'How you doing?' she says gently, touching my shoulder, and I nod. Suddenly, I am very tired. A shiver runs through me.

'Hubbie with you?' she asks, looking round the room. The nurses loved Tom and the way he remembered their names and teased them mercilessly.

'We aren't married.'

'Oh dear, well, you better snap him up before one of us tries to!' she giggles. I know she is only trying to make me smile, but it's a relief when she heads off down the corridor to fetch some water for us.

⋆　⋆　⋆

I watch Rae for a while, then quietly pull myself up and head out of the room. I can't put this off any longer. I tiptoe to the nurses' desk and ask to borrow the phone.

To delay what I am dreading doing, I contemplate ringing Dad for a second, then decide not to. He'll only panic and offer to come, and I can't let him do that. As every farming child in our part of Lincolnshire knows, there is no rock base under the fields. If Dad doesn't get his new potato crop out this week, the earth could become so sodden with this early summer rain that his tractor might disappear right through it.

I leave a message for Tom instead, telling him not to come back, that Rae is fine. The last thing I can cope with right now is Tom turning up and yelling at me.

And then, finally, the one I have been putting off.

'Guy,' I say, when his mobile goes to voicemail. 'Hope you get this message tonight — it's Callie. I'm really sorry but my little girl had an accident today, and I think she's OK, but I'm going to have to take tomorrow off to make sure. Hopefully, I'll be fine to get in on Friday. But I'll ring tomorrow when I know more.' I pause for a second. 'Um, Guy, I know this is a pain but please bear with me. I'll see if I can find a way to make up the hours at the weekend. And please say sorry to Loll for me. I really, really want to do his film. This week has been amazing. So . . . '

So what? I can't bring myself to beg, so I end the message.

I walk back to Rae's room and lie quietly back on my bed. A vision comes into my head of Tom and Guy's expressions when they hear my messages. I groan.

So close but yet so far. And now everything is messed up.

Why has that woman Debs not rung?

THURSDAY

21

Debs

Bang. Bang. Bang.

Three loud knocks on the front door woke Debs up with a moan. She rolled over, and tried to sit up.

Bang. Bang. Bang. The door went again. Her eyes felt stuck together with glue, her head sliding to the left. Forcing herself out of bed, she staggered to the window, pulled back the curtain and peered outside.

'Are you taking the piss?' the hazy shape of a man shouted up at her.

'Sorry?' she said, fumbling for her glasses.

'Nearly broke my fucking back,' he shouted at her, raising his arm in anger and walking through the gate.

What?

She pulled her dressing gown round her and took another look out of the window. A dustbin lorry was reversing back down their road with a loud bleep. Thursday morning. That's right, dustbin day. The man and two others were emptying the recycling boxes into it, him still shaking his head angrily. She looked down and saw that her box had been left, its lid half off, beside the bin.

Feeling like she was forcing her body to run

through water, she pulled on her slippers and went through to the bathroom to splash her face in an attempt to revive herself. She had to see the doctor about changing these pills. Even though her eyes told her she was awake, her mind still seemed trapped inside sleep. Woozily, she crept downstairs, holding on to the wall.

By the time she'd got to the front door and opened it to feel a rush of cold air, the lorry had backed all the way out onto the main road. Looking around to check no one could see her in her dressing gown, Debs tiptoed to the recycling box and lifted the lid.

It took her a second to adjust her eyes to the strange sight that met her.

The box was full of big, round, heavy pebbles. There must have been a hundred of them, lying like a shingled shore. She pushed the box with her foot. It was like trying to budge a brick wall.

'For goodness' sake,' she said out loud. Quickly, she stuck her head out of the gate to catch the angry recycling man, but he had gone. She tried to think clearly. The box had been full last night, with the cardboard that she had taken out.

She looked around, wondering where the pebbles had come from. A large bare patch of earth caught her eye. It lay in the front garden of No. 17, the house next door on the right, whose owner she hadn't met yet. The owner was a writer, she seemed to remember, who spent a lot of time in her cottage in Suffolk. Vaguely, she recalled that the woman had a pebbled area between three potted box trees that looked like it had been landscaped professionally.

So who would have done this?

Debs looked down. That was strange. Sticking out underneath the bottom corner of the box were strokes of green chalk.

It looked like writing.

She leant down and removed ten of the pebbles, placing them beside the box. Then, using all her effort, she pushed the box hard, inch by inch, till she could lever it off the paving stone.

The words started to appear in random order: 'your', 'head', 'back'. What on earth was this?

Puffing with the effort, Debs finally managed to push the box sideways until it dipped a few inches down into a flower bed, its heavy bottom lifting up off the paving stone.

She crouched down on the ground, and tried to make out the rest of the message.

Each word was written boldly in dark-green chalk. It was the calculated neatness of the writing that made the message even more insidious than it already was.

'BE VERY CAREFUL, BITCH, OR I'LL PUT YOUR TEETH THROUGH THE BACK OF YOUR FUCKING HEAD.'

'Oh!' Debs gasped, jumping up as though she had been stung. Desperately, she looked around her, peering round the hedge out onto the street.

The boy on the bike. He must have followed her. Was he watching her right now?

Debs put her head in her hands and shook it

desperately. She was right. The Poplars had found her.

They weren't giving up.

* * *

Her hands were still shaking ten minutes later. On autopilot, she moved round the kitchen, trying to make sense of the fractured images that spun through her mind from last night. What had that boy looked like? Was it the brother?

Her memories came randomly. There was the click of metal — maybe the bike changing gear? Then the slush of rubber on wet tarmac, followed by this sensation of a menacing presence behind her, coming close but not moving past.

She had turned round. She had. But that's where things went hazy. All that came to mind was the shape of a boy with grey fog where the face should have been. And then an overwhelming urge to lift her hand.

And then Rae lying there in the middle of the road.

Oh Lord. What had happened?

Grabbing her tea, Debs sat down at the table. How had the Poplars found her?

She pulled her dressing gown round her further, feeling unnaturally cold. Allen had made her take a pill last night to help her sleep after she had told him what had happened. It was him who'd gone next door last night and spoken to Jez on the doorstep.

'Her leg is cut, but she's fine,' he said on his

return, sitting beside her, and resting his hand on her arm. 'Apparently she has poor coordination. They're keeping her in tonight as a precaution. So try not to worry too much, love. Let's see what happens tomorrow.'

'Hmm,' she had murmured back.

His voice had been calm but she knew he was reaching the end of his patience. And she couldn't blame him.

So, today, much as she wanted to ring him, she didn't. Instead she rang a different number, already doubting her choice.

'Payroll,' said a loud voice.

'Alison, it's me,' she said, knowing her sister's tone would immediately change.

'Oh, hello,' Alison said flatly. 'What's up with you, then?'

'Um . . .'

'I have a meeting with the finance director in a sec, so you'll have to be quick.'

Alison was always about to do something important.

'I'm being harassed again,' Debs said.

There was a pause.

'What've they done?'

'I think one of them tried to frighten me in the street last night. The brother, on a bike. And I think he filled up our recycling box with stones. And left a very nasty note.'

Alison said nothing for a moment.

'What does Allen say?' she finally replied.

Debs gritted her teeth. How quickly her sister always got to her.

'I haven't told him.'

There was another pause from Alison's end as she spotted the weakness she'd been waiting for.

'Oh, I see!' she said. 'So you ring up poor old muggins instead!'

Debs bit her tongue.

'Listen, I just wanted to tell you. Don't worry. I'll — I'll ring the police if I have to.'

'You need to get that husband of yours to have a word with them,' Alison said. It sounded like a taunt.

'Better go,' Debs said. She couldn't help herself. 'I'm making dinner for Allen tonight. It's our six-month anniversary.'

Alison paused. 'I'll let you go, then.'

★ ★ ★

The ironic thing was that if it hadn't been for Alison, she would never have met Allen. And none of this trouble would have happened.

Maybe it had been her fault — for breaking the status quo between them. Before, her sister could keep the upper hand she had always demanded, with her better-paid job at the accounting firm and the more interesting hobbies. Ladies' choir was the best Debs could muster. Alison, on the other hand, learnt to sail and went on singles yachting holidays in Turkey. She'd showed Debs photos of one holiday romance, Graham, whom she said 'just worshipped' her. He had a red face, and a shirt opened to reveal a sunburned chest covered in grey hair to match his head, a bottle of beer in one hand, the other on Alison's thigh. She spent

200

a week torturing Debs with details about his proposed trip down from Peterborough. The day of the date came and went, and she never mentioned him again. Debs knew better than to ask. Oddly, it was that which prompted her to look in the *Guardian*'s Soulmates section.

'Shorter than you,' Alison had whispered the first time Debs took Allen round to her sister's new-build estate house in Palmers Green and he'd gone to the loo. She'd met them at the door with that flushed, hyperactive way she had when she felt under attack. 'You still look tired, Debs — is that the same cold sore or another one?' she'd exclaimed, grasping the bottle of Italian Chianti Allen proffered with a nod but no thanks. When Debs broke the news they were getting married, Alison hadn't spoken to her for two months.

Debs wondered sometimes if Alison had been pleased about what had happened at her wedding.

$\star$ $\star$ $\star$

In the end, Debs's mind had raced with so many dark thoughts that she'd had to leave the house and walk up the hill to Ally Pally, checking nervously every few seconds to ensure the boy on the bike wasn't following her again.

It was quiet today. Too early for the packs of teenagers who gathered at the school lunch-break, showing off how many swear words they knew in blaring voices; too late for the mothers who had taken their toddlers home from the playground for morning naps.

Debs set off and walked briskly round the boating pond three times, hoping the light breeze would clear her head. To distract herself, she watched packs of geese and pigeons fighting it out with the ducks for bread thrown in by a pensioner. Too late, she realized that the smiling woman trying to catch her eye from a table at the cafe was a parent from after-school. Dropping her eyes to the ground, she pretended not to see her. What would they all be saying? Lisa Buck had sounded hesitant on the phone this morning. 'No, that's fine, Debs. Let us know when you're feeling better — I think the Head will want to have a chat about what happened with Rae when you get back, but no hurry.' Debs knew what that meant. Take the week off and in the meantime the other staff and I will get together and talk about what happened and start digging into your past to find out if there is anything to be concerned about. The thought of them discovering the Daisy Poplar incident was so terrifying she started singing to herself to block the images from her mind.

It wasn't until she was back home, however, and filing the last few books on her shelves that she was finally able to force all the dark thoughts back into a box.

Books. Thank goodness for her books. They always calmed her. She looked down at the ones on the floor, wondering which to weed out from the packed shelves to make room for these final few. She picked out a couple of possibles and held them in her hands, weighing up what each one meant to her. From the age of eleven, thanks to Mrs Shaw at school who'd lent her a leather-bound copy of *Oliver Twist*, she'd loved books. For the beauty of their weight and shape as much as the escape their contents offered her from her mother's stuffy little Walthamstow flat, with its factory-moulded ballet dancers and TV guides.

There were two copies of *Tess of the D'Urbervilles* — one would have to go. The first was bought in a teetering old antiquarian bookshop that smelt of dust and sunlight on a lonely day trip to Oxford one Saturday before Allen, and had a hard green cover with gold lettering. The second was a battered paperback that fell open to reveal her name and the name of the teaching college she had attended two decades ago. The sight abruptly took her back to her coffin of a university room, and the German exchange student, Bruno, whom she'd let drunkenly grapple away her virginity after a party thrown by their lecturer with free wine. It had taken her two hopeful days to realize Bruno wasn't going to ask her out. Or speak to her again.

She threw the paperback on the pile for Oxfam.

The Poplars could not win. She could not lose Allen. She couldn't.

★   ★   ★

He had rung to say he'd be home early to see how she was, so she began to get a sandwich ready. Tuna and sweetcorn. That was his favourite. She had tried to learn all his preferences. No fabric conditioner on his shirts. 'Don't want to smell of flowers at the office, love,' he'd said, making her giggle unexpectedly. A nice dark ale, too. And a good crossword.

It took her a second to realize when Allen opened the door that he was speaking to someone.

She walked into the hall and saw a young policeman behind him.

'Love,' he called, seeing her panic-stricken face. 'It's OK, this officer has just come to ask you a few questions about the little girl across the road. Nothing to worry about.'

'Oh. Of course,' she mumbled, showing him into the front sitting-room.

He was young, probably in his twenties, but had a surprising confidence in his manner.

'We had a call yesterday from a witness who said a five-year-old girl in your care fell into the road in front of a bike on Churchill Road yesterday. I wonder if you could tell me what happened? I understand you're her teacher?'

The implication of his statement hung in the air.

'Officer, my understanding is that the child fell into the road probably due to poor coordination,' Allen said, sternly. 'Could we start from that assumption, please? My wife was not in her official capacity when the accident happened. She was helping a neighbour out in a medical emergency. She is very upset and has nothing to hide, but as you can see, she is shaken up by the incident.'

Debs looked at him. She hadn't seen Allen like this before. This must be how he got bus stops put in inconvenient places where elderly people needed them.

'OK,' said the young police officer. 'Do you want to tell me what happened in your own words?'

'Yes,' said Debs, trying desperately to think of what to say. 'To be truthful, I don't really know what happened. One minute she was walking beside me nicely and there was a bike coming up behind me, and the next she wasn't there and she was ahead of me, falling into the road.'

The police officer watched her carefully as if he were checking the moles on her face.

She dropped her eyes to the floor.

'Did you see the cyclist's face?'

'I . . . I am not sure.'

'And were you holding the child's hand?' he asked.

'I can't remember . . . No — I don't think so,' Debs said. 'She was walking nicely, I didn't need to.'

'But her mother says you'd been warned to hold her hand on the road.'

What was he saying? Debs looked at Allen, shaking her head.

'Was I? I know the mother worries about her health — all the teachers do at after-school club — but I don't remember being told I had to hold her hand on the road.' A tightness came round her chest, making her squirm to remove it.

205

'Things go blank sometimes.'

The police officer looked at his notes.

'Are you formerly Deborah Jurdon, formerly of Weir Close, Hackney?'

Oh no. She knew what was coming.

'Yes,' she replied weakly.

'Were you involved in an assault on a child at Queenstock Academy?'

Debs dropped her eyes to the floor. Her hands were shaking so badly she could hardly lift them to adjust her glasses.

Allen jumped up. 'Now, listen, this has absolutely nothing to do with that incident, officer,' he said crossly. 'Please leave my wife alone, you can see she is upset.'

Keep the lids on, she shouted inside her head. Keep the lids on. But she couldn't. The lids all flew off.

Panic-stricken, she blurted: 'Actually, whilst you're here, officer, and you are talking about the Daisy Poplar incident, I think I'm being harassed by her family. I know you don't like me talking about it, Allen, but last night. On the bike. I think it was the Poplar boy. The brother. Coming up behind me in the street, trying to frighten me. That's why I can't remember what happened with the little girl. I was scared. And now I think they are calling me on the phone all day. And . . . and . . . this morning someone filled up our recycling box with stones and left me a note on the ground. In chalk. A horrible note.'

Allen shook his head. 'Debs, no. You have to stop, love.'

'But Allen, it's true! You have to listen to me. I didn't want to worry you with this, but it's happening again, Allen. They must have found me . . .'

Allen looked harassed. Upset. 'Love, please don't bother the police with this — she's been suffering from anxiety since the school incident,' he said, turning to the young officer. 'Seeing a therapist.'

Debs glared at her husband. How could he?

'I am NOT imagining it, Allen!' she shouted. 'Please stop telling me that. If you don't believe me, come and look!'

'Mrs Ribwell,' the young police officer said, looking concerned. 'I have to say that I think it is unlikely that you are being harassed by the Poplar family. Our file notes show that the family have relocated to the Spanish coast after all the unwelcome press attention. Mrs Poplar works in a bar there now, owned by her brother, I believe.'

She stared at him, furious. Why would nobody believe her?

'So how do you explain this, then?' she shouted. She marched out of the room and opened the front door. Allen and the police officer followed her outside. Even as she went to fling open the lid of the recycling box she could tell that something was different. The lid had been replaced properly, not left half-cocked as she remembered from earlier.

Allen and the police officer peered over her shoulder as she took it off.

It revealed an empty green space, dotted with specks of black dust and tiny cardboard strips. Debs pointed inside it.

'The stones were there — and they'd been taken out of there,' she said, turning her finger to her neighbour's garden. But instead of the black earth from earlier, she could see the giant pebbles once again lined up.

She knew before she even looked that the chalk note behind her had disappeared, too, the dark-green powder wiped away.

'They were there,' she said. 'I think.'

22

Suzy

Suzy put her car in neutral, pulled on her handbrake and turned off the engine. With the flick of a long finger, she pressed the button that replaced the roof with a soft burr, took off her seat belt and pushed back in the seat. Five minutes. Just to gather her thoughts outside the hospital, before she went in. Callie had been difficult to judge yesterday. Sweet, passive Callie, with flashes of anger in her eyes, her voice louder, less hesitant than usual.

Suzy looked in her rear mirror at the red-brick Victorian hospital behind her. Last night was the first time she had been back since the twins were born. She'd never forget the shock she felt when the ambulance had pulled up at the emergency entrance of this grim old building, with its tired magnolia walls and belligerent drunk men and floors stained with dried blood and vomit, so far removed from the spotless white clinics of Colorado that, in heavy pants, she had asked a doctor if they were in the right place. Thank God, Callie, her new neighbour, had been there to tell her that it would be fine. That the doctors and nurses were fantastic. That she had given birth here, too, and that she would stay with Suzy in place of Jez, for those long five hours

209

until the twins burst into life in the birthing room with gulping, blue gasps.

She and Callie had locked eyes at that moment, dropping their jaws, laughing in delight at sharing this life-affirming moment. Suzy had gripped Callie's hand, tears flooding down her face, knowing that she had found a true friend in this woman who had witnessed her body and mind at their most vulnerable and shameful and exposed, and not left her alone.

And true friends, she thought, checking herself in the car mirror, forgive.

Callie was hurting, and it was logical for her to blame Suzy. All Suzy had to do was be there. Give her the time and space to realize she could trust her again.

A familiar shape passed Suzy's car, interrupting her thought. She turned her head to look.

The woman was in her seventies, perhaps, or had maybe just had a hard life. She appeared to have come out of the hospital, and was walking up Northmore Hill. She was average height, but heavy, her body bulking out the light-blue raincoat she wore over a pleated navy skirt. It was her legs that Suzy couldn't help noticing. They bore no relation to legs you saw in magazines. These were not the sinewy calves of children that helped them grasp their way up climbing poles in the park or run after a football. Neither were they the sculpted calves of women she was used to seeing in the city, colt-like in strappy sandals or black tights and tall leather boots.

No, she had only ever seen legs like these once

before. The calves were almost as wide as they were high, heavy with fat, the colour of raw sausages. Blue veins snaked across the deadened, pore-blocked skin. Lumps burst out in random spots, like broken mattress springs. There was simply no ankle. Instead the thickness extended down and was squashed into sturdy brown shoes, which the woman was currently attempting to move as quickly as she could. Her effort was palpable. She was leaning at forty-five degrees just to sway her bulk uphill, her wide, shapeless back dropping and rising heavily.

Why was she rushing?

Suzy looked around. A lithe young traffic attendant was racing up the other side of the road, fifty yards further down the hill, his long legs carrying him at an incredible pace. The old lady glanced behind her nervously. He knows her ticket has just expired, Suzy thought. He is chasing her. The cheetah and the warthog.

'Go on, hon, you can do it,' Suzy said under her breath.

The traffic warden bounced between two cars and stood rising and falling on the balls of his feet, like an athlete on the start line, waiting for a space to cross. Lorries thundered down Northmore Hill, thwarting him. Suzy turned to watch the old lady. She was slowing down rapidly now, her chest heaving to inhale more oxygen, her legs petering out in their task of propelling her massive bulk up the unforgiving gradient.

She put out a hand and leant on a blue Ford Fiesta, and took three deep breaths. She looked behind her, with a hunted expression, and saw

211

that she still had time.

Suzy checked. There was a two-second gap in the traffic as a bus slowed down to stop. Taking his chance, the traffic warden sprinted across the road. There was a bounce in his step, as if the tarmac was his own personal trampoline. In five great leaps he was across the road and racing towards the old woman.

With enormous effort, she was now squeezing herself through the small gap between the front of her car and the one in front, wincing as her body wobbled and shook against the hard surfaces. In her hand, Suzy could see a key. The old woman scrabbled to point it at a lock, her eyes searching out the traffic warden, who was now coming at twenty paces.

Her mouth opened, as if she was groaning. She managed to open the door and heave her body inside the car, using big, hammy hands to pull her giant legs inside.

The traffic warden reached the back of her car, his eyes wide and excited.

'Nearly there,' Suzy whispered.

With a final desperate effort, the old lady swung her door shut and started her car, just as the man dived off the pavement and attempted to walk in front of it to see her ticket. The old woman flipped on her indicator and began pulling out into the traffic as he reached her window.

It was too late. The wheels were already turning.

As the old lady was flashed into the traffic by a white van, the traffic warden raised his hand as if in salute. His mouth opened to reveal a great big gleaming smile. He'd lost the game this time. Next time she'd be his.

Suzy sighed. Time to go in and face Callie again.

★ ★ ★

Callie was sitting in a seat beside Rae's bed, staring out of the window. She looked up.

Suzy smiled, hoping for one back. There was definitely a movement around her friend's mouth, even if its intention was unclear. But it was something — better than yesterday, when she had refused to make eye contact at all.

'Where's Rae?' she asked gently, moving carefully into the room.

'In the playroom with another kid.'

Suzy leant down and gave Callie a kiss on the cheek. She smelled a little peaky. She was still wearing the same clothes as yesterday and there was a smear of make-up under her eyes. The hair that framed her forehead was sticking up as if she had slept with it pushed into a hard surface.

Suzy gave a big sigh. 'Well, that sounds promising.'

'They've put her on antibiotics for her leg,' Callie said. 'Her heart is OK but they're going to keep her till teatime.'

'I let the plumber in with your spare keys, by the way. He said the doll had got stuck on something and he'd have to replace the part. Shouldn't take long.'

'Thanks,' Callie said, distracted. There was

something about her face Suzy couldn't place. A firmness in her jaw line.

'Hon — what is it?'

Callie looked up at her. Suzy could see the battle going on in her friend's eyes.

'Suze — I'm just confused. A policeman's just been here about Rae's accident. He told me that he'd interviewed Debs this morning and she said you didn't tell her to hold Rae's hand? She said no one had told her that Rae mustn't run.'

Suzy opened her eyes wide with astonishment.

'What? That's crazy. I specifically explained that Rae falls over easily and that she had run away from you on Monday night. I swear to you, Cal, that's what I said. Jesus. Why would she do that? Ask Ms Buck. She must have overheard the conversation.'

'Apparently, she didn't — they've asked her. Anyway, he's gone to the canteen to get some tea — can you speak to him?'

Suzy touched her shoulder. 'Sure.'

Callie pulled away and stood up. She rubbed her eyes.

'Sorry — look. I'm just tired. And it's this place — I hate it. I'm just so confused. I mean, why she would have purposely ignored what you said?'

'I don't know.'

'It's just. Oh, I don't know. I just wish you hadn't asked her to bring Rae home.'

The accusation hung in the air. Suzy waited. She had to be very careful here. Callie clearly hadn't slept.

'Hon, listen to me. I know you're angry, and I

214

know you're worried. But you have to understand, I would do everything in my power to protect Rae as much as one of my own kids. I love her like family. I love you like family. And you don't think I wasn't awake all night wishing I hadn't asked that woman to do it? There's no way I would have asked her if she hadn't been a teacher. And sorry, Cal, but you had already allowed her to look after Rae at after-school club. You made that decision. Everything happened so quickly, I was just trying to do my best for you. You weren't there and I had to get Rae home . . . '

Callie looked at her and rolled her eyes. She shook her head.

'I know . . . ' she whispered. 'It's just, Suze, I am going crazy in that flat. You have no idea how bad things have been for so long. Then when I eventually try to change things — three DAYS after I leave her, this happens. And now we're back in this fucking place again.'

Suzy made sure that Callie saw she was listening intently to her. That was important. 'Don't blame yourself, hon. Blame me for trusting a teacher. Jesus, it just goes to show you can't trust anyone with your kids. I'm thinking of taking Peter and Otto out of nursery after this.'

She waited for Callie's reaction but her friend's face had changed. She wasn't listening to Suzy any more. She was looking past Suzy, down the corridor.

'Oh, great. Here we go,' she said quietly.

Suzy turned to where her friend's eyes were directed.

A big man with a deeply tanned face, Viking-white curls bouncing around his jaw, was striding down the corridor beside a tall, wide-shouldered girl with long, black hair. They were both wearing khaki jackets and had soft bags slung over their shoulders.

She had always thought Tom had an open, generous face. But the expression on it now was as far removed from that first impression as possible. His blue eyes were bloodshot with lack of sleep from the overnight flight and glittering dangerously. Callie shrank physically as he approached. Suzy moved beside her protectively.

'Where is she?' he demanded. Up close, he was unshaven, a faint blond fuzz around his jaw. Callie pointed towards the playroom at the end of the ward, gritting her teeth. She's trying not to cry, thought Suzy. She's frightened.

'I want to speak to the doctor,' he boomed, walking past Callie. At the sound of Tom's voice, Rae popped her head out of the playroom and came limping towards him, throwing her arms round his neck as he leant down. Kate stroked her arm. 'Hi, sweetie,' she said in her confident, well-spoken voice.

Callie stood frozen, watching them. This is what it would be like, Suzy realized, to see your husband with a new partner — with your kids. She shuddered, and reached an arm round Callie. The stiffness from moments ago simply melted away. Callie fell into Suzy's side, letting her hug her close.

That was better, Suzy thought. She knew it would just take time. Friends forgive.

'The way he speaks to you, hon,' she murmured. 'It's not right. Don't worry, I'll stay till he's gone. I'll go and find that police officer and get your tea.'

She left Callie in the corridor and headed towards the canteen, spotting a police officer looking for sugar beside the checkout.

'Hey,' she said. 'I'm Suzy Howard. Callie Roberts' friend — you wanted to speak to me?'

'Yes,' he said, looking at her, surprised, pointing her towards an empty table. 'I'll just put these down and take some details.'

She gave him what he needed, then talked through what had happened on the phone with Lisa Buck and Debs.

'So you are quite sure you told Mrs Ribwell that Rae had to be watched on the road because of her condition?' he said, pencil hovering above pad.

'Absolutely.'

'And can you think of any reason why she would deny that?'

Suzy sucked in her lips as if making a difficult decision.

'To be honest, between you and me, I find her a little strange. She seems a little confused and distracted. Maybe that's it. Maybe that's all it was?'

'OK,' he said, shutting the pad. 'Thanks for your help. We'll be in touch if we need anything else.'

'You're welcome,' she said, standing up and taking Callie's tea from him. As she took it her finger touched his by accident.

He gave her the type of smile that Suzy was used to men directing at her. Slightly too wide; eyes too searching.

Yeah, bozo, she thought. Get on with the job.

Returning his smile, she nodded and headed back down the corridor towards Rae's room.

She heard Tom before she saw him.

Turning the corner, she came across Callie slumped against the wall. Tom was back in the corridor, remonstrating with her, Kate silent at his side. Kate had a serious look on her face. She stood there in judgement, his ally, making it clear that she knew everything unsavoury there was to know about Callie; that she and Tom had picked her character and mothering skills apart at night in bed in whichever mountain cabin or jungle tent they happened to be sleeping in.

Two against one? Suzy thought, putting down the tea. I don't think so.

'What did you expect?' she heard Tom say as she marched over. 'She's in no position to be left with other people yet. It's too early. Just because you want to go back to work doesn't mean that you can! Just because you don't want things to be like this, doesn't mean they're not going to be.'

Callie's head was bowed. She turned as Suzy approached. Her eyes were fearful.

'Hey — don't speak to her like that,' Suzy said, standing in front of Callie and squaring up to Tom. He pulled his head back in surprise, his eyes still blazing.

'This is none of your business. This is between me and Callie.'

'What — and your girlfriend?' she said, motioning to Kate. 'Actually, it is my business. She's my friend, and she's upset and she's exhausted. And for your information, I spend much more time with Rae than you do, so I know how much you leave Callie to do everything. And she's a brilliant mother — all the time. You are away — what? — eight, nine months a year? Even when you're back you ring her all weekend, asking her stupid questions. If Rae says she's sleepy you're on the phone. Then you waltz off again abroad with your girlfriend here and sit around on a beach with your bloody baboons or whatever and leave it all to her, again. You know, if you actually took some of the strain off her, maybe she wouldn't need to be out working again just to feel she has a life.'

Tom went quiet. Then a smirk appeared on his face. 'That's how it is, is it, Callie?'

Callie kept her eyes on the floor.

He turned back to Suzy. 'I'm not going to insult you by taking to pieces what you've just said, because I actually believe that you believe it.' He looked back at Callie. 'You've done a good job there, Cal.'

Callie didn't react.

With a disgusted shake of his head, Tom turned back into Rae's room with Kate. Suzy reached out and pulled Callie towards her.

'Come on. Let's get you home for an hour, and get some clean clothes.'

Callie didn't speak, just walked numbly the way she was led.

'Hon, you are so well out of there. The way he

219

speaks to you is outrageous.'

'Is it?' Callie said quietly.

Suzy put a protective arm around her and pulled her back close.

23

Callie

I want to speak to Debs. I want to speak to her with an urgency that I haven't felt since the morning Dad rang, his voice stuttering and raw, to say that Mum had come home from her poetry evening class the previous night feeling fluey, and he had woken up in the middle of the night to find her covered in a meningococcal rash. She had died in hospital a few hours later as they desperately pumped antibiotics into her.

I sat on the train from London counting the minutes till I was back home to see for myself if it was true. To walk around the farmhouse numbly and see her glasses on the kitchen mantelpiece but no head to place them on, her wellies in the porch but no feet to put inside them, to take her to pick carrots for our tea. To shout, 'Mum!' when Dad was out at the funeral director's. 'Mum! Can you move your car? Mum! What's for tea? Mum! Have you seen my blue top?' Because in the millisecond of delay between my shout and the resounding empty echoing reply of the house, part of my brain still believed she might answer.

Suzy pulls into Churchill Road. You would never know anything had happened here last night. For a second, I hate London. Where

221

someone can be stabbed in the park and it doesn't even make the local TV news. When Mum died, our neighbours in the village were still discussing it a year later, bringing meals round, flowers, offers of help for Dad long after her anniversary.

Suzy parks outside her house, and we step out onto the pavement. The sun is dazzling today and hurts my eyes after nearly twenty-four hours in the fluorescent glare of the hospital.

'Come and have a look,' Suzy says.

She links her arm through mine and we walk to the end of Churchill Road, passing a couple in their fifties whom I recognize from further up the street. I try to meet their eye. They must have heard about what happened to Rae. The whole street must know a little girl had an accident here yesterday?

They cross over to the other side of the road, chatting.

'Yes, thanks — she's fine,' I mutter under my breath, sad for Rae. Suzy shoots me a sympathetic glance.

'What do you expect, round here?' she says.

We stop at the end of the road and Suzy points to the gutter.

'I think she was running down here — and fell or slipped about here.' Her finger moves to the corner of the kerb. 'The boy was turning there.'

There is nothing there. I am not sure what I was expecting. Perhaps a broken paving stone or flipped-up drain cover that says this was the type of accident that could have happened to any child, not just mine. Then something catches my eye. A little piece of yellow plastic. I lean down and pick it up. It looks like the hair from the ponytail of her tiny little doll that she carries around in her pocket. I check, but the rest of it is missing, probably carried off in the tread of the bike's tyres.

'Um. I'm going to go in now,' I say to Suzy, pulling my arm gently from hers.

'You OK, hon?' she says. 'What is it?'

I flinch. The word 'hon' is grating on me. 'Nothing. I just want to go and have a shower.'

She watches me carefully. 'OK,' she says, sounding hurt.

I frown. 'It'll be all right, Suze. I'm just tired, and fed up. I'll speak to you later.'

She nods, looking less than convinced.

'Do you want me to go and talk to that woman?'

'No — I'll do it. Thanks for the lift,' I say, and cross the road towards my flat, before she tries to hug me again. I can't help it. I just need to be away from her.

I open my front door to find a man in the hall. He is wearing white overalls and has grey hair that he has shaved to the skin, revealing a high forehead and a ridge across the top of his scalp.

'Hi. The plumber, right?' I ask.

'All right, love? Yeah. Come in. Nearly done but I've had to replace the U-bend so there's a bit of clearing up to do. Had to take a couple of tiles off the back, too, so I've just got to do a bit of plaster on that and we're done.'

'Great,' I say, following him back into the flat, not really caring.

The flat smells of chemicals and of him. A kind of male gym-locker smell of cheap deodorant. Tom always smelt of soap and warm skin.

'Actually, I've just realized — can I take a shower, or is the water off?' I ask. 'Sorry, it's just that I've been at hospital all night.'

'Course you can, love. Water's back on. Tell you what, I'll go up the caff for half an hour and leave you to it.'

I nod, grateful.

'How's your little girl, by the way?' he says. 'Your mate said she had an accident?'

His question takes me by surprise. Suzy must have told him. 'She wasn't hit or anything,' I start, then stop because I can't be bothered to explain. 'She's OK, I think, thanks. They're watching her now, and she'll get home this evening.'

'I've got one that age, myself,' he says. 'Have to watch them like a hawk, don't you?'

Yes, I think, you do, slightly testily. And I always do. And who's looking after your child right now?

He grabs his jacket and heads out, shouting into his mobile about being 'there at five o'clock, mate.' I shut the door, finally alone.

The shower feels good. It washes away the smell of hospital from my skin with welcome hot bursts. I stand for a while, letting water rain down on my head, soaking my hair into heavy tresses that press down onto my shoulders and across my eyes.

The thing is, I know what's coming.

But for this moment, standing here, I can pretend it's not going to happen. That everything is still OK.

The phone has been vibrating in my pocket all morning. It started at ten o'clock this morning, and I know who it is. It's not Dad because I rang him this morning when I knew Rae was fine, so he wouldn't insist on coming down. It's not Tom either.

There's only one person it could be.

I wrap myself in the only clean towel I can find and walk to the bedroom, where I sit on the bed and brush my wet hair. My work dress from Monday lies abandoned in the corner, the power of its silver sequins diminished now into a little soft lump of grey. I pull on a clean skirt and a T-shirt I find in the ironing basket, then with a heavy sigh stand up.

The phone sits on my chest of drawers, letting out an intermittent beep. I open it and press 'voice message'.

'Hi, Callie,' Guy's voice rings out. 'God. Sorry to hear what's happened. Hope she's all right. Ring us and let us know.'

Then there is the pause. The pause I knew would be there.

'God. Well. Listen. I think you know how it is. Unfortunately, Loll can't change his trip to New York, so we'll have to push on. I'll probably pass it on to Jerome for the meantime, because we're tight for time. Really disappointed, obviously — Loll loved your ideas. But, listen . . . take your time with what you have to do, then give us a ring when things have picked up. And we'll talk . . . '

'No,' I murmur. Oh no. He gave my job to Jerome. Jerome in his mid-twenties with no kids. Jerome who'll never have to run home when his kid's sick or take time off in the summer holidays.

What was I thinking? It is over.

Frustration makes me open my mouth.

'Aaaaaargh!' I scream. A great, big, angry scream that vibrates so hard from inside that it comes out like a roar.

'Shit!' I shout. All that. So close.

The bell rings, making me jerk my head upright. I take a breath and walk to the door.

The plumber stands on the step, eyes curious. 'Everything all right?'

'All yours,' I nod, picking up my bag.

'All right,' he says. 'Before you go, love, can you give me the details for the invoice?'

The invoice? I try to focus. 'You need to — actually, can you make it out to my little girl's dad?' I say, taking his pen.

'Good on you, love,' he says. 'Don't let him get away with not doing his bit. My sister's ex is a right slippery bastard. Never pays for fuck all, excuse my French.'

I write the details down, resenting every letter of every word I have to write. Guy's message hits me in waves. The implications form behind it. I've messed up the Loll Parker job. Guy will think I've become unreliable. I will not be earning my own money after all. I stare at the invoice. I cannot even pay this plumbing bill. When I subtract the cost of the clothes I bought at Brent Cross, there will be hardly anything left from my three days' fee.

'If she gets back in time, my neighbour across the road will collect the spare keys back off you; otherwise, just stick them back through my letterbox?' I call, on my way out.

I don't mean to — it's not his fault — but I slam the door and march to the gate. I look across the road at Debs's house.

One day, I think. One whole day since the accident and she hasn't even sent me a note or called or apologized. My daughter is in hospital, and now I've lost the only thing that makes me happy apart from Rae, because of that woman's carelessness.

Mum's temper surges out of nowhere and I find myself flying off the pavement.

24

Debs

Debs stood behind the voile curtain, watching.

She had seen Suzy and Callie arrive and enter their different houses, and now she was waiting to see what happened next. To keep herself busy she was rearranging her books in alphabetical order, moving Dickens up to the top and Hardy below. It helped. It was calming. Touching the books, smelling their comforting dusty covers. Getting some order back. Trying to forget what that young police officer had told her. Clearly, if the Poplars had left the country, some of their supporters, people who had read about the story in the newspaper, were doing the harassment. She just knew she wasn't imagining it. Why would no one listen to her?

A movement caught her eye just as she was turning away from the curtain again. Callie was emerging from her flat. For some reason she didn't lock the front door behind her, just walked straight out of the gate. Her hair was dark and flat as if she had just washed it and she was frowning.

Suddenly, she stopped and looked across at Debs's house. Debs gasped and fell back. Had she seen her?

She popped her head up for another look.

Callie was marching across the road towards her house, with a furious look on her face.

'Oh, help,' Debs said. She cowered down under the window sill.

Bang. Bang. Bang. The front door rattled, followed by two rings of the doorbell. Debs held her breath. She tried to make her body as small as possible. Looking up carefully, she saw Callie's silhouette above her. She was peering through Debs's window.

'Hello?' she was calling. The nervous little voice of the other day had been replaced by a confident tone. Shaking, Debs stayed where she was. What could the girl do? Apart from break the window, she couldn't get in. As long as Debs stayed here, she was safe.

She counted to ten, then heard her gate slam shut, followed by the sound of a car. She raised her glasses over the window sill and had another peek. Callie's old red Renault was heading off along the road.

It felt safe down by the tall pine skirting-board. She dug at the little bits of dirt stuck between the stained floorboards, wafting her hand over them to feel the faint breeze and damp smell from the cellar. The teapot was almost under here, she thought. A foot from Allen's nose and he didn't even know.

The door next door banged, making her flinch. She peeked again to see the American woman leave her house with some shopping bags and head off in her car.

Just to be sure, Debs waited another ten minutes, lying on the floor, sorting out the

Whitmans and Yevtushenkos on the bottom shelf. Now — it was probably safe. Crawling out of her sitting room on her hands and knees, she picked up the package wrapped in fairy paper that she'd left on the stairs beside the little girl's squashed doll and put on her shoes. It was the best she could do right now. She crept through her front door, popped her head round the hedge to see no one was around and briskly made her way across the road. The path up to Callie's door was a little different than she'd realized. The paint on the gate was scraped, and there were two bins, not one. Pieces of a broken box lay behind one, and weeds littered the front garden. That was odd. Not quite how she'd imagined Callie's home would be. She was such a smart young woman.

The best thing, Debs decided, was just to leave the package on the doorstep. That way it would be hidden by the bin, but still visible to anyone opening the door.

She was just about to lean down when she heard the noise from inside — at the same time as she saw the two doorbells. Oh. It was a flat?

Debs leapt back as the front door flew open. A young Somali woman in a veil started back, equally surprised. Debs lifted up her package to show her what she was doing. The woman grinned a wide, friendly smile and motioned Debs in.

'Oh, no,' Debs said. 'I was just leaving something . . . '

The woman smiled again and shrugged to show she didn't speak English. 'Please, please,' she said, motioning Debs inside.

Oh well. Maybe the package would be safer in the communal hall anyway. She nodded and went inside. The young woman closed the front door behind her, leaving Debs alone.

The hall smelt musty. Stairs ran up to a flat above, covered in a worn grey carpet.

Now, where was the best place to lay the package? There was a shelf where post sat. That should be fine.

She was just placing the package beside a tower of junk mail when the flat door beside her opened, too, and a burly, bald man walked out carrying a holdall.

'Oh!' she gasped.

'Oh, all right, love? You from across the road?'

She nodded.

'I was just going to pop these over,' he growled, placing some house keys in her hand. 'Tell her it's all sorted and that I hope her little girl's all right. Got one that age, myself. Cheerio.'

'Oh ... no ... ' stuttered Debs, trying to catch his attention as he swung open the front door and pulled it shut behind him.

She stood in the silent hall, holding the keys. Oh dear. What now?

She had really wanted to avoid speaking to Callie, till she had things sorted out in her own head about what had happened last night. Perhaps if she locked up the flat and waited on the pavement she could give the keys to the African lady. She might have been popping to the corner shop.

231

Deciding that was the best thing to do, Debs went to pull the door to Callie's flat shut. As she did, she caught sight of the inner hall.

That was odd.

No. This was not what she had imagined at all. She peered in. The walls of the hall were lined in woodchip that looked like it had been painted a beige colour many years ago, the tips of its knobbly peaks picked white in many places, possibly by a child. The floor was covered in vinyl that was supposed to look like tiles. Too many coats were crammed onto the hall hooks. There was a muddle of shoes underneath them that was overflowing, the heels pointing in all different directions. A few umbrellas, one with a broken spoke. A pile of hats and gloves bursting out from a plastic bag stuck on a peg. A child's reading bag, lying against the wall.

Curious, Debs walked in a little further. This wasn't how she imagined Callie lived at all. This flat was unloved, soulless.

She carried on into the sitting room and peered around.

A throw lay unevenly over an elderly sofa. The bookshelves either side of the fireplace were empty, apart from a few scruffy files, and piles of children's drawings, two of which had been stuck to the wall with Blu-Tack. One of the shelves sat at an angle, as if it had come loose from the wall and never been repaired. A few photos were propped up above the fireplace but not framed, one of Callie with Rae, and a man who looked like Callie's father; one of Rae dressed in a Halloween costume with the children from next

232

door, then another photo almost identical from a different angle. Everywhere Debs turned, there were more signs of Callie's resignation. A plant pot with no plant. Piles all over the coffee table of unopened bills and out-of-date school letters.

This was too bad. Debs wandered into the kitchen.

It was similarly worn and tired, with a pen-covered plastic cover on the table, and more piles of paper. A list drawn in blue on a whiteboard was out of date, with 'Christmas shopping' penned in faded blue ink.

Debs checked around. By the sink sat a dirty cup, probably left by the plumber. She looked for a dishwasher. There wasn't one, just an elderly-looking washing machine with a cracked door underneath a dryer. Absentmindedly, she found some washing-up liquid and a brush and cleaned out the cup and went to lay it on the drying rack. The wash rack was covered in the thin layer of white scale that the hard London water left everywhere. Not dirty, just unattended.

In a daze, wondering why Callie's home seemed in such turmoil, she looked under the sink and found some bleach and a scrubber.

Oh. What was she doing? She stopped herself.

Well, what harm would it do?

She swirled it round the sink and the taps and over the draining board, and began to scrub.

Scrub, scrub, scrub.

Five minutes later, the sink was gleaming.

Good, she thought.

It was when she put them back that she noticed the washing-up liquid had spilled inside the cupboard and dried, a thick green line snaking through the other cleaning bottles and underneath some damp plastic bags pushed to the back. 'I'll just do that, too,' she thought.

It was while she was on her knees wiping out the cupboard, cleaning down the other bottles and pulling out some old cloths, that she noticed the vinyl kitchen floor. It was clean in a perfunctory way as if it were mopped quickly every few days. That had not been enough, however, to eliminate the thin ridge of brown dirt that skirted the bottom of the kitchen units, almost in the crack in between.

Debs stood up. It would only take another minute. Now, where did Callie keep her mop?

★ ★ ★

She didn't know where the time went. One minute it was two o'clock, then it was six o'clock.

The flat smelled damp and fresh, as if someone had thrown a bucket of water over it. She stood back, pleased. It had only taken a second to pop home to fetch a few things. Every surface of the two-bedroom flat was polished and scrubbed. The windows sparkled. The toilet had been descaled and now flushed blue water. The sitting room was Hoovered and Shake-and-Vacced. A second wash was in the machine, the first in the drier. Old toothpaste tubes and empty toilet rolls had been removed from the bathroom, along with oddments of soap. A pile of junk mail and opened envelopes sat by the front door ready for recycling. Everything else had been sorted into folders marked with Allen's coloured labels. Urgent letters were now stuck to the old pinboard with red pins she'd brought from home. She had weeded out all the shoes that were smaller than a size eleven, or on their own, and put them in a recycling bag along with a couple of coats for 'Age 3', and a pile of old magazines and local newspapers she'd found down the side of the sofa.

Now there was only one more job to do.

She stood in the sitting room on a chair to close the windows, which she'd opened to let air flood through. It was then that she saw her. Suzy. The American woman was back home.

The window above Suzy's front door was framed in modern clear glass, as if the original stained glass had been replaced. Through it she could see Suzy sitting on the stairs of her house, halfway up, handset to her ear.

Debs stared at her. It had been on her mind all day. Had that woman told her to hold Rae's hand?

It took her a moment to realize she could hear something through the open window. It was a familiar sound. A phone ringing distantly. The world seemed to slow down for a second as Debs's brain tried to work it out. It couldn't be Suzy's phone because she was on hers.

So it must be . . . Debs's own phone.

Her eyes settled back on Suzy, her eyes and ears desperately trying to collate the information they had gathered, to make sense of it.

With her eyes, Debs saw the following.

235

Suzy replaced her receiver.

With her ears, Debs heard this.

The phone in her own house stopped ringing at the same moment.

How strange. Why would that woman be ringing her?

A shape moved to the right. Debs turned to see a figure walking up the street. It was Allen, wearing the smart raincoat she had bought him for Christmas. Gosh. Was it that late? She glanced at her watch. She'd need to finish up here quickly and put the tea on.

As she went to turn away from the window, Debs saw her husband slow down as he approached their gate. His eyelids were heavy behind the glasses that secretly Debs hoped he might change soon for lenses. He had nice eyes, Allen. Hazel, flecked with yellow, rimmed by long sandy lashes. But behind those old-fashioned frames with their thick glass, they took on a slightly bulbous look. The wiry hair of his eyebrows, which flew upwards of its own accord, was underlined and exaggerated by the black frames. She was the only person who ever saw what his eyes really looked like. The first time he'd taken his glasses off she had been so shocked at the exposed intensity that emanated from his naked pupils, she had blushed and looked away. It had just felt so strangely intimate.

A little flush of love ran through her now, too, for the way her husband made do with what he had physically without complaining. That mother of his had never shown him otherwise. Too scared she might lose him, Debs suspected. Well, she was here now. She would help him.

Debs watched Allen open the door, noticing how his shoulder drooped at what drama might be waiting for him on the other side. Not tonight, love, she promised him silently. Tonight, she would smile, and be upbeat, and not mention the Poplars or aeroplanes or the children next door. She would simply ask him about his day, and give him the attention he deserved. Today, at least, they would have one good day.

Debs was about to turn again when a noise caught her attention. It was her phone again, ringing out more loudly now through the front door Allen had just opened. She watched as Allen put down the briefcase she had bought him on sale from Debenhams. Idly, Debs noted how Suzy was now opening her own front door, and pushing her double buggy through it, with her older son holding on to the handle.

That was strange.

The American woman had a handset at her ear again.

Debs watched, hypnotized, as Allen straightened up and walked across the wooden floorboards of their hallway, reaching his arm out to pick up the phone.

With a sudden certainty, Debs knew what was going to happen. Her eyes darted to Suzy, who took the phone from her ear, and abruptly pushed a button.

Immediately, the phone in front of Allen cut off.

Debs froze. As she stood there, she saw her husband turn back to the door with a confused expression. Oblivious to Suzy's presence a few feet from him, he shut the door gently.

Suzy then placed the handset back in her house, shut her own door and walked to the gate with the three children.

A chill ran through Debs's body.

All week she had heard the children next door through the wall, thumping along the wooden floorboards of their hallway and up and down their stairs.

What if Suzy could hear their footsteps, too? What if she knew when Debs was about to pick up the phone?

25

Suzy

The park was very quiet when Suzy arrived with the boys.

They had already been here after school, but Henry was so restless this evening, making strange squealing noises and jumping at the twins till they cried, that she decided to take them out again.

As they reached the play equipment at the far end of the park, she recognized the little girl hanging off the monkey bars by the colour of her long hair. It looked like dipped gold. Not like Nora's red hair, of course. That would be pale strawberry blonde, her face sprinkled with freckles, her skin creamy-white like Suzy's.

The little girl was climbing up the monkey bars and leaning forwards, attempting to reach the first bar. Her mouth hung open with concentration, her summer dress lifting up unselfconsciously to show pants dotted with daisies.

Suzy looked around. The cafe had shut at 5.30 p.m., the schoolkids dispersed home for tea. Just a few dog walkers strolled across the empty football pitches, one throwing a red ball for a greyhound that whipped across the park at breakneck speed. Henry ran to the far side of the

239

play area and climbed on the pretend tractor, making growling noises as he turned the wheel. She could tell by how hyper he was when she picked him up from school that he was missing Rae. Rae was so good for him. Calmed him down.

The twins lay asleep in their buggy, their perfect little faces collapsed like old men's, mouths loose, cheeks soft and drooping. Suzy put the buggy brake on, and kissed them both on the head, while watching the little girl.

Where on earth was her mother?

'Can you help me?' the little girl called.

'Can I help you?' Suzy replied, pointing at herself.

'Can't reach it,' the child panted, trying again.

'It's Hannah, right?'

The girl nodded.

'Hon, where's your mommy?' Suzy asked.

'My mummy's running,' the little girl said, waving her arm towards the other side of the park. 'She wants to be thinner. She goes to Weight Watchers, too.' In the distance Suzy saw the back of a plump woman in black trousers and a white T-shirt jogging away from them, well out of shouting distance.

'Does your mommy leave you on your own?' she asked the little girl, incredulous. It would take a second to snatch the child. Even if the woman saw someone take her, she couldn't run across the park quickly enough to stop it. A few seconds. That's all it took to hurt a child for life.

'It's OK, I'm a big girl now.'

Suzy sighed. 'Well, hon, I'm sorry, I am not

going to lift you up just in case your mommy doesn't want you to do this. If you fell, she might be cross with me. But tell you what, you can ask her when she comes back.'

'OK,' said the little girl, jumping down. She ran past Suzy and began to climb up a ten-foot-high pole, using her bare feet to push her up the conical metal. 'Where's Rae?' she asked, looking down at Suzy with innocent brown eyes.

'Oh. Well, Rae is at the doctor's right now. She had a little accident.'

'Is she coming back to our school?'

Suzy paused. 'Well, yes she is. But, hon, I think you need to leave her alone for a little while. Rae is sick, you see. It would be real dangerous for her to do those things that you're doing right now. So when she gets back, you have to be gentle with her, maybe let her just sit down at playtime and not play games.'

She looked round. The woman in the white T-shirt had turned the corner at the top of the park, and was now crossing it, still running away from her child. This was ridiculous. Suzy looked around her. Surely everyone had heard about what had happened to Rae? Hannah's mother was being completely irresponsible. Quietly, she pushed the twins over behind a bush, beside the wooden building of the closed cafe.

'Hannah,' Suzy called. 'Do you want to come and see Henry's little brothers? They're sleeping right now. They look real cute.'

Hannah grinned and jumped down, and came behind the building. Suzy pulled the covers back.

'Oh, they're so sweet,' Hannah whispered. 'Hello, baby . . .'

Suzy looked out through the bush. The woman in the white T-shirt was running down the opposite side of the park now, looking anxiously over. Her pace was quickening.

That's right, lady, Suzy thought. This is exactly what could happen when you take a risk like that with your little girl.

'Hannah!' she heard her call faintly. 'Hannah!' with increasing urgency.

Hannah went to move. Suzy gently put her hand out.

'It's OK, sweetie, I'm here. Mommy will be here in a second and see you're safe with me.'

'Hannah!' The woman's voice was almost at a scream. Suzy saw her suddenly cut diagonally across the park towards them at a sprint.

OK, that should be enough.

She stepped out to see the woman running clumsily towards her, her face red and frightened.

'Over here,' Suzy waved, propelling Hannah gently forwards with her hands on her shoulder. 'Just looking at Henry's brothers.'

Caroline ran towards them, as if she couldn't stop now, trying to catch her breath.

'Oh. Thank goodness,' she panted. 'I thought she'd wandered off. Sorry . . . it's the only chance I get to run . . . John works late . . . she's normally fine . . .'

Suzy nodded as the woman tried to catch her breath.

'Well, you're right, you have to be careful. You

know, that teacher took her eye off Rae for one second, and . . . '

'Oh, yes. How is she?' said Caroline. 'We were so worried when we heard. I was going to drop round to see Callie. But I didn't know if it was a good time?'

'She's at the hospital a lot,' Suzy replied. 'She's pretty exhausted.' That would be the last thing Callie needed. These class mothers calling round, pretending they cared when really it was just another chance for a good gossip about Callie and her life.

Caroline looked at her, then nodded. 'OK, well, we better get back. Come on, Hannah.'

She turned as they left.

'Um, I know it's very late notice, but we're having an ice-skating party for Hannah's birthday on Saturday at four. We'd love Rae to come if she feels up to it. Even if she just wanted to watch, then have the birthday tea? She's very welcome.'

Henry walked up to Suzy and pinched her arm, looking beseechingly at her.

Caroline realized too late what she'd done.

'Oh — and Henry, of course.'

'Yeah, Mommy — I want to go to the party!' Henry shouted, pulling Suzy's arm. Hannah made a face at her mother.

'Thanks,' Suzy replied neutrally. Unbelievable. Inviting Henry and Rae at the last moment, out of pity, like they were a couple of charity cases. And now Henry had heard the invitation it would be impossible to avoid it.

'I'll pop the invitations through your doors,

then,' Caroline smiled, then headed off with Hannah.

Suzy watched her. Bet she wouldn't be leaving Hannah in a park on her own any time soon.

26

Callie

Rae looks bored when I return to hospital in my clean clothes. Her skin is glowing a normal colour, a hint of rosiness returned to her cheeks.

By 5 p.m. she is laughing out loud as Kaye pretends to 'steal' her nose, then Rae wants to try this new trick on me and Tom. At 5.45 p.m., Dr Khatam signs her off and humours me by letting me put words into his mouth that maybe she needs to rest for the next couple of days, when clearly Dr Khatam thinks she is perfectly OK. I look at Tom with a relieved grin. It was nothing serious. We're out of here.

But Tom is not finished. He grills the doctor for two more minutes about any symptoms we — or, most likely, I — should look out for once she's home, just in case. Bad mother, his behaviour says. Are you listening?

Thank goodness Kate and her judgemental expressions had gone by the time I drove back to hospital. Tom told me gruffly that as Rae was doing much better than Suzy's panicked call had led him to expect, they decided that Kate should return to Sri Lanka, and she is at their production office in Soho right now, planning how to reschedule the shoot to take over some of Tom's background shots for a couple of days till he is sure Rae is completely recovered and can go back.

Rae wants to walk out of the hospital.

'It's not sore, Mummy!' she cries, limping.

'Absolutely not,' Tom growls, and makes a big show of carrying her in his arms through the corridor and out to the car park, then lifting her into my car. What does he think she'll do next week when he's not here? I wonder, as I strap Rae into her seat and watch him climb into his Jeep.

As I drive back through north London, I realize Rae is waving to Tom in his car behind us. I caught her watching us today in the hospital room, darting her eyes back and forth, her face animated and twitching with a story she was clearly making up inside her head about us being back together.

'OK, sweetheart?' I say as we turn into Churchill Road.

'Hmm,' she says, sinking down in her seat.

I take the last parking place, so Tom drives straight past Churchill Road and turns right into the lane lined with garages that runs behind my flat. Rae and I get out of my car and walk to the corner.

'Where was it?' Tom says, emerging from the lane, car keys in hand. I point to the spot of her accident on the corner.

'Rae?' I say gently. 'Do you remember what happened last night when you fell into the road?' She has already told us she 'just slipped', keen, I suspect, to avoid a discussion about why she was running when I had told her not to twenty-four hours earlier. 'Were you thinking about your playdate with Hannah — were you upset? Is that what happened?'

'Cal,' Tom says. 'Leave it. Not now. She'll tell us when she's ready.'

I love the way that Tom tries to take control of me and Rae, as if he thinks we live in some sort of static state when he's not here, waiting for him to return from abroad with his opinions and thoughts, so we can move forwards again.

Tom picks Rae up and carries her to the door. Oh — keys, I think. I've left my bag in the car. I am just about to cross the road to fetch it when I see Tom walk straight through my front door.

'Did you leave it on the latch?' he calls.

'No.' That's weird.

I walk up behind him and Rae, and push past them. The inner door is lying open, too. I glance at Tom and frown. He puts Rae down gently onto the stairs, and walks in front of me, protectively.

'The plumber can't still be here,' I mutter.

'Stay there,' he says, walking into the flat. I follow him in, mouthing at Rae to stay on the stairs. There is a strange smell in the flat. It smells like cleaning fluids with an unpleasant damp undertone, as if stinking mould has been flushed out of the cracks of this neglected old house. It takes me a second to realize that something is different. There are only two coats hanging on the pegs, and the shoes underneath have been lined up.

'What the . . . ?' I say. Has Suzy done this for us?

247

Tom peers into the kitchen, shakes his head at me, then walks into the sitting room. I walk past him to my bedroom and push the door open.

Debs is standing there, singing, shaking a sheet over my bed, which has been stripped.

The sight is so odd, I have to shake my head and look again.

'Er . . . What's going on?' I say, bewildered. Did Suzy let her in?

'What are you doing here, Debs?'

She looks up, completely startled.

'Oh . . . ' she stutters, pushing her glasses up on her nose.

Tom comes up behind me, close, so I can feel his warmth at my back.

'What's going on?' he demands.

Debs stares up at him with frightened eyes. Even from here, I can see her hands are shaking.

'Um, Tom, can you take Rae into the sitting room?' I ask.

'Debs? Isn't that who . . . ?' he looks at me angrily.

'Just take Rae into the sitting room,' I say, pushing my hand gently on his chest. 'I'll sort it out.'

I shut the door behind him and turn round.

'Debs?' I repeat slowly. 'What the hell are you doing in my bedroom? What have you done to my flat? Did Suzy . . . ?'

I stop as I realize that my bedroom is so tidy it looks like someone else's. Old photos of me and Rae sit in two new frames on the chest of drawers. One of Mum's old lace tablecloths is draped over the pine dressing table. My pile of scarves and hair scrunches and necklaces has been sorted into different bowls on my dressing table. My new make-up from Brent Cross that I left scattered yesterday morning in a hurry is neatly stored away again in a bag, little red and black wands sticking up neatly.

'Um. Oh,' Debs mumbles. 'I don't know what happened. I brought over a little doll for your little girl — to replace the one that was broken when she fell. And then I saw that you were in a bit of a muddle . . . and . . . goodness. I am so sorry . . . '

'You did this by yourself?'

She stares, then nods.

'Er, Debs?' I say, confused. 'You need to go.'

'Yes. Yes, of course.'

Debs puts down the sheet and starts to walk out the door.

This is so bloody weird. I try to gather my thoughts.

'I don't understand. You didn't come and see her,' I say. 'In the hospital.'

Debs stops. She shakes her head, eyes to the floor. 'I wanted to. I was just trying very hard to remember what happened last night before I spoke to you. And I just don't know. One minute she was with me, and the next she was on the road. There was this boy on a bike, you see, and . . . '

'But Suzy told you that you had to hold her hand!'

Debs has a dazed expression in her eye that is starting to creep me out.

'Well, I'm afraid I didn't hear her.'

'But you're a TEACHER.'

'Yes, but not a mother, I'm afraid,' Debs replies. 'We usually have a group of children and we can't hold all of their hands.'

I shake my head. Maybe I'm exhausted but I actually feel sorry for her. Her skin close up is soft and pink and has a Vaseline sheen to it, like Mum's. The bags under her dulled eyes and thick greying eyebrows are heavy and sagging.

'Debs. This has been a nightmare. Rae was in so much danger last night. She's OK, but that's just luck — it could so easily have been a car, not a bike. Look, I am really worn out and upset. Thank you for the doll but I don't think you should have done this. I have to say I think it is a very odd thing to do and I'd really like you to leave now.'

Her bottom lip starts to tremble just as Tom walks in.

'Right, come on,' he says to Debs. 'Everyone's tired and we don't want to talk to you again till we've spoken to the police. OK?'

She doesn't resist as he steers her down the corridor and out of the flat. As she passes the sitting room, I see her glance to the side and smile at Rae. Rae looks back at her with wide open eyes.

'It's OK, Rae,' I say, going in and patting her hair. 'Mummy will be back in a minute.'

Sinking down on the unmade bed, I drop my head. The front door slams and Tom stalks back in, his arms lifted in an angry 'what the hell?' gesture.

'Oh, just shut up, Tom!' I blurt out. 'I know. I

know. I KNOW how crap it all is. My life's terrible — OK? I'm a mess. A terrible mother who lets weirdos look after her kid. You're right. A terrible bloody person.'

He turns and walks out the door. I sigh, and wait for the front door to slam again.

Instead I hear him murmuring to Rae, and putting a DVD on for her. I pick up the sheet Debs has dropped and put it on the bed, so I can lie down. I am tucking in the corners when the door creaks and I see him coming back in the room, two glasses of wine in his hand. He gives one to me and sits on the chair. He rubs his face with his big paw of a hand, and stretches out his long legs.

'Did you get the toilet fixed?' he asks.

'Yes,' I say uncertainly, sitting back on the bed.

He nods.

I try not to look at him. It's too painful to remember how I used to have the licence to walk over to that chair after a bad day, sit on his knees, and pull those big safe arms — those big farmer's arms that always remind me of Dad — around me like a roller-coaster harness.

He takes a sip, then another one.

'I know you hate me, Tom, but . . . ' I look at his face, wondering if I can say this to him. 'But sometimes this is just so hard. You know, I wasn't even sure I'd be a very good mother in any circumstances. And then I have this sick child, and then everything just disappears. And, you know, I try. I really do. But being here all the time . . . this mess I've got myself into . . . having no money . . . seeing nobody.' I can't help it.

251

Tears appear from nowhere and stream down my face. 'I am just trying to do something about it.'

There is silence. I wait for him to tell me it's my own fault, but he doesn't. He avoids my eye and stands up, throwing back the rest of his wine.

'Do you want me to put her to bed?'

I nod gratefully, wiping away the tears. He brings Rae in to say good night and I force myself to give her a big smile, and kiss her mouth and her cheeks and her hair. Her eyes shine at the novelty of me and Tom together at bedtime.

'Our house smells lovely,' she chirps. 'My teddies are all in a line.'

I only mean to sit on the bed for a minute. But I can't move somehow. It's nice just to rest for a moment, and let my arms fall heavy and still while Tom deals with Rae. Apart from the soft footsteps of the couple upstairs on my ceiling, there is silence, just the murmuring from Rae's bedroom where Tom reads Dr Seuss. Just a minute more, I keep thinking. Then I'll get up.

'I'll be over tomorrow to see you, babe,' I hear Tom say twenty minutes later. I jerk upright, realizing I have nearly been asleep. I walk into Rae's room and find him leaning over her bed to kiss her good night, looking like a giant in the tiny room. A giant who used to protect us but who isn't there any more. He protects Kate now.

He turns to look at me and the soft glow of the fairy lights takes me back to the first time I saw him, when he walked into Sophie's birthday party in our garden in Islington in the dusk with one of her old college friends, and sat round the bonfire we made in a dustbin and chatted to Sophie's visiting mum, whom everyone else was politely ignoring. And I remember how I'd had a bad week, and how as the evening went on his eyes kept straying over to me. How he made stupid faces across the garden, and it cheered me up a little. Then how he followed me into the kitchen, to find me, bum in the air, trying to reach my mobile phone, which I had dropped down the back of a radiator.

'Here, let me.' He smiled, reaching down to get it.

'Thanks,' I said coyly, reaching out for it.

'Yeah, right,' he said, holding it above his head and walking off, leaving me confused.

'Er, can I have my phone back, please?' I asked later, when I found him lying on the grass smoking a joint under the stars.

'You'll have to tell me why the sad face first,' he murmured, holding it up high again, while exhaling white smoke into the dark air, with these unruly white curls and blue eyes that dared me. And then I was reaching over, and smelling the soapy warmth of his skin, and feeling the breath of his laugh in my ear.

'I am going to marry that John,' I told Sophie later, drunkenly lying on her bed.

'Tom,' she murmured, removing her make-up.

And six months later, on that precious weekend to New York, at City Hall, with one hand on the bump that was already Rae, that's exactly what I did.

'We need to speak to the police about that

woman,' Tom says, following me out of Rae's room, the humour from that night in Islington long gone. 'What have they done about it?'

'I'm going to find out tomorrow,' I say. 'You know, I've been thinking. It might just have been an accident. She was probably upset about her playdate being cancelled. It might have happened even if I had been there. We need to talk to her about it.'

He shakes his head. 'When she's ready. But there's something not right about that woman. I want it sorted out.'

He turns to say goodbye, and in the bright light of the hall his face looks pained and worn and tired. I realize that he feels it, too. He blames himself for Rae, too. He wasn't there either.

★   ★   ★

I unlock the back door in the kitchen, and let Tom out through our scrubby little rear garden and back gate to the lane where his car is parked. I shut the door again, and stand in the kitchen, listening for his car to go.

I wait there for a while.

Then I remember I must redo the bolt on the garden gate after him. But before I can move, there is a knock on the back door.

I open it. My face gives it away.

Sometimes this happens. Sometimes, for months at a time, things between us are just normal and perfunctory, practical and functional, as they have to be. Then sometimes, there is a look.

He stands in the doorway, his large frame filling it. Without saying anything, he walks towards me, and shuts the back door behind him.

I know what's going to happen.

I walk ahead of him towards the hall in case I am wrong but he catches my hand and turns me round. I breathe a long, hard breath, followed by another. He looks down at me, his lids heavy, manoeuvres me into the wall, and pushes my skirt up. Trailing his hand up my thigh, he hooks one finger around the elastic of my knickers and pulls it, looking at me with eyes that have already gone.

'Take them off.'

We both know that this will be quick. No rosy-coloured, soft-focus, romantic lovemaking for us. This is about something else.

I remove them.

'And this . . . ' he murmurs, motioning to my bra.

I put my hands behind my back and undo the strap, feeling the weight of my breasts moving forwards as he lifts my top and pulls away the bra with one finger. I am breathing so fast I think I might faint. He sighs and rubs the flat of his hand across me till I moan, then lifts me up on to the table. He uses his knee to part mine.

The noise that comes from my lips next is a noise only he hears.

I know she's there, waiting for him to come back. But this is my child's father. And I know it's terrible. But sometimes, when everything gets too much, when I can't take the weight of all this responsibility, of all these mistakes I have made, of all this guilt, I need someone to take charge, just for a moment.

27

Suzy

Still no Jez.

Suzy arrived home from the park with the kids just before 7 p.m. to find an empty hallway. Had she done the right thing?

He had left at seven this morning for his digital technology conference in Birmingham. The second he had left, she had rung Vondra and asked her to run to Euston train station. A woman with a mission, Vondra had heroically made it onto the next train, and followed him up north.

Her first report came in three hours later: Jez was at the conference. Sasha was there, too. Her second report was more reassuring: Jez and two male colleagues had eaten lunch at an Italian bistro close to the venue, with Sasha nowhere in sight, then returned to the conference at 3 p.m. Everything seemed above board.

'You better come back, then,' Suzy had said. Vondra was expensive. There were only so many purchases of kids' shoes or car services she could fake before Jez became suspicious about where his money was going.

Yet now, as Suzy put the kids in the bath, she wondered if she had made a mistake. The conference finished at 4 p.m., according to

Vondra. He should have been back at Euston by 6 p.m. Now it was 7 p.m. and he wasn't answering his phone.

Vondra was right. It was always better to know when he was lying than suffer this agonizing guessing. Not only did it reassure her that she was not going mad — and that those anxious, sleepless hours were of his making, not hers — it was building evidence that would keep her babies safe if he ever did take her to a divorce court. More than once, she had imagined his face as her lawyer read out the proof of his infidelity.

As for the pain it caused her, well, she was learning to deal with that. If, for a second, she let herself imagine Jez with Sasha, his head tipped back, breathing heavily, Sasha's glossy brunette hair scattered around his thighs, she would jump up and move around quickly, finding tasks to do that distracted her from the nauseous sensation in her stomach.

Her main problem right now was keeping her evidence of his deception a secret from him. At times, the urge to blurt it all out and watch his face was overwhelming.

Last night, for instance, as they finally sat down to dinner together after visiting Callie in hospital.

'So, what was the banker guy's house like?' she said.

'Hmm?' he said, watching the news on the telly on the wall.

'In Hertfordshire. Is he loaded — was it a mansion?'

'It was OK. Big.'

'Did it have a pool?'

'Um — yeah, I think so.'

'Indoor or outdoor?'

'Can't remember. Why?'

She could have gone on, of course. What food did they give their guests? Did they have caterers? How old was the banker's wife?

But Jez was smarter than that. And she wasn't giving up. Not when there was a chance. So she had made herself stand up and walk to the kitchen on the pretence of fetching more water, and checked the calendar. Day fifteen. She might still be ovulating. Last night, after the hospital, she had tried again, after Tuesday night's dismal failure to seduce him. But he had gone to bed when she was in the bath and appeared to have fallen asleep before she climbed into bed in her new camisole. At least when he was asleep she could lie close beside him and feel his warmth against her. It helped, but it wasn't enough. Tonight she would have to be cleverer.

Suzy hung up the kids' coats in the hall and put on a DVD for them in the kitchen, promising herself she'd implement the normal rules again next week when her head was clearer.

She took off her own shoes and sat down on the floor in front of the telly, lifting Peter onto her knee and wrapping her arms round his warm, soft tummy. Henry shuffled over to lean his head into her shoulder, his hand resting unthinkingly on hers. Otto came, too, sitting up on the sofa behind her, with his chubby little feet dangling either side of her head, thumb in his mouth.

Cocooned by the boys, Suzy let herself relax. The room felt warm and cosy from the earlier sunshine. No. Nothing was over yet. If she stayed strong, this thing with Jez might pass. 'Lots of men go through something like this when the kids are small,' Vondra had told her when they first met. 'I like to keep in touch with my ladies, and you'd be surprised how many say it was just a phase. That he needed the woman and was jealous of the kids.'

So, who knows? Maybe Jez's train was just late. Next door, Suzy heard a door bang. Probably Debs' odd little husband going out. Who could blame him?

A vision of Callie and Rae came into her head. Had his wife even spoken to Callie yet?

Kissing the boys, Suzy stood up and left the kitchen. She picked up the phone and climbed up to sit on the fourth stair up. She punched in a number and waited. A second later, she heard a faint ringing through the wall.

The phone in her hand rang out, five or six times.

Suddenly, Suzy's letterbox flew open.

'I can see you! I can SEE you!' a woman called through the metal slit. It took her a second to realize it was the woman from next door, peering through with her black-framed glasses.

'Hey. What the hell are you doing?' Suzy shouted, slamming down her phone.

The boys appeared in the hall behind her, one by one, with big fascinated eyes.

'What's wrong, Mommy?' Henry said.

'You're calling my house!' Debs stuttered. 'Over and over. Trying to upset me. I will not put up with it. I had enough of it in Hackney and I will not put up with it now!'

'You what . . . ?' Suzy said. 'What the hell are you talking about? I'm calling my husband. You're crazy. You're scaring my kids.'

'But I can see what you're doing!' Debs called tearfully. 'Phoning me. Putting the phone down when you hear my footsteps reach the bottom of the stairs.' Her voice reached a high-pitched squeak. 'Why on earth are you doing this to me? Did the Poplar boy get you to do this to me?'

Suzy stared at her with wide eyes. 'Ma'am, I'm sorry, but there is clearly something not right with you. You're right — I did try to ring you earlier to ask you to ring Callie because she was getting upset that you hadn't been in touch — and I don't blame her. Now, I just told you, you're scaring my kids . . . Jeeez, and after what you've just done to Callie's little girl? Now go, or I'll call the police. I mean it.'

The woman from next door seemed to freeze. She let out a muffled gasp.

'I mean it!' Suzy said, getting up and flinging her front door open. 'Get away from my kids! Now!'

The woman stood in front of her. 'I did nothing to that Poplar girl!' she cried. 'She just twisted it around so that people would think . . . '

Just that second, her husband came out of the house next door holding a phone handset.

'There you are, love. British Gas is on the phone about our new account,' he said.

Suzy shook her head slowly. The woman stopped speaking and looked completely bewildered. 'But I know it was her,' she whined, pointing at Suzy. 'I know it was. Maybe the boy didn't say anything, but maybe she read about it in the newspaper?'

Suzy looked at the husband. His jaw was set firmly.

'Sir, you need to take your wife inside,' she said as calmly as she could so as not to frighten the children. 'She clearly needs help.'

* * *

The adrenalin was still pumping through her twenty minutes later. Suzy went into autopilot, putting the kids to bed without a bath, desperate to get across the road to tell Callie.

'Was that lady going to hurt you, Mommy?' Henry asked, curling up to go to sleep.

'No, hon, she's just not very well. You know how Rae has hurt her knee? Well, that lady is hurt in her head. But don't worry, Mommy told her to go away and she won't come back now. She won't hurt you or Rae.'

As soon as they were all asleep she ran around the house, making sure everything was turned off. She checked the clock: 7.50 p.m. Jez could be back any time but she'd take a chance he was out for the night now. She chewed her lip. She hated doing it, but sometimes there was no choice. This wasn't like running away from your children in the park. She'd only be across the road and could hear everything.

Ringing her own landline with her mobile, Suzy answered it and laid the handset on the upstairs hall outside the kids' rooms, beside their open doors, then took her mobile with her out the front door, shutting it gently.

Checking to see that the woman wasn't outside, she ran across the road and banged on Callie's door. When there was no answer she rang the bell twice, remembering at the last moment not to wake Rae up.

'Damn,' she muttered.

Callie opened the door. She looked flustered, and was wearing a bathrobe. Her cheeks were flushed, her eyes sparkling, like she'd just got out the bath.

She saw Suzy's face. 'What?'

28

Callie

Oh God. What is she doing here?

Suzy is standing on my doorstep, her eyes wild.

I pull my bathrobe around my half-naked body, hoping the glow in my eyes won't give away what I have just been doing in my kitchen. Why can't she just leave me alone today?

'Hon? Can I come in?'

'Suzy, um, sorry,' I say, looking back into the flat. The kitchen door is closing very gently, pulled from inside. I shift slightly to ensure Suzy doesn't spot the movement. 'Rae's asleep.'

'Sorry, hon, I forgot,' she says, lowering her voice. 'Listen. Jesus, I'm so freaked out . . . '

'Suze — sorry, I'm just about to go to bed,' I say, trying to keep the irritation out of my voice. 'Look — can we speak tomorrow?'

'Please. You got to hear this. That woman — Debs? You're not going to believe it. She's just started screaming through my letterbox.'

My shoulders slump.

'What do you mean?' I ask briskly.

'I was calling Jez to see if he wanted to eat when he got back from Birmingham tonight, and she suddenly pushed it open and started shouting through the letterbox that I was calling her to harass her because of some girl she knew.'

I relent for a moment. 'What? That's crazy.'

'I know, hon. Look.' Suzy holds out her hands. 'I'm shaking. I think she's nuts. You know, this thing happened, and I didn't know whether to tell you, but the other day, in the garden? I heard her husband saying something about how she shouldn't work with children again.'

What? I feel my face darkening.

'I know . . . I should have told you. I just didn't think, though. I thought he meant that maybe she was finding it too tiring. But now? Now I'm really worried that she's insane. I mean, what if she did it on purpose? You know. What if she pushed Rae into the road?'

'Oh God,' I murmur, looking back behind me into the flat. I want Suzy to go, but I can't help it. I blurt out: 'She's just let herself into my flat with the keys the plumber left. She's been here for hours and she's cleaned it.'

'What?' Suzy mouths.

'I know. I thought maybe she was trying to say sorry in her own weird way. But now, I'm not sure — and the creepy thing is, I'm sure something's missing, but she's moved stuff around and I can't work out what it is. What if it's a photo of Rae, or something?' Suzy covers her mouth and opens her eyes wide. 'Oh God. Should I tell the police?'

'I think you have to, hon. She's working at the school, for Christ's sake. We need to let them know. Maybe she did something, then lied about it on her application. I'm so sorry. I should have realized she was weird. I just assumed because she was a teacher . . . '

'It's OK, really. You wouldn't have known,' I say. 'OK . . . well, I'll do it.'

I wait expectantly for her to leave. But she just stands there, her eyes wide and concerned.

'Well, go on, hon,' she urges. 'I'll wait. You get the phone.'

This is getting ridiculous. 'OK, then — hang on,' I murmur.

I disappear into the flat. I pick up the phone and a piece of paper with the officer's number from the hall and walk back to the door, dialling the number, glancing up at Suzy.

'Hello.' He answers after three rings.

'Hi,' I say into the phone, nodding at Suzy. 'This is Callie Roberts. My daughter, Rae, was in the accident yesterday at Ally Pally?'

'Hi, Ms Roberts. What can I do for you?'

'Um, well, I'm a bit creeped out, to be honest. The woman who was with my child when she was hurt, her teacher, well, I've just received some information that this might not have been the first time a child has been hurt in her care . . . '

Suzy watches me, holding her breath. I hear the officer take a long breath of his own, before answering me. There is a strange tone to his reply, as if he is unsure of what to say.

'I'm afraid there is not much I am allowed to tell you. We've received no formal allegation from the cyclist or your child to suggest this was anything other than an accident.'

'Sorry, what do you mean, 'allowed' to tell me? That sounds like you know something.'

'Sorry, can you hold the line a minute?'

As I wait for the officer to speak to a colleague out of earshot, I see Suzy checking her phone every few seconds. What is she doing? Idly, I realize I can hear a faint cry coming from somewhere. It's not Rae. In fact, it's weird. It's like it's coming from Suzy's phone . . .

'Listen, I'm in court this week on a case,' the officer says, returning to the phone. 'Can I give you a call back tomorrow? I need to check back with the station before I speak to you about this.'

'OK. Tomorrow? Thanks,' I say, hanging up the phone.

'What?' Suzy said.

'That was weird.'

'What?'

'I don't know. He kind of hesitated like there was something he wanted to tell me, but he couldn't.'

We look at each other with wide open eyes.

'Shit,' I say, suddenly letting out a laugh. 'This is so weird.'

Suzy makes a face and pulls me forwards into her arms. Before I can help it, I stiffen, conscious she might guess what I have been doing. I push her away, freeing myself from her arms before I can stop myself. She looks at me, hurt.

'Oh, OK, hon. I know you're tired.'

'No . . . yes, I am — sorry.'

'But listen. We'll get to the bottom of it. Don't worry. Now, I gotta go. You OK? You need me to help when you go back to work this week?'

I shrug. I might as well tell her. 'I lost that job I was doing on the film, Suze.'

'Oh, hon,' Suzy says, taking my hands. 'I am so sorry. Maybe it's best at the moment, huh?'

I look at her quizzically. Now I know what's bothering me about her phone. It sounded like Otto or Peter crying at the other end. 'Who's with the kids?'

'Sorry?' Suzy says.

'If Jez is in Birmingham, who's with the kids?'

'If Jez is in Birmingham . . . ?' Suzy repeats slowly. She blushes, and gulps. I stare at her.

Is she lying to me?

'No. No,' she says, flustered. 'He just got back. Actually, I better get back, too, before he burns himself trying to put out the dinner. Listen, I'll call you tomorrow, hon. Give Rae a kiss from Aunty Suze.'

'OK . . . see you tomorrow.' I murmur, pushing an uneasy thought from my mind.

FRIDAY

29

Debs

The park was so quiet. It looked like the park that stretched out below Ally Pally that she'd wandered up to yesterday, with a path winding through tall ferns and nettles. So close to the city, and yet so empty and peaceful.

She followed the path, trying to remember where she was going.

The noise came suddenly behind her. A loud shriek. It sounded like it came from a girl. Not in pain. More like she was laughing. Turning quickly, Debs looked behind her at the oak and sycamore trees she had walked out of, but there was nothing there, just bark and dark spaces and curtains of green.

Then a roaring noise cut through the silence of the park.

She turned again, with a jump. What was that? It sounded like a car. But surely cars were not allowed down this track?

She spun around, looking through the trees that surrounded this clearing to spot where the noise was coming from. It seemed to come from all directions, moving through the woods. It had a roaring, vibrating pulse to it that for a second she thought she recognized.

Hang on. A motorbike. That's what it

271

sounded like. A motorbike.

As Debs turned full circle once again, two dirt bikes suddenly burst out of the trees in front of her and began bouncing across the uneven meadow towards her. They were driven by young boys who wore no helmets. A grinning teenage girl with a tight pulled-back ponytail rode pillion on one bike.

Debs gasped and looked around her. The clearing was empty, not a single dog walker or jogger in sight.

'Oi, love, got the time!' one of the teenage boys shouted above his dirt bike, making the others jeer with laughter.

'Oh, heavens,' she muttered, trying to move off the path, knowing the teenagers were not here for the time. She recognized that high-pitched jungle squawking they were making. She'd heard it the day she'd walked into her classroom to see a row of children's backs turned away from her, staring at a computer screen. She'd been a teacher long enough to know that that noise usually meant a joke had gone too far — individual responsibility had been thrown into a pile in the middle of the room and anything could happen.

She began walking quickly ahead, hoping that a jogger or dog walker would emerge from the trees and she'd be safe. The roaring noise stopped behind her. Please, God, she thought for a second. Had they gone away? She glanced behind her to see the teenagers throwing their bikes to the ground and bouncing towards her, grinning.

Oh no. They weren't going away. They were here to hunt her. Debs began to run blindly now, moving off the track and into the trees.

'Come on, love, we only want to know the time,' the girl shrieked, followed by laughter. She could hear their heavy footsteps closing in behind her, breaking branches and jumping on stones.

'Oh,' Debs panted, trying to push her way through the branches that seemed to be thickening and barring her way. She glanced, terrified, behind her and saw what looked like a flash of silver in the dull light.

Oh Lord. The boy had a knife.

Fighting a horrible heavy paralysis that seemed to be taking over her legs, Debs kept running, pushing through trees, feeling branches and thorns slapping her face and cutting her hands.

Suddenly a wire fence appeared before her. She was trapped.

It was no use. Everything was just going against her.

Slowly, she turned to look at the teenagers as their leering faces came closer. For a second, she imagined surrender. But then her body seemed to take over. Suddenly, she experienced the instinct she'd seen in a cornered cat or fox that writhed violently to get away from a trap. Her body wouldn't let her surrender. In desperation, she lifted her foot onto the nearest low branch of an old oak tree and reached up to the next branch to pull herself up. The teenagers stood with open, staring faces.

'She's climbing the fucking tree!' the girl screamed with laughter.

To Debs's surprise, she WAS climbing the tree. Her sore knee was no longer sore, neither was her sore neck. Her body lifted up easily, her hands and feet working in partnership as she pulled herself higher and higher. Adrenalin, she thought. It must be adrenalin. The teenagers gathered at the bottom of the tree, jumping about like baboons, laughing hysterically, taunting her with the knife.

'Just means it's going to take longer!' one of them shouted up.

Maybe, she thought. But at least up here they couldn't get her without risking a fall. Up here, she would have a few more seconds.

It was then she heard the noise again. The high-pitched screaming of the dirt bike.

How on earth? Were there more of the gang arriving? Helplessly, Debs looked down.

The girl was opening a large black bag, and pulling out something from inside.

It was the thing she pulled from the bag that was making the screaming noise.

'No!' Debs shouted. 'Please!'

I want to live, she thought, looking at the chainsaw. I want to live.

★ ★ ★

Suddenly, her eyes flicked open. The bedroom came into sight, so blurred she couldn't focus.

'Uh!' she moaned. Her body was boiling hot, her head felt like it was in a clamp.

274

A nightmare. It had been a nightmare.

So why could she still hear the screaming noise?

'Oh, goodness,' she moaned, trying to sit up. Was this one of those sleeping disorders she had heard about where people kept dreaming even when they were awake? Apparently they drove people so mad that they became unable to sleep.

She tried to sit up, fighting the semi-paralysis in her limbs.

What if she couldn't wake up properly? What if she was stuck in this waking terror all the time?

She forced herself to open her eyes and focus, despite the blurriness. Gradually, things began to come into focus. She reached over and found her glasses. Her face hurt if she moved it from side to side, as if fluid inside it was moving around and settling on her nerves.

'Ow,' she groaned, forcing herself to sit up.

The rosy light of the bedroom came into view. She could see a chair with her clothes folded over the top. The clock, which said 9.40 a.m. Her bottle of sleeping pills. She'd taken two last night to keep all the black boxes shut; to let Allen get some rest without her tossing and turning.

She shook her head. This was ridiculous. She would have to ask the doctor to change these pills. With colossal effort, she pushed back the covers with trembling hands and pushed her legs out of the bed. Clinging to the chair, she made herself stand up, swaying. She felt drunk.

It took Debs a minute to realize that she could still hear the high-pitched whining noise. It was real. It was a real noise, coming from the direction of the wall she shared with the American woman.

Holding on to the bed, then the wardrobe, she stumbled her way carefully across the room and dropped slowly to her knees beside the wall, wincing at the impact on her sore knee. She leaned her hot head against the wallpaper.

The whining increased twofold through the brickwork. What was it — a shower? An electric shower?

No.

No. She knew what that was.

That was a Hoover.

Ah. Relief made her sink forwards till her head touched the floor. She was safe. It was just a Hoover. It really was just a bad dream. She was safe, back in her house, the house she shared with Allen. The Poplars couldn't get her in here, at least.

Allen's mother's old clock ticked away in the corner, almost sending her back to sleep on the floor with its hypnotic beat. She would have to get rid of that clock. She could put up with his mother in most parts of this house if she had to, but not in the bedroom. Nothing was ever going to come right between Allen and her with that woman's presence in here on top of everything else.

Fighting the fatigue in her bones, she stood up slowly and pulled on her robe. Her stomach rumbled. Food. Food and a cup of tea would help, she thought.

Making her way carefully downstairs, she felt a slight dizziness play around her nose and eyes.

She held on tight to the banister till she reached the hall, then kept one hand on the wall till she reached the kitchen at the back of the house.

There was a cereal bowl laid out on the table for her, with a spoon and a teacup and a note written in Allen's big, clear handwriting.

'Couldn't find Mum's teapot this morning? Any ideas?'

* * *

She was just sitting down to the bowl of porridge she had managed to make when the squealing noise started again, this time through the dining-room wall.

She sighed. The Hoover again. Now it was downstairs. She was starting to hate these walls. They might have been fine a hundred years ago, before noisy household electrical appliances were invented, when children knew better than to tantrum, but now, she might as well be living in a cardboard box for all the sound insulation she had from the family next door. And especially that woman. That woman who was watching her and listening to her, and lying about it.

Debs sipped her tea, trying to ignore the noise. But it went on. And on. And on. It was as if the person with the Hoover was vacuuming the wall, running it along the skirting board, back and forth, back and forth.

Debs groaned. Her nerves could not take this today. She needed peace and quiet.

She poured another cup of tea then traipsed back upstairs to her bedroom and climbed into

277

bed, pulling Allen's pillow behind her head and the covers over her. Her robe sat snugly and softly around her shoulders. The robe Allen had given her.

It still felt strange that another person bothered about how warm she was or how much sleep she had. Once, before she had met Allen, she'd watched a programme about a sixteen-year-old boy who'd grown up in a children's home and had been taken into hospital with a burst appendix. 'The thing that's hard,' the boy had said, 'is that everyone who comes to hospital is paid to visit me.'

Debs had sat in her flat in Weir Close, clutching a cup of tea as the lorries rumbled past outside, tears spilling down her cheeks. She had known what the teenager meant.

She sat back on her pillows, lifted her cup of tea to her mouth, and . . .

'WOOOOOOOOOOOOO!'

The whining noise came out of nowhere. The Hoover. Back in the bedroom next door. The reappearance of the noise gave her such a fright she spilled her tea down her robe.

What was going on?

She sat for a second, using a tissue from her bedside drawers to wipe down her front. The noise did not stop. Like it had downstairs, it moved back and forwards. For one long minute, then another. Then another.

'Oh, no,' Debs gasped. She was not imagining it.

That woman next door WAS harassing her. Just like those people who read in the newspaper

278

about what she had done and put dog excrement through her letterbox in Hackney, leaving her to scrub the stinking, filthy smears from her floor.

She climbed out of bed as fast as she could and banged on the wall. The noise continued. 'Stop it!' she screamed. When nothing happened, she hobbled down the stairs to the phone and dialled a number.

'Allen!' she shouted. 'The woman next door. She's Hoovering all over the house. She is listening through the wall to find out which room I am in, then using the Hoover on the wall to harass me!'

There was a long pause.

'I'm in a meeting,' he said.

She hadn't heard that tone in his voice before. Flat and weary.

'Oh — why does no one believe me!' she shrieked, and slammed the phone down. She knew it was that woman who was ringing her, even if it was British Gas on the phone last night. And she had had enough.

Even if she'd wanted to stop herself, she couldn't. As if propelled by the force of a meteorite about to strike Earth, she pulled her gown round her, opened her front door, and flew out of her gate and through Suzy's.

She marched up to the front door and banged three times with hard, aggressive blows.

Suzy opened the door and peered down at her.

'Stop it!' Debs shrieked. 'I know it's you! I know you're doing this to me. Leave me alone!'

Just as she said it, a young woman with a dark

bun began to walk down the stairs behind Suzy, carrying a Hoover.

'Done those skirting boards for you again, Mrs Howard — what do you want me to do next?'

Debs faltered. Her head began to spin.

Suzy took one long step towards her. Her clear aquamarine eyes looked like they were carved from ice. She leaned forwards and took hold of Debs's robe at the shoulders and pulled her towards her, till Debs could smell the coffee on her breath.

'OK, ma'am, now you listen to me. You are acting a little crazy here. I don't know what is wrong with you, but I am warning you now. You come near my house again, and I will call the police. And the same goes for Callie. Go near her flat again, and we will both call the cops. We know things about you, do you understand? And we are going to tell the school. So I suggest to you that you get off my doorstep and go home right now.'

And with that she slammed the door in Debs's face.

* * *

She walked back through her gate, dazed.

It was strange, Debs thought.

For some reason the woman's threat calmed her down.

For the first time in months, she actually felt calm. Just like when Mum used to scream at her and slap her when she did something naughty. Back then, she knew where she was. Knew where the boundaries were, knew what the rules were. Inside Mum's rules she had always felt safe. She drew on the table, Mum screamed and locked her in the bathroom. She didn't go to sleep at night, Mum screamed and slapped her legs. She fought with Alison over a doll, Mum locked them out in the rain for hours and told them to 'get on with it'. Simple. They all knew where they stood.

It was strangely comforting being told off. Knowing what the rules were again.

The woman said she was crazy. Now there was a thought.

Her head was in such poor shape now, with boxes springing open and their contents flying everywhere, and blank bits, and the dizziness, that she really did not know any more.

Hmm.

She picked up the phone and rang a number.

'Alison?'

'What?' her sister said gruffly. 'I've got staff training in two minutes. You'll have to be quick.'

'Alison,' Debs said. 'I think I am in a bit of a pickle.'

There was silence.

'I think I might possibly be doing strange things. I don't know what to do because they don't seem strange to me but other people are telling me they are. And I don't think Allen can take any more of it. I am wondering what to do.'

There was an even longer silence.

'Aren't you seeing that shrink any more?' Alison said, her disdain of therapists clear in her tone.

Debs shook her head. 'I can't keep doing that. It was fifty pounds a session. And anyway,' she said, 'I was hoping I could talk to you instead. The thing is . . . ' Her voice disintegrated into a tiny, watery squeak. 'There is no one else I can talk to. And I'd just like to tell someone how I feel without paying for it . . . '

The implication hung between them on the phone.

'I've got to go. I'll ring you back after the meeting,' Alison said. 'Though I may be back late because the chairman wants to pick my brains about the new training course.'

'Thank you,' Debs said, taking a tissue out of her robe to quell the sob that was coming. 'And, Alison, I keep meaning to say, well done. You sound like you're doing really well in your job.'

'Hmm,' Alison said. Unsure. Wary. 'Well.'

'I think . . . I think Mum would have been proud of you,' Debs said, the oddness of the words feeling like hot spicy food in her mouth.

'Hmm,' said Alison.

They both knew it wasn't true. But perhaps it was something.

* * *

Alison rang back an hour later and they spoke for twenty minutes.

'So, you're telling me that this Poplar boy is harassing you because of his sister, but he's somehow coerced your next-door neighbour into joining in?'

Debs tried to ignore the teasing tone in her

sister's voice. She had never been able to help it.

'She could have read about it in the newspapers, Alison. Remember that first week, when people were shouting at me in the street?' Debs caught the sob at the back of her throat. She had long ago learned that crying had no effect on Alison.

'Right. Well, sounds completely unlikely to me. Nobody would care any more. More like your nerves making you imagine things. The boy you might be right about, though, so this is what I think you should do . . . '

Ten minutes later, Debs came off the phone with a list. Gosh, who knew what an organized mind her sister had? No wonder she was so sought after in the world of payroll.

Her sister's words rang through her head. She had to make a list of everything that was bothering her and work out a rational reason or a solution for each of them.

This was what she had to do:

1. Ring the phone company's nuisance department and ask them to put a trace on any incoming phone numbers. That way she could find out who was making the calls.

2. If it wasn't the woman next door, she should go round with a bunch of flowers and apologize. Explain she was suffering from stress and do her best to fix the situation. 'You could be living next to her for years,' Alison said, her voice rising to the occasion with the responsibility. 'You need to sort this out now.'

3. Depending on who was making the phone calls, she had to ring the police and make her complaint of harassment official, just in case it was supporters of the Poplar family.
4. She had to go to her GP and explain how she had been feeling, and ask to change her sleeping pills to help with her anxiety so that she would not overreact to normal neighbour noise — or passing planes.
5. She had to be honest with Allen and tell him calmly how she really felt.
6. She had to think very carefully about what had happened that Wednesday night with the little girl on the road, then go and speak calmly to her mother and Ms Buck.

Debs put the phone down, a new lightness in her step. Yes, all of Alison's advice made sense. She rang the phone company straight away and they promised to get back to her. Now, she knew the next thing she would do.

She opened the cellar door, walked down the stairs, then bent her head to cross under the floorboards towards the plastic bag that she had hidden there. She pulled the corner of the bag and it dropped down with the heavy weight of the china. She would tell him tonight. And while she was at it she would also explain how important it was to her that this was their new house, their first home as a married couple, and that his mother's possessions were making her uncomfortable.

And now she would go and have a cup of tea and have a think about what happened that night on the road back from after-school.

As she crawled back out of the cellar and headed for the kettle in the kitchen, she conjured up a picture of after-school club in her head.

Yes. That Wednesday. What had happened?

It had been completely full with thirty children, she seemed to recall, more tired and hyperactive than normal due to the fact it had been raining during playtime and they had been stuck inside for wet-play all day. The outdoor play area at after-school club was wet, too, which meant they had two and a half more hours cooped up. As a result, the atmosphere had been a little more frenetic than usual. She and Anne, the other teacher, had made thirty plates of pasta for them, then set up a drawing table, a crafts table and a homework table, made sure the boys were taking turns on the football table, and put on a DVD for those who wanted to flop on the cushions.

Had she seen Rae at all that afternoon?

Rae. Yes. That's right. Debs had noticed her. She had noticed how the little girl had looked physically smaller than all the other children in her slightly too-large blue school uniform. And she had behaved politely. Debs had been curious to note this — the puppet incident in Debs's hallway had given the impression that she was in fact fairly spirited. But while some of the older children ran around, whooping and teasing each other to tears, Rae and that other little girl, Hannah, had been whispering and giggling together, and holding hands sweetly. They had come to the craft table Debs had set up and made flower pictures for their mummies. Debs had helped them stick on some sequins. Then Hannah's mum had arrived early and told Rae she'd have to come to play another night as Hannah had a piano lesson. But it was Hannah who had a tantrum at the news, not Rae. Rae had just looked a little sad as Caroline had led Hannah away, stamping her feet.

So what happened next?

A cup of tea. That's right. It had been an exhausting afternoon, and she and Anne had rolled their eyes at each other after they had seen most of the children out of the door, and gone to turn on the kettle. They were in the kitchen having a well-deserved sit down when Ms Buck approached her with the phone, and Suzy had asked her to bring Rae home. She had buttoned up the little girl's coat against the rain. The little girl had seemed quite subdued as they walked along the wet pavement.

And then that boy had appeared behind them on the bike and . . . and . . . no, that was still blank. Debs sat down in her own kitchen with her tea, searching her mind for something, anything.

It was when she stood up to fetch some more milk that a thought dropped into her head with a heavy crash.

She did remember something else. Something, come to think of it, that was quite odd.

30

Callie

What has that woman done to my flat?

In the daylight, new revelations keep emerging this morning. I was too preoccupied in the kitchen last night to check around all the rooms properly, only noticing vaguely that my sheets smelled different as I collapsed onto my pillow and slept properly for the first time in weeks. But today it all becomes clear.

I nearly jump in shock when I walk into the kitchen to find a photo of Rae on the fridge door, which is now sparkling white. It is a photo I have always avoided looking at. Tom took it when Rae was a few weeks old, right after the first operation and she had lost so much weight. She is tiny, like a little baby rat, with wrinkly pink skin. Her chest is so thin it's almost concave. Debs has stuck other photos beside it with fridge magnets that she appears to have brought with her. One is from last year, of Dad and Rae on the beach at Skegness, their hair blown to the side, laughing, the wind farm in the background. A second shows Tom and Rae on a slide at the park, when she was about two, Rae tucked up in scarves and hats inside his arms. There is one from Halloween last year, too: Rae and Henry dressed as pumpkins, and me and

Suzy as witches pretending to be scary.

For a second, I stare, distracted. It's funny. When you look at all the photos together like this, my life, and Rae's life, look almost normal. You wouldn't know that she'd had two heart operations. Thoughtfully, I open the fridge to fetch milk for my coffee.

Jesus, what now?

All the old jam jars at the back have been removed; the newest ones now sit in neat rows along the top shelf, labels to the front. Withered vegetables have been removed from the drawer, which has been scrubbed and replaced.

I shut the fridge, shaking my head. That photo of Rae is bugging me. Where did Debs find it? I think for a second, then march across the kitchen to the drawers where I fling most things I keep meaning to file later. I pull one open and stare. Everything has been tidied. Debs has gone through my flat, gathered up all the loose photographs she could find, and sorted them out. Some she has placed in frames or hung on the fridge; the rest she has sorted into photo wallets and placed tidily in the drawer. I flick through the first one. 'Rae As A Baby', it is neatly titled. I feel sick.

Quickly, I start marching round the kitchen checking all the other drawers, cupboards and surfaces. This is unbelievable. She has used saucers and elastic bands to group paperclips, hair bands and pens. Current bills sit arranged in an old letter rack that the previous tenant left on the wall above the phone. Rae's school letters have been removed from the piles on the worktop and pinned neatly on the clipboard, replacing old hospital letters I forget to bin, which have been filed neatly in a paper folder marked 'Medical'.

Medical? I think. She's read our private stuff.

'Bloody hell. This is ridiculous!' I say loudly to myself. I walk in to check the sitting room. There is a clean jam jar full of dusky peonies on the coffee table, which has been cleared of the teetering piles that seem to accumulate round my flat and polished till it gleams. Even the skirting boards look brighter, as if she's washed them down. On the back of the door, there is a new display of Rae's best drawings placed inside pretty coloured paper frames.

'Unbelievable!' I exclaim. The cheek of it.

I say that because that is how I know I should feel. I should feel violated and angry and humiliated.

But actually, I want to cry.

'My pillow smells of strawberries,' Rae says, walking in, smiling. 'Can it always smell of strawberries?'

'Hmm. I don't know,' I mutter. Our newly laundered bedding always smells of nothing apart from hot radiators.

'It's like Granny has come from heaven and tidied it all up for us.'

I spin around.

She is watching me carefully, gauging my reaction.

More than anything, I am shocked. I've never told anyone this, but sometimes I pretend when Rae and I are walking into our

289

cold, dark flat in the evening that my mum will be there. She will have tidied up, and cooked us one of her roast dinners. The table will be laid, and she'll give us both a hug. And I'll sink into her, knowing that she'll take all the responsibility off me for a few hours. That she'll put Rae to bed for me, and read her a proper story instead of rushing through as fast as is decent. Then she'll feed me, and sit and listen when I tell her how scared I get about losing Rae. And she'll let me get it all out, then ask me what I think I should do, and let me work it out for myself, just like she did when Kieran Black chucked me for Jane Silvering, and I started a band with two boys at school instead and found that practising Blondie songs in our barn was much more fun on Saturday afternoons than Kieran's soggy kisses in the village bus stop. Or when I failed my maths GCSE and she suggested I do a week's work experience in a local recording studio in Lincoln, and I came home desperate to retake my maths exam and get to sound college as soon as I could.

Yes, if Mum was here. Maybe I'd find the space to work this all out myself. I'd find perspective. Perhaps I would never have lost Tom.

'Rae,' I say, remembering something. 'You know how we have a Friday night midnight feast like me and Granny used to do?'

She nods.

'There was something else we used to do too.'

'What?' she says, perking up. Her eyes are

bright today, sparkling.

I go to the drawer and pull out the packets of photos Debs has stored tidily, and bring them back and place them on the floor. Then I hunt in my room for a couple of old photo albums that I was given when we had Rae, but never used.

'This is what me and Granny used to do. We'd put in our family photos and write funny stories to go with the photos to make a history of our family.'

'I seen those at Granddad's house,' she shouts, excited.

'Good.'

We start with the earliest photos of her. The way Debs has grouped them, I am surprised how many there are. Tom used to take them, not me. I tried to stop him but he said we should take them in case we lost Rae; or to remind ourselves how far she had come later on.

She picks up a photo of herself when she is about three, after her big operation, finally, to repair the narrowing in her artery. Kaye is sitting on a bed with her, and she is holding a bowl and smiling.

'Hmm, what should we write here?' I ask.

'We could write that my favourite thing to eat at the hospital was ice cream and jelly,' Rae says.

'So it was,' I say, amazed. 'I'd forgotten. And Kaye brought you an extra one as a treat, which cheered you up, didn't it? Let's write that.'

'Mum,' Rae says. 'When Granny died, who

291

looked after Granddad?'

I look down at the photos.

'Um. Granny's sister, Aunty Jean, I suppose, and some of Granny's friends and their neighbours.'

She waits. I can hear her hesitate, wondering whether to say any more.

'Not you?'

I put down the photos.

'No. Not me very much.'

She touches my hand, and I look up.

'You know, Rae, Granny died the week after I started my new job in London. And I had just moved into my new flat with Sophie. And I probably should have moved back home then to look after Granddad, but I didn't know what to do. So I waited for him to ask me, and he didn't. And I didn't go.'

'Was Granddad very sad?'

Memories of that cold, dark year that Dad and I never discuss come floating back. 'I think he probably was sad, and now I think I probably should have gone home, but then I didn't ask him. I was very sad, too, and being in London and doing my new job made it better.'

'But then I got born ill and you had to look after me?'

I stare at her, realizing the implication.

'Rae. No!' I exclaim, grabbing her close to me till her hair pushes into mine, our curls merging into one mousey mass, just like mine and Mum's used to. 'Oh God. Is that what you think? Rae! That is not something you ever, ever have to worry about. Nothing will ever make me as

292

happy as looking after you and helping you get better. Not my job. Nothing.'

I rock her backwards and forwards as if she were a baby again, wondering what on earth I have been thinking. The sun's rays shine blue through Debs's gleaming windows.

31

Suzy

She didn't notice the blue envelope at first. It had come yesterday and fallen into the wire letterbox that hung on the back of the front door and lain there. Normally Jez sorted their mail, pulling out business letters to take up to his office, but he had returned late from Birmingham last night, blaming the trains — as she had suspected. Vondra was checking it out with the train company right now, along with the name Michael Roachley. Suzy was walking round the house, waiting with a sick stomach to hear back from her.

The reason she even noticed the blue letter was because of a white one that had landed on top of it today when the post arrived this morning. A white envelope with an American stamp attached. The front was handwritten and the stamp featured a white mountain and a skier jumping high off one of its slopes.

Just the sight of the mountain made her stomach twist with homesickness for the open spaces of home. The long narrow hall of her Victorian terrace closed in, the house's inadequate, cramped innards suffocating her. The handwriting belonged to her sister. Suzy frowned, opening it. Why wouldn't she leave her alone? The usual news about her kids and Denver, probably, written in a cheery, home-cooked style with endless exclamation marks. No — Faye, she was definitely not feeling homesick for.

Suzy removed her sister's letter, carefully tore off the stamp and threw it unread into the recycling box. Her sister could go to hell.

See how she liked it.

The stamp, however — she would stick that up on the fridge and show the boys.

She opened up the catch of the letterbox and five more letters fell out, plus a few junk mail leaflets and a local paper. She sorted through them. There were the usual brown typed envelopes for Jez, two bills, a children's catalogue she had ordered to buy the boys some clothes for summer, a charity request and a letter in a blue envelope.

She glanced at it to see whether it was business or personal.

The name on the front made her freeze.

Craning her neck up the stairs to check that Jez was firmly ensconced in his office, the door shut, she placed the rest of the mail into piles, took the blue envelope and sat on the bottom step. She looked at it again. Should she? Would he know it was due? Nervously, she used one nail to gently prise the glued flap open. There was a letter inside, also written on blue paper.

She took it out and opened it flat.

Through the wall, she heard an old-fashioned clock begin to chime midday with long, ponderous strikes.

By the fourth strike she thought someone had made a mistake sending this blue letter. By the ninth, she had realized that it wasn't a mistake.

By the twelfth, she looked up, and everything fell into place with a sickening thud.

With careful folds, she put the letter away neatly in her jeans pocket and wandered shakily into the kitchen with the phone, and dialled a number.

'Vondra?' she whispered.

'Suze? Hi, I was just about to ring you, sweetheart.' Vondra's warm treacly voice had a new triumphant tone to it. 'I've just found out who Michael Roshlé is. And that's not all.'

32

Callie

I look in our empty fridge, wondering whether I should ask Tom to bring over something for lunch for me and Rae.

I wonder what mood he will be in this afternoon.

The doorbell rings and I hear Rae jump up to the window.

'Aunty Suzy,' she shouts, and sits back on the sofa.

I open the front door. For the first time that I have ever known Suzy, her smile is missing. Her face looks gaunt, and her eyes red, as if she has been crying.

'Oh God, what's wrong?' I say in a panic.

She shakes her head.

'No, it's nothing.'

The muscles in her face are fighting to control her emotions. Tears spill down her cheeks despite them. My heart thumping, I usher her in.

In two and a half years, I have never seen her like this.

'Suzy. What is it?'

She wipes her eyes.

'Sorry, it's just something with Jez.'

'With Jez?'

'And his dad.'

'Oh. Oh, OK,' I burst out, relieved.

She looks at me quizzically.

'I just thought it was something I'd done. You know, being a bit stroppy yesterday.'

She shakes her head, and tearfully touches my arm. Fascinated, I can't stop looking at this new Suzy. Open. Vulnerable. Not so bloody functional. How different things might have been, if she had been like this from the start. Maybe if she had shown me her fragility, her flaws, I might have connected emotionally with her. Maybe then we could have been real friends. Maybe I could have been honest with her from the beginning about who I was.

'Hey, look what Henry sent you, Rae,' Suzy says, poking her head round the sitting-room door. She holds out the Disney DVD Rae was watching in hospital, and Rae limps forward to take it, grinning. Suzy bends down and takes Rae's face between her hands. 'You look better, hon,' she says. 'Pink cheeks again. Good girl.'

'Thanks, Aunty Suzy,' she exclaims, and hobbles towards the DVD player.

I touch Suzy's arm and lead her into the kitchen.

'What's going on?'

She frowns and shakes her head, then pulls out a chair and sits on it. For a moment I think she's going to tell me something, then she doesn't. Then she looks round the kitchen.

'Wow, she really did tidy up, huh?'

'Hmm,' I smile. 'Suze, tell me — what's going on? I've never seen you like this.'

She leans over to grab some kitchen roll and blows her nose.

'I think Jez wants to send Henry to boarding school.'

'What?'

'Yeah. And then Otto and Peter, probably.'

'That's ridiculous. Has he said so?'

'No — but he's meeting the headteacher of his old school at his father's club in a few weeks, and the other day he said that Henry wouldn't be going to Palace Gates Infants for much longer.'

'That's crazy. But that school sounded dreadful. It'll turn them into repressed . . .'

My words hang in the air.

'Like Jez?' she answers.

'No. Sorry,' I say. 'Look, just because he wants to send them there doesn't mean he can. They're your kids, too.'

'Have you met his father?' Suzy says ruefully. 'I think he's involved. He's probably offered to pay the fees. Jez always pretends like he is an old fool, but his dad has such a hold over him. He's never forgiven Jez for marrying me. I sometimes think Jez did it just to spite his dad.'

I stare. Suzy has never spoken to me like this about Jez, ever. In all the time I have known her, she has seemed blind to his faults, only ever harping on about how fantastic their relationship is, leaving me to hate myself for the little sting of jealousy it leaves.

She sits back with a long sniff and gives me such an intense stare with those incredible jade eyes that I have to look away on the pretence of checking that I turned the kettle on.

'It just feels like I'm losing everyone . . . '

'No, you're not,' I say, confused, struggling to find the right words.

She shakes her head. 'Argh. I need to stop talking.'

Guilt envelops me as I think of my own part in this and the pain I might have caused her. I can't help it. I have to know.

'Suze,' I say, taking her hand. 'Is this something to do with me, too?'

'In what way?'

I hesitate. 'Oh God. I don't know.'

There is silence.

'OK . . . ' I venture. 'Um, in the way I have been pulling away a little recently . . . '

She looks at the floor.

'The thing is,' I try, 'I've just been feeling really trapped at home and . . . ' I see her face. No. This isn't fair. I am not telling her the truth.

She looks up, curious. We lock eyes and I realize if I am not careful she will see the lies printed across my face.

The door opens and Rae limps in.

'Hey, Rae,' Suzy says, making an effort to sound cheerful again. 'I've got something else for you, too. Hannah's mum has invited you and Henry to an ice-skating party tomorrow afternoon at the palace.'

'Really?' Rae squeals, grabbing the invite from Suzy's hand. 'I love ice skating!'

I make a face at Suzy. What is she doing?

'Rae,' I venture. 'Darling, I'm sorry, but I don't think you're up to doing anything like that at the moment. The doctor said you had to rest

300

till at least Monday.'

'Mummy! You said that, not the doctor. He said I was fine.'

I stare at her, speechless, caught out in my own lie.

'Please, Mummy?' she whines. 'Please, please, please?'

Suzy doesn't meet my eye. Inwardly, I groan. She has put me in an impossible situation. She should have asked me first. I try to rationalize that she is justifiably upset about Jez's behaviour and not thinking straight. It is just going to be so difficult to tell Rae she can't go.

'Well, what about if you go to the party and don't ice skate?' Suzy says, looking firmly at Rae, and not me. 'You could wrap up warm and sit with Mommy, and watch the ice skating this time, then go to the birthday tea afterwards. Hannah's mommy said she was real excited that you might be coming.'

I look at her, astonished.

'We'll see how you are tomorrow,' I murmur, avoiding Suzy's eyes.

'In fact, I could stay and look after you when I take Henry up, and let Mommy have a rest here. She must be tired after being at the hospital.'

Something is happening right here in my kitchen that I am losing control of and I can't seem to stop it. I can't let Rae go. It's too soon. And Tom would kill me.

'Um . . . ' I start, torn with not wanting to upset Suzy any more.

'OK, that's settled then — gotta go. I'll come

301

and get her tomorrow,' Suzy says, touching my shoulder.

And she smiles and winks at me, then walks out, leaving me with a gleeful Rae.

★ ★ ★

It's lunchtime. I am so desperate to escape the flat, I ask Rae to wrap up warm and take her out for a ten-minute walk down a side road to the corner shop.

The road is quiet. 'Everyone else is at work; out having a life,' the empty pavements seem to say. Doors are shut and locked for the day, dustbins closed, curtains at half mast. Cats stroll across the road, looking like they have more purpose to their day than I do.

I don't notice the three scaffolders at first. I am only aware of a clink of steel and a matey, shouted conversation dropping away into an echo and then silence as we pass by. I bow my head, keeping my eyes on a red rubber band and old chewing gum circles stuck to the dirty, cracked pavement. But I know what is coming. In my peripheral vision, I sense the smiles as one makes an obscene gesture with his hands, and then sniggers.

What can I do? What power do I have to turn and ask them if they have not noticed I have a child with me? I have no power. Right now, I am nothing. Aimless, goalless, useless. Easy prey for the mean-hearted.

'Come on, darling,' I say, pulling Rae gently. Her fingers protest. They have been protesting since I took her hand as we turned out of the house. They lie stiffly in my palm, refusing to meet the embrace of my own. 'Let me go. I am not a baby,' they say. Which just makes me hold her hand even tighter, squeezing the little bones a little harder than I should. To show me I have not won, she juts out her bottom lip, and drags her feet.

'Don't, Rae,' I say. 'You know why.'

But the sulk continues all the way to the shop, around the vegetable aisle, and all the way to the till, only stopping when the Turkish owner gives her a free lollipop.

'*Hoşça kal!*' she shouts haltingly, as he has taught her, waving.

'*Güle, güle*, darling,' he laughs, waving at her as we leave the shop.

I smile back at him as if I am grateful, when in fact I am annoyed that he gave her a sweet when she was behaving badly. But he has already looked away. He doesn't care what I think.

On days like this, I know that however deep my guilt runs about Suzy, I can't give her up. Not yet. Because there are times when I crave her kindness like salve on cracked skin.

★　★　★

We arrive home, with bread and vegetables to make soup.

'Look, mummy, a note,' Rae says, picking a white envelope up off the mat. 'C-A-L-L-EE.'

She grins when I smile admiringly at her reading, and wanders off to watch Henry's DVD for a second time, leaving me to unpack the carrots and onions in the kitchen.

Who is this from, then? The writing is unfamiliar: rounded and neat, as if written for a child.

I open the envelope, take out the sheet of paper. The perfect script continues.

Dear Callie,

I know you are probably very upset with me right now, and yet again I must apologize for any part I played in Rae's accident the other night . . .

I check the name at the end

Debs.

What the hell is this?

But I really need to protest my innocence. I am convinced your friend did not tell me to hold your little girl's hand. And there's something else.

I read on, hardly able to believe what she has written.

I was concerned about a comment your child made to me as we left school on Wednesday. She said, 'When I see Mummy do I have to pretend to hate after-school club again?'
I was confused, as she had clearly had a lovely day with her friend Hannah. I asked

*her why she would pretend to you she had
not. And she replied, 'Because Aunty Suzy
tells me to.'*

'Oh, you bloody IDIOT,' I mutter under my
breath. 'She would have told Rae NOT to be
upset in front of me.'

*Please understand, I am not trying to escape
my responsibility for your little girl being
hurt in my care. I just wanted you to know
that you may want to check again with your
friend that everything is as it should be.*
   Debs

Is this woman insane?

I glance at the free newspaper on the kitchen
table. There is a story in there about a man who
was murdered by his mentally-ill neighbour, who
had stopped taking his medication. What if Debs
has done the same? What if she's dangerous?
Biting my lip, I phone the number on my
pinboard.

The police officer's phone goes straight to
voicemail.

'Hi, it's Callie Roberts again,' I blurt out
angrily. 'I'm sorry, but that woman Debs is
starting to scare me. She's just put this crazy
note through my door that basically accuses my
friend Suzy across the road of lying to me. And
also, last night, I didn't mention it, but she was
screaming at Suzy through her letterbox in front
of her kids. I need to know what is going on
— please. I mean, she lives right opposite and

305

she works at our school. Please call me back.'

I go to the window and look out. Debs is standing outside her house, peering, bewildered, from her front gate. She looks left, then right, then walks up to her recycling box and peers inside it.

'Crazy,' I whisper, hugging myself.

33

Suzy

Jez had worked upstairs all morning with his door shut again. She knew he would be down around one o'clock for a sandwich, so she cooked some penne with mushrooms and laid the table before he had any choice in the matter.

Almost on schedule, she heard his footsteps on the stairs.

'Hey,' she said quietly, keeping her back to him as she put out salad in a bowl and filled up the water jug.

'OK?' he replied. She felt his eyes behind her, glancing at the set table and the pot on the stove, trying to work out why she was cooking. Clearly deciding it was not worth asking, he sat down at the table, opened up the local newspaper she had brought in from the hall and flicked through it.

Purposely, she didn't smile. That would unnerve him. Normally she filled their silences with chatter directed at the kids, or questions to him about shirts that required ironing or how his train journey had been. Today, she would let him suffer. Out of the corner of her eye, as she ladled out pasta, she saw him glance at her twice.

'Here you go,' she said, bringing over two plates of pasta, then returning for the water jug.

'What's this in aid of?' he muttered.

307

She shrugged and sat opposite him, watching as he turned back to the newspaper, idly lifting a piece of pasta up to his mouth. Her cutlery remained untouched at the side of the plate.

'What?' he said, looking up from his newspaper to see what she was doing.

She shrugged.

'I was thinking,' she said, shaping each word firmly and slowly to ensure he heard her perfectly clearly, 'how nice it would be for us to have a little girl.'

Jez paused as he lifted a second piece of pasta up to his mouth, then pushed it inside and carried on eating. His eyes went back to the newspaper.

'Well?' she said, trying to catch his eye again.

'Well, what?' he said.

'What do you think, Jez? About the idea of us having a little girl? I mean, is that something you think would be nice?'

He stuck his fork in one, then two, then five pieces of pasta and pushed them in his mouth. As he chewed, he picked up another five pieces, clearing roads through the pile of penne.

'I'm amazed you're asking me,' he said quietly when he was finished. Even when Jez spoke quietly, his voice rumbled round a room. 'You didn't the first two times.'

The implication hung in the air, as he took another giant forkful of food and looked down at what was left. The accusation had finally been voiced. Her deception revealed.

'They were accidents . . . ' she said, trying to keep her voice calm. 'Accidents happen. They

308

happen quite a lot. Apparently, Rae was an accident, Callie said.'

He put down his fork and looked her straight in the eye.

'I won't be having any more kids, Suzy. And I don't want to talk about it again. Perhaps if you had to earn the money instead of just spending it at Brent Cross every day — the kids don't need any more shoes, by the way — you'd think twice about it, too.'

'Well, perhaps if you weren't planning to send all our kids to that stupid boarding school of yours, there'd be enough.'

'What?' he said.

'You heard.'

She stood up and slowly pulled herself up to her full height.

'Jez — you try to take my boys away and see what happens.'

Their eyes locked. It was finally said.

'The thing is, I think you've forgotten who I am, Jez,' she said. 'The girl out on the lake who had no fear?'

He dropped his eyes back to the newspaper. 'And I think you've forgotten that this is England, Suzy.'

'I'm going out now,' she said. 'I've lost my appetite. But this isn't over.'

★   ★   ★

She walked in long, deliberate strides up the steep avenues that wound precipitously to Alexandra Palace. Handsome terraced Victorian

309

houses like her own lined the route, any space in between them filled with side extensions and garages and six-foot high side-access gates. Through the windows she could see plasma tellies, modern art, leather sofas: the trappings of middle-class British affluence. Each door was painted a different colour, from cherry red to ice blue; door numbers ranged from traditional brass to modern slate in bold typography. Flower boxes tumbled over with blood-red geraniums and Japanese ferns and jewelled lobelia.

Each house a different variety, but all the same breed, she thought. Owned by people who had left behind family to come to the city in search of money and goals, prepared to live shoulder by shoulder in cramped, insufferable spaces to achieve it. An image popped into her head of butterflies pinned to a board.

What was wrong with these people, she thought, glaring through their windows? You don't do that to family. You don't just walk away from mothers, and fathers, and grandparents and cousins. They are your blood. And if blood doesn't look after blood, who does? You especially don't send your children away, either, as if they were worth nothing. Children are not worthless. They are precious.

Suzy marched up to an old kitchen cupboard that had been dumped overnight on the pavement, and kicked it with such force that its side splintered.

★ ★ ★

310

God, it was so hard to make her legs work properly here. Five minutes later she reached the palace entrance, turned into it and began the steep climb up the hill. That felt better. There was no room in London to stretch the sinews and muscles and skin, not enough clean air to refresh her lungs with gulping breaths. There was no big sky on which to rest her eyes, just a crushing grey smudge. It was impossible to find a clear path for more than a minute before it became blocked by children's buggies and bikes on the pavement and dogs on leads; by workmen endlessly digging up roads; by 4x4s squeezing through the narrow paths left by the workmen.

She pushed her body deeper into the steep gradient to feel the stretch.

Then stopped.

The action brought an image to her mind of the old woman outside Northmore. She shook her head furiously, trying to release it.

Those legs. Those legs. Those great hammy legs.

And now her sister's letter.

No wonder she had woken in the night, gasping for air.

She tried to lose the images in her head by forcing herself on, up past the deer park and duck pond, to where two skater boys smacked their boards down on the runs and ramps of the skate park underneath the glowering palace wall.

For a second she paused to take a breath. Grateful for an audience, the boys pushed back their floppy fringes from serious faces, and put in extra effort as they lifted their skinny knees high and twisted full spin. The dark-haired one reminded her of Henry. Henry would be his age before she knew it. Except this boy still lived at home. He would leave this park in a while and open the front door of his house with a grumpy 'hi' followed by a reluctant kiss for his mother, before heading up to a bedroom that smelled of feet and mouldy cups and that hid his teenage secrets. A room where he felt safe. Henry would be long gone from her home by then, moulded into a little Jez, having hid his tears for his mother's kiss in a dormitory pillow in the middle of the night.

'No,' she moaned under her breath.

* * *

It was no good. The memory of those legs would not go away.

'Mommy, where are we going?' she had asked that hot afternoon. The cracked leather seat of the man's dirty old Buick burned the backs of her knees. In the afternoon glare of a Colorado summer, the oil smell in the car worsened and made her head swim. She pushed away a pile of the paint-strewn clothes and black-streaked mechanical manuals that littered the back seat, and tried to sit up higher.

When her mother didn't answer, she glanced at the man.

He looked back at her in the rear-view mirror. His eyes reminded her of the eyes bandits had in cowboy films.

'Where are we going?' she asked, looking

through the grubby windows at an area she didn't recognize. This didn't look like the way to the store where they sold ice cream. The street they turned into was wide and quiet. Nettles grew in front of single-storey houses. The pale grey road looked like it had dried out in the sun and cracked. One front yard was full of rusted cars and motorbikes, an American flag hanging. There was a faded picture of a gun in the window. 'Beware of the owner!' it said underneath. As the man drew into the driveway of a small house with a collapsing wooden porch, paint peeling off it, she felt herself sink down.

'Come,' her mother said, opening her door and taking her hand. Glancing over, Suzy saw the man bring a bag from the car. The long arm of her Pink Panther drooped from an opening. Hypnotized, she allowed herself to be led to the door. She never saw it open. She just looked up to see the monster. As wide as she was tall, short man's hair, eyes that bulged behind dirty glasses. The monster's chest sank to her waist, shrouded in a dirty tent of a dress. Her mouth moved like Suzy had seen her friend's baby sister do on its mother's breast. Wet, in a repetitive sucking motion.

'No . . . ' she began to whine as her mother pushed her towards the woman and a smell inside the house like dog food.

'It's just till the baby's born, hon,' her mother said, and then she was gone.

'Nooo!' Suzy had screamed, trying to run after her. But before she knew it, the monster had dragged her inside, pushed her to a sitting position and those hammy, stinking legs were coming round her from behind, squeezing her cheeks together till they hurt. Squeezing her face till the tears couldn't come.

'Quiet, you!' the monster barked. 'Quiet, you.'

⋆   ⋆   ⋆

Oh, today, Suzy could cry. She really could. She could march up to those skinny skater boys and scream and bawl right in their faces. But if there was anything the monster had taught her, it was this. There was no point crying.

She had tried, of course. She had screamed and yelled for her mother, and flown at the monster's soft stomach with her little fists. But then the monster had just smacked her round the head with a sweaty paw and locked her in a cupboard with spiders and roaches. For hours she'd been in there, having to pee in the corner and eat the candy in her pocket, stolen at a school half-filled with other children that nobody seemed to care about. She had tried screaming, too, when the monster held her head under a tap, in the hope that a police officer would come and take her back to her mother and tell off the monster. But a police officer never came to this street. Monsters, Suzy soon learnt, got away with things. Just like the one with the giant legs, panting up the hill outside the hospital yesterday. How she had prayed that traffic warden would catch that disgusting old woman, but deep down she had known he wouldn't. Monsters always win.

So, Suzy thought, kicking a stone as she flew past. There really was no point screaming. Locking her jaw, she turned right down a path.

No. There was a much better way to deal with people like her mother, who betrayed the very people they were supposed to love.

Skirting the back of the palace, she entered the ice-rink car park and crossed it, before emerging at the front of the palace and taking the stone steps that descended steeply down to the road. She waited for a bus to pass before she crossed, then dipped down into the parkland. Continuing down the steps, far into the trees, she turned left into the stalky woods that led to the wildlife area. There had been a hidden lane here, she remembered, when she and Callie had brought the kids one day in spring to see the wildflowers. Down in the trees, without a hill or view to guide them, they had become disorientated and found themselves on a lane so narrow they had been forced to pull the kids into the centre to keep their legs from being scratched by brambles and nettles. She stopped. Now where was that? She tried a few different ways, trying to recall its exact location. A holly tree caught her eye. Beside it there was a gap.

There it was. Good.

Checking that no one was watching, she turned right beside the holly bush, and walked down the lane. Yes. This was fairly hidden. Dog walkers and joggers would use the wider lanes. This one was nothing but a back way down to the cricket club. Only the park maintenance people and young people with reasons to hide away would use it.

And there was an old bench, over there under an oak tree with thick, low boughs. Perfect.

This would do.

This is where she would do it.

★ ★ ★

She made it back to nursery by 3 p.m. to pick up Otto and Peter and their buggy, then carried on to fetch Henry at school. The twins were happy to gabble cheerfully to each other all the way, giving her time to plan.

When she arrived, most of the other schoolchildren were already outside the classroom, putting on their coats. Suzy ignored their parents and walked to the door.

Ms Aldon was waiting. Normally, she would see Suzy coming and call for Henry. But not today.

'Mrs Howard, have you got a minute?'

Suzy steeled herself. That was never a good sentence to hear.

'Yes,' she said.

From this angle at the classroom door, she could see Henry sitting at the far end of the classroom by himself, his shoulders hunched, his eyes on the floor.

'I'm afraid we have had another incident,' Ms Aldon said quietly. Her face was apologetic and irritated at the same time. 'Henry pulled Luke's head back very hard at playtime. The sticker chart we discussed doesn't seem to be working,

I'm afraid, so I think we are going to have to arrange a meeting for you and your husband with the head to discuss what happens next. For instance, I am sorry to ask this, but is there something happening at home we should be aware of?'

Suzy stared at her. 'How dare you?' she whispered.

Ms Aldon went pale. 'I'm sorry, but we have to ask . . . '

'For your information, no. There is nothing happening at home, not that it is any of your business. I presume you are taking into account that he's very upset that Rae isn't here?' she said. 'Henry finds it very difficult when Rae is not around.'

'Well, that's something I wanted to talk to you about, too,' Ms Aldon said, looking increasingly pained. Her eyes darted behind Suzy as if hoping to find an ally.

'I've had reports from the playground assistants that Henry is being quite disruptive about Rae's other friendships. He seems to think that she should only play with him. I'm not sure if this is something you encourage at home, for example? He becomes agitated when she plays with other children, like Hannah, for instance. I can't corroborate this claim, but Hannah did tell the playground supervisor that Henry had threatened to spit at her if she didn't leave Rae alone.'

Suzy chewed her lip.

'I'm sorry, Ms Aldon. But I've had enough of these accusations. If Henry is playing up, perhaps you should look at the way he is treated by the other boys in this class. Henry is always being left out of everything by the other children — and Rae, too, by the way. They don't let him play football or invite him to parties. So if you are going to single out my son, I suggest you look at the way you supervise all the children in your playground and in the meantime I will arrange my own meeting with the head to talk about what I am beginning to perceive as negligence in the care of my son. Not the best time, I would imagine, with one of the after-school staff already being investigated for what happened to Rae in her care.'

And with that she motioned Henry over, took his hand and marched away.

* * *

Nobody spoke on the way home. Henry was crestfallen and tripped beside her quietly. Even the twins seemed to sense it was not a good idea to play up, and sat back in their buggy with dreamy expressions on their faces.

Suzy marched into the house, unstrapped the twins and placed them on the sofa beside Henry with beakers of juice, turned on the television and walked back to the stairs.

'Jez?'

There was no answer, so she shouted twice more till he appeared at the top of the banister.

'What?'

'I'm going out, you'll have to look after the kids.'

318

'Are you joking?' he growled. 'I'm waiting for a conference call.'

'Tough,' she said.

'Suze. Don't even . . . '

But she was gone, slamming the front door.

34

Callie

Rae is so excited about Hannah's party tomorrow she cannot sit down. She has changed her outfit three times before settling — with my strict approval — on her silver fairy party dress that Kate bought her for Christmas, jeans with warm socks and trainers, and a fleece. I watch Rae taking off her dress carefully for tomorrow, trying not to think about it. I think I am hoping that the party will be cancelled. Or that I will still come up with a really good reason not to let Rae go that will not leave her prostrate with grief on the floor and upset Suzy any more than I clearly already have. I am frozen. I wish Tom was here to help me decide. He is twenty minutes late.

The doorbell rings, making me jump. I open it nervously to find Suzy. Her cheeks are bright pink.

'Thank God it's you,' I say under my breath. 'I keep thinking it might be Debs.'

'Why?'

'Oh, I'll tell you in a minute,' I say, nodding at Rae.

Suze gives me a sympathetic frown and rubs the side of my arm. 'Hon, you look exhausted. Listen, I'm going to Brent Cross for an hour, you want anything?'

A figure moves behind her on the doorstep. Tom walks in through the front gate. He sees Suzy and hesitates.

Things need to be said, his expression says.

Suzy is talking but I can't hear her words.

'Suze?'

'What?'

I point behind. She stops talking and turns to see Tom. They regard each other without expression.

'Um, Suze,' I venture. 'Would you mind sitting with Rae for five minutes while Tom and I, er . . . ?'

'Sure, hon,' she says cheerfully, ignoring Tom and walking into the house.

I lean into the small hallway, pull the inner door to my flat shut behind Suzy then come back outside, pulling the exterior door gently behind me.

'You're looking very serious,' I say, warily.

He glares.

'Really. And why would I be looking serious, Cal?'

'Er, I don't know, Tom . . . ' I say, a joke in my voice, trying to regain the connection we made yesterday.

'Last night, perhaps?' he says bluntly.

'What do you mean, last night?'

'I mean, last night.'

What is he talking about?

'What about last night?'

'You're going to keep that up, are you?'

'Really,' I mutter, confused. 'Tom, I don't

321

know what you're talking about.'

'OK. Well, what about how when I left here, I sat in the car for ten minutes, talking on my phone.'

'So?'

His eyes burn into me. And then I realize. A thousand pieces of jigsaw are thrown up in the air. They fly through the air, turn, then head back to the ground, randomly scattering into places out of my reach.

'So — you know what I saw.'

'What?' I murmur, already knowing it's pointless.

'You KNOW what.'

35

Suzy

Suzy walked into the sitting room and sat down beside Rae, with a beaming smile. Good. Ten minutes alone.

'Hey, babe,' she smiled, lifting Rae's feet onto her legs.

Rae smiled and looked back at the television.

'Henry's so excited about the party, he can't wait,' Suzy said.

Rae smiled and nodded.

'I'm sorry, hon,' Suzy continued, taking one foot and rubbing it gently. 'I really thought Mommy would let you go.'

Rae shot her a look. 'What?'

'Turn round, watch the telly. I'll rub your feet.'

Rae did as she was told. 'But I want to go,' she whined.

Suzy shrugged and made an apologetic face. 'I'm sorry, I know. She's just being a little mean. I don't know why.'

Rae shook her head tearfully.

'Poor little boo-boo. I know Hannah will be disappointed you're not there.'

Rae's bottom lip jutted out.

Suzy sighed. 'I know, hon. It's hard. If you were my little girl, I'd let you go.'

Rae kept her face to the screen, but her eyes

slipped sideways towards Suzy.

Suzy took her other foot and rubbed it gently. 'You know, Rae, I'm going to have a little girl one day, too. I can't wait. I'm going to take her shopping for clothes, and to see all her favourite films, and I'm going to give her the biggest birthday party in the world. Even bigger than Hannah's. And I'm going to be there to pick her up every day from school with a cookie and a kiss. She's going to be the most loved little girl in the whole world.'

Rae was looking straight ahead, her eyes glistening, brow furrowed.

Suzy leaned forward and stroked her face.

'Poor boo-boo. It's not your fault. Listen, I can't promise anything, but do you want me to see if I can fix this with your mommy?'

Rae nodded.

'OK, well, I'll do my best. Leave it with me. But you might have to help, sweetie. You remember what we said to do. Like, when you didn't want her to go to work? You remember what you did?'

The little girl turned. 'But I did want her to go to work. Hannah's mummy goes to work.'

'Rae, Hannah's mommy leaves her in the park for bad people to hurt her body. Do you want your mommy to do that?'

Rae shook her head, tearfully.

'Good girl, so you know what to do.'

A noise from outside made Suzy bring her head back up and look out the curtains. Callie was standing on the porch, her face ashen, as Tom slammed the front gate and walked off.

36

Callie

Friday evening is spent in a state of terror. I chat to Rae, I make her favourite tea of pasta with tomato sauce and cucumber. I read her a story, and change the plaster on her leg, and lie with her for a while, talking about tomorrow's party. All the time, I see her scrutinizing me closely, but I brush it off.

Because I am forcing myself just to breathe.

Tom has done it. He has found out the worst secret of all; the ghoulish truth that I keep hidden in dark corners. The one that keeps me awake the most at night.

It is 9 p.m. before I can close Rae's bedroom door and pick up my mobile.

'It's me,' I say. 'We have to talk.'

I can hear from the grunt in his voice that this is not a good time.

'I'll see what I can do.'

I walk around my flat, tidying up with fingers that seem large and clumsy. I put a mug on a shelf carelessly, knowing I have not placed it firmly enough and let go anyway. It falls heavily and smashes on the floor. I take it out to the dustbin in the back garden, and unlock the bolt on the back gate, before returning to the kitchen.

I am standing, waiting, hands on the worktop,

when there is a knock on the back door.

And I open the door. And there he is. My child's father. Just like last night, his big frame filling the door. But this time the expression on his face is tense and serious.

'Come in,' I whisper, checking the garden behind him to make sure no one is watching this time.

And in Jez walks.

★ ★ ★

I usher him through the hallway where I stood last night in my dressing gown, trying to deal with Suzy at the door as Jez hid in the kitchen. We enter the sitting room.

'What is it?'

Shutting the door, in case Rae hears, I turn round to look at him. The physical awkwardness is back, as quickly as it disappeared last night. When Jez returns to being distant like this, he has this way of pulling himself up to his full height, towering above me. His body becomes a sheer cliff once again, unclimbable.

'Jez, can you sit down?' I ask, wishing he didn't need to make this show of re-establishing the boundaries every time. I know where the boundaries are. I know who I am. The treacherous liar who pretends to be his wife's best friend.

Jez raises his eyebrows, then lowers himself into my sofa, causing the cushions to ride up gently either side of him. He opens his knees and places linked fists between them. The hands that held my wrists so firmly last night are out of reach again, his actions tell me. Tonight they are locked into expensive cufflinks. The dark curls that fell furiously onto my hot skin are restrained once again, swept off his face. The shine of his leather boots patronizes my shabby old green carpet. In case any of this is not clear to me yet, Jez makes a show of picking away a piece of fluff that has attached itself to his trouser leg.

'So,' he sighs heavily. 'How's Rae?'

'She's fine.'

'No complications?'

I shake my head.

'Good. You need anything?'

I shake my head.

'I put two hundred pounds in the account this morning, just in case.'

I nod a thanks.

'So what is it?'

When I say nothing, he lifts his heavy eyebrows impatiently, and scratches at one of his immaculate, dark sideburns. Don't do it, the expression in his eyes says. Don't pressurize me.

'I need to tell you something,' I say, trying to hold my voice steady.

'What?'

'Tom saw you here.'

A slight tremor passes across his face.

'Last night? I could have been borrowing coffee. I live across the road.'

I blink.

'Jez. He's not stupid. He's furious that this is happening again. He's especially furious that you were here when Rae had just got back from hospital.'

'Right,' he mutters. He pulls at his cuffs, takes a deep breath, and then gives a second sigh so heavy that the movement brings creaks from my sofa. I try to catch his eye, but this is what Jez does. He looks at you for a second with those eyes as dark and secret as a forest at night, and just when you think you have him, he brings down his heavy lids, shutting you off, and you are left instead to gaze at long lashes resting on a sweep of cheek that runs down to the curl of his top lip, annoyed with yourself for wanting more. Of anything.

'So, what's he going to do?'

'I don't know. Nothing, hopefully, but I don't know. He's furious. When he came this afternoon, Suzy was here. I thought he was going to march in and tell her. He left without seeing Rae.'

Jez shakes his head, looking at the floor, as if admonishing a naughty dog.

'You can't let him do that, Callie. The boys?'

'Jez!' I say. 'It is not exactly an ideal situation for either of us, is it? But I can't control what he does. So I'm just warning you, so you know.'

He stands up.

'What — is that it?' I snap. 'Where are you going?'

'Nowhere. I need a drink.'

Suddenly, I notice how rattled he is. He paces beside the curtain, pulling it even more tightly closed. I go to the kitchen and return with the last glass of wine. He takes it without thanks, gulps it back and looks at me.

'There's stuff going on you don't know about. With me and Suzy.'

'What? The boarding school stuff?'

He glances at me, surprised, then shakes his head.

'No. Yes. Other stuff. But the thing is, Callie, if she finds out at the moment, it would just . . . '

He finishes the wine in a second gulp, then finally looks me in the eyes.

'This has just occurred to you now, has it, Jez?' I say bitterly.

'No. But this has to stop,' he says.

'What, like last time?' I mutter.

He shrugs, moving his downturned eyes towards the window.

'And the time before,' I continue.

He puts the glass down and frowns. A gentle sigh pushes his lips apart, and it's all I can do not to go over and kiss them, hating my own weakness.

'No, I mean, all of this has to stop completely. This, between you and me. And you and Suzy being friends. It's too risky.'

I stop breathing.

'What do you mean — completely?'

He groans. 'I'm not sure, but someone's been trying to get into my bank accounts. Asking around. And I have to think about the boys.'

'What do you mean, 'trying to get into' your accounts?'

'Someone Suzy's hired. Or maybe not. I don't know. But I do know I need to nip this in the bud. Sell the house. Move. Before she puts two and two together.'

His words hit me like knuckles in the face.

'But what can she find out?' I say weakly. 'Tom's name is on Rae's birth certificate. And if he tells Suzy we're sleeping together, we just deny it. Say it's Tom being nasty. She thinks he's horrible to me, already.' The words roll off my tongue with ease. I have, after all, worked all of this through in my head hundreds of times in the dead of each restless night over the past two and a half years.

'It's too risky,' he mutters, shaking his head.

Jez stands up and walks towards me. Under the bright sitting-room light, I realize how puffy his face looks. There are dark circles under his eyes. One long wave of hair has worked its way loose and gently falls across his forehead.

I continue, fighting desperation. 'Look — let me just do what I was trying to do. I go back to work. Get some money. Stop relying on her so much. Move to a different road. Gradually, break it off with her. I get back on my feet. Then . . .' I drop my eyes to the floor, ' . . . see what happens.'

Jez sighs. 'I know you think you know her, Cal, but I'm telling you, if she finds out about this, the way she's been recently — I don't know what she'll do.'

'You mean, she might take the boys?'

As Jez goes to answer me, his mobile beeps. He checks it. 'That's her. I told her I was getting wine at the corner shop.' He starts to walk into the hall.

'No. Don't.' I shake my head, panicked. 'Don't go. Not like this. I . . . I . . . '

I peek carefully through my sitting-room curtains. I see the lights of Suzy's house shining across the road.

For a second, I imagine that light extinguished. I see a future where she is no longer there, and neither is Jez. When there is nobody there to run to when I need to talk after an empty day, and no one to touch my body when I am so lonely I think I might die. Air squeezes from my lungs as my chest tightens.

'Jez?' I whisper loudly, following him into the kitchen. 'Jez.'

He stops.

He knows that tone in my voice. That pitiful ache.

He turns.

'Please. Stop. Just stay, for a few minutes. Don't say that, not till . . . '

He takes my hand, and the touch of him does what it always does to me, however much it makes me hate myself.

I inhale deeply, and exhale slowly.

He bends down and looks me in the eye, finally. Jez knows the power his eyes have over me. The dark forests part to reveal hidden pools at witching hour.

His lips drop close to mine. They brush along the skin. They are warm and taste of wine, and make my body arch in a way I can't control. I push my face up towards him, unable to hide it. But I should know better than to ask Jez for anything. He sees me, and stops. With one hand, he takes my hand and without warning pushes it behind my back, trapping me against the wall.

I stand there, unmoving. Then Jez moves his feet closer to mine. He pushes the heavy weight of his body against mine. Not Tom's sweet, comforting weight with its safe places to hide. Jez's body is like armour.

He drops his face down to my ear and breathes heavily. 'Callie, I have to decide when and how,' he whispers.

Still pinning back my arm, he uses his other hand to run down and up my left side, from my breast to my hip. One long stroke, up and then down.

I wait, frozen, to see what he has decided to do right this minute. His features slacken, watchful and unhurried.

I hate myself. I hate myself that he does this to me. I hate myself that by the time Jez decides when and how, I am so weak that I have no control.

Then without warning, he lifts my T-shirt and kisses me hard on the mouth. Teeth scrape skin.

37

Callie

It is a few hours before I can bring myself to go to bed after he leaves.

The oven clock ticks against the hum of the fridge.

I walk around my flat, slowly, aimlessly, licking my scraped lip, hating these walls that someone else painted. Vaguely, I recall there was something nice about this flat once. Something to do with the light. And then Suzy asked me to fetch some things from her house while she was in hospital having the twins, and I walked in with Henry and Rae in tow to find Jez walking around naked and jet-lagged, straight off the plane from Australia. Jez, the man I never thought I'd see again. Then this flat became a place with no light. A place of secrets. A place where lies are locked away at night.

I survey each room, mentally packing all that Rae and I own. It doesn't come to much. All that work, for so little.

So, this is it. The end.

Can you have an end to something that had no beginning?

I wander into Rae's room, sit down and rest my head on her duvet to watch her sleeping.

She murmurs. The curl of her top lip is lying

sweetly pushed up against the pillow, and I drift off into darkness, recalling the first time I saw it.

★ ★ ★

Friday night in Soho. I am sitting in Ellroy's with Guy, Sophie and all the boys from the studio, so drunk that the street outside is now just silver flashes of moving light streaked with the red lights of late-night cars and the blue neon of a lap-dancing club opposite.

'Oh-weyo-wey. Oh-wey-yo-weh!' Sophie sings, grabbing my hand and making me hold up the sound design gong I received at tonight's advertising awards.

'Sh!' I admonish as Guy glances over. He is shaking the hand of a man who has just walked in, with a hearty laugh, while shooting stern looks at me. However pleased he was with me, and however much champagne he bought us all tonight to celebrate, I know he expects me to represent Rocket at all times and that does not include me or my paralytic flatmate throwing up on the floor of his private members' club.

'Right, guys, taxis are outside,' Rob behind the bar shouts, leaving us to drunkenly organize ourselves into different London postcode groups for the ride home.

'Give me a sec, Soph,' I say. 'Got to get my coat.' I arrive back to find they have all gone.

'Sophie — you twat,' I murmur, knowing she'll think I've gone in the other cab to north London with Guy, and won't even notice I am missing till she gets home. And she's left my award on the table.

The bar is still half-full, so I wander to the counter, ask Rob to order me another taxi and buy a fizzy water to sober up with while I wait.

I sit holding the silver block, finally allowing myself to look at it. I can feel the tears welling, and know that once I get home I can crawl into bed and let them flow, away from the eyes of my colleagues who think I should be pleased to have my work validated so publicly.

When all I can think is, Mum won't see it. And without Mum, pushing me to take all those opportunities she never had, I wouldn't have this stupid thing.

As I stare at it, I become aware of a tall man taking the seat next to me, where he takes off his coat and orders a bourbon.

'Yours?' he says after a minute, looking at the award.

I nod.

'Congratulations,' he says.

'Hmm,' I mutter, sipping my water. 'Were you there? At the awards?'

'Me? No. I'm staying here,' he says, nodding upstairs. 'On business, from the States.'

I turn to focus on him, as best as I can. He is wearing a sharp-cut suit, and from this side angle I can only see a dark sideburn and a tanned jaw under a sweep of hair.

'Funny, you sound English,' I murmur into my water, wondering whether it would be polite to rest my chin on the counter till my car gets here.

'I'm from London,' he smiles, taking his whisky from Rob with a nod. 'I live in Denver.'

'Denver. Really. Wow. So what's wrong with London, eh?' I mumble in a drunken attempt to make a joke. I decide to rest my chin on my hand instead.

'No, I like London — I have a business over there.'

'God, I love London,' I slur. 'I love it.'

And with that my face slips off my hand. He smiles and points at my empty glass. 'Can I get you another drink?'

'Um . . . ' I mumble, trying to compose myself and finally getting his face into focus.

When I do, I think at first that I know him. And then I realize that I don't. It's just that his face is a face I was always going to see one day. There is some familiar combination of skin and colour and bone that was always on its way to this moment. And for a second, just for a second, being so sure of that one thing takes away the pain of Mum.

'Sorry, Callie,' Rob says. 'Taxi's going to be another forty.'

I nod, as if I am annoyed. But all I can think is that I want the pain to go away some more.

It is only as I wake the next morning beside the man upstairs at Ellroy's that I notice his wedding ring, on the hand lying on the pillow.

It lies pointing up at his mouth, which has fallen open in sleep. There is an indolent curl to his top lip, which I have already learned to love brushing hungrily between my own, and I shake my head as I realize that even though I have now seen that gold ring, it does not stop me wanting to do it again.

So I leave before he wakes. Before I can find out his surname or his mobile number. Because that way, if I am gripped by this mad notion of wanting to kiss this man again, I'll never be able to find him, however much I want to.

And I sneak out, unaware of the mark he has made on me.

★ ★ ★

Rae shifts her head and rolls over. So I stand up and then crawl into my own bed, still in my clothes.

I lie on the bed and stare at the ceiling. I lie there for a while, realizing it is two and a half years since I looked at this Victorian ceiling rose and thought how pretty it was. I stare at the intricate latticework of the plaster, my mind slipping forward to four years after that fateful night in Ellroy's.

It is a rainy day in Greek Street. I am running down the street in a blur of tears, searching in vain for Sophie in the Coach and Horses because her mobile number is no longer working. And then there he is, in the middle of the street — Guy.

'Bloody hell, mate, what's up with you?'

'Tom wants me to move out,' I whisper, as he pulls me into a steamy cafe where two girls with beehives and red lipstick sit drinking tea. 'He's given me a week to find somewhere else.'

'Oh, mate,' he murmurs, unable to help himself glancing at his watch, his mind half back at the studio. 'Must be in the air. You heard me and Claire have split up?'

I nod a sorry, sipping my tea. Tom and I had already heard through the Soho grapevine about Ankya, the leggy Polish photographer.

He pulls out his mobile. 'Listen, bloke opposite me in Ally Pally's got a cheap flat for rent — it's a bit run down but it would do you for a couple of months.'

I nod tearfully while he begins to make calls to neighbours to track down the landlord's number.

'Here you go,' Guy grins, writing down the number for me and standing up, his duty done. 'Shame. I've just sold my place to a bloke I used to be at school with, or we'd be neighbours!'

It was a month later as I walked back into my new flat in Churchill Road, reeling with shock after bumping into a naked Jez in Suzy's house, that an image finally came into focus in my mind.

The night we celebrated my sound design award in Ellroy's bar.

Of Guy shaking the hand of a man who walked in with a hearty laugh of surprised recognition, just before he and everyone else left to go home.

A tall man, in a black coat, who five minutes later would remove his coat and offer to buy me a drink.

The bloke who, four years later, would bump into his old school mate, Guy, in Ellroy's again, and mention he was moving his family back from the States to London and would be looking for a house.

Apparently, Guy told me, the private sale

saved him a couple of thousand pounds in estate agent fees, so he and Jez split the difference.

What a deal.

★ ★ ★

Is it cold tonight, or is it me? Pulling the duvet over me from the side, I turn off the bedside lamp and try to shut out any more images of this mess I have made of my life.

But there's one I can't shut out. Of the shock on Tom's face, when I met him by the bright lights of the London Eye for a drink on a freezing, dark night and tearfully told him I was stupidly, unbelievably pregnant with Rae, two months after we started seeing each other at Sophie's party.

'But I had really bad mumps when I was a kid,' he said in disbelief. 'The doctor says this wasn't supposed to happen.'

I meant to tell him about my one-night stand with Jez, I really did. Then Tom smiled, bewildered. His smile grew, full of shock and wonder. Around us, armies of tense-faced commuters marched to Waterloo. The Thames roared beside us, streaked with the liquid-gold leak of river lights along the banks. Things became distorted in all that blinding light and blackness and noise. Tom mistook my tears for fear about him and his intent. He pulled me into the railings, away from the crowds, and whispered into my ear that whatever happened, he would look after me and this baby for the rest of his life.

339

I hid inside his big arms, and allowed myself to hear what he was saying. It was going to be OK.

So when I opened my mouth to tell him the truth, I hesitated. And as I hesitated, I watched the truth float silently out of my mouth in a misty cloud of frozen breath and disappear into a pitch-black sky.

A second of hesitation that turned into a life sentence, for me, for Rae, for Tom.

I lick a small spot of blood from my lip again. Jez likes to leave his mark. And, not for the first time, it hurts.

SATURDAY

38

Debs

Debs started to hear noises at 9.45 the next morning, when the American woman's children and husband had left the house.

It started with a tapping on the wall. A gentle tapping that followed her up the stairs and then into the bedroom.

'It's nothing,' Debs whispered to herself, recalling Alison's words. 'You're anxious. It's in your imagination.'

Then the Hoover joined in. Leaning against the wall upstairs, its tortured whine vibrating through brick. In the kitchen, it was the liquidizer. Every minute, for one minute, shrieking with high-pitched hysteria. A radio started in the downstairs hall at such a volume that the Radio 4 speaker's clearly enunciated consonants were obliterated into a sibilant rumble.

'Stay calm,' Debs whispered to herself, cleaning the bathroom blinds one by one with a wet cloth, wiping dust from one end to the other and back again. 'It's just normal noise. This is the type of noise families make.'

But by 1.30 p.m., there were no more gaps between the noises. A television was now blaring upstairs, along with a hairdryer. They had harmonized into one continuous, painful drone, like the work of some new young avant-garde composer, percussion provided by an explosion of banging doors.

Then, at 2 p.m., there were new noises.

At first Debs didn't know what she was listening to. As she lay on her bed, trying to read a book, it crept through the walls with vicious intent. Horrified, she put the book down. Unmistakable.

'No,' she moaned, stuffing her earplugs further into her ears till the cartilage felt stretched, pulling the pillow more tightly round her head.

She couldn't be imagining this. She couldn't be.

39

Suzy

Shortly after she turned off the TV in her bedroom, Suzy walked slowly downstairs, running her hands through her freshly dried hair, checking that Jez had not arrived back from lunch at his parents' in Hampstead with the kids. Typical, the first time he had ever taken all three kids at once by himself, and yet all she could feel was unease.

The house stood empty and quiet. Funny that. If a stranger walked in now they would see a home. But if you looked carefully you would start to see the big fat lie. It was just space. Space that lay between brick and plaster, glass and tiles. Space through which people moved, kidding themselves smugly that they had created something special out of all this air; meaningful and permanent. A home.

But this wasn't a home. It was an illusion.

She sat on the stairs looking up at the photo of the three boys, and pulled the blue piece of paper out of her pocket for the twentieth time since yesterday.

A night drifted back to her from two years ago, when she had got drunk for the first time since she'd had the twins. She'd been sitting at her kitchen table opposite Callie, trying to keep her eyes open, as her new friend emptied their second bottle of wine and moaned about how tonight's meeting with Tom when he came to pick up Rae had finally made her realize he would never take her back.

'I can't believe he called me Callie,' she slurred. 'He's never called me that. Tom never calls people their real names. When he heard my name was Calista, he called me Flockhart, like the actress, and then it was just Flock. And now tonight he called me Callie again, like we're strangers.'

Callie had been so drunk, she had fallen asleep on their sofa. So drunk, Suzy thought, opening the blue piece of paper she was holding, that she had presumably forgotten what she told Suzy that night. Suzy had been sick herself that night, having completely misjudged how much alcohol she could handle after a long break. It was only now she remembered herself.

The plumber's invoice stared back at her, 'Flock Ventures' scrawled in the corner, with Jez's address underneath. It had taken Vondra two minutes to confirm her worst fears, with a phone call to the plumber on his mobile. 'Wanted me to make it out to her kid's dad,' he shouted down the phone. 'Thought I'd pop it through the door — save her a bit of trouble.'

Her kid's dad.

Suzy looked up at the photo of the three boys, and at the soft curl of Henry's lip. The one he shared with Jez. And with Rae. So obvious, now she saw it.

And she had trusted them both. Jez and Callie.

'You never learn, Suzy,' she whispered to herself as she stood up and walked into the kitchen.

40

Callie

Rae wants to go to the park, but I decide that another day on the sofa can only do her good. I know I'm just being anxious. I don't care.

She lies there, watching the film Suzy gave her for the fourth time. Tom is due in five minutes.

I dry my hair, dipping my head forwards so that the wet strands fall in front of my face like a curtain. I stay there as long as I can, running my tongue over the new bruise on my lip.

My eyes are puffy from where I haven't slept. Where I lay in a waking nightmare of my own making.

'Mum! Dad's here!' Rae shrieks.

I push my hair back and look at my reflection in the mirror. My eyes are watery with fear. I hear Tom walk into the flat. I try to pull myself together. At least I can stop Tom telling Suzy.

I walk to the hall to see Tom closing the door and giving Rae a big hug.

'So, how are you today, monster?'

'OK,' she murmurs, hugging his legs tight and peering up at him. 'But Mummy's making me stay in all the time.'

'Rae?' I say. Jesus. I don't need Tom's view of me tainted any more right now. 'I just want to make sure you're . . . '

'Mummy's right,' Tom says, tickling Rae under the chin. 'You'll be back at school on Monday with all your mates. Now go and watch telly for a minute and let me talk to Mummy.'

'No . . . want to stay with you . . . ' she whines.

'Off you go, mate,' he says, pretending to kick her bum. 'I'll come in a minute.'

I stand in front of him, feeling like a child myself. Defenceless, and dependent on his mercy. He motions me with his eyes into the kitchen, follows behind me and shuts the door.

I walk to the worktop, and turn, arms folded in front of me, trying to control my nerves. Tom sits at the table.

'What?' he says after a second, when I don't say anything.

'I need to know what you are going to do.'

'No cup of tea first?'

I shrug uncertainly, and switch the kettle on, noticing I am shivering. What is he doing?

'Oh, for God's sake, Tom,' I say, spinning round. 'Tell me. I need to know.'

He shakes his head. 'What I don't get, Cal, is — what are you doing with him? The guy's a wanker. Not only is he married — to your friend, by the way — but those fucking suits and the hair gel, for God's sake.'

I turn angrily, to see his hands at the sides of his head as if he is outlining a huge quiff. His sleepy eyes gently slope to the sides.

Is he teasing me?

For a moment, I allow myself to settle my gaze

349

on his face. It's a long time since Tom has teased me.

'Don't judge,' I say, sitting down next to him and putting my head in my hands. 'I've never judged Kate.'

'She's not my best mate's wife.'

'Suzy's NOT my best friend,' I say defensively.

'Really?'

'No. She's someone I rely on. Company when I'm lonely. I haven't had much choice, you might have noticed.'

Tom watches me. 'What about Sophie?'

I shrug.

He sighs. 'It just fucking annoys me, Cal. Apart from the fact he's sniffing round Rae, it's the fact that he's using you like that. He knows you're on your own. He knows you can't tell his wife. For fuck's sake. When you were at Rocket you used to go up against the arsiest blokes in Soho if they tried to mess with your work. What are you doing letting him walk all over you?'

I shrug and keep my eyes down.

'He doesn't walk all over me.'

'Sure?'

I sigh. 'It's complicated.'

'I bet it is. One minute you're telling me he's some bloke you had a one-night stand with the week before you met me. Then I find the guy living across the road, back in your bed.'

'Oh, for God's sake!' I exclaim, slamming my hand down on the table. 'I've told you. It's a coincidence. It's all because of Guy. But if it makes you feel better, he didn't recognize me.'

'So why the fuck did you tell him?'

'I had to! What if the twins had heart problems, too?'

'All right — so what's he doing here late at night, if it didn't mean anything?'

I pause.

'I don't need to explain that to you.'

'Yes, you fucking do. When my daughter's lying in the next bedroom, you do. When his wife's across the road.'

His words hang in the air. The sharp click of the kettle breaks the silence.

'What, you think I'm breaking some kind of rule?' I snap, standing up and marching to the worktop. 'You know, Tom, you're talking to someone whose mother got flu, and died. Someone who worries every single waking moment that her daughter's going to be next.' I reach up and slam two mugs down on the tiled worktop with a crack. I throw teabags into them and start pouring the hot water on so furiously that it splashes, and burns my hand with tiny hot stings. 'I mean, what rules are these, Tom?' I ask, grabbing a spoon and squeezing the teabags again and again. 'Everybody around me — I see them, planning holidays, what secondary school, what book group, what car. And when I'm among them, it's like I'm feral. I have nothing. A horrible flat. No job. No future. And they sense it. They didn't even invite me to the parents' class party last term. Do you know how that feels? They act like I don't exist.'

I extract the squashed teabags and throw them so hard into the sink that they smash onto the stainless steel and burst open to reveal a thousand tiny leaves. Next, I grab the milk out of the fridge and pour it in so fast it spills over the top. Without putting it away, I walk back to the table and bang the mugs down in front of Tom, and little beige streams of tea run down the sides. I stay standing, glaring down at him. 'So, you see, it doesn't feel like I'm breaking a rule because there aren't any in this nightmare that I live in. I just scrabble around, borrowing money from Dad. Asking you for money to get the car serviced, Jez to get the toilet fixed. Being friends with anyone who is vaguely kind to me — and believe me, there aren't many. And in all of this mess, he's the only thing that makes me feel good. Just for a moment.'

'Does he?'

'Yes.'

I stay standing. Furious. Watching him.

Tom takes a sip of his tea. Then there is a long pause. It looks like he's trying to decide whether to say something.

'What?' I say.

He screws up his mouth thoughtfully.

'Hmm.'

'WHAT?'

'Think your milk's off.'

'What?' I look down and see nasty white lumps floating in my own cup. 'Oh, for God's sake,' I shout, spinning towards the door. 'Yeah, OK, you win, Tom. I'm a total mess. I can't even make a cup of tea properly. So just fuck off!'

And I start to march towards the door. But

before I reach it I feel his hand on my sleeve, pulling.

'Cal, stop it. Come here. It doesn't matter. Look, sit down,' he says. I stay where I am, obstinately, taken aback at the hint of smile I can hear in his voice.

I turn to check. He tugs my sleeve again, motioning with his head towards my chair. I roll my eyes and I sit down, biting my lip.

He sighs and runs his hands over his face. 'Look, it's not that I'm judging you, Cal. I . . . '

'Sounds like you are.'

'I'm not. As I say, it just pisses me off. That he's taking advantage.'

It takes me a moment to realize that it is concern I can hear coming out of Tom's mouth. I watch, fascinated, as his nostrils flare in that way that used to make everyone laugh in the pub because we knew there was a joke coming.

'I didn't tell you, but she got really ratty with me the other night, when I was putting her to bed . . . '

'Rae?'

'Hmm. She told me she was cross that I had carried her out of the hospital because it felt like I was treating her like a baby. And that she hates being small because everyone treats her like a baby. And she said that . . . '

'Uh-huh . . . ?'

'That she liked it when you went to work and she was cross with me for telling you not to.'

'Did she?'

Tom's grin finally appears. I can't help it. I smile back. Embarrassed, I cover my mouth with my hand. We haven't smiled together about Rae for a long time. I shift uncomfortably on my chair.

'Tom?' I say. 'If you are going to be kind to me, I've got to warn you that I'm going to cry. I am feeling like pretty much the worst person in the world at the moment.'

He screws up his mouth as if trying to decide whether to speak.

'OK. Well, look, Cal. I'm going to make you an offer, but it's got conditions.'

'What?'

'Well, I was talking to Kate last night on the phone . . . '

'Yeah?'

'And . . . she said she thought you looked exhausted . . . '

'That was nice.'

' . . . and that she thought you had too much to deal with. And she said she'd be really pissed off if she had to give up work.'

Oh.

'In fact, she reminds me of you sometimes,' he continues. 'She's good, you know. And desperate to get on. I know she's my girlfriend, but you should have seen her face when she realized she was getting to do some of my shots in Sri Lanka.'

That was nice. Of Kate.

'So . . . ' he carries on. 'I've decided . . . '

'What?'

' . . . that when this Sri Lankan contract is done, I'm going to look for a studio-based job. Here.'

I stare at him.

'London?'

He nods.

'But you do wildlife. It's what you do.'

'Yeah, well, as I say, I've decided. So, if I'm around a bit more, I thought maybe you could go back to work. I wouldn't be earning as much, so you'd probably have to anyway.'

I can't believe what he is offering. A rush of possibilities come at me. We could be a family again. Not in the same house, obviously. But a family who meets on Sundays for walks and Christmas and Rae's birthday parties. And if Tom helped me more with Rae, I could take another contract with Guy. I could get out of this mess. Start to fix things.

I blink back the tears again.

'Everyone's always asking me if you're working again, you know. They still rate you. Ring Guy and see what he says. If you want, I'll take a few weeks off and have Rae for the summer to get you going — then we'll sort something out in September.'

The tears come. I lift my hands to cover my eyes.

'You don't have to . . . '

'Yeah, well, she's still my little girl.'

I keep my hands in front of my face. Because I know if I looked at him now I would see the pain in his eyes, remembering what I did to him.

* * *

It is a cold winter evening. Rae is three years old. I am cleaning my teeth in the bathroom mirror when the door opens and Tom walks in, removing his coat, his skin pink from walking along the freezing road from the Tube.

'Good night?' I ask, waiting for him to do his usual: shove his cold hands up my T-shirt to make me laugh, or kiss my head to say thanks for letting him have this Saturday night out with his old mates from the wildlife unit. 'How was everyone?'

'Good,' he murmurs.

But he doesn't come near me. Instead, he wanders around the bathroom as if he is looking for something.

I watch him in the mirror as I work the brush around my mouth. His face is unsmiling, his shoulders rigid as if trying to carry a heavy weight.

'You all right?' I mumble through the foam of the toothpaste. 'What's up?'

Tom avoids my eye. He turns round again, and again, restlessly, like a dog trying to find a comfortable spot, before finally sitting down heavily on the side of the bath. He leans forwards and puts his head in his hands.

'Tom!' I exclaim, turning round. 'What's the matter?'

He shakes his head, eyes to the floor.

'Tom? What?'

He sits back up but keeps looking at the floor.

'Just something Gordon said.'

'Which Gordon?' I say, confused. 'Vet Gordon off the programme?'

He nods.

'What did he say?'

Tom exhales heavily and becomes very still. I have never seen him like this before.

Then he opens his lips.

And my life changes.

'Gordon went to the bar . . . ' he murmurs.

'Uh-huh . . . '

'And while he was there, Jamie showed us a photo of his kid and we were all taking the piss, because the kid's got blue eyes and Jamie and his girlfriend have got brown eyes . . . '

The blood inside my veins turns to ice.

Please no.

I turn quickly back to the mirror and continue brushing my teeth. If I brush my teeth everything will stay normal, I think.

'And we were all making jokes about how the milkman had obviously been doing his rounds when Jamie was away filming . . . '

Tom pauses. His cheeks are rigid with the difficulty of saying what is to come.

' . . . and then Jamie turned to me and said, 'You can talk, mate . . . ' '

My spare hand reaches out and grips the sink.

' . . . at which point, Gordon walks back from the bar with a round, and hears Jamie telling everyone that Rae has brown eyes, and you and I have . . . '

His voice breaks off.

I am brushing my teeth so hard now I can feel my gum bleed.

'And Gordon, who thinks that Jamie is just talking about genes in general, says, 'No, that's extremely unlikely. The gene for eye colour is autosomal recessive. Brown-eyed parents can have a blue-eyed child, but very rarely the other way round. A brown-eyed child usually has to have at least one brown-eyed parent.'

And finally our eyes meet in the mirror.

Our blue eyes.

★ ★ ★

Tom stands up in the kitchen to go and see Rae.

'Tom,' I say. 'I know you'll never believe me, but I really wasn't sure.'

He looks at the photo of Rae on the fridge. 'Yes, you were, Cal.'

I can't help it. I reach out and touch his arm. And for a second he lets me.

'You'll always be her dad.'

He pulls his arm away.

'I don't need you to tell me that.'

'OK, but please don't tell Suzy,' I whisper.

He drops his fingers on the table, and drums them.

'I don't want that guy near Rae again. That's the condition,' he says, walking to the kitchen door and opening it.

I bite my bruised lip.

It takes me a moment to realize that he is saying something else. But this time there is a catch in his voice.

'Or you, Cal. I don't want him near you.'

Surprised, I look up, but he just walks away, into the hall.

'Tom . . . ?'

'I said, that's it.'

41

Debs

At 3.20 p.m., she stopped hearing the noises. The American woman's front door banged, and then it was over.

Debs sat on the floor of the spare room in a praying position, her head in her hands, barely daring to move.

For ten whole minutes, she sat there counting. When birdsong from the garden and distant traffic gradually filled the room again, she slowly unwrapped from her head the swaddling she had made from Allen's woollen scarves, and removed the earplugs. The cartilage inside her ears felt red and swollen. Tentatively, she stood up, trying not to make a sound. At the door, she gently grasped the old Victorian knob and turned it, holding her breath, cringing when the lock made a muffled click. She leant her head into the upstairs hallway for a second just to make sure.

Nothing.

The silence bathed her ears like the warm olive oil Mum used to pour in when she had an earache.

Biting her lip, she experimentally took a few tiny steps across the upper hallway to the banister, and leant her weight against it to lighten her footsteps. If she moved like this, stretching her arms down the wooden rail, bit by bit, leaning on it, she could ease her body down with minimal tread.

Three minutes later, she was tiptoeing across the downstairs hall into the back kitchen, her eyes turned away from the wall she shared with the American woman, like a hostage avoiding eye contact with a bank robber. In the kitchen, she realized her throat was raw, and turned on the kettle, holding one hand over the switch so that she could dampen the click of the 'on' button.

Finally, she let out a long breath, and felt brave enough to reach up for a cup and a teabag.

CLICK. The kettle switched off.

'Argh!' she exclaimed in hushed tones, before covering her mouth with her hands.

It was then she caught sight of her reflection in the silver kettle. Crazed eyes, two hands over her own mouth.

Oh Lord. What on earth was happening to her?

She poured the tea quietly, took out the milk, shutting the fridge with a soft 'shhh', and recalled last night. Allen had carefully laid out the pieces of his mother's teapot on the worktop after tea, as she stood behind him, ashamed.

'I must have made her a thousand cups of tea in this thing,' he said, fitting together two pieces of the handle.

'I didn't do it on purpose, love,' she had said. 'But while we are on the subject . . . '

She had finally managed to explain her feelings about his mother's belongings. The way they intruded in her new marital home. How she would like to sell them or put them in storage.

'Whatever you want, love,' he'd said, turning his back and sitting down with his *Guardian* crossword.

It had felt so good. She had taken control, just like Alison suggested. Overcome her fear. Fixed something.

And now she was tiptoeing towards her own kitchen table, terrified again.

Debs, she thought.

This could not go on. This needed to be fixed, too.

Desperately, she searched around in her mind for a solution. In a moment of clarity, she knew what she'd do. She'd persuade Allen to sell the house. Tonight. She'd persuade him tonight. Yes, it would cost thousands to move again — probably everything she'd ever saved and put into this house would be lost in another round of stamp duty, and solicitor and estate agent fees — but this time she would take control; make sure they got it right. They'd move out of London, perhaps to the Hertfordshire country-side, and then Allen could commute. And this time, they'd go detached. Find a bungalow. Maybe with a large garden, up a lane, where the Poplars couldn't find her. Where she wouldn't be able to drive herself insane wondering if her neighbours were persecuting her, because there simply wouldn't be any neighbours.

The decision calmed her shaken nerves for a second. It was a solution. A terrible one, but a solution nonetheless.

Then a thought hit her. Wasn't Luton Airport

near Hertfordshire? Wouldn't there be planes flying over the . . .

'Oh!' With a sharp intake of breath she suddenly, finally, listened to the madness in her own voice.

'No,' she said, shaking her head at what she had become. No more.

42

Callie

Twenty minutes after Tom goes, I am taking the rubbish out when I see Suzy coming out of her house. Caught unawares, I hide my face. I'm not sure I can control it right now.

'Hey there,' she calls, crossing the road.

'Hi,' I say, keeping my eyes on the floor, as if I am looking for something I have dropped.

'You OK?' she replies, bemused.

'Yeah,' I say, 'just tired.'

'Rae, honey?' she calls, walking straight past me and into my flat.

Where's she going? I stand up and follow her.

'Hey, did the police guy ring back yesterday? About Crazy Lady?'

'Oh. I'd forgotten about that. No.'

'You need to chase him, hon. I'm telling you' — she points to her head — 'nuts. I won't let the kids in the garden.'

'Really? OK.'

'Anyway,' Suzy gives me a sympathetic frown and rubs the side of my arm. 'You OK? It's all going on this week, huh? I saw Tom over here earlier. You guys OK?'

'Yeah . . . um, he's decided to come back to London full-time to help me with Rae — so I can go back to work.'

Suzy opens her eyes wide and smiles. 'That's great, hon. It's about freaking time.'

And she keeps rubbing my arm. The warmth of the friction seeps into my exhausted muscles, and my shoulders slump like collapsed tent poles. Fatigue courses through me, and all of a sudden I need to sit down.

'Hon,' she murmurs, 'you look done in. Let me take her?'

'Who?'

'Rae. Up to the ice rink? Jez is stopping at the phone shop in Muswell Hill on his way back from Hampstead with the boys. I'll get Henry straight from him at the roundabout on the Broadway, then drive Henry and Rae to the palace.'

Hannah's party. It's today. It's now.

'Oh. I don't know, Suze, I haven't even got a present . . . '

'Who says Aunty Suzy rocks?' Suzy exclaims, pulling a Polly Pocket box out of her bag. 'I got it at Brent Cross. I figured you wouldn't have time.'

'Thanks,' I mumble. 'But I don't know. She's tired and . . . '

I don't want her out of my sight.

Suzy stands up and takes me by both shoulders.

'What is it? Don't you trust me with her?'

I look up at Suzy's kind face and all the emotions of the last twelve hours come crashing together. I remember what Jez said, about the strain she was under. And I realize I am done. I simply cannot hurt this woman any more.

'Yes. Yes. Course I do . . . '

'Well, let me take her for you. You've had a crazy week. Put your feet up, watch a film. Then if the police guy rings you can speak to him properly without Rae there. It'll be so noisy up at the ice rink.'

Last night, when I finally fell asleep, I dreamt Rae skated past me with blue lips and I kept shouting to her to stop and she wouldn't turn round.

'Oh — don't you look beautiful, sweetie?' Suzy calls over my shoulder to Rae. 'You ready?' And she winks at her.

I turn to see Rae dressed in her party outfit, her cheeks radiant with excitement. Panic grips me.

'Actually, no, I'm sorry, Suze. I just don't . . . '

'No!' Rae yells, looking at Suzy. 'Mummy, no! I want to go. It's not fair, I never get to do anything good, EVER. I never get to go to parties. Hannah wants me to come.'

Her lower lip is jutting out, threatening to wobble. Last week, all I could think about was how I wanted Rae to have a real chance at life, at last. And now I am doing precisely the opposite. Letting my own anxiety about remote risks ruin her life again.

'Hon,' Suze says, taking my shoulders. 'Listen to me. Listen to Aunty Suzy . . . ' I give her an unwilling smile. 'You know I will protect her with my life. If you feel worried, just follow us up there when you've spoken to the police. Jez will come up later with the twins so there will be two of us anyway.'

Rae starts whooping and jumping up and down.

'OK,' I murmur, resisting the voices in my head.

I walk to the airing cupboard, pull out a bag Debs has marked 'winter' and take a Puffa jacket from it.

'Suzy, it's cold in there. If she looks chilled can you put this on over her fleece?'

'Sure, hon.'

She looks at me and touches my arm again.

Suzy lifts Rae up and gives her to me. Rae and I kiss on the lips and I think how soft her kiss is. Gentle and sweet like a little peach. I want to devour her. Keep her here with me. Safe.

'Say bye to Mommy,' Suzy says.

And I let Rae go.

43

Debs

Even though the noises had stopped, Debs needed to escape the house. So she took some golden marigolds Allen had picked up at a nursery in Cruise Hill on his way home from cricket last Saturday, and settled down to plant them in the small bed in their front garden, trying to relax.

It took her a minute to realize she could hear voices.

The American woman.

Hunkering down, Debs peered through the tall hedge. Suzy was standing on Callie's doorstep, Rae held tightly in her hand.

Through the leaves, Debs saw Suzy and Rae wave to Callie, and heard the front door shut.

'I did it!' Rae giggled. 'Mummy let me!'

'Clever girl. I told you.'

'Are we walking to Ally Pally, Aunty Suzy?' she heard the little girl call.

She didn't hear Suzy's reply, but they crossed the road and stood close to where Debs was hiding. Debs lay paralysed like a mouse in the clutches of a cat. They were so close she could have touched them through the hedge. Then there was a beep, and the sound of doors opening. She saw a small set of feet disappear off the pavement and heard the rear passenger door shut.

Then she heard a whisper. A strange whisper.

She strained and heard the American woman talking to herself in a squeaky falsetto. It took her a second to realize it was an unpleasant imitation of Rae's voice.

'Ma-mee let meee!' she whispered. The voice dropped back to her normal tone, but remained quietly under her breath. 'Yeah, well, let's see what Ma-mee does when Aunty Suzy gets real tired of being fucked around, sweet cheeks.'

And with that, she opened the driver's door, her feet visible climbing inside. Debs instinctively moved forward, pointlessly, to reach out to the little girl locked in the car. Her movement rustled the hedge, making her gasp.

The American woman's feet stopped.

They climbed back out of the car — and pointed towards Debs.

Debs shut her eyes tight.

'Look at me.'

The words were cold and clear. Debs opened her eyes to see Suzy staring at her through the hedge.

'I'm watching you,' the American said coldly. 'Spying on our kids. You didn't get my note, huh?' She lifted her arm and formed it into a fist. 'Teeth through the back of your fucking head, lady. Not going to say it again. Want me to leave it on your answerphone this time?'

And with that, Suzy turned round, got into her car, started up the engine and drove off.

Oh my Lord.

Debs sat on the paving stones of her front garden.

Oh my Lord.

She had been right all along.

Desperately, Debs's mind flickered around. The woman was a monster. What on earth was Callie thinking letting her take Rae away? Debs's eyes flew to Callie's front door. For a second, she imagined running over there and banging on the door, telling Callie what Suzy had just said. What Debs had heard through her wall this afternoon.

But the young woman hadn't even replied to her note from yesterday yet. If Debs turned up on her doorstep ranting about green chalked notes and funny phone calls, she'd probably call the police.

This was terrible.

There was Allen, of course . . .

She contemplated running to the hall and picking up the phone. Would he believe her?

'Oh,' she groaned. What was the point of having a husband who didn't believe a word you said?

A door clicked open on the other side of her house, making her look up in surprise. A scraping sound started. Curious, Debs glanced through the hedge to her right, and saw a woman in her sixties, a perfect white bob framing wide cheekbones, kneeling down in the garden of No. 17, staring at something.

'Oh, hello,' the woman said, looking up at her.

'You've just moved in?'

'Yes,' Debs said, embarrassed to be caught staring through a bush. She stood up quickly and walked to a gap in the hedge between the houses. 'Hello — Debs.'

'Beattie,' said the woman, wiping a muddy hand on her brow then holding it out to shake through the cypress branches. 'You know, it's the strangest thing. I've just arrived back from Suffolk, and someone has rearranged all the pebbles in my front garden.'

'Oh,' gasped Debs.

'What is it, dear?'

'I . . . I . . . ' Debs tried to get the words out but instead they stuck there, and her breathing became erratic.

'I . . . I . . . ' she blurted, giving up, as great tearing sobs pushed past her words and tears spilled from her eyes.

'Oh!' the woman exclaimed. 'What is it, you poor thing? Are you OK?'

Debs shook her head, unable to speak.

'Look, come round here,' Beattie said, motioning her round to her gate. 'Come in for a second. Let's see if we can help.'

Dropping her shoulders, Debs did what she was told. She exited her gate, and found her new neighbour waiting at hers, hands held out to take Debs's shoulders.

'I'm so sorry,' Debs sobbed. 'It's just . . . '

'No. Don't you worry at all,' the woman said. 'Now come in and have a sit down.'

She led Debs by the arm into a house that smelled of fresh baking. Its walls were painted expensive, muted greens, and tasteful drawings and paintings of nudes and landscapes hung on the walls. Debs found a tissue in her pocket and tried to dry her tears as she followed the woman into the back of the house, which, unlike hers, had been knocked through to make a big, cosy, Shaker-style kitchen with a long pine table, a giant bowl of fruit on top of it, and a laptop, open and running. Photos of grandchildren sat on the dresser and books lined the shelves.

'Now, what can I get for you?' Beattie said kindly. 'Cup of tea?'

'That would be nice, thank you,' Debs sniffed. 'I'm so sorry. You must think I'm mad. I've been under a lot of strain recently. I'm afraid I was already a little under the weather when Allen and I moved in and now I seem to have got myself in a horrible confrontation with the woman next door, which has made everything a great deal worse.'

'The American woman on the other side?' Beattie asked gravely. Debs nodded.

'My husband thinks I'm going crazy, that I'm imagining it, but I really do think she's quite unstable. There have been all these noises in my house, and my phone has been ringing non-stop, and I think she filled up my recycling box with the pebbles from your garden. And the worst thing is I think she put me in a situation where I almost hurt another neighbour's child by accident, which is terrible because I'm a teacher and the one thing I'm good at is knowing how to look after little children — and the little girl's mother is so upset with me, and I will probably lose my job over it, and . . . '

She took a gulping breath.

'And you think this woman did all of this?' Beattie asked.

Debs hesitated. Oh no. What had she done? Now this pleasant woman would think she was insane, too.

'Wouldn't surprise me,' Beattie said, nodding.

Debs wiped her nose.

It took her a second to realize what Beattie had just said.

'Sorry?' she whispered.

★ ★ ★

Beattie walked over to the kettle and poured them both a cup of tea.

'I said, it wouldn't surprise me. Right. Let's have a piece of cake.' She laid out a rectangular lemon cake on a pretty china plate and brought over two steaming mugs.

'I'm afraid she's a very strange woman. The Hendersons left because of her, although they probably wouldn't want me to tell you that. She banged on their door just after she arrived here a couple of years ago and asked them not to park their car outside her house. Mr Henderson thought that maybe it was because she was American and didn't realize that on a street like this with no parking restrictions you can park where you like. But she apparently became very unpleasant and repeated that she didn't want his car outside her house. She wanted the space for their cars. They thought it was a bit silly, but the

372

next time they parked outside her house she came out of the door and screamed at them. Sheila Henderson said it was quite frightening. Then she put the Hoover next to their wall and left it on all day. Sometimes she flushed her toilet all night when they were trying to sleep. Then she put the radio on at top volume in the summer with the windows open. They think she might have tried to poison their little Highland terrier, too. They found grapes and chocolate in the garden one morning, which are toxic to some dogs. They called the council in the end but they said they'd have to catch her doing it. She was too clever for that. I'm sure you've realized, but this is a very friendly street. Everyone's in and out of each other's houses, so all the neighbours heard about it. Soon, even the women were parking out on the main road in the dark late at night just to avoid the space near her house.'

Debs went cold.

'But she's looking after the little girl from across the road.'

'The little girl who had the bump with Mary's son?' Beattie said.

Debs stared.

'Mary's son?'

'Yes, Mary in the next road. Her son fell off his bike the other day — only told her yesterday that the little girl was there. Mary popped round yesterday to check she was all right but the mum was out.'

Debs's face turned ashen.

'What's the matter, dear?'

'Oh my goodness. It's her. All of it.'

'What do you mean?'

Debs put her hands over her mouth. How could she have been so stupid? Her silly paranoia had stopped her seeing what was right in front of her eyes. She'd been right all along. The American woman was crazy, and possibly dangerous, too.

And she had Rae.

'Beattie,' she said, looking up. 'This is very important. You need to tell me now everything else that you know.'

44

Suzy

The ice rink was busy when they arrived at 4 p.m. The huge car park to the right of Alexandra Palace was almost full with the weekend crowd, as well as people using the mini-golf and skate park and the pond cafe. Henry and Rae, full of excitement at what was to come, had shouted all the way from Muswell Hill, where Jez had been waiting, unsmiling, in his 4x4 at the roundabout with the boys. Suzy had had to ask them to quieten down so she could concentrate on the road and arrive there safely.

'You're a bumpy-pointy nose!' Henry yelled.

'You're a pinky poo-bum!' Rae squealed in delight.

'Guys!' Suzy called out as she put the handbrake on. 'You're going to have to behave nicely if you go to this party. Hannah's mummy has lots of children to look after so she's going to need you to be real good.'

They giggled wildly and banged their legs together, helpless with excitement.

Now, what was the best way to do this, she thought. She drove round till she found a space near the gate. The kids threw off their seat belts in the back and jumped around the car. Suzy got out and opened Henry's door so they could both scramble out. She reached into the front seat and took out the presents for Hannah and gave them to the kids. They took one each, giggling, and walked hand in hand to the entrance.

'Be careful,' she called as she locked the car.

She opened the tall blue doors and the kids ran through. Caroline was waiting at the far end by the entrance that led into the ice rink. She was smiling her big toothy smile at everyone, the legs that would always be heavy however much jogging she did ensconced in tight black slacks.

'Hi there,' she grinned, waving at the children. 'Hannah's so excited to see you!'

Suzy came up behind the children and put her hand on Rae's shoulder, reminding her to hand over her present.

'Thank you so much,' Caroline said, the smile slipping a tiny but perceptible amount as she turned it on Suzy. 'Callie not with you?'

'No. She's resting.' Suzy waited till Rae and Henry had run over to see Hannah, who was standing in a princess dress, beaming. Hannah gave Rae a hug, and they jumped up and down.

'Actually, Caroline,' Suzy said, 'sorry, but actually I'm going to have to take Rae home again, too. I'm starting to feel she's not up to it.'

Caroline looked over at Rae. Her face was animated and bright, her eyes sparkling.

'Oh, that's a shame, she looks so full of beans.'

'Hmm. That's the problem,' Suzy said. 'If she gets over-excited it can make her ill again.'

'Oh, OK. Well, we'll take Henry to get some skates, then,' Caroline said, frowning a little.

Henry was only here because of Rae, and they both knew it. 'We'll be finished at five-thirty.'

Suzy smiled. She caught Rae's eye and motioned her over.

'Hon, you look tired,' she said.

'I'm fine.'

'I'm not sure. Can you come out to the car for a moment so I can check you?'

'Um. OK,' said Rae, confused.

Suzy took her hand and walked over to Henry.

'Hon, give Mommy a hug, OK?' The little boy was too excited, his face already turned eagerly to see what the other children were doing. 'Henry,' Suzy repeated. 'Look at me. Give Mommy a kiss.' He turned his cheek to her, but not his lips, his eyes flickering over to the ice rink. She could feel his muscles flexing against her, pushing her away. Just like his father. 'Henry — listen to me. Daddy will be up to get you later. Listen, I want you to be a good boy for him, OK?' But when he didn't respond, she took him in her arms and hugged him tight again. 'I love you, baby,' she said.

But Henry was already half out of her arms, squirming to release the rest of his body.

'Let me go!' he shouted, hitting her arm.

She saw Caroline's face.

'OK, hon, let's get out of here,' she murmured to Rae, leading her back out of the entrance before Caroline had second thoughts about keeping Henry.

Outside, the bright sky of earlier looked like it had been shaded in by pencil. Heavy drops of rain hit them on the head. Rae twisted her neck around.

'But I want to go to the party,' she began to whine.

Suzy opened the car door and ushered her in.

'Not right now. Now we're going for a little drive.'

45

Callie

I can't stop looking at the clock. It's just before 4 p.m. and the party will finish at 5.30 p.m. It will take them fifteen minutes to say their goodbyes, find the car and drive home. One hour and forty-five minutes. I can do that. Suzy will be there, and Jez. If they need me, I can drive up in five minutes.

I need to let Rae do this. I gave her life, now I have to give her the chance to live it.

To take my mind off her absence, I trawl around the flat, tidying up. It is strange. Since Debs has put it all in order, grudgingly I have to admit I like it better this way and am already starting to use her files, opening my latest gas bill this morning, recycling the envelope and pinning the bill to the pinboard. With the flat tidy, my mind is clearer. The haze is lifting.

Unexpectedly, my phone rings. I grab it in case it is Suzy calling from the ice rink. The number is marked private — it must be the police officer ringing back.

'Sorry it's taken so long,' he says. 'There's not much I can tell you, I'm afraid. Because there is nothing we can charge Deborah Ribwell with — no evidence that she pushed your little girl into the road, and your little girl hasn't implied

379

that it happened — I can't say anything else at the moment.'

'But when I told you that I had concerns about her behaviour, you sounded like you knew something connected to that.'

'I'm sorry, but any prior knowledge I have about Mrs Ribwell falls under the Data Protection Act,' he repeats, in an annoyingly professional way. 'So there's not much I can do.'

'But that's ridiculous! She's running round this street screaming at me and my friend, and frightening our children. What else does she have to do? Actually hurt someone?'

He pauses and I hear him take a deep breath. 'Look. First of all, nothing can happen unless you report it. So, has she been verbally abusive or physically abusive to you?'

'No.'

'Has she made any threats?'

'No!' I say, frustrated. 'I mean, she tidied up my house without asking.'

He says nothing.

'And she just makes me uneasy. I don't trust her.'

'Well, there's not much we can do about that, I'm afraid. We can't arrest her for tidying up or making you uneasy . . . '

To his credit, he doesn't say it with an audible smile.

'But she teaches at my daughter's school. Listen, you've got to tell me what you know. There is no way I am letting my daughter near after-school club again while that woman is there.' As I talk about Rae, I start to crave seeing her. As soon as I finish this phone call, I am going to head up there.

Another pause. 'Look. Have you ever just Googled her?' he asks.

Google. Of course.

★ ★ ★

Two minutes later, I am standing at Jez and Suzy's door, ringing the bell. No answer. Jez must still be in Muswell Hill with the twins.

I twiddle the spare keys to their house in my hand, wondering what to do. Suzy's mobile is going straight to answer-phone which means she must be in the ice rink with it turned off.

Would she mind? It wouldn't be the first time I've let myself in to borrow the computer if I've needed to book a ticket to Dad's or something. It would be the first time I've done it without asking first, though.

Hmm.

I stare at the front door. It was Suzy who told me to chase Debs up with the police, after all.

OK. Grimacing with uneasiness, I slot the key in the lock and pop my head round to check there is no one inside.

So they're both out. I'm sure in the circumstances they wouldn't mind.

Still tiptoeing, I pad up the two flights of stairs to Jez's study, open the door and walk across the carpet to the computer. It smells of him. The faint fragrance of something expensive that he uses when he shaves. Goosebumps break out all over my body. I push back into the worn leather,

381

allowing myself just for a second to imagine that the soft leather encasing my body is him.

The computer is on. Gingerly, I reach out and type 'Deborah Ribwell, teacher', into Google.

It takes me a minute to realize what I'm looking at. It's a news story repeated by all the national newspapers in various forms.

February this year, it says. Four months ago. My eyes drop to the headline:

HACKNEY TEACHER GUILTY OF COMMON ASSAULT

And there. There is Debs's name. In the online archives of a local newspaper.

18 February

A Hackney schoolteacher today pleaded guilty to a charge of common assault against a minor at Hackney Magistrates' Court.

My mouth drops open.

Deborah Ribwell, an English teacher at Queenstock Academy, admitted to striking a 15-year-old student, known as Child D, twice in the face in Victoria Park on December 10 last year. Sentencing was suspended in order for Mrs Ribwell's solicitor to present a plea of mitigation. The case continues . . .

A door bangs outside, making me jump. I stand up and look out of the attic window to see Debs slamming her next-door neighbour's gate.

She marches out onto the pavement, across the road and up to my front door.

'What the . . . ?' I whisper.

'Callie!' she shrieks, banging on my door. 'Callie!' She bangs over and over, pushing the doorbell three or four times. I sink back from the window so she can't see me, and keep watching. When no one answers, she turns back to the gate with this wild look on her face.

'AAAAAAAARGH!' she screams, banging the gate behind her, and marches off up Churchill Road.

Oh my God. Suzy was right — she's crazy.

Is that why Rae fell in the road? What if Debs lost her temper at Rae — for running down the street without her on the way home from after-school?

And hit her?

*   *   *

Horrified, I return to the computer to read the rest of the news reports only to see a small instant message has popped into the middle of the screen.

Where did that come from?

Curious, I read it.

'U there . . . ???' it says.

I look around, awkwardly, as if the writer can see me. Whoever sent it must know that Jez's computer has gone online. There is no signature on it but then I see the messaging address on top of the note. 'SassySasha' it says.

I wait but nothing happens.

A note for Jez. From SassySasha.

Wondering if he is here.

* * *

Trying to ignore the uneasy feeling it gives me, I scroll down to read the next report from the newspaper. I am just hitting the link when my phone rings. I answer it without looking, assuming it is Suzy.

'Hey?' I say, answering. 'Where were you? I couldn't get through. Listen, you won't believe this but . . . '

'Callie?' The voice is familiar, but I can't place it.

'Yes?'

'It's Caroline here, Hannah's mummy.'

'Oh — hi,' I say, surprised. 'Is everything OK?'

'Sorry, Callie. Not really. I'm afraid Henry is, well, playing up a little. He pushed another little boy over on the ice. Quite hard. I'm afraid I just don't have time to deal with it. I've tried Suzy but her phone's off. Is Rae well enough for you to come and pick him up?'

'Sorry, Caroline, what did you say about Rae?'

'Has Suzy dropped her off with you?'

'No.' I stand up and look out the window again to see if they've just arrived, but nothing. Suzy's car is not on the road, either. 'Sorry, why would she? Sorry, Caroline, I don't understand.'

'Oh. That's odd. Suzy took Rae straight home

384

when she dropped Henry off. She said Rae was unwell. I'm sorry, I just assumed she was bringing her back to you.'

Frantically, I check my watch. They've been gone half an hour. Where are they?

'Caroline, what sort of unwell? Was she breathing funny?' I bark.

'No, no. Callie, really, I thought she looked fine, actually. I was a bit confused why Suzy was taking her home, to be honest. Listen, don't worry about it. I'll keep Henry here till I hear from . . .'

But I am not listening any more. I am running down the stairs.

46

Debs

The rain was coming down heavily. As Debs reached the palace, she wiped her glasses, only for them to steam up again the second she replaced them on her nose.

Panting, she began her search. Everywhere she could think of, she looked: in the car park outside the ice rink, the grass areas beside it and along the walkway in front of the palace. She even went into the ice rink and peered through the tall glass doors, but there was no sign of Rae's mousey blonde curls in the whirl of children circling the rink. She ran to the back of the palace next, and scouted around the play park, which was emptying rapidly of parents and children, disappearing in a flurry of wellies and wet coats as the downpour persevered.

'Where are they?' Debs muttered.

She completed one circuit of the duck pond, but the only movement there was rain smashing into it, throwing muddy water back up in the air. Then the skateboard park with its slick, silent ramps. Nothing.

Everywhere was empty. The palace was like that. One minute teeming with life; the next, a rolling empty park, dotted with shadowy corners and menacing gaps between bushes, and blind bends and hills with who knew what over the ridge, all of it uncomfortably far from the eyes of passers-by. Debs's wet cardigan felt vacuum-packed to her limbs, as did her trousers. Her bob was plastered round her face. The rain had found its way inside her lace-up shoes, rendering her socks damp and uncomfortable.

Where were Rae and that woman?

She turned and shrieked as a bull terrier bounded towards her with a lolloping bounce. Its owner, a man in a waterproof hood with a sullen face, called it away without apology.

Damn her nerves. She was fed up with being intimidated.

'Rae!' she began to shout weakly, as if this would help.

She climbed back up to the palace again, and looked out across London and over the steep drop of parkland in front of the palace. Surely they would not be down there? In this rain there would be nothing to do. No park, no shelter. Just trees and paths through the woods.

Woods.

She shuddered. She hadn't been in any woods since the day that dreadful Poplar girl from Year Ten and her disgusting boyfriend had cornered her in Victoria Park, as she took a walk on Saturday morning to clear her head. Shouting abuse and laughing, and waving those photos that she couldn't bear to look at. Repulsive images of something that had been so timid and careful and precious, yet had been turned by this disturbed young girl and her leering boyfriend into something so public and repulsive and horrific, that Allen was on the verge of moving into the spare bedroom to avoid Debs ever having to contemplate doing it again. Why he would even want to try again — why he had even stayed with her after that humiliating nightmare — was anyone's guess.

Debs's heart beat fast. Oh, she was so tired of this. Of being frightened. Of living her life depending on the behaviour of others. Why had Mum not given her any backbone?

This afternoon the American woman had played pornography loudly through her wall. And Debs had let her. She had let her turn up the volume and torture her with disturbing panting and groaning sounds that made Debs sit on the edge of the bed, holding her ears.

She looked out across London. Enough, Debs, she thought. It is time to stand up for yourself.

Pulling out her mobile, she sat down on a bench and dialled Allen at his cricket match. Expecting it to be turned off, she was surprised to hear his voice answer.

'It's me, love,' she said in the most confident voice she could muster. 'Now listen, please. I know it's been a difficult few months for you since everything happened, but I'm afraid you are wrong about me imagining things. The woman next door has confirmed it. I have proof. And now she's taken the little girl and I am pretty sure she is frightening her. I'm up at Alexandra Palace right now looking for her.'

She heard his sigh.

'Allen. Why did you stay with me? You know, after what happened.'

It was a question she had never dared to ask him. They had fumbled their way from that first meeting in a restaurant holding copies of the *Guardian*, Debs so nervous she had nearly been sick in a plant pot, to marriage without much being said directly at all.

'I'm up next to bat, love, when the rain stops,' he murmured.

'I mean it, Allen. Tell me now. Was it better than just being lonely?'

'No.'

'Well, what?'

'Oh, Debs, please, love . . . '

'Urgh,' she said under her breath, stamping her foot a little. She shook her face from side to side, making her glasses shift on her nose. 'Allen. Love. I'm sorry, but if you and I are going to make this marriage work, then you are going to have to talk to me. Because . . . because, I'm sorry, love, but I've, I've . . . ' Her tone began to rise. 'I've just had enough. I've had ENOUGH. I'm scared stiff of you, if you want the truth. I tiptoe round you all the time, just waiting for you to tell me it was a mistake. And I can't take it any more. If you don't like what I am, Allen, then, well, maybe you should tell me and we'll be done with it. I can't live this way, feeling judged every day for my silliness and the way I wash socks and notice things, and for what my sister did . . . '

'Don't say that,' she heard him murmur. 'Don't say that.'

'But you do! And do you know what, maybe

you're right. Maybe I'm just a bad bet, Allen. Just like Mum said Dad was. I'm a bad bet. You should never have got involved. No one should be involved with me. And I think the only reason you are still with me is that by the time you realized that I was a bad bet, you were too polite to get out of it. Because that's the type of person you are, Allen, isn't it? Someone who looks after other people. Damaged people. And that's what I am — damaged.'

She heard him take a long breath.

'No.'

'What?' she sniffed. 'Don't lie.'

'No. Debs, I married you because of the opposite.'

'No, you didn't.'

'Yes, I did. I married you because . . . well, the way I saw you working so hard with those kids when so many people gave up on them. And the way your sister is so difficult with you, but somehow you always forgive her. And because of the way you love your books, even though there are so many I have nowhere to put my cricket trophies.'

She couldn't help it. A smile played at her lips.

'I admire that, love. How much you know about them and how passionate you are about them. And it annoys me that you won't take up my offer and take a year off to do your MA in English, because I know you've always wanted to do it. It's not something I could ever do, but I'd love to see you do it. And you're not bad at crosswords, either. Maybe not as good as me, but . . . '

To her surprise, she suddenly chortled at his unexpected joke.

'Debs. You mustn't worry, love. It's going to be OK.'

'Is it, Allen? It's just, I am so tired,' she sighed.

'I know you are.'

'No, Allen. You don't. I am just so tired of being bullied by people who do not take the time to try to be even a little bit kind. I feel that I want to stand up to them, whatever it takes. I want things to go back to how they were, between us. Do you remember? It took us both so long to find each other and then, and then that girl . . . What right did she have to . . . ?'

'Yes, love.'

'OK, Allen. The thing is, I need you to believe me. That's how we make this work. I need you to believe me. So I am asking you this once. Will you please leave now and come up to Ally Pally and help me?'

He paused. 'This is what you want?'

'Yes. It really is. In fact, Allen, I think it might well save me.'

'OK.'

'Thank you, Allen. I'm sorry if it causes a problem with your match.'

'It's only cricket, love.'

There was a pause as they both smiled at his accidental joke. She put the phone down, trying not to cheer. She had done it.

Now, to find that woman.

Debs walked down the stone steps that dropped into parkland, forcing herself to leave her fear behind as she disappeared from sight of the road into the trees that led to the wildlife area. She was going to find that little girl and check she was OK, if it was the last thing she did — even if Allen had to get her sectioned afterwards.

47

Suzy

The rain landed on the car windscreen like the water bombs Henry threw in the garden. Hundreds of gentle water bombs. You didn't get rain like this in Colorado. There it came in great, elemental waves that soaked the plains and then hung between the mountains in curtains of heavy mist. It beat you with no mercy, washing the land with a parade of drumming rain that would, from time to time, blast up into the clouds and twirl violently into a black tornado that you could see for miles. No, the rain at home was wild, alive. It wasn't this polite British rain. You couldn't fight it off with a little plastic umbrella.

Homesickness for Colorado was coming now in long, regular contractions. London was supposed to have been a fresh start. A place to be a normal person, finally, with a normal family and normal friends, far from the liars and betrayers and users and demons of home. Yet, it turned out, the liars and betrayers existed here, too. At least back in Colorado, she could drive out into the wilderness and hike hard till everything turned numb with exhaustion, and peace finally descended in the expansive silence of the plain. In London, there was nowhere to escape. She could hardly breathe in this toxic air.

393

Suzy started up her yellow convertible. Finally, the path looked clear. The rain had driven away the joggers and dog walkers and left her alone at last. She drove slowly off the main palace road and down into the lane that ran through the parkland, hidden behind tall rows of trees. 'Perfect,' she muttered, turning right over a large pothole further down towards the wildlife area, the car door lightly scraping wild raspberry bushes, sprinkling red fruit on the road. She kept driving slowly till she found the entrance to the hidden lane. When she reached it, she slowed down and looked behind her. There. No one could see from here.

'OK, hon?' she said.

Rae looked at her with her curious big eyes. She was shivering a little in her thin silver party dress, the fleece tossed forgotten on the ice-rink reception-area floor.

'Can I go to the party now?' she said meekly.

'No, hon. It's too dangerous for you at the moment. Mommy wants me to take you home. She's being mean again, I'm afraid. But do you know what? I've done something very silly.'

'What?'

'Well, I went the wrong way when we came out of the palace, so I turned in to the park lane to turn round, and there was a big van in the way.'

'Was there?' says Rae, confused.

'Uh-huh, so I had to drive past it, but then the lane got very narrow, and I couldn't turn round, so I kept driving trying to find somewhere to turn, and now we're really stuck!'

'Are we lost?' The little girl looked out of the window at the wet bushes around them with fearful eyes.

Suzy took Rae's hand, which felt ice cold. She stared at her for a long moment, watching as tears started to form in the child's eyes. Leaning forwards, she stroked Rae's cheek.

'I think we might be.'

Then she turned and looked at the bench under the tree.

48

Callie

I reach the door of the ice rink, soaked in rain, my chest heaving.

'Any sign?' I gasp, pushing through the main doors and running up to Caroline.

'No,' she calls, looking concerned, while trying to hand out cake to the children who dance around her, arms outstretched, all decorum lost in their quest for more sugar. Henry sits in the corner, sulking. 'What can I do?'

'Can you keep Henry?' I say. 'Please? I need to find out where they are.'

She nods again, doing a good job of hiding her irritation.

I stand, gulping air, dripping water, pushing buttons on my mobile. Suzy and Jez are still not answering. I leave a message for Tom. I ring A&E at Northmore, too. Nothing.

Where is she? I fly back out the door.

'Rae!' I scream into the car park.

I rush to the wall that looks over the city, and down onto parkland. Left and right. 'Rae!'

Nothing. The long walkway is clear. Huge raindrops pummel my face. Spray flies up as a car races past through puddles below.

396

Where is she? Where the hell is she?

Great sobs burst from my mouth.

I need her. I need to know she is safe. I need to protect her.

49

Debs

Allen rang her when he reached the entrance to the ice-rink car park.

'I'm down in the woods, love,' she panted, pushing away a branch. Leaves were sticking to her hands and face. Her trousers and shoes were soaked now. 'Can you find the cricket club? I'll meet you there in three minutes.'

She managed to climb out of the wet bramble bushes onto the rutted, one-car track that led from the palace road down into the football and cricket fields at the bottom of the parkland in front of the palace. A minute later, she heard Allen's car crunching along on the stony road.

'Over here!' she shouted, waving a wet, woollen arm.

He stopped and opened the passenger door.

'You're soaked, love.'

She jumped inside, sending rivulets of water all over the interior. He sat, watching her expectantly. She looked at him, brushing water from her arms, then leaned over and took his face with both hands. To her relief, he didn't flinch. Bravely, she lifted his glasses and met his gaze.

'Allen?' she said.

'Hmm,' he muttered.

'I don't like these glasses. I want to see your eyes. They make me feel safe.'

He nodded.

'Right. Will you carry on looking down here?' she asked, pulling away. 'I haven't been round the nature reserve yet — it starts over there at the edge of the cricket field. I'll take the car, if that's OK? I could do with getting warm for a second. I'll take it to the other side of the palace, where the garden centre is.'

'Course, love,' he said, looking slightly dazed. He stepped out of the car in his green anorak. 'What are you planning to do, if you find them?'

'I don't know yet,' said Debs, opening the passenger door and walking round to the driver's side. 'Maybe just watch them till she gets Rae home safely. Then I'm going to get that woman Beattie next door to talk to Callie.'

'OK, love. Well, be careful.'

'Thank you, Allen,' she squeaked, touching his arm. His glasses were dripping with water, just like hers. They look at each other through their steamed-up lenses.

'What a pair,' he said.

And to her surprise, he leaned forwards and planted a rain-drenched kiss on her lips.

'I'll be back down to get you in ten minutes,' she squeaked, blood rushing to her cheeks. 'If you see them in the meantime, ring me.' She climbed back in the car, adjusted the seat for her longer legs and drove off, a smile tugging at her lips.

* * *

Debs reached the T-junction at the top of the rutted road. She turned as if going right onto the palace road. She was just about to continue when something back down on the track to the right caught her eye.

She pulled over sharply onto the kerb and had another look. A flash of bright yellow was moving behind a tree, down into the woods.

That was them! Where were they going?

Debs looked around wildly. There wasn't enough room to do a three-point turn here. Without time to think, she turned off her engine, jumped out of the car and ran back towards the trees.

There it was. Yellow. Yellow metal.

'Oh!' Debs gasped, chasing after it.

She ran into the trees, making her way along a little path that took her ahead of the car, then steeply down onto the lane.

She ran blindly, not knowing what she was going to do when she got there.

Pushing through spiky wet branches, she emerged onto a little lane.

A noise behind her made her turn.

Suzy was sitting at the top of the lane in her car, talking to Rae behind her.

Then she turned round to look at the road — and saw Debs.

The women's eyes met through the rain-soaked windscreen.

50

Callie

'Hello. You're the mother, are you?'

I jump as the shout comes out of nowhere. I am running down the hill blindly, trying to work everything out. If Suzy left the palace and didn't arrive home, where could she be? At least if I retrace the route she would have taken by car, I can be sure they haven't crashed or broken down. My ears strain to hear sirens.

I stop and see the odd little man from across the road waving at me.

'Have you lost a child?'

'Yes!' I shout. 'Have you seen her?'

'Come over here,' he motions through the rain.

I dash across the road, missing cars by a whisker. Close up, he looks like a wet mole, with a long nose and kind, sad eyes.

'Do you know where she is?' I shout above the drum of water.

'I don't, I'm afraid, but my wife is pretty sure that she's with your neighbour in this park,' he says, pointing towards the dark, wet trees. 'She's looking for her right now. Why don't we go this way together?'

I stare at him, horrified.

'What are you talking about? Why the hell is

your wife looking for my child?' I shout. 'What the hell is wrong with you?'

Before he can answer, a high-pitched scream of 'No!' comes out of the woods.

51

Debs

What was the American woman doing? She started the car and began to rev it, staring at Debs like a monster through the windscreen. Her face was fixed in a grin, her eyes wide and angry.

With precision, she pushed a button and watched Debs as the window came down.

'I need to speak to you,' Debs shouted nervously. 'Could you turn the engine off, please?'

But the American woman just kept staring at her, revving the car. Her turquoise eyes shone fiercely out of the grey shadows cast by the wet trees above. Horrified, Debs watched as Suzy revved the engine even more loudly this time, and slowly turned the wheel until it pointed in her direction. She could see the little girl in the back seat, crying, pulling at her seatbelt.

'Please,' Debs shouted, 'could you turn the engine off, Suzy? Or could you at least let Rae out, please. She's scared.'

But before Debs could say anything else, Suzy slammed her foot on the accelerator and came flying the thirty feet towards her, the car's wheels scrabbling on the wet path as they picked up momentum, shooting up grit and leaves.

'No!' Debs screamed, jumping to the side.

The car missed her by three feet and slammed into a bench with an enormous bang that sent its bonnet flying up in the air. An airbag burst open with a blast.

There was a moment of silence, as steam rose high into the air with a hiss.

Debs stood blinking.

Suzy slowly lifted her head up. Blood dripped from her nose. She looked at Debs again, eyes still shining.

52

Callie

'There!' Allen shouts, pointing to where a puff of white smoke is rising from between the trees.

I run through tall wet grass so fast that each time I trip the step just throws me towards the next obstacle, and I make it through the woods, legs and arms flying in all directions, body almost horizontal against the wind.

'Rae!' I scream.

We reach the path and look desperately left and right.

'Callie — help!' I hear Suzy's voice shouting. 'Please help us!'

'This way,' Allen shouts, taking my arm as we stumble down through wet undergrowth onto a smaller path.

I stop, helpless.

Suzy's car is smashed into an old bench, the yellow metal of its bonnet split into violent curls. Debs is standing in front of it, hands out, shaking her head.

'Call 999!' I scream at Allen. I run to the back door. 'Rae? Rae?'

'Callie, help us. She tried to kill us,' Suzy sobs from the front, her face pressed into an airbag. 'Argh. I think my arm's broken. She ran out screaming at us, and made me crash. Is Rae OK?

Please, Cal. Check her first.'

I look up to see Debs walking tentatively towards the car.

'You!' I scream. 'Get the fuck away from my daughter!' I pull frantically at the back door, trying to see through the dark glass.

'It's locked, Suzy,' I shout.

'OK, hon,' she murmurs, moving her hand around to find the lock. It springs open.

The door pulls out with a heavy clunk, and I force my head inside, terrified.

And there is a moment. A wondrous, peaceful moment when I see that Rae is not there. That the booster seats are empty, the back seat vacant, the seat belts neatly clipped in their slots. Not today, I think. For once, it is not us. Not me, not my daughter, not my family.

It is only as I put my head between the front seats in relief to tell Suzy that Rae is not here, that I see a flash of silver.

A silver dress crumpled in the footwell.

And then bones collapse inside me. A tidal wave of blood rushes through my veins. Systems close down.

53

Debs

'Allen, I didn't, I didn't . . . ' she stuttered in the rain as the ambulance pulled away.

He put his hands round her wet face and smoothed down her hair.

'I believe you, love. I believe you.'

And then he pulled her tightly into his soft, fleshy arms and she stayed there, weaving backwards and forwards, but he didn't let go.

54

Callie

'Where is she?' Toms screams in my face.

He barges through the doors of A&E, his eyes raw. I just stare at him and point towards a door.

'Jesus Christ!' he shouts. He rams his elbows either side of his ears. 'What the fuck happened? That fucking woman, Cal. I told you.'

I stand waiting, unable to move.

'Where is Rae?' he yells, grabbing my arm.

I take two, then three, deep breaths and force out my words.

'Cardio have just taken her. She went into the back of the passenger seat.'

'What are they saying?'

'She's in the MRI. They're worried that . . . '

'What?'

'That because the impact was on her chest — the old aortic repair has . . . '

' . . . ruptured?'

I shut my eyes and nod.

'Oh, Jesus Christ!' He puts his hands on his face.

This is my fault. I've done this. The Saturday night drunks are already arriving in A&E. One man who smells badly of urine falls over and is left there by the nurses, cursing in our direction. Another sits with his mate, with a towel pressed to a bleeding arm, the expression of a vicious dog on his face.

Demons, I think. Here for me. Surrounded by demons. For what I did.

'Why didn't you report that fucking woman?' Tom says, looking at me with a desperate look on his face. 'I told you there was something wrong with her.'

'Why didn't you, Tom?' I murmur. 'There are two of us.'

He rolls his eyes, and we lean against the wall together. Helpless.

* * *

'There's a shadow around her heart,' the young A&E doctor says. 'And we can hear a murmur.'

'That's normal,' says Tom, trying to find hope. 'Lots of kids have murmurs after the surgery.'

'I know,' says the doctor. 'But in this situation, with the shadow, we want to transfer her to the . . . '

'Paediatric cardiology unit, we know,' I say.

He looks at us sympathetically. 'Just to be sure.'

We both nod.

'We've rung upstairs and Mr Piper is on standby.'

We both just shrug, defeated.

'Try not to worry,' he says, walking off.

And I stagger a little, and the tears start to tumble down my face, and I sway back and forth in this horrible corridor. And it's then, when I feel I can't keep myself up any longer, when everything is about to give way, that I feel the roller-coaster harness of Tom's arms come down around me.

★ ★ ★

I thought if I imagined the worst thing that could happen, every day, then it would never happen. I heard that once — that people who imagine the worst often survive because they are constantly prepared. They have their plan of escape from the plane ready in their minds. The fire escape route out of their hotel room committed to memory. The tree branch that they would hold on to if they fell in the roaring river picked out.

But it seems I am wrong.

'Not good news, I'm afraid. We think the shadow is blood leaking from the aorta. In which case, we'll have to repair it again,' the surgeon says.

Numbly, we nod.

Here again.

Open heart surgery. This was supposed never to happen again.

With Tom's arm round me, we walk back to Rae and take her hands tightly. She lies sedated, quiet.

My own heart aches like it is being stretched.

'Rae, you're such a strong girl,' I whisper. 'I'm sorry it's taken me so long to realize that. But I promise you. This operation is going to go fine this time. And you're going to get better. And when you get out, the first thing we're going to do is plan your birthday party, OK? Hannah's mummy just rang to say Hannah can't wait to see you. So you're my precious girl, and be strong.'

And I lean over to kiss her hair. It is damp and pushed back from her face. The pink cheeks have gone. I hold Rae's hands, pleading with her silently to stiffen her fingers and pull them defiantly away from me again. But they lie limp in mine.

Oh, my baby. Our little Rae of hope.

And then Tom is beside me, kissing her face, and the nurses try to wheel her away. But I can't let go of her hands, and Tom and the nurses have to make me.

55

Callie

I don't know how long I am waiting for Rae to come out of theatre. It could be ten minutes or ten hours. Time, I have learnt, goes at a different pace in hospital.

Tom and I sit side by side, gripping our seats, our arms touching. I rock gently against the warmth of him. I concentrate on the sound of my breath. Each one seems to last an eternity. Deep and slow, like wind across an empty field.

We have been here before.

I remember this now. This limbo. This flying through a storm. Trying to stay up in the turbulence and lightning. Gripping seats. Praying to land.

Just waiting and breathing and praying and waiting.

★   ★   ★

I don't know what time Suzy appears, but it must be long after midnight. As she disturbs me from my trance, I notice suddenly that Tom is not there. I wonder if she waited for him to go to the toilet or find a doctor to ask what is happening for the tenth time.

There is a plaster across her nose. The skin

around her eyes is bruised, and her arm is in a sling. Seeing her makes me want to sink into her. To go back to the normal life of twenty-four hours ago, of home, of Churchill Road, of Rae wanting to go to a party.

'Oh, hon,' she murmurs, taking Tom's seat gingerly. 'I can't believe this. I'm so sorry.'

'How is it?' I ask, pointing at her arm.

'Broken,' she says. 'Hurts like hell. But they've given me something.'

I wrinkle up my mouth in sympathy.

'Oh, hon,' she repeats, resting her head on my shoulder. 'What can I do? I just don't understand why she didn't have her seat belt on. I did it up at the ice rink.'

I shake my head and sniff. 'It's probably my fault. The one in the back of our car gets jammed against her chest — it's so old. I let her take it off to un-jam the strap.'

She nods, stroking my arm.

'Jez with the kids?' I ask.

'His parents just arrived to help out.' She rolls her eyes. 'God help us. At least they're off to South Africa on Monday.'

'Have you seen the police?' I ask.

'That guy, the young one, just got here. They've been questioning Crazy Lady. Cal, you need to give that guy a hard time. I mean, how many times did you try to speak to him about her this week?'

I look at her. 'Three?'

'And what did he do?'

'He got me to Google her.'

Suzy's mouth drops open.

413

'That was it? That was the extent of how seriously he took you?'

As I watch her annoyed expression, suddenly I remember. I jump up, and bring my hands to my face.

'Oh God, I haven't told you.'

'What?'

'I did look her up. She's been in court. Debs. She hit a child.'

'I knew it!' Suzy cries. 'What did I tell you?'

'Oh God,' I murmur. 'You're right. I shouldn't have let him fob me off like that. Especially when you told me what her husband said in the garden. Honestly, Suzy, I think you might be right. I think she might have hit Rae and that's what made her fall into the road on Wednesday.'

Before I can stop myself, I groan out loud, and my hand flies up and I slap it hard on my forehead. The sting makes my head fly back. Before Suzy can stop me, I do it again and again.

'Hon?' she shouts, shocked. 'No! Don't do that.' She leans forward, wincing with the movement, and grabs my hand. 'Sit down. Come on. You weren't to know. You were all tied up with work shit. You just had too much going on. Look, we know now. The police can't ignore this. You need to forget about it, and think about Rae right now. She's going to be out of theatre any minute, and when she is, she's going to need you to be strong.'

But a volt of panic has started running through me, making my limbs jerk like a puppet's. I stand up again and pace the room.

'I should have seen it, Suze. I'm her mother.'

As I pace past the clock, I look up for the hundredth time and let out a long groan. 'Jesus. Why's it taking so long?'

Suzy sighs and pulls herself up to standing, nursing her broken arm. She stands in front of me to stop me moving, and with her good hand firmly pulls my face to look at her. 'Listen, Cal, sweetheart. Look at me. I know this is a nightmare. But listen to me. Rae is going to be absolutely fine. She really is. And we will get this sorted with Crazy Lady, and the police. But tonight, you've got to focus. I'm here for you. Just like you were for me when the twins were born. And, I promise you, this is all going to work out. This isn't the right time to talk about it, but I've decided — from now on, I'm going to look after Rae after school. That way, you'll know she's safe. And if you need to go up to your Dad's or something at the weekend, she can stay with me then, too. It'll give you a break and it'll give me the chance to really spoil her. We'll do it when Jez is at his parents' with the boys. Then me and Rae will have a proper girls' weekend.'

But her words don't calm me. They just deepen the current of panic pulsing through me. A pounding starts in my ears.

I turn to see Tom in the doorway with two cups of coffee. He and Suzy survey each other silently.

'I need air,' I gasp, pushing past him out of the door.

415

For a moment I don't know which direction I'm going in. I just stumble down a dark corridor lined with children's murals that seems to go on for miles, like a tunnel under a mountain.

My lungs feel as if they are filled with something heavier than air.

Eventually I reach the end and turn into the new modern wing, with its tall glass atrium, and march along the white corridors, looking out of black windows. All the corridors on the floors above and below me are empty, too, clear of the people who have the luxury of coming to hospital during the day, and those who perhaps come a couple of times in a lifetime. It is just the people like me and Rae and Tom who are here in the dark hours, moving along these white corridors with black windows like pieces on a chessboard.

As I climb up a set of stairs, a large sob bursts from my throat. I hate this place. I hate being back here. I hate the fact that I know these corridors as well as the un-signposted country roads back home. I hate the fact that I know everything. That I know it's quicker to walk to the fifth-floor vending machine than take the lift, which becomes congested on the fourth floor with patients coming for blood tests. I know that the disabled toilet one flight up is always cleaner than the public toilets on our floor, and that no one minds if I use it in quiet hours. That I know the best seat to choose for Rae in the ECG waiting room, where she won't get her legs banged by passers-by using the corridor, but we can still see her number come up on the wall-monitor without cricking our necks.

I hate the fact that I have brought Rae here again. That I did all those things to protect her, and then I made one bad choice. I went back to work and let that woman near her.

I march up to a metal waste bin sitting against a wall and bang my fists down on it. A metal clatter explodes into the night-time silence.

'Rae . . . ' I sob into its echo.

* * *

'Are you all right?' a man's voice says.

As I come to, I realize I am standing on the tiles, polished and ready for tomorrow, beside the blackened windows of the closed flower shop full of empty vases, shaking.

I turn and see a tall man with dark hair in the shadow of the door of the canteen. For a second, I think it's Jez. And for a second, I am relieved. Because if it is Jez, then I can pull him down one of these dark corridors to some dark room, and let him take the pain away for a while.

'Are you OK?' the young police officer repeats, walking towards me.

I stand, shaking. Of course. Of course, it's not Jez. Because Jez is not here. Jez is at home with the boys.

'Come on. Let's get you a seat and something to drink,' the police officer says.

I watch his face and I want to scream at him that this is his fault, too. That he should have

417

warned me earlier about that woman. But right now there is no point.

It was my job to protect my daughter. And I didn't.

So I let him gently guide me through the door into the empty cafeteria, where chairs are stacked neatly on tables and dim night lights illuminate a few drinks machines in the corner. A female officer is already seated at a table, on the phone. There is a folder on the table in front of her. She sees me and finishes the conversation, quickly closing the folder.

'Any news?' she says, standing up and pulling down a chair for me.

I shake my head numbly, and she gently takes my arm from her colleague and guides me down into the chair.

★ ★ ★

It is a few minutes before the police speak to me. I sit silently as they move around behind me, fetching me a can of lurid soda from the machine. The cold liquid feels like a razor blade on my dry throat. I become vaguely aware of a muttered conversation elsewhere.

Then they sit down opposite me, and smile again. The male officer starts to speak.

'Deborah Ribwell's saying the same as last time. That it wasn't her fault. She's saying that Suzy Howard crashed the car on purpose to hurt your child, and that before they crashed, she made it clear to Mrs Ribwell that this was her intention.'

418

I look up at him. 'What are you talking about? That's just ridiculous. You know Debs has already hurt a child. Why are you even listening to her?'

I roll my eyes and look out of the dark window. In the reflection, I see a look pass between them.

'Miss Roberts, do you have any reason to think that Deborah Ribwell's allegations have any truth to them?'

'I can't believe you're even asking me this. Suzy wouldn't hurt anyone, especially not Rae.'

He shrugs. 'We'll speak to Mrs Howard in the morning. See if we can get to the bottom of this. But as far as you know, she has no reason to lie?'

'Of course not. How many times?'

The female officer surveys me closely. She takes her time, choosing the right words, I suspect. 'Can I just ask how long you've known Mrs Howard?' she says gently.

I shrug. 'Two years? Two and a half? We're neighbours.'

'And you know her well?'

'Yes.'

She says nothing. I notice she has her hand firmly on top of the folder in front of her.

'Well, as much as you can do, I suppose. I mean, we look after each other's kids.'

'And you trust her to do that?'

I look up at the young woman's face. Probably years off having kids of her own.

'It's London,' I say, trying to keep the testiness out of my voice. 'You don't have much choice, do you? With neighbours, other mothers? I

419

mean, you can't know everything about anybody you just meet in a city. But, yes, I trust her. She's never given me any reason not to.'

'Has Mrs Howard told you much about her background? From before she came to London,' the male officer says.

'What do you mean?' I snap.

'Can I ask what she's told you?'

I can't help it. I laugh. 'Why are you asking me this?'

'Please. If you could try, it might help.'

I shrug. 'OK, what do you want to know? She grew up with her mum in Denver. Her mother was a hairdresser, or a beautician or something. Uh, the two of them used to hike a lot in the mountains, they skied, that kind of thing. I don't know. How can this possibly help? Suzy went to business college, I think — worked in an office. Met Jez when he was over on business. Had three kids. That's it. She likes swimming. Good at making biscuits. Does that help?'

I throw myself back angrily in my chair.

They both smile empathetically.

'OK, well, let me ask you this,' the male officer continues. 'Why do you think Deborah Ribwell would want to hurt Rae, in particular? Had you or Rae done anything to provoke her?'

'No, of course not,' I say, shaking my head dismissively. Then I jerk forwards in my chair. 'Hang on, yes. Oh shit, I've just remembered. Rae hit her on the nose with this horrible toy she gave her when we first met her. Maybe that was it. And also, me and Suzy think she might have been angry that Rae ran away from her on the pavement and pushed her or slapped her, and that's why she fell into the road. I think Rae didn't tell me because she thought I'd be angry that she was running.'

'Right. So you think these two incidents — being hit on the nose with a toy and running away on the pavement — made Deborah Ribwell angry enough to try to hurt or even kill your child?'

His words hang in the air, seeming to mock me.

'I don't know,' I snap. 'Why are you even asking me that? You know she's got a record. You told me to look her up yourself. She hit a child at another school.'

The male officer looks confused and shakes his head. 'Deborah Ribwell received a conditional discharge for that incident.'

'What does that mean?'

'The magistrates let her off.'

I glare. 'Not in the news story I read.'

'Well, you maybe didn't finish the reports.'

I sigh and bite my lip.

The female officer sits forward. 'Callie, Deborah Ribwell was the victim of an extremely vicious Internet harassment campaign.'

I shake my head.

She continues. 'It was quite a big news story, so I'm not telling you anything here you couldn't find out yourself. What happened was that a girl in her Year Ten class took offence to a comment Mrs Ribwell made about single mothers with lots of children by different fathers that was actually quoted from a play written by inner-city schoolchildren. She misunderstood and thought Mrs Ribwell was 'disrespecting' her mum. So she got her boyfriend involved. They posted ads with Mrs Ribwell's private details on sites where people advertise for sexual encounters.'

I sit up.

'I think you can imagine what happened. Then they really stepped it up. The boyfriend, who's quite a bit older, wormed his way into Mrs Ribwell's wedding reception and charmed her sister into letting him leave his laptop in Mrs Ribwell's honeymoon suite to keep it safe. What he actually did was set up a hidden camera and filmed Mrs Ribwell on her wedding night.'

They see my face drop.

'And then the girl posted the footage round school.'

I bite my lip. 'Oh my God. That's awful. Poor Debs. I would have slapped the girl, too.'

The officers smile.

I sit back. 'OK, I take your point. But that still doesn't mean she's innocent here. What if she was so traumatized by that girl, she's gone nuts around kids? Suzy heard her husband say she shouldn't be working with kids any more.'

The policewoman shrugs. 'There's absolutely no proof. In fact, her employers used their discretion to let her work in the after-school club because they accepted it had been a very unusual case of extreme provocation. Her record was unblemished before that. In fact, she was highly thought of. And you have to remember, as the cyclist hasn't come forward we have no witnesses to either incident.'

I sigh, and take a long gulp of my drink, trying to clear my mind.

'No! Wait!' I say suddenly, slamming down the can. 'Hang on. There is someone else. There was a woman there, on Churchill Road that night — the night Rae fell into the road when she was with Debs. Suzy told me — she said a neighbour rang the police. Why don't you ask her? She must have thought it was serious enough to call you — that's why you interviewed Debs in the first place, wasn't it?'

The officers swap glances again.

'What?' I snap. 'Why do you keep looking at each other like that?'

'It's just that . . . ' the male officer starts.

'What?'

The police officer holds up his hand to halt the conversation, and instead takes out a notebook. He flicks through it for a second, then turns it round and shows me.

'The woman who reported the bike incident was her — Suzy Howard,' he says. 'There was no other witness.'

I stare at them both.

'And that's why we wanted to ask you what you know about Suzy Howard,' says his colleague. 'Because right now, in both cases, it's her word against Deborah Ribwell's.'

SUNDAY

56

Suzy

'*Hush, little baby*,' Suzy sang gently to Otto as he fell asleep in his cot.

Her arm was agonizing, the cut on her forehead throbbing.

Didn't matter, though. Not any more.

Thank God she'd managed to get rid of James and Diana, sending them off to the park with Jez and the two other boys. She'd actually come down at 7 a.m. to get her painkillers and found Diana trying to give the kids grapes without cutting them up. Grapes! Children could choke on grapes. You could tell the woman hadn't brought up her own son; had left him to nannies and school matrons.

Suzy walked downstairs and along the hall, wondering how quickly Jez could persuade his parents to go home. He'd rung the hospital at nine and told her that Rae was out of surgery but in intensive care.

'OK, well, we'll just wait and see, hon,' she'd said, glancing up at the photograph of the boys in the hallway.

When they were finally on their own later, one of the first things they'd talk about was getting that photo redone. With Jez in it, this time. No arguments.

They'd have some nice dinner, and chat about the plumber's invoice, which she had ready to place on the kitchen table for him to see. Then they'd go upstairs and he'd finally give her what she wanted.

All of a sudden, she heard footsteps in the house next door. That was interesting. Crazy Lady, back from the police station. Wonder how that went?

She wandered back into the kitchen, smiling.

57

Callie

The taxi drops me off outside Suzy's.

I can see from my reflection as I pay the driver, and from his expression, that I look a sight. My hair is bushing out from getting wet in the rain yesterday. There are bags under my eyes. An ugly patch of coffee is splashed randomly down my white T-shirt from when the surgeon suddenly appeared in the doorway at two o'clock this morning and Tom and I leapt up.

'Thanks,' I say to the taxi driver, refusing to meet his inquisitive eye and walking off.

The street is quiet. I stop for a moment on the pavement, and listen.

In the distance the early-morning weekend traffic rumbles like waves crashing on a shore. The staccato, piercing whistle of a greenfinch bursts above my head. I shut my eyes and listen more deeply. The hum of electricity wires. A distant cry from a child in the park across the road. A rustle of little feet behind a bin.

It calms me. I let the sounds wash over me till finally, from somewhere inside, I find a tiny bit of strength.

I turn and look at Suzy's front door.

The window boxes are bursting with deep-pink geraniums. I think of the trips we took to the garden centre in the spring with the kids to buy them, and how me and Suzy helped the kids plant them, and how I held up the trellis as she nailed it to the wall, and how together we twisted wisteria around her front door. How I watched her creating this welcoming, nurturing home with her kids and Rae, and looked across at my dusty old window boxes full of dried-up roots.

Slowly, I walk towards her gate, and step up to the doorbell.

'Cal? Oh, thank God. I've been so worried,' she cries, flinging the door open. 'They wouldn't tell us hardly anything. Is she still in intensive care?'

I walk in, my head bowed.

'There's a lot of blood round the heart. They're waiting to see if it drains.'

She pulls a horrified face, then pulls me into a hug.

'Oh, hon. Listen, it's over now. It's done. You just need to give her time. Come on, you're exhausted. I'll make you some eggs, then I'll get Jez to drive you back to the hospital after you've changed.'

But I don't move. I stand where I am inside the hall, with the front door still open, and place my hands behind my back. I lean firmly backwards into the wall, trapping them.

'Suze. I only came for a moment. I've got to get straight back. But there's something important I need to ask you. There's something I don't understand.'

'Uh-huh?'

'Actually, a couple of things.'

'Like what, hon?'

I go to open my mouth and nearly stop. If I say it, I might not be able to go back.

She watches me carefully, her face set in a concerned expression.

No, I think. It is time.

'OK, well, I spoke to the police last night. And they said something weird. They said that you were the person who reported it when Rae fell into the road.'

She watches me, expressionless now.

'And I have this memory that you told me it was someone else. A woman. A neighbour. And I don't understand.'

Suzy sticks out her lower lip.

'Hon. You're not listening to me. That guy's an idiot. How many times do I have to tell you?'

I stare at her.

'But I saw it, Suzy. I saw your mobile number in his log.'

Suzy screws her face up and shakes her head oddly. Quickly, again and again.

'Cal — what is this? I know you feel guilty about Rae, but it feels like you're kind of taking it out on me.'

I take a deep breath.

'No, Suze. I'm not taking it out on you. I'm just trying to sort things out. Like, while we're at it, for instance, I still don't understand why you took Rae away from the party, or how you ended up getting the car stuck in the park. When Caroline rang me at hospital yesterday she said that Rae had been fine when she arrived at the party. Jumping up and down, excited.'

431

Suzy goes bright red. Her eyes grow wide.

'Oh, my God, Callie. Who are you listening to — that woman's an ass. She's been a total bitch to you the whole time you've been at school. I didn't want to tell you this, but it's her who turned all the parents against you. She's a snob, Cal. I heard her make a joke about your accent once. I've tried to warn you.'

I stay pressed into the wall.

'And then the really weird thing was that Ms Aldon rang Tom's mobile this morning to see how Rae was. And she mentioned to him that on Monday, Tuesday and Wednesday she'd had to tell Rae and Hannah off because they were so excited about after-school club that they ran out of the classroom before they were allowed to go. I mean, that's completely different to what you said, Suzy. Why are all these things different?'

Fascinated, I watch as the muscles on her face ripple. It is as if the flesh lifts in slow motion, then suspends mid-movement in an expression that frightens me. It is not unlike the faces of the stone gargoyles that glare down from the palace walls.

Instinctively, I find myself shrinking further into the wall. Then she opens her mouth.

'What — you think I'm a lying pig, Cal?' she says in a strange voice.

'No,' I murmur, taken aback. 'I'm just saying that I'm getting confused at how many people seem to be telling me different stories. That's all.'

She snorts.

'And you believe everyone else but not me? The friend who's stuck by you all this time?'

'No. Of course I don't.' But then I make myself meet her eye. 'Well, actually, Suze, if I'm honest, I don't know.'

My words hang in the hall. Spoken out loud. There is definitely no going back now. I look nervously up the stairs, wondering if Jez is here.

'Oh. That's interesting,' she says. Her voice starts to rise alarmingly. 'That's REAL interesting, Callie. That you would accuse me of lying.'

'What do you mean?'

And without warning she stomps down the wooden floor away from me into her kitchen.

Hypnotized, I follow, and find her standing at her kitchen table. There is nothing on it but a blue piece of paper. She stares at me with an odd smile on her face.

My eyes drop down and suddenly I know. This is what was missing from my flat.

The plumber's invoice.

And then I feel my legs give way, and I grab the table to steady myself.

*　*　*

'Where did you get it?' I ask, trying to control the tremor in my voice.

'Your friendly plumber. Said he saw the address on it and thought he'd help you out by dropping it in for — now, how did he put it — that's right . . . *the little girl's dad.*'

Rae's dad.

I look at it. There, in my own handwriting. 'Flock Ventures', with Jez's business address — his home address — underneath. The invoice

I meant to hand to him in private, as normal, when he paid for something to help me out. I was so tired from the hospital, it didn't even occur to me that the plumber would see the address and take the initiative to post it through Jez's letterbox, without asking me.

How could I have been so careless?

Unsteadily, I reach out for a chair. The adrenalin that has pumped through my body for nearly twenty hours now is draining away fast, leaving my limbs so weak I can hardly move them.

'Suze. He's not her dad,' I mumble, trying to pull the chair out from the table. 'Tom's her dad. Jez is a bloke I met in a bar six years ago when I was upset on the anniversary of my mum's death. It happened before you, Suzy. Long before.'

She nods her head. 'Uh-huh, and it didn't occur to you he might be married, Cal? You didn't bother to ask?'

'I was drunk . . . '

'Oh yeah, of course, that delightful British habit of drinking till you puke. Course you were, Cal. But if you hadn't been, and you had done the decent thing, you'd have found out that I was back in Denver, four months pregnant, wondering when he was ever coming home.'

I turn my eyes away, ashamed. 'You'll have to ask him about that, Suzy,' I say, taking a seat as my legs threaten to give way.

'Oh, I plan to,' she says in the same cold voice. 'Trust me, I do. And yeah, take a seat. Make yourself at home. I mean, that was always the plan, huh?'

I try to manoeuvre my legs under the table, then realize I can hardly move them any more. I am trapped.

'Of course, I couldn't leave it there, though,' Suzy continues, moving into the kitchen area. Vaguely, I am aware that she is taking something from a drawer. 'Got a friend of mine to do a bit more checking around. And guess where Jez was the other night when I was waiting for him to come back from Birmingham? And you know what, Cal? I only realized later, but I could smell him on you.'

I lift one thigh with my hands, trying to make it work. Nothing happens. I can't get up. A burning desire to get back to Rae overwhelms me. I can't cope with this. What have I started? I have to get out of here.

Suzy lets out a sharp breath, and I look up. Her eyes are staring down.

'Suzy. This isn't just about me,' I say, desperately trying to use my hands on the table to pull myself back up. 'You know as well as I do that there's something wrong with you and Jez. I know you try to hide it, but I can see it now. I don't know what it is. But I do think that he's lonely.'

'Lonely?' she smiles, looking back up. 'Really? You think you're the only one he sees, Cal? You should speak to my friend Vondra. There's at least two more like you. Probably loads of little Raes, all over the place.'

She shakes her head when she sees my

shocked expression.

'Yeah, so any plans you had to move in here and steal my husband are on hold. Looks like you got competition, hon. And one of them's quite a bit younger, apparently.'

'That's never what I was trying to do. You and me had become friends before Jez even turned up. I didn't know how to tell you and then it was just too late and . . . '

All of a sudden, there is a knocking at the front of the house. We both turn to see Debs, peering nervously round the open door.

'Callie?' she says hesitantly. 'Are you all right, love?'

'Debs,' I call. 'Please. Not now.'

Suzy throws her hands up in the air.

'Oh, great — now we got Crazy Lady, too. You see this, Cal? See her screaming at my doorstep? You know, even after I found out that you were sleeping with my husband — did you know that, Debs, that our good friend here was banging my husband — I still tried to protect your child from this nutcase. Because that's what friendship is about. And instead of thanking me — because Lord knows, Callie, you haven't got any other friends, probably because you never shut up talking about yourself, by the way — you accuse me of lying. Unbelievable.'

I turn to see Debs's face frozen in uncertainty. Her eyes flicker from me to Suzy, and back to me.

She comes further into the corridor, hesitantly.

'Callie — you're having an affair with Jez?'

'Debs, please, will you go away, that's not your

business. I'll talk to you later.'

But she stays put.

'Callie,' she stutters. 'You've got to listen to me. Suzy's telling lies. About me, about everyone . . . '

Suzy gives a little yelp. She walks purposefully out of the kitchen area past me towards Debs, and physically stands in front of her in the hallway.

'Quiet, you. Out of my house.'

But Debs persists, peering at me around Suzy's waist.

'Callie, please listen. My neighbour, Beattie, will tell you. Everyone on the street is terrified to speak to you because of her . . . '

'Out!' Suzy yells at her, trying to herd her to the door, but Debs won't stop, her little head with its big glasses popping out either side of Suzy.

My exhausted brain struggles to understand. What is she saying?

'And she's done it at the school, too. Beattie's daughter says that she's told terrible lies about all the parents to each other.' Suzy keeps inching her back towards the front door, using her full height, but Debs won't give up. From somewhere I finally find energy to push myself up onto my feet and start to follow them out into the hall, curious, holding on to the sofa for support. 'The school's had to speak to her about it,' Debs continues, her voice taking on a desperate tone as Suzy gets her to the door and tries to push her out. 'And she's told people terrible lies about you, too. Apparently all the

437

parents knew Rae had been ill and that you were on your own, and they were desperate to make you welcome at the school, but she stopped them. She told them that you've said terrible things about their kids. And that Tom is violent, so that no one allows their children to come and play. And she even started a rumour that you slept with a divorced parent at the school — Matt, is it? — then said he was bad in bed.'

I reach the kitchen door and stop.

'What?' I call. 'Suzy, stop! Leave her. What did she just say? I've never even spoken to that guy . . . '

Suzy turns. Her face is bright red; her eyes wide and furious. She is trying to push the front door shut across Debs's body.

'I said, stop it, Suzy! How could she know that? How could she know any of this?'

Suzy crosses her eyes and does this stupid comedy face.

I stare at her. 'Suzy. Tell me you didn't do this? Tell me you're not the reason this whole neighbourhood has ignored me and Rae for two and a half years?'

A stupid, silly smirk crosses her face, like a schoolgirl caught passing a note in front of a teacher. She lets go of the door and pulls back. Debs shakes herself down and moves back inside.

'What is wrong with you?' I gasp. 'Why would you do this to me, Suzy?'

Suzy gives this long, comedy sigh. As I watch her, it is as if she is deflating, all the anger seeping out of her.

'She's jealous, love,' Debs calls. 'I think she did it to me because she thought you and I might become friends. I think she can't bear you to have a relationship with anybody but her. And I think she didn't want you to go to work and see other people so she tried to scare you into thinking that something might happen to Rae if you weren't here. It is a terrible thing, jealousy. I should know, love, my sister . . . '

I stand there, confused. Trying to work it all out.

And then the blood drains from my face.

'But even if that's true . . . I mean . . . Rae. Suzy, you wouldn't . . . Not Rae? You wouldn't hurt Rae. Not on purpose . . . ?'

Debs looks up at Suzy. 'Are you going to tell her, or am I?' she says, a brave new tone entering her voice. Suzy slumps slightly to the side, saying nothing.

'She drove the car at the bench, Callie,' Debs says. 'With Rae inside. And I think she was going to do it whether I'd turned up or not. I'm sorry, but it's the truth.'

But my thoughts are elsewhere. There is something odd on the floor. Small red dots running down the hall towards Suzy.

Then Suzy lifts up her hand, and finally I see what she was doing in the kitchen. 'Debs,' I gasp.

'What?' she says.

I point my eyes at Suzy's hand. In it, she is holding a small, sharp vegetable knife. Debs's eyes follow. At the same time, we allow our eyes to drop down to Suzy's left trouser leg, the inside of which is rapidly turning from khaki to deep burgundy. I become aware of a tutting noise, and realize it is blood hitting the floor.

'Suzy,' I whisper. 'What have you done?'

Without hesitation, Debs marches straight up to Suzy and holds her hand out.

'Give it to me, Suzy. Now, please,' she says in a gentle voice. 'You're all right, love. It's going to be OK. Callie, call an ambulance.'

And I watch in horror as this tender expression crosses Suzy's face, and she turns to me and gently slumps against the wall.

'I just thought you were it,' she says, her voice draining away to a tired murmur. 'You know, you and me, Cal. Friends forever.'

MONDAY

58

Callie

I sit by Rae's hospital bed, watching.

She opens one eye, sticky with sleep, and tries to focus on me.

My face bursts into a smile as big as the sun.

'I'm thirsty,' she says. 'I want Ribena.'

'Better to have water at the moment,' I answer, avoiding the ongoing temptation to climb into her bed and hold her warm little body so close that it becomes part of mine again.

'Kaye gives me Ribena.'

I smile. 'Does she now? Well, I'm glad to see you're trying it on again, anyway. Listen. I've got something for you.' I reach down into my bag and pull out a white envelope. 'It's from Hannah.'

Rae's face lights up. She rips open the envelope and pulls out a card. On the front is a drawing that Hannah has done. It is of her and Rae. Rae has enormous eyes that fill most of her face, and curly hair jutting out in a ball, and a big grin with jaggy teeth. Hannah has bright orange hair and is holding Rae's hand. She has put Rae carefully on a box so that they are the same height. There are hearts all over the picture with 'BF' written inside them.

'That means best friend,' Rae says breathlessly.

I stroke her cheek, pleased for her, and together we open the card. 'To Rae. We'll Always Be Together, love Hannah xxx' it says.

Rae giggles. 'Hannah sings that song a LOT. It's from *Grease*. She says I can watch it at her house.'

I smile at her shining eyes, and look again at the words.

We'll always be together.

And I lean over and hold her tight, and hope in her case it is true.

'Rae, darling, listen. I've got to go and ring Granddad to find out what time he's coming this afternoon. I'll be back in a minute.'

I pop my head out of the door and motion to Tom, who is chatting to one of the doctors in the corridor, and he nods and comes to take over, placing his hands on my shoulders as we pass in the doorway.

'OK?' he says, rubbing them.

'Hmm,' I reply, leaning my head into him a little as he does it.

'Where are you going?'

'I won't be long. There's something I have to do.'

We turn to see Rae sitting up, radiant. Watching us.

And we roll our eyes at each other, and I leave.

★ ★ ★

I wander down to the cafeteria, thinking how different it looks in the daytime. Sun streams in through the glass atrium. In the distance, I can

444

see the London Eye. The doctor says Rae is doing well. That she won't be here too long. We could be free of this place again soon. And for good, this time. Forever.

The cafeteria is a different place today, I note. Crowds of people queue for lunch; visitors, young doctors in striped shirts with stethoscopes proudly hung round their necks; exhausted-looking surgery staff in scrubs; patients with tubes and sticks and bandages. I didn't notice on Saturday night, but the cafeteria has been done up since the last time we were here. It is bright and fresh and clean. The air is full of chatter. Of purpose. Of things moving forward. Of hope that things will heal.

And then I see him. In the far corner, his head slumped down over a newspaper, a large plastic coffee cup in his hand. Still in his bloody suit. But this time, his hair has a greasy sheen to it. It falls forwards onto a hint of a dark shadow around his chin.

He doesn't see me at first. I watch and I think. I think about how Jez has always taken the pain away.

And then I focus on the hard line of his jaw, and I allow myself, finally, to accept that this is not actually true. Because after the euphoria, Jez does other things to me. He creeps around my system, collapsing veins, suppressing my breathing, slowing the neurons in my brain, poisoning my heart, and clogging the arteries that keep me alive.

No, I think, watching his eyes, and starting to walk towards him. If I am honest with myself,

445

apart from giving me Rae, Jez has never done me any good at all.

* * *

'How is she?' I say, pulling up a chair beside him.

His head jerks up in surprise. He immediately looks behind me. Looking for Tom, probably. Wondering if there's going to be a scene.

'They're keeping her in. For observation,' he says.

'What — in A&E?'

He pauses. 'No. The psychiatric unit.'

I raise my eyebrows, and he looks away.

'How's Rae?'

'Good.'

He nods. 'That's good to hear.'

I sit and say nothing. I just keep looking at him.

'So, what is it, Jez? Why did you ring?'

He taps his fingers on the table and attempts a smile.

'I need to ask you a favour.'

I stare at him. 'You want to ask me a favour?'

He rolls his eyes. 'I know. Not very apt in the circumstances.'

I sit back.

'Well, I tell you what, Jez. Before you ask me that favour, why don't you answer a few questions for me? Then we'll see.'

He looks at me, and I realize something. For the first time, I have the upper hand. There is a softness around his face that I have never seen before. Jez is scared, I think. Lost. Suddenly he

446

looks like a big fat child dressed up in his dad's suit.

A wave of revulsion takes me by surprise.

'OK . . . '

'OK. Well, first, I want to know something about Suzy. I want to know where you met her. Did you meet her at work?'

He lowers his eyes. 'In a way. Yes.'

'At your office, in Denver?'

He wriggles uncomfortably in his seat. 'No. At her work.'

'Which was . . . '

'In a cl . . . I mean a bar. Near my office.'

He looks uncomfortable. 'A bar or a club?' I ask carefully. 'Which was it?'

He sighs. 'A club.'

'And should I be asking what sort of club?'

'Probably not,' he murmurs.

I nod, taking it in. Thinking of the folder the police officer had in front of me when she asked me about Suzy.

'OK. Well, and you married her — why?'

He purses his mouth. 'She got pregnant in the first week. On purpose. Then it just seemed like a good idea. Pissed the old man off.'

'And at what point did you realize your gorgeous, sexy new wife that you married to piss off your dad was a total nutcase?'

He glances at me sharply. 'Cal. I know what she's done to you. But you're talking about my kids' mother.'

I hold his gaze.

'I said, at what point, Jez?'

He sighs and leans forward, picking fluff from

447

his sleeve. 'It started pretty soon after. She started turning up at my office, giving dirty looks to the women I worked with. Following me to bars. Screaming at me in front of friends. She slapped me once in front of the boss I was contracting for in Denver when he got his driver to drop me back home late after a work thing.'

'So, why didn't you leave?'

'I thought it was the pregnancy. But after Henry, it got worse. She wouldn't let anyone near him. She wanted me and him in the house all the time with her. I tried to get a child-minder in to break it all up a bit, but Suzy said she heard the woman threatening to put Henry in a microwave if he didn't stop screaming. The woman denied it, but I had to let her go. And then Suzy got pregnant again. That was when I brought us back and started working from home. At least if I'm around she calms down, then she can't track me down when I go out and see clients and friends. I can have a life.'

'Well, from what I hear, you've certainly been having that,' I say. Jez bites his lip. 'But you knew. You knew she was crazy?'

'What's crazy? Jealous, maybe, mixed up. It was all about her sister. She . . . '

'Sister?' I exclaim. 'What bloody sister?'

'Faye. She lives in Denver. Suzy doesn't speak to her, but she tracked me down one day at work and told me everything. She reckons that's what caused it. That she stayed with their mother and Suzy got sent off to some old nutter of an aunt. The mother only ever turned up for appearances' sake if the school or social services started sniffing around.'

I take it all in. 'So this is why you were always on her back to put the twins in nursery? Is that what the boarding school thing is about, too? To get them away from her as much as possible? And what? Get them away from her completely at some point?'

He fiddles with a sugar packet.

I shake my head.

'So what was the favour you wanted to ask me?'

He sits up and attempts a smile.

'She's going to be in here for weeks, maybe months. My parents left for South Africa this morning and won't be back for two weeks. I don't want them to know what's really going on. So, I'm going to try to get the nursery to extend the twins' hours from nine to six, and get Henry into after-school club. I just wondered if you'd be able to help out. I've got to get this Vancouver contract bid finished and I'm not going to be able to find a childminder that quickly.'

I stare at him.

'Let me get this right. You're asking *me* to look after your kids?'

He tries the lowered eyebrow and lips combination he used the night of Rae's accident, clearly hoping it will do the trick. 'I mean, the boys and Rae,' he says in a voice meant to convey some sort of sentimentality. 'I mean, they are family. Sort of.'

'Family,' I snort. 'Is that right, Jez? That's how

449

you see Rae, is it? Family. That's why you were at home snoring your way through the night while she was having her chest cut open.'

I stand up and have to fight the urge to smile. 'You know, Jez, the thing is, you let that insane woman near my daughter, even though you knew what she was capable of. So, as far as I'm concerned, all of this happened because of you. Because it suited you to have me and Rae keep Suzy busy and off your back. Even though you knew what she might do.'

His face darkens.

'So, I tell you what I'm going to do. I'm going to decline your kind offer. Because what I think you should do, Jez, is pull out of your Vancouver contract and look after the kids yourself for a while. You might not have enough money for a nice new suit, but you'll survive. After what the boys have been through, they could do with having their dad around for a while. And, as we both know — you never know who you can trust with your own kids.'

He thinks for a minute. Then reaches out one of his cufflinked hands and touches mine. 'I know what you're saying, Cal, but I'm in a bit of a situation here. If you don't think of us as family, then I'm asking you to help me as a friend.'

I pull my hand away and resist the temptation to laugh. 'Jez, you know as well as I do what we've been doing, and it has nothing to do with friendship. But, if you get stuck, I'm sure Sassy Sasha would be delighted to help.'

And with that I march off through the

canteen. The clatter of steel pots and pans from the kitchen sounds like wild cheering in my ears.

★ ★ ★

I arrive back in Rae's room to find Tom on the parent's pull-out bed, snoring softly. Rae has rolled over again and their faces lie opposite each other, a few feet apart, noses and foreheads and chins pointing in different genetic angles to each other, but fixed in the same tranquil father-and-daughter expression.

I shut the door to the room, walk over to Rae's bed and climb gently onto the end of it, so as not to wake her.

Then I look at Tom and I look at Rae, and I look at my own reflection in the sunlit window, and I lie down between them, a hand drifting close to both.

Acknowledgements

This is my first novel so there are many people to thank.

First, my husband, for supporting me through the 'year' I decided to take off to write a novel, and then not complaining when it stretched into two . . . and to my kids for never complaining when I made tea late and hogged the laptop.

I doubt I would ever have got there without the invaluable encouragement and expert guidance of my agent Lizzy Kremer at David Higham Associates. I've said it a thousand times but thank you, again, Lizzy — and to Laura West at DH, too. A big thank you also to Katy Regan for her generosity and inspiring ways, and to my magazine fairy-godmothers Marie O'Riordan, Vanessa Thompson and Charlotte Moore, for setting me off on this path to fiction.

I am very lucky to have a wonderful publishing team at Pan Macmillan. In particular, I am indebted to Maria Rejt for taking an interest in *The Playdate* at the early stages, and to my editor Trisha Jackson for making publishing my first novel so enjoyable. Also, for their sterling work selling *The Playdate* abroad, Harriet Sanders, Liz Johnson and Jon Mitchell, and to Thalia Suzuma for her much-appreciated enthusiasm.

As for the content of the book, I am very grateful to Dr Iain A. Simpson for helping me to understand infant aortic coarctation, and to Dr Beth MacMillan and Dr Neil Mantan for taking the time to diagnose my plot needs, early on. Any errors in the use of that information are mine.

I'd like to thank Ingrid Holmquist and Simon Natas for lending me their professional expertise in psychology and law. Also, Dan Weinberg, for doing an admirable job of helping a technophobe like myself understand sound design. I'd also like to mention David Holmes at Rocket Music in Australia who was so nice about me inadvertently copying the name. The two Rockets and their staff are, of course, completely unconnected.

My thanks, too, to the friends who shared a contact or an experience, from potato farming to Turkish translation — Astrid, Flic, Gary, Sonja, Kat, Pete, Wes and Anita — and to the writer friends who guided and cheered me on — Sita Brahmachari, Wendy Jones, Wendy Hatton, Jonny Zucker and Karen McCombie. I doubt also I would have got there without my family heroically flying in from north and east, as deadlines loomed, or my very own 'Beatties': Lara and Fran — the kind of London neighbours I hope Callie has now.

We do hope that you have enjoyed reading this large print book.

Did you know that all of our titles are available for purchase?

We publish a wide range of high quality large print books including:
Romances, Mysteries, Classics
General Fiction
Non Fiction and Westerns

Special interest titles available in large print are:
The Little Oxford Dictionary
Music Book
Song Book
Hymn Book
Service Book

Also available from us courtesy of Oxford University Press:
Young Readers' Dictionary
(large print edition)
Young Readers' Thesaurus
(large print edition)

For further information or a free brochure, please contact us at:
Ulverscroft Large Print Books Ltd.,
The Green, Bradgate Road, Anstey,
Leicester, LE7 7FU, England.
Tel: (00 44) 0116 236 4325
Fax: (00 44) 0116 234 0205

Other titles published by
The House of Ulverscroft:

THE CHILD THIEF

Dan Smith

December 1930, Ukraine. Luka, a war veteran, wants a quiet life with his family. Their village is hidden from the advancing Soviet brutality — until the stranger arrives pulling a sled bearing a terrible cargo. When the villagers' fear turns deadly, they think they've saved themselves. But their anger has cursed them: a little girl has vanished. In these frozen lands, Luka has the skills to find the one who stole the child. With his sons, he sets out in pursuit. They track down a skilful hunter who uses the child as the bait in his twisted game. Battling harsh conditions, Luka must stay ahead of Soviet authorities. His toughest enemy is the man he tracks, yet his strongest bond is a promise to his family back home.

DEFENDING JACOB

William Landay

Andy Barber's job is to put killers behind bars. And when a boy from his son Jacob's school is found stabbed to death, Andy is doubly determined to find and prosecute the perpetrator. Until a crucial piece of evidence turns up linking Jacob to the murder. And suddenly Andy and his wife Laurie find their son accused of being a cold-blooded killer. In the face of every parent's worst nightmare, they will do anything to defend their child. Because, deep down, they know him better than anyone. Don't they?